# FRACTURED

## A TALE OF APPARATUM

# FRACTURED

## A TALE OF APPARATUM

by Keith Robinson and Brian Clopper
Copyright © 2013

Printed in the United States of America
First Edition: February 2016
ISBN-13 978-1530020966

Cover by Keith Robinson
All rights reserved.

No part of this book may be reproduced in any form or by any electronic or mechanical means including information storage and retrieval systems, without permission in writing from the author. The only exception is by a reviewer, who may quote short excerpts in a review.

Visit www.WorldofApparatum.com

# FRACTURED

## A TALE OF APPARATUM

CO-AUTHORED BY

### KEITH ROBINSON

unearthlytales.com

AND

### BRIAN CLOPPER

brianclopper.com

*Chapter 1*
## Kyle

Kyle Jaxx leapt from his bed, rushed to the window, and peered out through the blinds. The morning sky was a hazy blue, and the sun glinted off the smooth, rounded glass walls of high-rise apartment towers standing across the block from his own. Looking down from the eighty-fourth floor, the silent maglev train far below eased its way into the city center. People crawled like ants on the streets, clustering on the corner where gleaming white transport pods disappeared into the ground. Police cruisers whined through the air. The mayor's election campaign blimp turned slowly, its silver surface flashing as it caught the sun's rays.

It would be a perfectly normal morning except that today was Kyle's fourteenth birthday. Today he was eligible to receive the implant in the back of his head.

He dressed quickly and hurried along the hall to the kitchen for breakfast. His parents and younger brother were already seated around the table, and the stream screen on the wall played the morning news, though the volume was low.

"Here he is," his dad said gruffly. He was peering at his tablet, his finger poised over the screen. "I knew the birthday boy wouldn't sleep in this morning."

"Happy birthday," Kyle's mom said over her shoulder as she took the muffins out of the oven. "Are you ready?"

"For the implant?" Kyle said. "Yeah, I'm ready."

"Any last bets?" his dad asked. "I've still got you pegged as Librarian. You have that pasty-faced bookworm look about you." He peered at Kyle, his nose wrinkling with distaste. "Then again, Librarians are usually presentable. When are you going to get that greasy hair cut, boy? It's as long as a girl's. And why do

*1*

your shirts always look like you slept in them?" He sighed and shook his head, returning his attention to the tablet. "Perhaps a Lab Geek is a better fit. Scruffy bunch, the lot of 'em."

Kyle self-consciously pushed his hair out of his face. "It's not greasy," he mumbled. "Anyway, I'm gonna be a Robotics Engineer. Or better still, Cybernetics Engineer."

"So Lab Geek, then."

"Lab Geeks look through microscopes all day. I'm going to be working on artificial body parts—starting with Byron's upgrade."

A brief silence fell as his mom placed the hot muffin pan on the table and took a seat. Kyle glanced toward his younger brother Byron, who sat perfectly still, looking on impassively, his small mechanical body having no desire to fidget the way ordinary eight-year-old boys might.

"What do you say, Byron?" their dad asked. "Think Kyle's going to end up in Cybernetics?"

Byron's smooth plastic head tilted slightly to one side, and his orbs flashed a soft, pale green. "I hope not," he said in his synthesized voice. "I've only got my brain left. I don't want that getting messed up as well."

Kyle and his parents laughed. Byron remained impassive, but the soft flickering of his eyes indicated that he was chuckling internally.

"Implant today, then ten-day training," Kyle said, counting off on his fingers, "and then graduation. After that, I'll get started on your new parts. I know I can make them work. I got those two mods working okay, didn't I?"

"They were EasyInstall mods," Byron said. He raised his right hand and flexed the digits. "Adding a short-range laser isn't the same thing as fixing on new legs and arms."

As if to prove the simplicity of his mod, a short beam of red light suddenly projected from a fingertip as though he were extending an inch-long claw. It was nothing more than a cheap utility tool, able to slice through thin plastic and wood but requiring a two-minute recharge after ten seconds of use. The other EasyInstall mod, an electronic lock decoder, was more subtle. Technically speaking, they were supposed to have a license for that one.

"Mmm," Kyle said in answer. He turned and gazed longingly at a pile of components tucked into a corner of the lobby under the coat rack, a collection of limbs and parts bought dirt-cheap from Uncle Jeremiah over in East Morley. Byron was overdue for an upgrade. While his mind had naturally advanced in the four years since his accident, his small body had slowly degenerated.

Three of the family reached for the muffins. Byron watched, his head making micro-movements from time to time. When Kyle was halfway through his first muffin, his dad gently put his own down and pushed his tablet aside. "Seriously, son, I don't want you to be another fixer-upper like me. I'm hoping for Military."

"Speaking of which, Josef," Kyle's mom said, "will you *please* fix the air purifier before I choke to death."

He sighed, pushed back his chair, and wandered over to a flat grey panel almost as large as the nearby window. "It was working fine last night," he muttered.

"No, it wasn't. It's been on and off for days."

Kyle's dad opened the panel and peered inside. There wasn't much to see: thick pipes, a filter system, and a box of electronics in the corner. He placed his hand over the box and frowned. The muffins lay forgotten while he mentally diagnosed the problem, his eyes narrowed. Eventually he clicked his tongue and returned to the table.

"You can't fix it, Dad?" Kyle asked.

"No. Diagnostics indicates a faulty logic board. I'll pick one up later this morning." He grabbed his half-finished muffin, but before biting into it, he jabbed a finger at Kyle. "And that's what you need to remember, son. Every piece of tech in the city, every tiny device with an electronic brain, is receptive to human manipulation. But only a few can pull it off. That's what implants are for. Implants boost the signal. They help connect your brain to microchips. You can diagnose problems, control entire systems, override malfunctions."

"I know, Dad."

His dad barreled on. "What you *can't* do is replace broken parts like logic boards. Not with your mind, anyway. If a physical part is broken, if the hardware itself is faulty, even Grade-A Diagnostic Technicians like me aren't worth anything."

"I *know*, Dad, but—"

"And that's why you need to quit dreaming about that pile of nuts and bolts in the lobby." He patted Byron affectionately on his smooth, cold shoulder while he spoke. "Sorry, Byron. We'll get you some new parts one of these days." He returned his attention to Kyle, his expression hardening. "Even if you get into Robotics, you can't just make parts work unless they're in good order."

"But the parts *are* in good order."

"What, because Uncle Jeremiah said they were?" He rolled his eyes. "Yeah, like all the other trash he sells at remarkably knock-down prices." He gave up on his muffin and glared at Kyle. "Son, *everyone* wants to be in Robotics. But it's a low-paying job, and you'll likely end up doing more paperwork than hands-on testing or diagnostics. Those robot shows you keep watching on the stream screen are about a handful of guys who got really lucky and have the dream job of designing and deploying advanced machines. Not many end up in a job like that. So get your head out of the smog, son. Instead of aiming too high and falling short of your dreams, aim for something tangible—a job you can apply all your skills to in some form. Think Military."

"Dad," Kyle said, shaking his head, "I'm not—"

"City troops are paid well. You can help deal with some of the nonsense on the streets." He turned toward the stream screen and barked, "Sound up!"

A news reporter blared, "... *demonstrators outside the Repurposing Factory all week, and they're not going away. Mayor Baynor stated, 'They have every right to their opinion,' yet a strong troop presence . . .*"

"See? People are always moaning about something," Kyle's dad said, his voice raised. "I wonder how the mayor puts up with it. Sound down!"

He turned back to Kyle. "Or if you really want to be in Robotics, Kyle, consider Traffic Droid Maintenance. The city will always need traffic droids, and those rust buckets keep breaking down. You could be on call, setting 'em right, keeping the traffic flowing. City employment means amazing benefits, and even the lowest maintenance worker reports directly to General Mortimer."

Mention of Mayor Baynor's right-hand man reminded Kyle of something. "Hey, General Mortimer has a cybernetic arm. Maybe I could work directly for him and keep it in good running order." He looked at his mom and smiled. "Or maybe sabotage it so he strangles himself."

"Well, that would be a relief," she murmured.

"Don't disrespect the man, Kyle. Nor you, Loreena."

"No," Kyle said, "or we'll end up standing against a wall being shot to death. Or worse, being repurposed."

His dad thumped the table. The muffin pan and three plates jumped, and Kyle almost choked on his mouthful. "That's enough!" his dad said, suddenly angry. "Both of you. Walls have ears." He gently tapped the dimmed screen of his tablet, and it lit up at his touch. "I've been reading about it on the datahub. That kind of talk is dangerous. It gets around. Next thing you know, neither of us have jobs and the landlord is throwing us out on the streets—and you know how I feel about those who can't contribute to society. Deadbeats should be repurposed."

"Or exiled," Kyle said quietly. "By law, deadbeats have the option to — "

"Bah!" his dad interrupted. "Enough talk. Eat." He glared at the clock on the wall. "We're leaving in ten minutes. Your appointment is at nine sharp, and we're *not* going to be late."

\* \* \*

Kyle wanted to take the pod, but as usual his father said it was a waste of good money and only a benefit to those who couldn't be bothered to plan ahead and leave in good time for their destination.

"The maglev is perfectly adequate," he grumbled as they boarded and found seats. "A quarter of the price, and the station is right below our apartment. Besides, the minimum requirement to make Pod Controller is only 60%, which means passengers need to cross their fingers and pray to the three moons they get where they want to go. Anyway, by the time you factor in the time it takes to get to the nearest pod depot . . ."

He droned on, but Kyle tuned him out. He'd heard the same speech a million times before. The maglev train was slow, stopping dozens of times en route to a destination that was just eight or nine blocks away. If you wanted to get to the far side of the city, pods were more expensive but *so* much faster—literally half a minute compared to about an hour.

By fifteen minutes to nine, Kyle and his father had arrived at the local Implant Clinic, checked in, and were sitting in the waiting room. Despite his father's laced fingers and relaxed posture, Kyle fidgeted and tapped his foot, forever twisting around to peer at the clock.

Eventually, his dad grabbed his arm and snapped, "Will you sit still!"

"I can't," Kyle moaned.

The receptionist continued to stare at her screen, flashing through pages of text on the datahub as she filed her nails. Sifting through endless patient records was not what Kyle considered an ideal job. This woman probably sat unmoving all day long, checking the error log, analyzing implant data transmitted daily from every eligible citizen, trying to keep her hands busy while her mind did all the work.

A silent stream screen on the wall behind her showed the latest headlines and live pictures of a wreck on one of the city flyovers: several injured and three casualties, the dead being transported to the Repurposing Factory.

Just after nine, Kyle's dad began to grumble about punctuality. He remained outwardly calm, though, even when a door swung open and a white-coated technician stepped through, looking at a clipboard. "Kyle Jaxx?"

"That's me," Kyle cried, jumping up.

"Restraint, son," his dad whispered, reaching out again to grip his arm. "Show some self-respect and—"

"This way, please," the technician said.

The semi-circular room Kyle and his dad were led into was exactly as depicted on infostreams—pure gleaming white with a single aluminum chair in the center and several small machines hanging on stiff rods from the ceiling. An array of screens adorned the curving walls. Three technicians sat at control panels on one side, while another two waited by the chair.

Being seated in The Chair, as it was referred to in awed tones by citizens, was the single most exciting, anticipated, and revered moment in every child's life. It marked the end of useless childhood and the beginning of purposeful adulthood. When Kyle rose from The Chair, his new implant would allow him to access technology with the will of his mind. It would allow him to *connect*.

"Take a seat," the technician said. "Dr. Pollard will be right in. Your father may wait in the viewing room."

Kyle was barely aware of his dad being ushered away into a small adjoining room with a glass wall that looked very much like one of the giant monitor screens. He was focused instead on the moment he'd been waiting for—being seated in The Chair.

It wasn't as comfortable as he'd expected. The padding was a little tough and dug into him. But when the technician lowered the backrest to a horizontal position, the whole thing seemed to alter to fit his contours. Clamps slid into place around his ankles and thighs, then his wrists and chest, and finally around his forehead. Each clamp was padded, and they tightened carefully with a gentle hiss until Kyle was unable to move at all. He stared up at the machines, wondering where the implant was actually stored, where it would emerge from, wanting to know every detail of the procedure but knowing that he wouldn't see any of it.

A technician pressed something on a keyboard, and the horizontal chair started to tilt to Kyle's right. He could barely suppress a grin as he turned like a wild boar on a spit—and for a moment he wondered where that particular image had come from. Seconds later he hung upside down, facing the floor, the weight of his body straining against the clamps. It was a strange feeling, being supported like this, but not unpleasant.

A small panel in the seat behind his head lifted away. He felt a draft on the back of his exposed neck. At that same moment, another man entered the room. Kyle could see his shiny black shoes and black pants, and the white coat that flapped casually as he walked.

"Ah, Dr. Pollard's here, Kyle," the technician said. "Are you ready?"

"I'm ready," Kyle said, trembling with excitement.

*Chapter 2*
## Logan

Logan eyed the path and frowned. It was too obvious, the grasses thoroughly trampled and his partial footprints splayed across the muddy patches. This would be the last time he entered the Broken Lands by this route. Not that anyone followed him out this far from the Fixer Enclave. They were all too afraid of the ruins.

Of course, this might be the last time he entered the wastelands at all.

He stepped carefully onto the muddy path, not wishing to sink his boots farther than necessary in the yielding terrain. In another minute, the confines of the forest would fade away, and he would be out in the open, crossing the wide expanse of bone-dry land that marked the outskirts of the Broken Lands.

As his feet began kicking up dust, he thought of what others his age were doing. All who had turned fourteen in the last two months in his village were also entering the ruins, but far south of his one-man expedition. Today would be the first and only day they would set foot in the ruins. It was Tethering Day. It was to have been his Tethering Day, too, but he knew better than to lump himself in with the others.

Logan glanced back to see if anyone was hiding in the thin brush at the forest's edge. He gripped his spear tighter, knowing there were physical threats out here in the wastelands.

In Apparata, reaching fourteen years of age was a milestone. Each enclave youth achieved citizenship and with it the obligation to become tethered. One could only do so out in the Broken Lands where the spirits roamed free. To be tethered to a spirit was a noble act and a requirement of becoming an adult. It was unthinkable to pass through life without being paired with a spirit—a prospect Logan faced.

He was entering the truly broken area of the wastelands. Remnants of archaic buildings stood in ramshackle piles, their design and purpose long forgotten if ever known at all. No one remembered what had happened in the Broken Lands or even who had lived there. Some said their ancestors, while others claimed another race of beings entirely. How else to explain the twisted forms of the spirits that were bound to the ruins until their tethering? One only entered to become tethered to a spirit and then never set foot in the Broken Lands again.

Logan allowed a crooked smile. *Shows how much they know.* He had been sneaking into the Broken Lands since he was ten. And in all that time, not a single apparition had seen fit to sync with him.

He had done it on a dare at first, several classmates in his learning circle having goaded him into it. They had watched from afar as several spirits approached him. But the ghostly figures had merely circled around, sniffing distastefully. Not even the invasive Breakers came near. And he had been an easy target. Normally, those under the age of fourteen were too weak to tame a spirit. Logan, on the other hand, was of no interest to them. He was lacking in some fashion.

The destroyed buildings grew more populous around him. He walked down a distinctive street now, the rubble reaching above his head. Most of the first floors in this part of the ruins were intact with the upper levels lying in shambles.

He glanced back, the safety of the woods far behind him. He liked it that way. While others claimed entering the Broken Lands filled them with unease, he felt something that was missing back at the Fixer Enclave: acceptance.

Not that the spirits radiated this emotion. Above him two Weavers ducked and bobbed alongside each other, playing some form of tag. They looked to be young, their eyes wide and dark. They ignored Logan, disappearing over the roof of the most intact building along the street. To be tethered to a Weaver was well regarded. They were the builders and creators. His people always put special emphasis on any of the spirits that were productive, that contributed.

A Breaker ghosted through the roof of a nearby structure, its long tusks leading the charge. It spun about and glared back at the roof, outraged at not having disturbed the building. Breakers thrived on destruction. Anyone tethered to them had to have supreme resolve. Controlling a Breaker, bending its will to excavate and clear the forest, was a demanding duty. This particular spirit swam in cruelty and malice. Logan shivered at the thought of its power. Without hosts, spirits could not affect their environs. If an unfettered Breaker could, the result would spell massive destruction and chaos. It took another run at the roof, ignorant of its inability to deliver even the simplest physical touch.

The Breaker dove into the ground, its sheer mass daunting in spite of its semi-transparent appearance. Logan half-expected to feel the earth shake and fissures to appear to mark its passing, but none did. Had it been tethered to one from the Enclave, the dirt would've been thoroughly gouged and churned up. His father, moored to a Breaker, was always on edge, never content.

Logan marched to his left and climbed a slight rise of a wall, hugging close to the section that was largely intact. He straddled the top of the wall and let his legs hang, rocking back and forth with contentment. He opened his canteen and took two deep pulls.

He kept telling himself he didn't need to tether, but he knew that wasn't true. Anyone who remained untethered past the age of fourteen faced two paths: banishment to the Broken Lands—or death. Resources were finite in their tiny realm, and none of the enclaves had room for those who could not contribute. Still, there was life outside the enclaves, wasn't there? Although bordered by the forbidden wastelands to the west, Logan often wondered why no one had built a vessel to leave Apparata by

*11*

water to the north, east, or south. Surely there were other lands? Their world could not be just one solitary land mass lost in a sprawling ocean. Logan often thought of leaving by sea but didn't feel an affinity for the water like he did the ruins. Given the choice, he would pick exile to the Broken Lands over death.

But he didn't have a say in the matter. His fate lay in his father's hands, and that likely meant something rather more final than a shameful exile.

*Maybe I should just stay out here, never go back,* he thought. He could make the decision himself to make the ruins his home. He took stock of his supplies: a simple hunting knife, his spear, a fishing net, and flint. Along with the canteen, he had the basics. He could fashion what he needed from the debris in the ruins. Many of the buildings were cleared of anything remotely useful here on the outskirts, but what if he went deeper?

His attention went to the west, into the heart of the ruins. What awaited him there? Back home offered nothing more than awkward goodbyes. He would miss his younger brother, but Kiff was strong for an eight-year-old with a lame leg. He had overcome much in his short life, and Logan was infinitely proud of him. But was that enough to force Logan to return home and risk hearing his father call for his death? He thought not.

While his father would brand him a coward, Logan wouldn't let him decide his fate. He would stay in the Broken Lands and make it his home.

Maybe there were others like him ... But that thought quickly dissolved. He knew of no others in the past two generations to go untethered. He was unique.

At least for now.

*Chapter 3*
**Kyle**

Dr. Pollard glanced over the patient information on his clipboard. It was said that every man, woman, and child in the city was born with the power to connect remotely to technology, to bond with a microchip from several feet away using only the power of the mind. But channeling thoughts was supremely difficult, and the tech-link was always weak—hence the implant, which boosted the signal and allowed recipients to flourish, to recognize their calling in life and contribute to Apparati in whatever technological field suited them best.

Some young patients showed more promise than others. Even before the implant they could switch stream screens off without verbalizing the command, or open doors without touching the pad. And on extremely rare occasions, along came a recipient with a command of tech so finely tuned that an implant was unnecessary. On Mayor Baynor's orders, such recipients vanished from the public eye and became special operatives working directly for General Mortimer.

Kyle Jaxx was no such recipient. In fact, he lacked even the slightest hint of focus.

The doctor stifled a yawn. Just another routine implant, then. He gave the technician a nod and got to work on his first procedure of the day.

He stared up at the delicate robot arm and focused. The arm responded immediately, and the implant—a tiny flat device no bigger than a fingernail, with a slightly curved, needle-thin tail—descended in the gentle grip of fine pincers. There was very little for the technicians to do. Most of the white coats were for show; the patient's father was, after all, watching from the viewing room. This work was all about Dr. Pollard, an experienced Grade-A Surgeon with a perfect score in most of his field tests. The work was easy, though he tended to screw up his face in concentration to make it look difficult. He leaned in close, nodded, made a meaningless scribble on his clipboard, glanced at the hanging monitor, and refocused on the microchip.

Under his direct mental guidance, the robot arm positioned the implant at the back of the patient's neck, which was visible through the opening in the chair. A red laser dot marked the exact point of insertion. The robot arm had several built-in appendages, like miniature arms folded up alongside the primary. At Dr. Pollard's command, one unfolded with a soft hiss, wielding a tiny syringe. It quickly injected a numbing agent next to the laser dot.

A scalpel blade appeared and made a swift and barely perceptible incision. Next, the main arm lowered and pressed the implant against the skin where a speck of blood was forming, causing a red smear. The tiny tail stuck upward like a random hair.

When the robot arm released its needle-sharp pincer grip, the tail began to thrash—and the chip disappeared into the incision, worming its way deeper.

The monitor beeped, reporting fluctuations in the readings. All perfectly normal. Just for show, Dr. Pollard nodded again, peering at the screen and making random marks on his clipboard. He smiled and complimented the technicians.

"Um," one of them said.

Dr. Pollard glanced at him, seeing a puzzled frown. "What's wrong?"

Rather than say it out loud, the technician pointed at one of the large monitors on the wall behind him. It showed digitized schematics in real-time, and the chip, blown up to about a foot in size, was right there at the base of the brain where it should be. Only . . .

"It's not activated," he said quietly. "Is it faulty?"

The doctor could see that the chip's tail had bonded with the brain stem. As far as he could tell, the implant was like every other, working correctly and ready to channel and transmit the patient's thoughts. Yet no data was being received.

"The implant is in send mode," the technician confirmed. "We have a strong, perfectly normal signal from it. It's just not receiving any data from the patient."

"So it must be a faulty connection," Dr. Pollard mused. He'd overseen a thousand or more implant procedures in the last decade, at a rate of two a week. It was such a simple five-minute job that dozens of similar procedures could be crammed in every day if ever there was a need. But the city and its population were finite, and so were the number of children turning fourteen. How many faults had he run across in his time? Exactly twelve. He'd easily repaired the three bad connections and two damaged chips, but the remaining seven had simply been poor candidates, their brains unreadable.

Seven poor candidates. Could Kyle Jaxx be the eighth? Dr. Pollard hoped not. "Check the connection," he said quietly, knowing the technician was already running diagnostics.

The tech shrugged. "It's good. The chip is responding and transmitting properly. Everything is fine."

So the patient was indeed his eighth poor candidate, Dr. Pollard thought sadly. Poor kid. He glanced toward the viewing room and saw Mr. Jaxx pressed against the glass, a frown on his face.

"What's happening?" a shaky voice called.

Dr. Pollard knelt to peer at the boy hanging under the chair, whose overlong dark brown hair hung limply. "Sorry for the delay, son. We're going to sit you up and run a few routine tests, okay?"

"Okay."

The doctor allowed the technicians to manually retract the robot arm. They turned Kyle's chair over and sat him up. The boy's face was red from being upside down, and when the clamps pulled back, padded though they were, he had indentations across his forehead.

"Let's see what you can do," Dr. Pollard said, nodding toward the wall screen directly opposite.

A program was launching. Normally it wasn't necessary; the data transmitted from most patients' brains right after connection usually provided a stream of information that meant instant classification and dismissal. This time they'd have to run the manual calibration tool. One of the technicians would get to make use of his own implant for a change.

"Coming up on the screen is a series of classifications," Dr. Pollard said as calmly as he could, his heart thumping. He dreaded the upcoming talk with the child's father.

As he spoke, rows of circles flashed across the screen, dozens of them, each with a label and progress bar. In theory, some of these classifications should match the patient's disposition. The strongest match would determine the boy's future.

"Run your gaze across the labels," Dr. Pollard told him, "and see if you can connect. It's a very simple test. The screen acts as a conduit to a multitude of simulators spread throughout the complex. Your brain will attempt to manipulate those simulators as though you're in the same room. If successful, the progress bar will show something more than 0%. If you reach 100%, that means you've found your calling in life." He smiled tightly. "Start with the classifications you think you're suited to, for example Mechanical. When selected, it will drill down to subcategories such as Vehicles, Appliances, and so on."

"Okay," the young recipient said, sounding both excited and nervous.

Dr. Pollard allowed one of the techs to step in for the one-on-one walkthrough and hand-holding. Sometimes this manual classification took a full hour. The test was usually reserved for those who were suited to many tasks and needed actual statistics to determine their strongest match. Unfortunately, when it came to boys like Kyle Jaxx, with no data whatsoever being received via his implant, it usually took the full hour just to prove that he was simply a poor candidate, unable to connect to anything.

In which case, the boy had no future in Apparati.

\* \* \*

"It's been two hours," Dr. Pollard stiffly told the patient's father. Mr. Jaxx looked ready to explode, and security guards were already standing by outside the room.

"It has to be a mistake," the man growled. "Why won't you try another implant? How do you know for sure it's not just faulty? If you can just try another one—"

"You have to believe me when I tell you that the chip is in good working order. We've run full diagnostics three times. It's transmitting fine. It's just not receiving any data from your son's brain. The implant was successful. Your boy just isn't a suitable candidate."

"Meaning he's worthless?" Mr. Jaxx snapped, his face a deep red, fists balled. "Is that what you're saying? That my son is of no use to this city? That he's a *deadbeat*, fit only for *repurposing*?"

Dr. Pollard nodded. "Unfortunately, that's exactly what I'm saying. Look at him. He's been trying his hardest with the classes. He managed to squeeze 2% out of Robotics, but only because he tried extra hard with that one. Still nowhere near the minimum requirement of 55%, though. Otherwise he's a flat zero across the board. I'm afraid he has no future in Apparati, Mr. Jaxx."

"Maybe he just hasn't found the right class! Maybe you don't *have* a class for what he can do! Did you consider that?"

Dr. Pollard gave a curt nod to one of his techs, and the man returned the nod and opened the door. Three security guards filed in. In the larger room beyond, still sitting in the chair looking scared and confused, Kyle Jaxx persisted in staring at the screen trying to make *something* respond.

"You need to make a choice, Mr. Jaxx," the doctor said quietly. "You may of course have the rest of the day to say your farewells to your son. Your family is welcome to visit the clinic. But your son will be incarcerated here until midnight, the end of his fourteenth birthday, at which point he will be turned over to the Repurposing Factory. Unless, of course, you'd prefer that he be exiled to the Ruins."

Mr. Jaxx didn't answer. His shoulders slumped as though he were suddenly tired. The expression on his face went from anger to frustration to pain and finally to reluctant acceptance. He seemed like a decent law-abiding citizen, Dr. Pollard thought, and would likely do the right thing no matter how difficult. He would, with great dignity, accept the fate of his deadbeat son and grieve in private when it was all over.

"Mr. Jaxx? You don't have to decide right away. The law allows you, on your son's behalf, to opt out of repurposing anytime before midnight, after which the decision is no longer yours. If you decide he should be sent to the Ruins—"

"He won't," Mr. Jaxx grunted. "Deadbeats have no place in this world, neither here in the city nor outside its walls. He'll go for repurposing, and he'll go with dignity."

Dr. Pollard nodded. "I understand. Security is here. He'll be taken to a holding cell." He reached out and gently placed his hand on the man's shoulder. "I'm sorry, Mr. Jaxx. There's no known reason for these rare defects. It just happens from time to time."

*Chapter 4*
## Logan

Eight-year-old Kiff sank back into the tall grasses, pleased that his older brother had not detected him and sent him home. Logan usually had an uncanny knack for knowing when he was being followed, but today he seemed distracted. Kiff had managed to follow him all the way to the fringe of the Broken Lands.

It was well known how often Logan broke the law and snuck out to the ruins. Kiff was always being harassed by his classmates about his older brother's perilous transgressions. It had been going on for years. But while Kiff was fed up with everyone in school whispering about it, he was beginning to see his brother's point of view. Today was Logan's fourteenth birthday, and he couldn't tether. He was already considered an outsider to the enclave; after today he would either be exiled or put to death unless he tethered in the next few hours. Kiff was worried for his brother's plight . . . but more than that, he was intrigued.

He knew what grim fate their father would choose for Logan—that is, if he got his way. Breakers like his father tended to think and act aggressively. The berserker nature of the spirit always seemed to create more strife in their family than anything else. Not many could tame a Breaker, and those who did were revered by all. They were the ones who cleared the land, dug new fields for crops, or blasted away any rocky obstructions that stood in the way of expanding the enclaves. Their father had been outspoken about further expanding their village. He had an important job, working long days and spending far too much time synced with his Breaker. No one else would ever say it, but Kiff was convinced his father's gruff, overly authoritative demeanor was a direct result of the Breaker's hold on him.

Kiff winced as he stood, his left leg a constant reminder of his misfortune. He traced the scars that ran its length, finding their pronounced aspect on his skin both soothing and unnerving.

A kaliback had expanded its hunting territory to include the field near their home. The grey and yellow-furred predator, with its distinctive double set of eyes and mouths, was the size of a market wagon. It had smashed Kiff's leg with its twelve-foot armored tail. Logan had come to his aid, beating back the animal with a simple stick until their father arrived and killed the creature with the assistance of his Breaker. In Kiff's mind the spirit's tusks still looked stained with kaliback blood.

His mother, matched with a Fixer, was the serene one, offering her healing talents to all. A pity she couldn't mend her own son's damaged leg more than she had. But thanks to her, Kiff could at least hobble. Before she and four other Fixers worked on him, his mangled leg would have kept him from ever leaving the house again.

When Kiff turned fourteen, he wanted to be a healer like his mother. He had the right temperament for it, accepting and giving. He shivered, thinking of being tethered to a Breaker like his father. He would do anything to avoid that. It was too much. He would rather wink out than become tied to the destructive spirits.

Returning his attention to where his older brother sat on the wall, Kiff could make out two Weavers dancing through the air. The apparitions didn't look so populous here. Probably most were south, attracted by the presence of those entering the Broken Lands on their Tethering Day.

Kiff swallowed. He was afraid for his brother, not because of the risk of being tethered to a Breaker or attacked by numerous predators, but because Logan had crossed into the ruins with the solemn resolution of one who never intended to return. Kiff knew his brother faced exile or death for remaining untethered after today.

He knew these same thoughts rattled through his brother's head. That's why Kiff had chased after him. He wanted to talk to Logan one last time, try to convince him to approach the Tribunal and make a case for something other than the two dire outcomes he faced.

Kiff leaned against the Banisher marker, a three-foot-tall wooden post driven into the ground. Tied to its top was a simple blue ribbon. These posts ran along the periphery of the Broken Lands. How long since a Banisher had been by to work their magic? Thanks to their adeptness, they cast spells at each post in order to keep the spirits out of the enclaves. It was a shame his brother hadn't been a girl. Then 'she' could've been a banisher. They didn't tether to a spirit. It was part of their acceptance into their order. Not that Kiff would want to have a Banisher as a sibling. They were always odd, detached. He knew Mora Vil in his class was one. She radiated the perfect creepy vibe for it.

His brother had hopped down from the wall and was walking deeper into the ruins. Logan appeared at home in the barren landscape, his tanned skin and lean musculature speaking of an untamed wildness that somehow fit. His shoulder-length brown hair scattered in the breeze. Logan had an intensity fueled by curiosity and not fear like their father. If exiled, Kiff knew his brother would manage. But what sort of life would that be?

Kiff drew in a quick breath as a lone Creeper spirit slithered over the ground to his left a good three hundred paces off. He waited another second, eyeing with disgust the numerous tentacles protruding from the Creeper's midsection.

Their neighbor was tethered to such a spirit and always snuck about. Kiff found it unnerving. Creepers were limited in their options. Most elected to use their stealth to help patrol, a task Kiff found thoroughly boring. Slinking around tethered to a Creeper held little attraction. There were very few threats to the seven enclaves other than canyon clackers and kalibacks. The oversized rock worms rarely left the steep rocky confines of their home, and kalibacks almost always fled when outnumbered.

He touched his scar again, a phantom pain stabbing through its entirety. His kaliback hadn't fled. It had only stopped its attack after being gored by their father's Breaker.

The Creeper was now much farther away. Seeing no other spirits, Kiff stood and limped into the wastelands.

He almost expected to feel some sort of jolt upon his entrance into the Broken Lands, but felt nothing other than the familiar numbness that christened his every other step. He scanned constantly as he hobbled after Logan.

Kiff knew his plan wasn't well thought out, that at any moment a phantom could slip out of the ground or from the nearby rubble and attempt to tether with him, but he sensed his path to Logan was clear. Once he caught up, he had no inkling how long it would take to convince Logan that his plan to face the Tribunal could work. He stumbled over a twisted hunk of wood, kicking a pile of stones in every direction with his good leg.

He crouched and slowed his progress, alert to the volume of his disturbance.

Behind him the Creeper was out of sight. No other spirits roamed free. Most were probably drawn to the Tethering farther south.

Logan continued, oblivious to Kiff's presence. He was only another hundred paces ahead.

Kiff considered calling out, but thought it better to go deeper into the ruins. If a spirit made an appearance, he might be able to lose it in the maze of half-standing buildings.

He passed his brother's former perch on the long wall. He was surprised at how intact the buildings were farther in, even spying some vegetation in spots. Maybe there was enough here to survive. Maybe Logan would be okay out in the Broken Lands. Could exile actually be an option?

Kiff shrugged and continued forward.

Ahead, his brother had dropped to his knees, scrutinizing something metallic on the ground. Kiff was surprised that the object wasn't covered in rust. It appeared to be a large sphere with black markings, and a long pole jutted from its underbelly with a triangle of some sort at its tip.

Logan reached out to touch the triangle. Kiff wanted to shout out a warning, but didn't.

Instead, he let out a shriek on his own behalf.

Coming up fast on his right was the distinctive bulk of a Breaker. Leading with its tusks, it zoomed toward Kiff, a wicked grin splayed across its broad crimson features.

Kiff lurched to his right, scrambling to put any sort of distance between himself and the spirit. He tripped over a ragged root.

He whipped around to see his brother racing toward him, spear held high and ready for battle—not that it would be any use against a spirit.

The Breaker was upon Kiff. It let out a moan and pounced on him, its tusks dropping into his body, but not tearing at his flesh.

Despite the absence of injury, Kiff let out a heart-rending scream, for the attack was not on his broken body but on his mind.

He was being tethered.

*Chapter 5*
## Kyle

Kyle sat on the edge of the bed in his cell, utterly miserable. The unfairness of it all, of the system, the *law*, burned him up from inside and threatened to overcome him. He wanted to scream—and had done so already for an hour before finally slumping onto his bunk in exhaustion, his throat raw.

He wasn't some sadistic killer convicted of heinous crimes. He was simply one of those rare and unfortunate souls who couldn't connect to any part of the city's technology. But his fate was the same as a violent criminal—to be repurposed.

His parents and little brother now sat with him in the so-called holding cell—more of an expensive hotel room, the sort his parents could never afford, and the sort his dad would never pay for even if he could. It was certainly luxurious . . . but he didn't care. He just wanted to curl up into a ball and cry.

There was nothing his parents could say or do to settle his nerves or cheer him up. He'd woken that morning with the certainty this would be his best birthday ever, but nothing had been farther from the truth. He wished he'd never crawled out of bed. Of course, then the authorities would have come looking for him. Kids sometimes ran away on Implant Day or were held back by nervous parents. In those cases, the parents risked imprisonment and the implant went ahead anyway. It was the system.

Still, even though the procedure was mandatory, the number of failed implants was so small as to be hardly worth fretting about. Kyle certainly hadn't been worried when he'd woken that morning. He had good genes, or so he thought. Two decades earlier, his dad had passed with ease, a full 100% score in Appliance Diagnostics and Repairs. His prowess as a repairman was well known, and many neighbors in the apartment called on him to figure out what was wrong with the dish ionizer or laundry press. Of course, being a stickler for rules, he always made his neighbors write out work orders and go through the proper channels. There was no cutting in line with him.

Kyle's mom was less strict. She'd made 86% in Pharmacy, and she occasionally cobbled together pills off the record at far greater legal risk than repairing a neighbor's faulty drink dispenser. Kyle knew she often worked off the books because he'd seen people come in, have a light and pointless conversation, and leave shortly after grasping a mysterious square envelope. Kyle had opened one before, finding inside a clutch of tiny pills made with her home-installed pharmacy press.

And here was Kyle, barely able to muster 2% in Robotics and a flat zero on everything else.

His parents tried to talk in soothing tones, but his mom was overwrought, leaving the room several times in tears, unable to look at him. He told himself it was because she would miss him and not because he was a worthless deadbeat.

Byron managed to get a word in from time to time. He sometimes wobbled around the cell on his thin mechanical legs, his oversized feet keeping him balanced, but mostly he stood still. One of these days he would get an upgrade to a bigger body as Kyle had promised. The accident had happened when Byron was four, and so his robot body was that of a four-year-old. But he was eight now and often commented that he would like to be taller to match his age, with a faster processor. If Kyle had passed in Robotics, got his official license and security clearance, he might have reconfigured the spare limbs lying in a heap at home and programmed them to work for his little brother.

Not anymore, though. His dreams were dashed.

Still, repurposing brought money into the family. A small consolation. Maybe after Kyle was gone, there'd be enough money for his dad to go ahead and pay someone to do the upgrade. Someone who wasn't a deadbeat.

"I don't *want* to be repurposed," he said suddenly, bolting upright and cutting through his dad's latest speech about how right and proper it was to contribute body parts to society.

"We've been over this," his dad said with a sigh. "In an ideal world, implants would be optional—"

"I want to go out into the Ruins."

This brought a grimace to his dad's face, though his mom's lifted briefly with hope. "No, son," he said, shaking his head. "Repurposing is painless and an honorable way to go. Only your brain dies, leaving every part of your body to be put to good use for those who need transplants."

"Didn't help Byron, though, did it?" Kyle retorted. His forthcoming death emboldened him in the way he spoke to his father. It wasn't like he was going to be grounded for being disrespectful. "Where were the spare body parts when he was crushed under a ton of bricks?"

The uprising on that fateful day four years ago had led to twelve deaths and dozens of injuries. Poor Byron had been standing in the wrong place, on the other side of a wall, when a bomb had gone off inside the mayor's reception office. Mom had suffered broken bones, too, but she hadn't even noticed her pain as she'd dragged Byron's shattered body from the rubble.

Curiously, the number of wink-outs had spiked that day as well; several men and women had simply vanished into thin air, never to be seen again.

"Let's not go through this again," their dad said softly. "Kyle, it's not just about doing the right thing for society. It's about making things easier on you. Repurposing is painless. Your brain is put to death while your body lives on, hooked to a machine. Avoiding unnecessary shock and trauma to the body is paramount, so you can be assured that you'll be put to sleep with—"

"I don't care about that."

"You should," his dad said sharply, a deep frown setting in. "The Ruins is a slow death. You've heard the stories of bodies laid out across the wastelands. How do you think those people died? From thirst? Attacks from predators? Torture and execution by gangs?" He nodded and leaned toward Kyle. "Try all of the above, and worse. I can assure you that no good comes from being out there. It's bad enough for grown men, murderous convicts who choose to be exiled. But an innocent fourteen-year-old boy?" He shook his head. "I can't allow it. I won't do that to you. As your father, you have to trust that I know what's best for you."

"But I want to *live!*" Kyle shouted, leaping off the bed. "Why don't I get to choose for myself?"

"Because you're a minor. The law says—"

"It's not fair!" As his mom's sobbing intensified, Kyle fell to his knees and grabbed his dad's large hands. "Please. Send me out. Give me a chance. I might survive in the Ruins. You never know, I could get past the famous Tower on the horizon, and then—"

"There's nothing out there, son. Nothing but death. The place is littered with old machines that don't work and abandoned houses where people used to live before the city was walled up. There are gangs and predators, and that's all. If you go out there in the morning, I guarantee you'll be turning on a spit by dinnertime."

Kyle remembered how, during the implant procedure, he'd been clamped into his chair and rotated just like a dead animal on a spit over a fire. How fitting that image seemed now.

"Mom?" he said, turning his gaze to her.

She buried her face in her hands and sobbed harder. But after a while she got herself under control, wiped her eyes, and looked at him through a film of new tears. "Your dad's right, honey," she said shakily. "I can't bear the idea of losing you . . . but it's for the best."

Kyle released his dad's hands and climbed to his feet. He stared hard at his parents. "It shouldn't be about what *you* want," he whispered. "But if it makes you both sleep better at night, go ahead and sentence me to death."

His words cut through the air like daggers and into both his parents' hearts. He saw their eyes widen, their mouths drop open, and instantly knew he'd gone too far and wished he could take it back.

But he didn't. Instead he stared at them defiantly for a second before turning away.

"Just go," he said.

Kyle heard them shuffle across the floor, heard the rapping of knuckles for the guard, and the door hiss open. "We'll be back soon," his dad said tightly. "Come on, Byron."

Kyle realized that he hadn't heard the familiar sound of the whirring servos in his brother's spindly legs. "No, he can stay," he said, turning to see Byron standing perfectly still in the exact same spot he'd been standing most of the day.

His parents left, and the door hissed shut. Byron tilted his head. "Sorry," he said simply. Somehow, even his artificial voice box held more warmth and sympathy than their dad's.

Kyle sat once more on the edge of the bed and motioned for his brother to join him. Since it was a chore for Byron to maneuver himself onto anything higher than a child's stool, he remained standing, stiff and absolutely still. "I'm gonna miss you," Kyle said. "I really wanted to work in Robotics and build you a proper upgrade." He sighed and shook his head. "I wish I didn't have to be repurposed."

Byron leaned closer, his orbs glowing softly. "Want me to help you escape?"

*Chapter 6*
## Logan

The scream sent chills down Logan's spine. Even before he turned, he knew its owner—his brother!

He spun, hoping to spy Kiff at the edge of the Broken Lands, wailing about a plucky lurk bird harassing him. Sadly, the scream had been too close to make that scenario true.

Less than a hundred paces away, Kiff rolled in the dirt, flailing his arms and legs weakly at a Breaker. The spirit loomed over him, its intent unmistakable. It wanted to tether.

Logan sprinted closer, his spear raised. He screamed at his brother, "Get away from it!"

The Breaker dove into Kiff's midsection, its spirit form passing through his far smaller body with ease. Kiff flinched as the long, deadly tusks entered him first. He squirmed about as the phantom's long muscular arms merged with his leaner appendages. The Breaker spun around inside its host, situating itself as if arranging its bedding. Its ethereal limbs splayed out, imitating the posture of its host's far weaker arms and legs.

Logan had only ever seen a tethering from a distance. Usually the spirit funneled into the citizen, for a time occupying the same space. Most spirits were either the same size or smaller than their hosts. Breakers and Hunters were the exception. Breakers, especially, could be as much as twice the size of those they tethered to. Only when the process was complete did the spirit blend with the physical form of their host.

Logan dropped his spear. He risked harming Kiff if he plunged his weapon into the spirit. He had to try and yank the spirit out. Was that even possible?

Kiff stopped flailing and lay still, his arms spread, palms upward as though offering himself to the gods. Logan watched as the spirit's more massive arms shimmered, to all appearances resembling a protective shell for Kiff. Usually it was not the spirit that exerted control, but the host. With Kiff being so young, the roles were reversed. He was losing himself to the spirit, and if that happened—if the spirit took control—the result would be a deranged monster that would have to be put to death, after which Kiff's body would be buried and the spirit would resume its mindless roaming in the Broken Lands.

Logan fell on his brother, receiving a facefull of the breaker's torso as his own body passed through the spirit's larger form. He went numb from the cold sensation rushing over every part of him immersed in the spirit's dimensions.

Kiff screamed, "Get it out of me!"

Being engulfed in the Breaker had not just numbed Logan's muscles—his thoughts were more random and far less pressing than he wanted them to be. Logan lifted his head, unnerved by how sluggish his thoughts were.

With his head no longer mired in the Breaker, reckless courage overtook him.

"Take me, I'm stronger." Logan yelled at the spirit. He straddled Kiff and the phantom at the waist. He looked back to see Kiff's legs engulfed by the thick thighs and calves of the spirit's. Again, being far more in volume, the creature's lower appendages encased Kiff's. The two were becoming one—but which would win out in the end?

The Breaker let out a wet growl. Logan snapped his head back around and stared into the eyes of his brother's attacker.

The wide visage of the spirit was extremely flat, with eyes sunk deep into massive sockets and small tusks curling up from its high cheekbones. It held its head back to rest inside Kiff's. Logan knew it desired to thrust its long tusks mounted atop its head into him, but couldn't. It was too occupied with flooding Kiff with warped thoughts to give Logan's invitation any serious consideration. The spirit rejected him.

He didn't know what to do. Spirits were immaterial until tethered. Once linked with a citizen, they could be conjured up outside of the body and given substance in order to perform tasks. Would Kiff cease to exist and the Breaker take physical form? Would Logan soon be wrestling with a very large Breaker instead of his brother?

He peered past the spiteful features of the spirit and into Kiff's eyes. Their lively orange hue was muted, growing steadily dimmer as he looked on. His brother couldn't handle it. He was too young, his will too yielding.

Logan couldn't best the spirit, couldn't rip it free of his brother or coax it to take him instead. Kiff had to expel it, something that had never been done before by anyone under fourteen, or drive it deep down inside him, suppress it long enough for Logan to race him back to their enclave and beseech them to help. Maybe all five Fixers could do something. They had to. With their mother leading them, they could fix Kiff. It wasn't like a Banisher would be visiting their enclave anytime soon. And they usually only drove the rare untethered spirits back into the Broken Lands. Logan didn't want any creepy Banishers working on his brother.

He relaxed and talked firmly but with a soothing tone. "Kiff, you have to stay awake. You have to take charge. You can't let it overwhelm you."

Kiff spoke, but his words sounded slurred and muffled from being swamped by the Breaker's magnitude. "Its thoughts are so angry! It wants to wipe out all of me. It wants to take my memories."

A thin trail of drool slipped out of the corner of Kiff's mouth. His cheeks slackened. Logan was losing him.

Logan reached into the spirit and shook his brother's head. "No, you're the strongest person I know. You can do this. You always find the strength, Kiff!"

His brother's eyes lightened, their normal spark returning briefly. "I know why I came. You can't run. You have to face the Tribunal. I'll help you. I'll stand by you."

Logan flinched. Because of him, Kiff had entered the Broken Lands and was now merging with the Breaker's slippery, malignant essence. Logan bristled at this, but didn't falter. If anything, he grew more determined to make things right.

"You are the one it will serve. It doesn't matter your age. You have it in you to put the Breaker in its place. Shove it down deep! Lock it up and don't let it run free!"

Kiff smiled, his lips a smaller mirror of the grim apparition's sneer hovering just scant inches above his much softer features.

"Beat it down and we can stand before the Tribunal together!" Logan shouted.

His brother squinched and gritted his teeth.

While Kiff lay still, it was the Breaker's turn to thrash. It howled as its host exerted his presence.

Logan held his ground. "Bury it deep so we can go home. We'll make this right together."

Kiff gasped. "I'm trying, but it's ... fighting ... me." Sweat flicked from his forehead and he rocked his head back and forth with increasing vigor.

"Fight it! You're Kiff Orm! No one puts you in your place, much less a creepy Breaker!"

Kiff screamed and abruptly sat up.

The Breaker moved with him, its tusks slamming into Logan's jaw. He flew back, landing on his back several paces away. The Breaker had been solid!

Logan wiped the trickle of blood from his chin, not caring that he was injured. What did it mean that the Breaker now had density? Was it now in control?

His younger brother sat up, planting his arms firmly behind him to stabilize his upright posture. Kiff whispered to himself. "Get in. Get in."

The Breaker's more massive shape shuddered then dissipated into Kiff's smaller frame. It was disturbing to watch the Breaker's larger proportions disappear into his brother. The last to go were the phantom's long tusks. They vanished into Kiff's forehead.

Kiff wobbled slightly then grinned. "I did it."

Logan rose to a crouch and reached toward him. "Yes, you did."

"I feel like I went up against Iggy Norvil. You know that guy?" Kiff arched an eyebrow as he wiped the growing sweat from his forehead. He looked feverish and ready to keel over.

Luckily Logan caught him before he dropped back to the ground, unconscious.

He held Kiff for a long time, fearful the Breaker would animate his brother like a puppet and viciously attack him.

When no such attack came, Logan secured his spear to his knapsack and gently lifted his brother, surprised at how frail and light he was. He marched away from the Broken Lands toward their enclave.

He had to fix this. He had to make things right before he left for good.

*Chapter 7*
## Kyle

Byron struggled to keep up with his parents and the guards. His short legs and large feet weren't designed for long, brisk walks, especially since his bearings were worn. Because he was so slow-moving, other families had gone on ahead.

He couldn't imagine life without his older brother. Who would oil his joints and tighten his screws without Kyle around? Sure, his dad would take on the job, but low-grade mechanical limbs were finicky and required fine adjustments. Even the wrong kind of lubricant felt weird.

Of utmost importance was his nervous system. He had rudimentary sensors attached directly to his living brain tissue within a casing of cerebrospinal fluid, and those tiny signals gave him clues as to when he was missing a step, grasping something in his hand, or even bumping his head. He felt no pain, but avoiding damage was important when replacement parts cost so much.

He clicked and clanked along the metal grid flooring, winding through a maze of corridors. His left orb had been flickering for months, and recently it had started showing a blurred spot in the middle, but otherwise his vision was excellent even if he didn't have the same periphery range as normal people.

As they rounded the final bend, he saw far ahead a door that read REPURPOSING CHAMBER, and in smaller lettering underneath, ALL VISITORS MUST BE ACCOMPANIED BY AUTHORIZED PERSONNEL.

When a guard swiped his access card, Byron's built-in camera whirred and took sixty-four pictures. He sifted through the images, zoomed in to the clearest, identified and extracted the swipe card's printed serial number, captured the bar code, stored the data on his hard drive, and deleted all the pictures—all in less than two seconds.

The door opened, and the Jaxx family entered yet another corridor, this one with glass walls and overlooking the main factory from thirty feet up. The long, closed-in gantry led straight to the Repurposing Chamber. The rounded corridor walls muffled the humming of huge machines, the bubbling, hissing vats, and the rattling conveyor belts carrying sturdy crates of all sizes, each leaking freezing cold vapors. Byron asked what was in them, and though his parents hunched their shoulders and looked away, one of the guards waved his hand around. "Those are from yesterday's repurposing. We had a pile-up on the 87 Flyover, three lives lost. Those crates? Body parts. You see, we bring the bodies in and carefully dissect them—"

"Enough!" Byron's mom said, raising her finger in warning. "He's eight. Spare the details."

The guard pursed his lips. "Still, it's worth pointing out to the young lad that all these parts will be used. There's a heart transplant ready to go, a girl who needs a new eye, an old woman looking forward to a healthy pair of legs that are ten years younger . . . Be assured that your son's parts will be put to good use, too. We repurpose bodies every day—accident casualties, murder victims, the murderers themselves when they're sentenced to execution, and then of course those like your son who fail to display any aptitude and don't fit into our society . . ."

He trailed off when he saw her withering glare. Byron had seen his mom's withering glares before, but this particular one was a killer. Neither guard spoke again.

Infostreams suggested there were repurposings pretty much every day, so the entire operation—preparing the donors, playing host to grieving loved ones, dissecting the bodies afterward—must run as smoothly as clockwork. There were occasional reports of a father frantically trying to reverse his decision and send his child to the Ruins instead, or a prisoner breaking free, but for the most part a repurposing was a simple, routine experience shown on the stream screen every morning at eleven just before the weather forecast.

The gantry ended at a door just like the last one. A guard swiped his card, the pad lit up green, he pressed it, and the heavy steel door rolled sideways. "Full house today," he said, ushering them inside.

Kyle and five other donors were lying on sturdy tables, spaced a few yards apart, in what was known as the Repurposing Chamber. The Jaxx family was the last to arrive; the others were already crowded around their loved ones, sobbing freely but otherwise strangely composed, stiff and formal. Infostreams claimed this to be a place of peace and tranquility, a final resting place where the so-called donors could make peace with the gods—which was about all they could do because of the drugs they were on.

Apart from the family entrance and a separate door marked PRIVATE, the chamber was simple and bare, circular and domed with an enormous glass viewing pane that took up half the room and was currently blocked by a steel shutter on the outside. That shutter would be opening in just over eight and a half minutes according to Byron's internal clock, after which an audience would peer in through the glass while the mayor finished running through his routine speech.

Mayor Baynor's voice could be heard even now, echoing around the chamber from speakers in the domed ceiling. He was just outside, on the other side of that shutter, addressing the city.

Byron declined his parents' gestures to come over and say goodbye, and instead stood patiently while they whispered in Kyle's ears. The minutes ticked by. Around the room, other parents and family members now seemed to be patting hands and nodding as though they'd transitioned from anguish to acceptance.

Kyle most likely wasn't scared. The glass mask covering his face hissed softly, and though his eyes were wide open, he grinned inanely as if he had no clue of his predicament. Which he didn't. "Peace and tranquility," the infostreams always said proudly. "The happiest moments of any person's life are those final minutes in the Repurposing Chamber."

With his orbs on the door marked PRIVATE, Byron shuffled around the perimeter of the chamber, taking his time. Guards glanced at him, looked him up and down, but he was used to that kind of scrutiny. When he reached the door, he openly pressed the release pad. It beeped rudely and lit up red, then dimmed again.

A guard wandered over. "That room's private."

"I know," Byron told him, unmoving. "That's what I need. A private room."

"Private means you can't go in."

Byron swiveled his head around. "Oh."

The guard frowned down at him. "Are you, uh . . . are you the Jaxx kid?"

Byron inclined his head.

"I've read about you." The guard knelt in front of him. He seemed friendly enough. "I recognized you from an article I saw. Byron Jaxx, the city's most mechanical boy. Most people have a cybernetic arm here, a robot leg there, a bionic eyeball, a few plastic components . . . but you're the real deal, a fully robot boy with a brain encased in fluid." He squinted as if that would somehow help him see right through Byron's face. "You're pretty amazing, kid. How old are you now?"

"Eight."

The guard pursed his lips. "You're kind of small for an eight-year-old. I guess it costs money to replace parts, huh? Longer legs would be a start—"

"I need to shut down for a minute," Byron interrupted, trying his best to make his voice sound weak.

"What? Why?"

"System failure. I need to reboot my system. Why can't I go in here?" He raised his hand again, pressing on the pad and making it beep rudely. It glowed red under his palm, then dimmed. This time he kept his hand where it was, placed on the pad.

The guard shook his head. "Sorry, kid. There's a restroom, but it's way back along the gantry—"

"I'll just reboot here, then," Byron said, and affected a heavy sigh that came out with a soft reverberation. "My limbs have locked up. Please don't disturb me."

"I'd rather you came away from the door . . ."

Byron slumped as much as his robot body would allow and bowed his head, feigning a reboot.

"Kid?"

Rebooting was something Byron rarely did. The guard, however, was not in a position to question him, and after a moment he clicked his tongue and quietly walked away. Byron waited thirty seconds, feigning a complete shutdown, then set to work on the electronic lock. He knew security cameras were watching him, but his hand was already frozen in place on the pad as though he were leaning against the doorframe in the middle of rebooting.

He retrieved from memory the access card's serial number he had captured from the talkative guard earlier. With that number, a scan of the barcode, and a simple electronic signal from his EasyInstall mod, he could fool the lock without effort. But instead of opening it, which would make the pad glow green and alert security, he would just reset the clearance level. Resets were usually followed by fresh programming; until then, the lock would be a free-for-all.

It took only twelve seconds. When he was done, he jerked and backed away, then looked around as if wondering why he was there. The guard he'd spoken to earlier raised his eyebrows questioningly, and Byron raised a plastic thumb in return.

Ignoring the private door, he slowly edged around the room to where Kyle was laid out on the table. This time he accepted his parents' invitation to say his farewells, though he needed help climbing onto a chair so he could lean across the gurney and gaze into his older brother's vacant eyes. "It's all good," Kyle said dreamily, not quite focusing.

"Can we be alone?" Byron asked, aware that his parents were standing right behind him in case he fell.

"Son—"

"Please, Dad? Just let me say goodbye on my own."

Reluctantly, his parents sidled away.

"You've got four eyes," Kyle mumbled, squinting up at Byron. "They keep moving around." He let out a childish giggle.

Acutely aware of twelve guards standing around the room, plus several security cameras, Byron leaned over his brother and pretended to say his farewells while studying the hose that protruded from the bottom of Kyle's mask. It snaked down past the crook of his neck into a hole in the table.

Byron waited for the nearest guard to turn away, then activated his small short-range laser. It buzzed lightly, extending an inch from his index finger like a glowing red needle. He quickly lasered through the light plastic hose as close to the table's surface as possible. The top portion of the hose sprung free. His receptors detected the increased hissing as air and gas escaped from the stub of hose sticking out of the table, but nobody else heard thanks to the mayor's booming voice.

"Time to wake up, Kyle," he murmured.

*"Two minutes, folks,"* a lady's voice said over the P.A. system, briefly interrupting the mayor's speech.

Byron waited as long as he could, leaning in close to his brother and shielding the severed hose from prying eyes. He was aware of his dad sidling up behind him.

"*Please make your way to the exit, folks,*" the lady's voice said. "*The shutter will be opening in one minute and thirty seconds.*"

Byron allowed himself to be helped down, and he tried his best to make a fuss so that his dad was too distracted to look back at Kyle. Several guards looked his way, and on impulse he started yelling in his tinny voice so that *everyone* swung to face him, including the guards who were going around checking on the donors. "Leave my brother alone!" he yelled, turning up his volume full blast.

"*Please vacate the chamber.*"

Guards hurried around, urging families from the room. Byron found himself surrounded by half a dozen armed men—as if someone so small was likely to cause any trouble. They were big and ugly, ready for action, their hands hovering over their weapons. "Get your son under control," one of them said in a low, threatening voice.

"He's just upset," Byron's mom said angrily.

Out in the corridor, Byron managed one last sneaky glance into the chamber before the door rolled shut. The domed room was empty except for the donors. Nobody had noticed the severed hose, and the shutter would be opening in about a minute.

Now it was all up to Kyle.

*Chapter 8*
## Logan

Logan stumbled into the enclave with Kiff unconscious in his arms. His brother had roused twice on the long trek home, both times speaking a language Logan had never heard before. Had it been the Breaker talking in its native tongue? Did the spirits have a common language? Fortunately, the unruly spirit didn't re-emerge in any other way. Logan had feared the Breaker would escape and attack him, but it hadn't.

Even though Kiff was asleep, he was tense, battling the Breaker. How long could he keep the spirit contained?

When Logan walked into the center of the village, the marketplace was empty other than a few odd vendors manning their stalls. He examined the sun. It was creeping past the halfway point. Most citizens must still be at the Tethering.

Kreeb Lang, the proprietor of a fruit stall and the Fixer Enclave's busybody, raced over to him. "Logan Orm, what's happened to your brother?"

Logan didn't have time for his inquiries. "Where's my mother?"

Kreeb blinked, making a show of his reaction. His thick grey eyebrows danced up and down. "Why, at this month's Tethering, of course. Wish I could have gone, but the Sovereign deigned it necessary that a few of us stay back. Don't want any folks pilfering more rations than they deserve." He jerked his thumb back behind him. "Pity. It's always fun watching you kids wrestle with your untamed spirits."

Three Hunters stood at attention off to the side, keeping watch over the marketplace. Logan knew there was probably a Creeper or two skulking around as well, an added pair of eyes to catch any breaking the law.

Kreeb started to slip his arms under Kiff's limp legs. "Here, let me help you."

Logan yanked his brother away from the older citizen. Kreeb was tethered to a Skimmer. He wanted to grab hold of Kiff not out of a sense of coming to their aid, but because it was physical contact that allowed Skimmers to read the thoughts of others.

Logan hoped he had pulled his brother away in time. Judging from Kreeb's frustration, it was clear he had. The man hadn't gotten enough of a read to know what had happened.

"You must learn to let others help you, Logan," Kreeb said.

One of the Hunters approached—Greer Melb's brother, Lanak.

Lanak's spirit eased out from his back, peering over its host's shoulder. The distinctive narrow eyes and long snout combined with its rows of jagged teeth and the solitary horn that emblazoned its muzzle were all the hallmarks of a predator. While many in the Enclave envied any who became Hunters, Logan found them unsettling. Again, much like Breakers, but less so, they were unpredictable apparitions, difficult to control.

Lanak said, "What did you do now, Orm?"

Logan squeezed his eyes shut, willing himself and Kiff to be anywhere else but here.

The Hunter unsheathed his sword and eyed the stand of trees Logan had exited, alert to any threat that might come barreling out of the woods. His spirit disengaged and roved over Kiff's still form. It sniffed around, froze, and glared back at its host, barking in disgust. Obviously something was off.

Lanak seemed to understand. "Your brother has no outward injuries."

"No." Logan didn't know what to do.

"Then what happened? A fall? Did he hit his head?" Lanak said.

Kreeb's spirit exited his body and snaked around the man's neck. Skimmers appeared as serpents, their movements

*42*

measured and often mesmerizing. Logan watched it slide about, fascinated by its undulations.

Lanak snapped, "Answers, Orm! I cannot act on your behalf if I don't know what happened."

Logan shook his head, breaking free of the Skimmer's hypnotic pull. "I was out in the Broken Lands. Kiff followed me."

Kreeb gasped. His spirit retreated inside him as the man took two steps back.

Lanak said, "Did he enter the ruins?"

From the look of dismay and disgust, Logan knew the Hunter had realized what he would say next.

"Yes."

"And a spirit tethered with him?"

Logan's shoulders slumped. Suddenly, his brother felt far heavier. "Yes."

Kreeb gasped again, this time more for the attention than out of shock.

"Which spirit?" Lanak asked, his tone grim.

"A Breaker."

Lanak remained impassive, but Logan knew the Hunter was upset. It was painted all over his tethered spirit's face. The apparition reared up, extending upward the pair of skin flaps behind its ears, a sign that it was about to pounce on its prey. The bright purple markings stretched across the webbed flaps were designed to still its prey, to overwhelm them visually.

It had the desired effect on Logan. He felt his knees buckle. He pitched forward, losing consciousness.

\* \* \*

Logan awoke, his skin cold and clammy. His mother sat at the foot of his bed stroking her spirit. Once tethered, spirits sank in and out of solidness at the beck and call of their host. The Fixer sat in her lap, its plump furry frame quivering in place.

"Mother, where's Kiff?"

The Fixer zipped up to his mother's shoulder on tiny stalk-like legs, its three tails coiling and uncoiling constantly. Logan didn't like how the spirit's long ears twitched and tracked his voice. The Fixer's wide eyes, always moist and leaking, peered at him expectantly.

His mother slipped her long hair to her other shoulder, giving the spirit more space for its perch. "He's in his room. Two of my colleagues are seeing to his comfort. Their Fixers are more adept at sedating than my twitchy fellow."

Her Fixer bounded into the air and landed atop her head. Its thin lips sputtered humorously as it ran in circles on her head.

Logan sat up. His words rushed out. "I brought him back so you could heal him. I thought if all five Fixers did something together—"

"It's not possible. Brink's Fixer and mine can't be in the same room together." She placed a slender hand on his knee and offered him a cloth to wipe his glistening brow.

He took it but didn't bring it up to his face. "But in such an extreme case, you can make them get along, can't you?"

"No, it's been tried before. It won't work. You were too young at the time, but four years ago there was a tragic incident with the canyon clackers. We tried then, and our Fixers almost tore each other to pieces." She pulled up her left sleeve, revealing a scar running from her wrist to her elbow. "It was the only time I ever lost control."

Logan had wondered about his mother's injury. Every time he had asked her about it, she had given him a different, blatantly false story. He hadn't felt dismissed by this, merely coddled. But he had never called her on any of the stories no matter how laughable. Now she was sharing. *Too little, too late.*

She quickly rolled her sleeve back down. "Your father is with him as well. He knows about Breakers. He can give some valuable insights, but the outcome is not good." She sniffled and wiped the corners of her eyes with the back of her hand. Her

Fixer hopped back down into her lap and rolled on its back, its six legs stuck high into the air as it stretched.

Logan grimaced.

His mother's words came out as no more than a whisper. "Why did he follow you?"

"I don't know. He's foolhardy."

He regretted his insult, but his mother didn't call him on it. "He thinks the world of you. I knew he wasn't at the Tethering. He had told me he wasn't going as a form of protest. He was bound and determined to march into Sovereign's Hall and demand they change the law. And I think he would've if not for all this." She nodded in the direction of Kiff's bedroom.

Logan fought back the tears. His voice cracked. "I should never have gone today. I should've stayed home and awaited my fate."

His bedroom door crashed open. His father stood in the doorway, his Breaker looming above him, all snorts and growls. "Yes, you should've, Logan."

He thrust himself into the room, not bothering to duck through the doorway to allow his tethered spirit easy entry. The bulk of the Breaker from its waist up ghosted through the wall above the door. It looked displeased at having to discorporate. It glowered at Logan.

"You tempted him. You lured him out there to die!" His father's face reddened, his Breaker's presence swelled.

"I didn't!"

Logan glanced over to his mother's Fixer. The smaller apparition ducked into the safety of her body, only sticking one eye out from her neck to keep tabs on its roused kindred.

"He's always following your lead, always straying. Almost made me wonder if I was raising two who would embarrass me at their Tethering." His father's face softened as he glanced over his shoulder. Through the open door, Logan could see his brother's door still hanging open and the two Fixers fretting over Kiff.

"Can they do something?" His mouth was dry.

His father's voice dropped. "Only aid him in containing the Breaker. They cannot help him best it. It can't be done."

"Just because something's never been done before, doesn't mean it can't." Logan tensed, knowing he was treading on familiar ground. So many of their arguments centered on his hopeful nature and his father's absence of such.

As always, his father sought to dash his hopes. "He will not get better. He will eventually fall. And then he will join you in your fate. The Tribunal has called you to the hall tonight to hear my decision. You know what I will say." His eyes narrowed. "Death over exile for you."

Logan's mother shivered and pressed her hands to her face, smothering her grief. Her Fixer sobbed, completely buried in her body.

His father's Breaker glided along his thick outstretched arm and added the length of its immaterial arm to his. It was pantomiming his father's outrage. How could he be so tied to something laden with such contempt?

Logan tore his eyes away from the linked pair. Let the Tribunal prattle on as they must.

He had no shortage of what he would say back to the bloated sovereign and his loathsome chancellor.

*Chapter 9*
**Kyle**

Kyle stared up at the domed ceiling and studied the tiny black security camera, amazed at how terrified he felt right now compared to just a few moments earlier. He knew it was the happy gas that had relaxed him for the past hour, and he also knew that Byron must have done what he'd promised and cut the hose. Kyle barely remembered his family's visit; it was all a blur. But here he was, waking from a dreamlike state, the happy gas escaping harmlessly into the room instead of hissing directly into his mask.

Suddenly, he was no longer happy.

That was a good thing, though. He blinked rapidly, trying to collect his thoughts. He remembered a sleepless night after Byron and his parents had left. He remembered daylight coming through the small window, the guards coming to fetch him, a walk along a featureless corridor with other donors ahead and behind him. A medical room full of equipment. Three doctors—two men and one woman. The woman had been all business, unsmiling as she slipped a portable mask over his face and told him to relax. And he had. He remembered nothing after that except faces swimming in and out of view, and something incredibly funny. His face ached from laughing so much.

But whatever it was he'd found so hilarious earlier was long gone. Now he saw a chamber of death where countless others before him had died.

As full lucidity returned, he was aware of a commotion by the door. There had been a disturbance all along; he was just now waking to the tail end of it. He twisted his head to look, but a heavy door slid shut just then, and the shouting was extinguished. Now he was alone in a silent room.

*47*

*The Repurposing Chamber*. Fear shot through him, and suddenly his focus was razor sharp.

He wasn't quite alone. Five others were here, all murmuring nonsense and grinning inanely at the ceiling. And the chamber wasn't quite silent, either. The mayor's voice echoed through the speakers. "... And in just one minute, citizens, this morning's donors will be revealed." The voice softened. "Now, you know me. I've been mayor for thirty-nine years. I've run unopposed for the last twelve elections. Why? Because, as I like to say in all my campaigns, I *get it*. I understand the people. I understand our great city. I understand the problems of overcrowding. Our system has no time for criminals and laggards, and no room for those unable to contribute in a way that we, the people, are accustomed. The very moment we relax our laws and start giving handouts to those who fail to contribute ... well, my friends, that's when our city begins its decline."

Realizing that time was ticking away, Kyle bolted upright and fumbled with his mask. The moment his feet hit the floor, an alarm sounded, far noisier than it needed to be. He clapped his hands over his ears, and as he staggered away from his table, donors twisted their heads to look at him, giggling and laughing at his antics.

A heavy roller door slid open, revealing a long gantry beyond. Kyle had seen the Repurposing Chamber on the stream screen enough times to recognize that door. It was usually shut, as was the mysterious door marked PRIVATE. He knew the gantry was the main route in and out of the chamber for visitors and guards. He caught a glimpse of a dozen civilians, but his view was quickly blocked by a stream of guards stampeding into the chamber.

"... And so, my fellow citizens of Apparati, I would like to introduce you to this morning's wonderful donors. As you know, all who give themselves to the city in this way should be celebrated, even revered, for what they offer our society. Today we have tragic accident fatalities as well as a criminal and a rare recipient failure . . ."

*Scratch that last one*, Kyle thought as his bare feet slapped across the metal floor. He made for the door marked PRIVATE. Had Byron unlocked it for him?

"Our donors are, as always, heroes. As hard as it is for loved ones to let go, in the end there's really *no need* to let go— for our donors aren't going anywhere. They're all around us, probably standing among us now, and within us . . ."

Kyle had almost expected the mayor's grand reveal to be delayed until the escapee had been detained, but apparently nothing got in the way of a good ceremony. With a sudden thunk and clang, the giant shutter outside the glass wall started to rise, and a dazzling strip of daylight appeared along the bottom, spanning nearly half the chamber.

"And now . . . I give you . . . our donors."

Even though the alarm continued to blare, the glass wall was thick and soundproof, and the audience outside would look in on a silent room as the shutter rose. Kyle glimpsed a sea of expectant faces as he made it to the small door marked PRIVATE. The pad turned green, and the door hissed open. He fell through the doorway, turned, slapped the pad again, and watched as a sea of guards hurtled across the chamber toward him, their eyes widening as the door hissed shut in their faces.

Most security doors had an override lock on the inside. This one was no exception. He pressed the button half a second before the guards slapped at the pad outside. The button under Kyle's thumb lit up red, the word LOCKED emblazoned across it.

"You can't be in here," a woman's voice said.

Kyle spun around. The room was long and narrow, a door at the far end. Security cameras fed images to this small room, and there were three people seated at monitors on the right-hand wall—two middle-aged men and, nearest to him, a woman in her thirties.

So this was it. The place that nobody ever got to see on the stream screen, the infamous room behind the door marked PRIVATE. Somewhere here was a button or switch that responded only to a certain type of implant, that activated the poison. The Death Switch, as it was known.

Fists were pounding on the door behind him. Kyle, dressed only in a light gown, felt weak and vulnerable. But these three lab geeks, if they even qualified as that, looked nervous. "How did you get in here?" one of the men asked. He was bald and sweating.

Kyle spied a pair of scissors, a ruler, and some pens sticking up from a holder on the desk next to the woman's monitor. He leapt for the scissors and thrust the sharp end toward the woman's face. With a scream, she fell off her chair and scrambled across the floor while her colleagues jumped up and yelled at him to stop before someone got hurt.

"I'm gonna die if they catch me!" Kyle yelled, shaking with terror, adrenaline surging through his body. He advanced suddenly. "I'm coming through. Back up or I'll start stabbing."

He gave them no time to think, to *calculate* with those scientific, manipulative, conniving, murderous brains. They stumbled and tripped over their own feet as they hurried out of his way.

"You can't possibly escape, Kyle!" the woman squawked. "You're just delaying the inevitable."

Kyle hated that she used his name. He supposed it was better than being just Table Number Two, but still, using his name as if she were his friend, as if she *knew* him—it was too much. He darted forward and shoved her hard, and she stumbled against the wall as he shouldered past the others.

The pounding on the locked door behind him had ceased, but somehow that was worse. The guards were fumbling around, trying to override the lock, probably waiting on their Class-A Locksmith to arrive.

Kyle burst through into the room beyond and stood there in horror while the door hissed shut behind him and cut off the blaring alarm. He saw bright lights, gleaming walls, rows of patients on gurneys, and dozens of what looked like mist-filled glass coffins standing upright around the walls, with dark figures barely visible inside. There were crates, too, some of them with faint wisps of vapor drifting from the cracks. Kyle instantly knew they contained body parts.

White-coated doctors and masked surgeons spun to face him as he dithered by the door. For a couple of seconds, nobody spoke or moved. Then the deathly silence was broken by someone saying, "Subdue him!"

Doctors advanced as Kyle dashed along the aisles between gurneys, changing direction and skidding around as his route was blocked at every turn. Panting, he snatched glimpses of the patients as he ran, most of them in deep sleep, some attached to machines and drip stands: a woman with a missing arm, a teenage boy with bandages across his eyes, many hooked up to complex breathing equipment—all hopeful recipients awaiting their turn for new body parts.

*You're not getting mine*, Kyle thought savagely.

The doctors were still yelling, telling Kyle to get out. Spotting the exit at last, he found it unguarded. As he dashed for it, he realized his pursuers had been herding him this way all along. They were doctors, not guards—they just wanted him out of the room.

The double doors hissed open as he approached. He took off to the right down a corridor. Glancing over his shoulder, he saw guards spilling around a distant corner.

He felt oddly detached from reality as he sprinted along the polished floor of the empty corridor. He passed one surprised nurse and an elderly janitor, then a group of student doctors. All of them moved aside for him, shock on their faces. Escape from the Repurposing Chamber was rare, but Kyle felt sure there must be some kind of lockdown procedure. Nobody could expect gentle doctors and nurses to tackle a frantic scissor-wielding refugee; that was the guards' job—if they ever got their act together and caught up to him.

He passed a room with a glass wall. Inside, technicians walked around checking instrument panels on the ends of floor-to-ceiling cabinets. Some of these cabinets were glass-fronted, their shelves filled with what looked like eyeballs and brains floating in containers. Kyle wondered idly how many new people could be cobbled together using all these spare body parts. He shuddered when he thought about what would happen to him if he was caught—his own brain-dead but living body stored in an upright coffin until needed, or his body dissected and organized into cabinets.

After skidding around several more corners, heading to the right each time, he let out a gasp of relief at an overhead sign pointing the way to an emergency exit. He pushed through into a dingy, concrete passage and toward an external door sharply outlined by light.

Could it be this easy?

The emergency door had a standard horizontal bar to push up against. Kyle threw his weight on it but bounced back, winded. Rattling the bar with frustration, he realized it had been electronically sealed by some unseen security operator seated at a remote computer screen. A panel to the side had lit up red with the word LOCKDOWN.

It was too late to go back. Kyle knew guards were pouring into the corridor. They'd be on him in seconds. He was trapped in a short, dark emergency passage, his freedom and escape from death foiled—by a single door!

He banged on it, slammed up against it, pounded it with his fists, rattled the bar again and again until he heard voices in the corridor behind him. He went quiet, listening, his heart thumping. Heavy footsteps approached, and someone called, "He's at the emergency exit."

And then Kyle heard a whirr and clunk. He glanced at the panel to the side of the door. The red light had turned green, the word LOCKDOWN dimmed. His mouth fell open, unable to make sense of it. A system error? Or was someone watching out for him?

When Kyle pushed on the door again, it opened. He stepped outside, blinking in the sun, his gown billowing in a breeze.

Hundreds of people were standing there, some turning to stare at him in amazement.

*Chapter 10*
**Logan**

Logan entered Sovereign's Hall alone. His parents had already taken their seats along with most of the enclave. To either side, there were rows of simple wooden benches angled so that the audience could observe the proceedings. Nearly all were occupied.

No sooner had he appeared than two Hunters fell in step alongside and marched him to the center of the great hall.

The building was the tallest in the village, its steep roof reaching three times the height of the closest structure. The exposed rafters, thick beams carved by Breakers out of helmstone, the hardest trees in Apparata, reminded him of looking up at some creature's sheltering ribs. Only he didn't feel protected by them.

He had faced the Tribunal back when he was ten, answering to the crime of entering the Broken Lands. That first judgment at the Tribunal's hand had been harsh, but he had tried to block it out. Not being a full citizen yet, his parents had spoken for him then. Not that his father had stood up for him very much, begging forgiveness, all the while spouting condemnations about Logan. The sovereign and his chancellor had punished Logan's family with half rations for almost a year.

The Hunters stopped at the base of the circular stage. Logan ascended the four simple stone steps with determination. A glance around told him that those newly tethered were in attendance and grouped in front to his left. Only two of his classmates had Breakers, while the rest had synced with a wide variety of the other spirits. There were an overwhelming number of Hunters, but only one Fixer, his friend Nomi. She looked at him with sympathy. Her Fixer looked as rambunctious as his mother's. He wondered if his mother would take Nomi under her wing and teach her mastery of the healing arts.

He dropped to one knee and bowed his head. Seated in two tall chairs made of cricken wood were Sovereign Lambost and Chancellor Gretin. Both stared at him with fiery intensity. The sovereign's spirit, a Hunter, was submerged except for its head, which sprouted from his right shoulder as he sat hunched forward, eager to begin the judgment.

In contrast, Gretin, tethered to a Creeper, held his thin and shriveled frame stiff and straight. He scanned the crowd as he took in the spectacle of his office. "Before we begin, a moment of silence for three of our own who winked out earlier yesterday."

Everyone in attendance, including Logan, bowed their heads.

Winking out was a horrible fate. No one understood the phenomenon. It wasn't the same as death. Citizens died all the time, from old age, accidents, and occasionally murders. Their passing made sense in that context. But winking out was a mystery. Citizens young and old simply disappeared, sometimes right before the very eyes of their loved ones. No one had yet found a suitable reason for this tragic end. The most comforting theory held that one was less likely to wink out if they were tethered, that linking with a spirit somehow grounded you to the world in a more resolute manner. Logan didn't believe that, because tethered and untethered alike had been known to wink out. Not that he ever voiced his opinion.

The last person to vanish had been Frink Loom, a regarded Hunter and a close friend of his mother's. That had been two days ago. With the three wink-outs yesterday, the overall number was getting close to thirty for the month.

After a suitable pause, Gretin said, "The Tribunal has been called tonight to decide the fate of two brothers. Is the Orm family in attendance?"

Logan didn't look back. He knew his father was on his feet as was customary. "Leet Orm and Prima Klin Orm are here, Esteemed Chancellor."

The chancellor licked his lips. "And who will speak for these children?"

"I will," Logan's father said.

Logan held his tongue. He would let his father say his piece, but his words would not be the only ones from Family Orm tonight.

Gretin nodded at the sovereign. "Loyal to the Enclave and its laws, who will deliver the judgment tonight?"

Lambost cleared his throat. His spirit slipped farther from his frame. "I, Sovereign Lambost, will decree the fates of the accused. It is with solemn duty that I undertake the actions that have served our people for so many passings of the seasons."

Chancellor Gretin filled the silence with his voice, dithering in a manner that evidently bothered Lambost, whose spirit looked ready to rip Gretin's to pieces.

Logan knew that true strength had nothing to do with intimidation. He waited patiently.

Lambost glared at Logan's father. "Your son is fourteen years of age, Leet Orm?"

"Yes."

"And he was not present at his Tethering today?"

"No, Sovereign."

"Where was the boy?"

His father drew in a breath then launched into his reply. "He crossed into the Broken Lands separate from his classmates for reasons I cannot fathom."

"And did he come back tethered? Did he come back a citizen granted a responsibility through his new spirit?" Lambost switched his gaze to Logan.

He looked up at the sovereign, determined not to shrink back.

"No. He cannot tether." His father's voice didn't waver. "Not today or after all the other times he broke our laws and messed about in the ruins."

His father found him shameful. Logan knew he had secretly hoped to never enter Sovereign Hall to face the Tribunal on his son's behalf again. Not because he wanted to spare his son, but because he didn't want to grant the Fixer Enclave another opportunity to tarnish his family name. With Logan unable to tether, his father would sooner have him wink out.

Lambost said, "Those who cannot tether face exile or death. What say you of the fate to be brought on your kin, Leet Orm?"

Logan did not turn to look at his father or mother. He kept his back straight.

His father's voice was surprisingly shaky. "We grant him death. We see no merit in throwing him into the Broken Lands. We deny exile."

None in the crowd reacted, but their spirits certainly did. Chortling barks arose from numerous Breakers and Hunters along with the hissing of the Creepers and Skimmers. Most of the racket came from the newly tethered spirits, since their hosts were new to controlling them and their reactions weren't tempered.

"So be it." Sovereign Lambost shot his arms out, quelling the crowd with his gesture. "As to the matters of Kiff Orm, the Tribunal asks to know the particulars of his condition."

Logan's mother surprised him by answering, "Prima Klin Orm requests a voice."

His father would be bristling at this outburst. Logan almost turned to gauge the level of his father's outrage, but refrained.

No one responded. Chancellor Gretin and his Creeper looked mutually aghast.

His mother reiterated her request, strong but strained. "I will speak for my youngest."

The sovereign slipped his tongue out, almost testing the air for the possible reception allowing her to speak would bring. It was a fat, slovenly tongue much like its owner. "We will hear Prima Kiln Orm, spouse of Leet Orm. Her voice will suffice."

Logan turned to see what his mother would do.

"Kiff Orm, my son, went out into the Broken Lands. He is only eight." She drew her hand to her chest. Her Fixer clung tightly to her neck, looking befuddled at all the eyes on its master.

The crowd tensed. They knew his fate already.

"A Breaker attacked him, attempting to tether." She paused, then said, "He has quelled its influence for now, something I never thought possible. I ask this tribunal to grant him amnesty until such time that it is clear only the Breaker is in attendance in his small, innocent frame. In the meantime, I beseech you to let his struggles become ours. I ask that you let him have a chance to break his spirit."

Logan was surprised his mother dared so much. His father's gaze was directed to the ground, his face red.

No one spoke for a long time.

"And how did he happen to be out in the ruins? What would provoke a child to risk so much?" Lambost again shifted his gaze to Logan.

*He knows the answer. He wants the spectacle of a mother branding her son with accusation.*

"He followed my other son, Logan Orm. But that is not relevant."

Chancellor Gretin yelled, "But it is! We don't want one so feckless, so contemptuous that they would lure their kin into the ruins, to breathe any more of the blessed Apparata air than he deserves. I say it marks Logan Orm as highly dangerous to all. I submit that his death not be in the standard two days, but tomorrow, at midday."

Lambost sent his attendant a shriveling look. Gretin didn't flinch, gazing back at the sovereign expectantly. Logan sensed a power struggle at hand.

Sovereign Lambost could not scale down the consequence without appearing weak. Gretin had escalated the sentence, and Lambost had to go along with it, that much was clear. He declared with deliberate slowness, "Logan Orm is indeed a danger to the utmost. His family will witness his death at midday tomorrow."

Logan's mother sobbed.

Lambost added, "As for the younger brother, we must err on the side of caution. No one under fourteen has ever mastered a spirit. Mercy dictates we end his misery tomorrow as well."

Logan leapt to his feet. "No, you can't do that!"

Sovereign Lambost froze, and the hall fell silent. It was not tradition to have the accused speak if another had already been assigned to speak on their behalf. Logan was once again breaking the law. But he wasn't disputing his own sentencing.

"Silence!" the sovereign spat.

"No, I won't be silent!" Logan trembled with rage. His original screed was to have been on his behalf, but having seen his mother speak out for his brother, he knew which battle should be fought. "I ask the Tribunal to agree to my mother's terms, grant my brother the chance to best his spirit."

Both Lambost and Gretin lurched back, beside themselves that Logan had not whined about his own sentencing.

"I ask that you let Kiff prove you wrong. If anyone can quell a Breaker, it's him. I know his strength of conviction. He can do it. Let him."

Glaring at Logan, Lambost's cheeks reddened as he rose from his seat. His Hunter loomed over him, gathering hatred and spite into it.

A murmur broke out among the citizens. Soon there was chanting. It started out weak, but grew slowly in volume. "Give Kiff a chance!"

The chant reverberated through the hall, quickening as it gained in volume. The air was awash in something new—change.

Lambost's Hunter shrieked over the chanting. Its guttural wail sent chills down Logan's spine.

Lambost shouted, "Logan Orm will die tomorrow! His brother, Kiff Orm, will be given a stay of six days. If during that time his Breaker subverts him completely, a determination I will make and all will honor, then he too will part this living world."

The crowd did not respond. They were clearly fearful they had overstepped their bounds.

Sovereign Lambost announced, "Return to your homes and prepare for tomorrow. Prepare yourselves for another day of serving all in the enclave. May wisdom and loyalty be at your side." The sovereign swept his arms up and down, signaling the end of the gathering. He and Gretin marched pompously through a separate doorway.

Logan smiled at his mother. His father saw this and turned his back.

Logan's Hunter escort marched him to the Pens. He would spend the night there resigned to his fate, knowing that possibly his brother might make it through. He hoped for his mother's sake that would be true.

*Chapter 11*
**Kyle**

As Kyle blinked in the sunlight, the emergency exit door closed behind him, and an old man—bald on top with flowing white hair around the sides, and an equally long white beard—nudged him aside. He placed the palm of his hand on the greenlit pad fixed to the doorframe. Bolts whirred and thunked into place, and the pad glowed red as its LOCKDOWN status resumed. Seconds later, Kyle's pursuers started pounding and shouting from within.

"That'll hold them for a minute," the old man said with a wink. "But you need to hustle. Hurry now."

At that moment, voices yelled from somewhere in the surging crowd. "There! Get him!" People automatically started moving aside, creating a passage to allow the factory security guards to apprehend their escaped donor. For a moment, several of the armed brutes came into Kyle's view, and his heart sank, knowing he wouldn't be able to outrun them barefoot on the litter-strewn sidewalk.

But then the mood changed. Some of the spectators deliberately got in the guards' way, making them fumble and yell. Another brief surge in the crowd swallowed them up.

Kyle turned to ask the old man what was happening, but he'd vanished.

Instead, a rotund and red-faced spectator gestured urgently. "Run, boy! You have a chance. Get out of here! Stick it to the mayor!"

Kyle ran, bewildered by the unexpected help from complete strangers packing the street, overflowing the factory entrance and sidewalk in both directions. The crowd only ever got this big when there was a repurposing of a fourteen-year-old who had failed to implant—like today. Kyle was big news, a rare case. A short line of demonstrators waved boards that read CHILDREN SHOULD BE CHERISHED NOT PERISHED, but they were outnumbered by glaring city troops.

Kyle weaved in and out of the crowd, putting distance between himself and the factory. Hands patted him as he went, and people cheered.

The mayor's voice boomed out on the public address system while his face filled enormous stream screens on sides of buildings. One of his eyes was a different color—deliberately so, for the man was proud of his artificial orb and wanted to show it off. It had a slight glow to it, and rumors said it could feed him images directly from the datahub.

He was in rare form, making light of the confusion in the Repurposing Chamber. "Looks like our young donor forgot to bring his favorite toy. He'll be right back, folks." He laughed, and a few in the crowd did, too, but it was polite, somewhat uncomfortable laughter.

Kyle stopped dead as a small man jumped out in front of him. "Here, kid—take my coat."

"W-what?"

The man thrust his jacket at him. "Take it. Blend in."

Stunned, Kyle accepted the jacket, suddenly aware that his light gown was probably flapping open at the back. As he slid into the thick leather jacket, a boy in his late teens hurried forward as barefoot as Kyle was, holding out his shoes and socks. "Put these on."

And a woman shoved a plastic bag into his hands. "I just bought these pants for my son. Take them, Kyle. Here, let me get you some money . . ."

While she was digging in her purse, several hands emerged from the crowd, stuffing bills and coins into the plastic bag that Kyle now held to his chest. People were patting him on the back, touching the top of his head, squeezing his shoulders. It was a most bizarre and unexpected experience.

"Seriously," Mayor Baynor continued, his voice still uncomfortably close, "the situation's under control. Our young donor had a reaction to his medicine and has gone a little wild. Factory Guards will have him under control in just a moment. And the city troops have been alerted. But if you see the boy in the crowd, folks, please do hold onto him—for his safety and yours."

That last statement was a thinly veiled threat. Kyle heard it clearly, and so did everyone else. "Go," a sea of faces told him. "Take the pod. It's just around the corner."

In a daze, Kyle hurried on, finding that the crowd parted just enough for him to pass, and then sealed up behind him. He imagined the guards and troops would have a tough time navigating the seemingly mindless crowd.

Dressed in a thick leather jacket, with shoes and socks clasped to his chest along with a bag stuffed with cash and some mystery items straight off a clothing rack, Kyle felt as though life had just been squeezed back into his chest.

The streets opened up, and a bright yellow transport cab veered and bounced on its cushion of air as he ran in front of it. It hovered there while the driver yelled angrily at him. Kyle dashed across the road and around the corner to the pod depot.

The crowd was thin here. Many people had no idea what was going on and stared at Kyle in amazement as he hurried to buy a ticket. "East Morley," he panted to the clerk behind the small ticket window. He could have mentioned any number of suburbs along the Wall, but East Morley was one he happened to know. His Uncle Jeremiah lived there. The wily businessman got most of his junk from the Ruins. In fact, having the Wall in his backyard was probably why he'd moved to the dumpy area in the first place.

The clerk looked bemused as he placed a fingertip on the ticket machine. It beeped, and a small red card emerged from the side. Without saying a word, the clerk gestured toward the price displayed on the screen.

Normally, Kyle would have gasped. His dad was right—the price of pods was ridiculous. Did he have enough money? He dumped the shoes and socks on the counter, then turned the bag upside down. Bills fluttered out, more than enough to pay for the ticket. With shaking hands, Kyle shoved some across the counter. "Keep the change."

He scooped his possessions—remaining cash, shoes and socks—into the bag and hurried away. Behind him, something buzzed on the clerk's desk, and a screen lit up. Kyle knew it was the city troops calling to be on the lookout for a fugitive. He already had his ticket, but they might still shut down the station and halt the pods.

The depot was narrow and dark. There was a line of about ten people and three gleaming white egg-shaped pods. A couple entered the first pod, and the door silently closed, its seams virtually nonexistent. The vessel eased along the track, then stopped and sank back into a recess in the wall beyond. When a panel closed over it, there was a sucking sound from within, and when the panel reopened, the pod was gone. A person was already entering the second pod, which was now the next to go.

More pods arrived, two of them joining the ranks. Kyle waited anxiously, knowing that guards or troops could show at any moment.

When it was his turn, he stepped inside, sat on the circular bench seat, and with a shaking hand slipped his small red card into the slot. As he was buckling up, a soft female voice said, "Your destination is East Morley."

"Yeah," Kyle said, wiping his forehead on the sleeve of his gown. Why wasn't the pod moving already? "Let's go," he demanded.

There was a long pause, and Kyle heard shouts outside. Worry gnawed at him. This was the end of the line. The pod technician, an unknown woman with a soft voice sitting in a cubicle somewhere, literally held his life in her hands. Not even in her hands—implants could be used without physical contact.

So she held Kyle's life in her *mind*. She could easily send him on his way to East Morley, or simply open the door and let the guards and troops get at him.

"Please?" he said.

"You're wanted by the City," the woman said, sounding troubled. "You're all over the datahub. The system is flagging you as a fugitive."

Kyle looked for a spy-eye of some kind but saw nothing obvious. "If you can see me," he begged, "you'll know I'm no danger. I'm fourteen. I've never harmed anyone in my life. Please—"

"I could lose my job if I let you through," the woman whispered, her voice strangely intimate in the soundproof pod.

"I could lose my *life*," Kyle said.

Someone banged on the door. A voice yelled, "Open it up!"

For a long half-minute, Kyle sat there waiting for a faceless stranger to decide his fate. He could barely sit still, and he glanced around searching for a tiny black dot that might indicate a spy-eye camera. If he could move closer to it, stare into it, put on his most sincere and pleading expression, perhaps this woman might—

And, just like that, the pod jerked. It was moving.

It had been years since Kyle had used a pod, but he remembered the thrill as it sank back into its transport chute and then plummeted into the ground. He felt himself lifting out of his seat as it went. He gripped the harness, but almost immediately the fall stopped. Kyle felt the pod turn to the right. On the screen, a helpful digital compass backed this up, its needle shifting to the east. Then the pod accelerated and Kyle was pushed back against the seat.

He'd only made short hops before. It was all his dad had been able to afford—or waste—on pod trips. This was a long run, about half the city's diameter, a route that started in the inner southwest quadrant and ended at the very edge of the city to the east.

He arrived five seconds later. Mayor Baynor was far behind, but General Mortimer and his pack of city troops would be hot on the trail shortly. Kyle had no time to spare.

Despite the urgency, he paused and looked again for a camera. "Thanks," he said, trying to smile as he searched. "You saved my life."

"Go. I'm erasing this record. If anyone asks, say you took a cab." The operator's voice dropped to an urgent whisper. "Go now—city troops are here."

Kyle said nothing more. If the pod technician was found out and arrested, there was nothing to stop her replacement from closing the door and trapping him again.

He leapt out of the pod and ran for the depot exit.

Once outside, he gasped and turned in a slow circle. This part of the city was worlds away from the center—run down, forlorn, and smelly. People barely looked at him as he rummaged through his bag, dug out a brand new pair of pants, and pulled them on. A little big, but no matter. He tucked his gown into the pants as though it were a shirt, and instantly felt better. The socks were fine, the shoes also a little big, but better than too small. He transferred his cash into his jacket pocket, ditched the bag in the nearest trash can, and went to look at a wall-mounted street map.

Finding the route he was looking for, he took off across the road.

He could have gone to his uncle's house, but he suspected his uncle wouldn't want city troops following a fugitive to his home. Kyle was finally beginning to believe that he had escaped his repurposing, but now he had two options: life on the run in the city with troops on his trail every minute of the day—or exile to the Ruins, that vast and deserted landscape outside the Wall.

*Turn right after two blocks,* he reminded himself as he ran along the sidewalk. A gang of youths stopped their conversation as he passed, and Kyle suspected they might have crowded around and harassed him had they not been so surprised. He refrained from looking back over his shoulder in case that would spur them into giving chase.

*One more block*, he thought as he crossed an intersection and resumed his sidewalk sprint.

The cars here were old-style road-rumblers with wheels and exhaust fumes. The mayor maintained that the smog over Apparati was caused by dozens of poor districts just like this one—filled with ancient vehicles and their gurgling combustion engines—but he never said a word about the factories on the north side belching smoke into the sky, probably because that was where all the fossil fuels were burned to generate the enormous amounts of power needed to run the city. The mayor constantly praised the evolution of technology and cruised around in his high-tech hovercars and airskimmers while turning up his nose at the stench emanating from the slums. Yet everyone knew the truth. This rundown area was the true Apparati, where workers inhaled toxic fumes, sweated grime, and got their hands dirty to provide a clean, sleek, high-tech city center for Mayor Baynor and his self-absorbed elite.

Kyle turned right at the next corner, and the Wall came into sight three blocks ahead. The news stream often showed the structure from the other side, which was far more impressive to look at. He felt a stab of terror as he slowed to a jog and held his aching sides. He'd made it this far, but now that he was here, he wasn't certain he could follow through.

Walking as fast as his weary legs could carry him, he weaved in and out of passersby and considered his options. What if he didn't leave the city? Could he live here? What if he waited for the dust to settle and headed over to his Uncle Jeremiah's place?

He wrinkled his nose, remembering his uncle's ugly apartment block with its smell of urine in the elevator, the graffiti in the dingy corridor, and the paper-thin divider walls that did nothing to mask the noisy neighbors. Kyle's dad had worked hard to leave these slums, moving closer and closer to the city center. No wonder he was so set against the idea of a deadbeat in the house! Maintaining a lifestyle in the shiny high-rise towers in the mayor's squeaky-clean neighborhood involved precise management of finances—and an unemployed youth sponging off his parents was likely to bring that dream crashing down.

Kyle couldn't go back home. He wanted to live, but not out of his father's pocket. And the idea of trying to find a low-grade job in a place like East Morley filled him with horror. He'd almost rather take his chances in the Ruins—but not quite. He'd be a fool to turn down a helping hand.

The problem was that he had an implant in his neck. It might not work the way it was supposed to, but it was still operational. He was being tracked right now. In fact, wasn't that the whine of police cruisers in the air? He squinted, searching the sky, wondering if those specks just above the rooftops in the distance were cops coming straight from the city center to pick him up. He could ask his uncle to take a knife and cut out the probe, but not before the troops were onto him.

Panting for breath, he finally arrived at the Wall. He found some steep steps leading up, a short climb that landed him on top of the twenty-foot-thick structure with a fence running its entire length. It was a thirty-foot drop down into the Ruins on the other side, offering an impressive view for visitors. People often stood here with their faces pressed to the iron railing, gazing with awe and wonder at the derelict buildings and wastelands stretching to the east.

But Kyle had no time for sightseeing. He clambered over the railing. Technically speaking, he was violating the law just by standing here on the wrong side of the fence. He laughed to himself. What were they going to do to him that was worse than being repurposed?

The Ruins sprawled below. He knew there were safe places to jump down; he just had to find one. He hurried along the top of the wall, staying close to the fence. It wasn't a huge drop, but a broken ankle in the Ruins would kill him for sure. It was a place where he needed to stay on his feet to survive.

Sirens in the sky caught his attention. Yes, there they were—four regular police cruisers and three of General Mortimer's military escorts, whining through the air above rooftops and between ugly apartment towers. They would be here in a matter of minutes. Kyle couldn't escape them, not with the tracker in his neck. He had to go.

He searched frantically for a safe place to jump down into the Ruins.

*Chapter 12*
**Logan**

Logan lifted his head, his thoughts murky. How long had he been asleep? He stretched, allowing his feet to press against the opposite side of the pen. His prison was made of stout twindle branches and secured in place at key bracing points by staunch vines. Earlier, he had tried to untie several of the vines, but had earned a flurry of cuts from the thorns riddling them. He rose to his knees—any farther and he'd knock his head against the pen's ceiling. He looked up to see Apparata's three moons high in the night sky. *Probably more than halfway through the night*, he thought.

The wooden bowl that had held his last meal sat where he had thrown it. The Hunter who had been on the receiving end of its contents was nowhere in sight. Logan thought that odd. He looked for the other Hunter, whirling around to see if he still sat in the high crook of the tree to the north. He was missing as well.

The Pens were a place that didn't require guards most of the time. Very few broke the laws of the enclave. The six other pens arranged to his left were empty. The last to be housed here had been Sleak Rumtoff for stealing from his neighbor. He had weathered a week in his pen. He wondered if Sleak had been thrown in the same cell he now occupied. He had a hard time imagining the large man could even fit in any of the pens.

The crackle of a branch directed his attention to the area where the tree Hunter had been posted. Was he returning from a break?

A slender figure emerged from a low copse of young trees, pushing aside their flexible trunks with ease. Logan recognized the long flowing blond hair of his mother. She slunk across the small clearing leading to his pen.

"Mother, what are you doing here?" he hissed.

"What needs to be done." She clutched a small load saw. Her Fixer hovered above her shoulder, eyeing the implement with fright.

Realizing what she was intending, he held up a hand. "No, you risk too much."

She scampered forward and dropped to her knees, driving her long skirt into the mud before Logan. "I have risked too little up to this point."

He didn't interrupt. She had more to say.

Her eyes glistened. She held the saw in her lap and leaned closer. "You and your brother are my world. I can't bear to lose you both."

Did that mean she thought Kiff was lost to her? Was she freeing him because his brother had lost to his Breaker already? "Kiff?"

She rubbed her eyes. Her Fixer cooed at her, hoping to pacify the storm of emotions it detected seething inside its host. "He is back home resting under the watch of three Hunters. The sovereign comes this morning to check on him. I fear he will not honor his word."

"What happened to the Hunters watching over me?"

His mother smiled weakly. "Out cold. While I lack the precision to properly sedate an injured patient with my Fixer, I could certainly muster taking out two healthy specimens."

Logan knew this to be true. His mother was the enclave's most compassionate healer but not its strongest.

The longer his mother lingered, the more likely it was she would be discovered. "What if they posted a Creeper? It'll slink off and report you."

"Did you see one?"

"No." Not that they were easy to spot. They were good at staying hidden, spying on one's comings and goings.

She looked behind her. "Then I'll take my chances."

"If you free me, what happens to you?"

She gripped the saw and lifted it. "Nothing. Lambost would not dare to cast further punishment on our family. If he lashes out at me, he risks completely upending your father, his most powerful Breaker. If he takes me away from him, there's no telling what the Breaker will spur him to do. It's been years since he lost control. I doubt our enclave could withstand another of his fits."

Logan nodded. "But won't losing Kiff send him over?"

An unbridled intensity gripped her. She smacked the saw blade against the pen. "He will not lose Kiff." She began to saw the closest branch. "And he will not lose you either."

"But . . ."

"Let me focus on what needs doing." She sawed, leaning into each motion with all of her slight weight. The wood shredded, but it was slow going. Beads of perspiration formed on her forehead.

Logan put his hand on the saw handle. His mother stopped sawing and looked him in the eyes. "Let me do this," he said.

She released her grip. He pulled the saw into the pen and attacked the branch with fury. He wanted to be done with this escape so his mother could flee. The longer she stayed, the greater the chance she would be found out.

She cradled her hand. Blisters had already formed. One had popped and oozed clear liquid. Her Fixer scurried down her arm to hover over her injury, huffing and puffing in frustration. Logan knew a Fixer could not heal its host. That was a shortcoming. His mother had to have her injuries tended to by another Fixer. He doubted she would seek treatment. It would mean trusting one of the other four Fixers with her injury. The others were loyal to the sovereign and would rat out his mother's injury to Lambost in a heartbeat. What about Nomi? She was now a Fixer. Could she lend her healing talents to the mix? He dismissed the fragile plan. Her abilities were too new, unfocused.

His mother sighed, rousing his mind from its wanderings. He finished sawing the first branch and kicked at it. It slid upward slightly, but he needed to cut through a few more in order to make good his escape.

"I can't have you put to death," she said with a stuttering breath. "Exile is what needs to happen."

Logan knew she meant for him flee to the Broken Lands. "If I go, I can't return. Ever."

"I know that." She pointed to a large tree off to her right. "I squirreled away some supplies for you over there, enough to last a week. Any more and you wouldn't be able to carry them."

"Thank you, but—"

She shushed him. "You will fend for yourself, forge a new path out there."

He had another branch sliced through. He kicked at it, dislodging both halves from the frame. He set to work on the branch next to that one. "You sound so certain."

"I am."

Just then, a man tethered to a Creeper slunk out from behind a tree only feet away from them. Neither had heard his approach. His spirit hissed.

Logan's mother said, "Bisron, please don't."

The man glared at Logan. "You shouldn't be out here, Prima. Step away from your son."

Her eyes pleaded. "You know this isn't right, Bisron. Please don't stop me. Look the other way."

"I would if I could, but the sovereign would just use a Skimmer to pull the truth out of my head. I can't."

Logan slipped the saw behind him.

She rose slowly. "I understand. You can escort me back." She walked past him. His Creeper hissed again.

"We have to obey the law," Bisron said.

"I know. This was just a moment of weakness."

"Here *and* speaking out in Sovereign Hall? They will not forget, Prima."

Bisron glared at Logan and then turned to follow her.

She said, "I don't know what came over me. I couldn't let them take away my son."

"I understand, but the sovereign is looking out for all."

Suddenly, she dropped to all fours, scooped up a fallen branch, and sprang onto her escort.

She slammed the makeshift weapon into Bisron's head twice. It was over in seconds. The man lost consciousness and fell to the ground. The Creeper snapped at her before merging back into its host, unable to take action without him.

She raced back to Logan's pen. "Hurry. Others will find us, and I don't think I'll get that lucky twice."

He nudged the saw back in place and resumed hacking at the wood with greater intensity.

"You have to go out into the Broken Lands, Logan. They will not dare follow you there."

The saw parted the branch. He grabbed the top half and wrested it free. He kicked at two of the other branches, pushing them outward. He dropped the saw and squeezed through the opening. Once out, he retrieved the sharp tool from the pen and handed it to his mother. She wrapped her arms around him and hugged him tight.

"There are answers for you out there, I feel it deep down. Your place is no longer with our enclave. It pains me to let you go, but you can't stay here any longer. Something important awaits you in the Broken Lands. You must face it with the strength and love you direct toward your brother every day."

He pulled back and looked into her eyes. Tears welled up, maybe even more than hers. "It doesn't matter what I find out. You will always be my mother. I want to—"

Off to the left, leaves rustled underfoot. Either the Hunters were awake and scuttling back to their posts or reinforcements had been called in. Getting his mother out of there was top priority. He stood, willing his tired muscles into action, grabbed her hand and launched them away from those approaching.

She pulled him off course, surprising him with her strength. "We must get your supplies."

He almost resisted, but thought better of it. He hopped over several exposed roots, being mindful that his mother did the same. She stumbled on a small rock outcropping but quickly righted herself. Her Fixer chattered nervously and sent Logan a noxious look, blaming him for his mother's misstep and near pratfall.

"I heard voices. Over here!" shouted a deep voice from the woods behind them. Whoever it was, they were almost to the pen clearing. If Logan and his mother didn't disappear into the woods now, they would be seen fleeing. Hunters were fast, hard to outrun.

His mother broke free and vaulted over a bush to land behind the large tree. She bent down, scooped up two canteens and a large satchel—*his* satchel—and waved him over. He darted into the underbrush, but not before looking back one last time for a sign of who was about to descend on them. She didn't wait for him, taking off immediately, pressing deeper into the woods. She expected him to follow.

His father broke into the clearing. He spied Logan and waved for him to leave, to disappear.

Logan didn't react. He stood still for a second, then slipped into the woods, his mother already far ahead. He didn't look back, but heard another voice. "He's gone! Did you see where he went, Leet?"

He heard the faintest of hitches in his father's response. "No, he must be long gone."

Logan could hear no more of their exchange. He was too far away. He had heard enough. His father had sided with him. His father had allowed him to escape. *What does this mean?* he thought as he crashed through the woods with more abandon, no longer caring if those behind him heard.

\* \* \*

No one gave pursuit. After a time, they slowed to a walk, catching their breaths in fits and starts. His mother looked far less haggard than himself. She crested the hill and stood framed in the starlight, with her arms crossed over her stomach, smiling.

"Your father was there, wasn't he? Leading the charge?"

Logan nodded, bending over as he gulped in several breaths. "He saw me."

She waited for him to say more.

"He covered for me."

"Of course," she stated.

The Broken Lands spread out before them. He saw a slender Creeper floating not more than fifty paces ahead.

He said, "There's more out there than just broken buildings?"

She nodded.

He took a drink from one of his canteens. He offered her the other. She declined.

"I can't come back." He wanted it to sound strong but feared he phrased it as a question.

"There are answers out there. I know it," she said.

"What about you?"

"Your father and I will be fine." She slid close and dropped her head against his chest. Her small hands fell between her cheek and his collarbone.

"I'll never forget you," he said.

"No, I wouldn't hear of it." She lifted her head and kissed his cheek. "But don't look back. Your path is ever forward. You were meant for more than just a simple tethering. You are not one to be so easily tied down."

He sobbed and nuzzled his nose in her hair.

He pulled away first, keeping his hands touching hers as he took two steps into the Broken Lands.

Her fingers squeezed tight, then let go, releasing him.

He turned, taking heavy steps into the Broken Lands.

He abided by his mother's wishes as he quickened his pace; he did not look back.

In his mind, his mother stood on the rise until he disappeared into the ruins.

In his heart, he felt her presence and knew that would never change.

*Chapter 13*
**Kyle**

The Wall was a thirty-foot high barrier of steel and stone stretching from north to south—literally from coast to coast, though it was only a day's walk from one end to the other, or roughly half a day in either direction from where Kyle stood on top of the structure. With the smog-covered city of Apparati behind him and the silent, eerie Ruins stretching as far to the east as he could see, he felt a moment of strange calm. It was as though the light breeze became still, and the noise of traffic and whining police cruisers decreased to a dull murmur. The city held its breath, waiting.

Kyle dropped down into the Ruins.

He landed on the sloping rooftop of an old, single-story building that looked like it might once have been a small house in the forgotten past. It seemed to cower under the Wall, dwarfed by its ominous presence. One entire corner of the house had been demolished to make way for the Wall's construction hundreds of years ago, just one of many such buildings that had fallen victim to the decisive ruling of a straight line on a map back in the days when the Wall had first been conceived. Pretty much everything west of the Wall had long since been built upon, the city of Apparati rising high into the sky. To the east, the Ruins lay forgotten, crumbling in the wind.

Panting and shaking with the fear of being captured, Kyle slid carefully down the warped, slate-tiled roof, twisted and hung for a moment, and dropped lightly to the ground.

The narrow streets were claustrophobic and packed with derelict structures, many with great sections of wall missing, revealing iron bars sticking out like ugly black bones. Most of the windows were glassless, but a few shards stuck up.

The silence was unnatural. The breeze high on the Wall was nonexistent down here. The neighboring city was so quiet it might as well have been a hundred miles away. All Kyle heard was the whine of cruisers in the air.

Would they come out over the Ruins? They might. It was well known that technology continued working for quite a distance beyond the Wall, slowly becoming more and more temperamental farther out until engines and computers stopped working altogether. The cruisers wouldn't have a problem operating this close to the Wall. Kyle had to move—to get as far away from the city as possible, heading east through the Ruins. At some point, machines would be unable to follow him and he'd be safe.

Safe from the city, anyway.

He darted along the streets, knowing that others were out here, people that had been here a long time. Convicted murderers and the like were always repurposed rather than exiled—Mayor Baynor knew better than to allow such violent offenders to simply walk out of the city—so there was little chance of bumping into anyone of that nature. Still, there were many other criminals who had been given the choice to opt for exile, and of course the many voluntary Leapers, all of whom were a real threat out here.

Pausing for a second in a doorway, Kyle was struck by a terror so deep that it paralyzed him. Was this really his life now? Dashing from door to door trying to avoid lawless deadbeats? How was he going to survive? How would he find food and water, and stay warm at night? He didn't even know how to make a fire.

For the first time, he fully understood why his dad had wanted him to be repurposed. The shame of having a deadbeat of a son running around was probably part of it, but mainly it was the thought of what could happen to a fourteen-year-old boy dumped in the wild. What if he was beaten half to death and abandoned? Or just left to his own devices, alone and afraid, cold and starving, cowering in some dark corner of an abandoned building for the rest of his miserable life? What kind of life was that?

He shook his head. *Get a grip. One thing at a time.*

It wasn't yet noon, but the sun was high. He had no cover of darkness to rely on; he'd just have to dash around in full daylight. Or loiter in the shadows of a ruin for the rest of the day and make a move at dusk.

*No way.*

He hurried on, darting from doorway to doorway, staying close to the walls, wary of deadbeats who might jump him at any second. He couldn't worry about everything at once. His most pressing concern were the police cruisers and, worse, General Mortimer's military escorts. One whined by directly overhead, and Kyle dove through a doorway and stood just inside, wrinkling his nose at the smell of something dead and rotting.

He moved on as soon as he could, channeling everything he had into his mission: to get clear of the Wall and out of range of the cruisers. How far would he have to travel before tech stopped working? He couldn't remember. Much of what he knew about the Ruins was hearsay and varied from source to source. The Ruins were often mentioned on the news, but it was usually when people were exiled, or on rare occasions when people took it upon themselves to leave. They were called Leapers, though Kyle was unclear whether that was because of their leap from the Wall or their huge leap of faith that something better awaited them.

Hardly anyone was allowed back in no matter what. In recent months, a young woman had been thrown from the Wall by unruly louts. She'd survived the thirty-foot drop with a broken leg, and spent days begging to be let back in, screaming until she was hoarse while cruisers hovered above, keeping tabs on her, dropping her food and water, and shooting at any deadbeats who wandered near. Finally her family had persuaded the mayor to intercede and bring her home.

For fugitives, returning to the city was not an option.

The ancient city sprawled all the way to the distant horizon in the east where a single, almost mythical structure stood. Kyle had viewed the Tower through his miniscopes, so he knew it was real, but to the naked eye it was a thin, shimmering smudge as though a landscape painting had been scratched.

*The Tower.* Kyle knew that was where he was headed. It was where *everyone* said they would make for if they were ever exiled. Leapers headed that way, too. It made sense, really. It was far from the city, far from working technology, and there was a sense of mystery about it. And everyone knew there was land *beyond* the Tower. The rest of the Ruins lay far out of sight, long forgotten. If anyone had ever made it that far, they had never returned to tell about it.

Kyle kept moving. Once in a while he came across a piece of machinery—a rusted hoverbike, a dismembered service droid, a busted assault rifle with just a skeletal hand still attached. He paused when he found a dented sphere about three feet across. Its black military markings were clear. This was one of General Mortimer's scouts. Normally they buzzed around, spying from a safe height, twisting and beeping, clicking and whirring. This one looked like it had come across a band of deadbeats. Nobody liked being spied on.

He knew he'd run into more of these, and they'd most likely be active, darting around the rooftops, searching for him and reporting his position. He slapped at the back of his neck as if bitten by a bug. They didn't *need* to report his position; his tracker was doing that already. Another reason to get away from the city. Once he was out of range, the tech would naturally stop working.

When he saw movement ahead, the flicker of someone ducking out of sight to his left, he immediately took an alley to his right. He wasn't taking any chances. He'd spin off on detours all day long if he had to.

He realized too late that he'd just been played. Two deadbeats eased around the corner at the end of the alley, and when he turned to hurry back the way he'd come, two more appeared. Where had they been hiding? Their clothes, and even their faces to a degree, were the same dull grey as the buildings. They might have been standing in full view against a crumbling wall as he passed by.

Now he was trapped. His foray into the Ruins was going to be much shorter than he'd imagined.

*Chapter 14*
## Logan

The street ahead was cluttered with weeds and grasses encroaching on the ruined city, staking claim to every crack and fissure. As the morning sun cast long shadows from the standing structures before him, Logan realized he had gone farther than any of his other forays. Several buildings had their second stories intact. He was struck by the desire to explore inside but wondered if such an endeavor would risk a cave-in. Would he find anything to help him within their dark interiors?

He had already inventoried the supplies his mother packed. Enough food for five days, seven if he stretched it. He was concerned about water. Two canteens might make it three days but not much more. He stopped and settled on a stone bench outside a building. The large window of the structure yawned before him, tempting him to enter. Small shards of glass stood upright or poked out at odd angles along the window's rotted frame. Glasswork didn't come easy to his people back in the enclave. Most homes relied on wooden shutters. Only the sovereign had all his windows sealed off with expensive glass.

He grasped hold of a large piece of glass, wary of its sharp edges. It pulled free with little effort. He held it in his hand. His mother had given him a hunting knife but not his spear. Could he fashion a weapon with the shard? He scanned his surroundings and spotted a length of staunch vine growing up and over a collapsed wall. He removed his knife and eased closer. Carefully, he shaved off a suitable length of vine then went to work lopping off its knobby thorns. Satisfied the vine wouldn't cut him, he searched for a long branch.

It felt good to allow himself this simple task. It helped to take his mind off the larger picture. For the past hour, that had been all he could think about. He was alone in the Broken Lands searching for a link to his past, something to tell him where he'd truly come from. As he had progressed, his frustration mounted. He had no clue what he was looking for. His mother's words rang true, but that truth instead of being liberating felt like an added weight. Already he was an exile. Now he was expected to find what? An inviting home of people just like him that could survive out in the Broken Lands? All unable to be tethered to a spirit? That dream seemed hollow, false.

He found a large wooden stick half buried under a wall. Its surface was rough but still looked like it had been shaped and sanded. He withdrew it to find its length too short for a spear. It was a handle of some sort. There was clearly a slot carved into its top where some head or prying attachment had been embedded. All that was left was the shaft. It was a cheap softwood like gleek only darker and more knotty. Logan cautiously rammed the glass shard into the slot. So thick was the glass that it barely fit. He took that as a good sign. Maybe his makeshift weapon wouldn't break with its first real use.

As Logan wound the vine repeatedly around the glass, making sure it held it snug against the wood, he looked to the rising sun to his west. An immense tower rose far off, a structure he had caught glimpses of from the outskirts only on the clearest of days. That was another aspect of the Broken Lands that many found unnerving: it was almost always shrouded in a perpetual fog further in.

He was heading to the heart of the ruins. The Tower was important. He realized that now. Maybe it was the fact that its shape was now unmistakably present despite the fog. He had no idea if it lay a day away or a week. Anything more would make the trek impossible with his current supplies.

He tied off the vine a number of times then held the weapon aloft. He swept it through the air. The balance was off, but he would have to work with what he had. He took another swig of water.

He froze, the hairs on his arms standing. A large Breaker ghosted through the façade of the building directly across the street. It hadn't seen him. Why was he so antsy? It wasn't like the spirit would attempt to tether. He flashed back to the image of Kiff being overtaken by another Breaker. There it was. Despite knowing the spirit couldn't do anything to him physically, its presence tugged at him. He felt anger at the spirit but knew that was wrong. The spirits were only acting as they had for hundreds of years. It had been his fault Kiff was there. He had not been careful enough. He had allowed his brother to trail him.

Despite feeling weak in the knees, Logan stood. He couldn't let the past keep him from surviving. He had to move on. He watched the Breaker charge at a decapitated statue in a nearby courtyard. It plowed through the stonework, its passage disturbing not even the dust that layered the sculpture. Logan was curious what the statue depicted. With its head missing, it was hard to tell if it was a likeness of his own people or another race entirely. The torso and lower body could certainly pass for any citizen of the enclave, but what if the head had hideous horns or antlers? He thought to wait for the Breaker's departure so he could zip over and examine the ground around the statue. Maybe the head was still lying there intact.

He grew flush with excitement at the idea of learning who might have built the civilization and then left it abandoned under centuries of dust. He padded to a large pile of rubble and crouched. *Just leave*, he thought, sending his demand to the Breaker knowing it wouldn't be moved by his mental urgings.

The Breaker took two more passes through the statue before engaging in a mid-air tantrum. After flailing its arms and legs far longer than Logan thought was necessary, the spirit tore off for parts unknown.

He counted to one hundred before starting across the open street. As he was about to step through the entry to the courtyard, a distinctive warbling shattered the silence.

He spun to see a pack of kalibacks hunched atop the roof of the building he had retrieved the glass from. There were five, and all ten pairs of eyes glared at him.

The leader kaliback's left and right lower jaws dropped. From the left, its distinctive yellow tongue flopped out, its tip festooned with poison-laden barbs. From its right mouth the keening warble barreled outward.

The entire pack dropped to the ground together, landing on their thick front legs without a sound.

Logan gripped his hunting knife in one hand and his newly fashioned glass weapon in the other. He abandoned his inspection of the statue, a mystery for another day, and tore down the street toward the creeping fog.

*Chapter 15*
## Kyle

The deadbeats closed in on Kyle, two in front, two behind. A fifth appeared—the decoy, the one who'd manipulated him into heading down this alley in the first place.

They were just about the scruffiest individuals he had ever seen: several layers of unwashed, threadbare clothes, long straggly hair, and dirty faces. Three were men, one a woman, and the fifth a girl of about ten.

"Give us what you got," the woman said softly as she edged closer.

Kyle shuffled from side to side, judging the width of the alley, wondering if he could slip past the deadbeats if he was quick enough . . . and then debating whether he would be able to outrun them afterward.

By the time the gang closed in, he still hadn't made up his mind, and then it was too late. They pressed in, so close that he could smell them.

Rather than repeat herself, the woman reached out and pulled his jacket open, feeling it with her thumbs. She patted the pockets, came across the wad of cash, and gently pulled the notes free. After a quick count, she calmly placed them in her own pocket.

"Anything else?" she asked, looking him in the eye.

"N-nothing," Kyle said. "Just these clothes. I was supposed to be repurposed, but . . ."

"You escaped?"

Kyle nodded.

Under all that grime, she had clear green eyes. Her teeth were straight though yellowed. What had she been like before coming to the Ruins? How had she ended up leading this gang?

The others exchanged glances. The three men looked like they could tear a fourteen-year-old boy in two, yet they seemed oddly calm, clearly respectful of the woman in charge. The young girl looked bored, staring off into space. Just how many times had she helped ambush newcomers that it had become routine to her?

The woman looked Kyle up and down and fingered his jacket again. "Respect to you for getting away," she said. "We'll take the jacket. You can keep the pants and shirt." She peered at his shoes. "What size are those?"

The fact that she had said he could keep the pants and shirt told him they planned to let him go, which eased his terror somewhat. It also fueled his anger—that they intended to take his jacket and maybe his shoes as if they had some kind of right.

The woman sighed. "Come on, kid. Jacket and shoes."

One of the men had a short, stubby weapon hanging from his belt, a military handgun with a built-in chip that, once locked with a user's DNA, was no good to anyone else. For the gun to be working for him, this man must be a dishonored military man—or perhaps a locksmith.

One of Kyle's friends, Cayden, was always boasting about his dad's locksmith abilities, able to disengage electronic locks of all kinds just by looking at them. If Kyle's implant was working, and if he was a locksmith, he'd be able to unlock the weapon right now and set it to free-for-all, then make a grab for it. Better still, if he had some military disposition as well, he could wrangle with its deliberately complex software and fire it from where he stood, blasting that man's foot off and causing a distraction . . .

Kyle sighed. Who was he kidding? Very few were multi-talented like that. Those who were worked for the mayor. Kyle had no skills at all.

"I won't ask you nicely again, kid," the woman said, raising her voice. "You've got three seconds. After that we'll take what we want and a bit extra for our trouble."

"Get lost," Kyle said.

Where his sudden bravado and perhaps stupidity had come from was a mystery, but the words were out before he knew it. The woman's eyebrows shot up, and the men sighed and shook their heads.

"Okay, kid, if that's how you want to play it . . ."

Kyle never knew exactly who clubbed him on the back of the neck. In the next instant he was on the ground being tugged this way and that. His jacket and shoes were stolen while he was still struggling to wake from his daze. "And this is for giving us lip," the woman said, at which point she drew a long knife.

Kyle yelled, but the men pinned him down. The woman cut through his shirt—his light repurposing gown—and tore it free of his body, then tossed it aside. She pulled his socks off and flung them, then grabbed the top of his pants and paused with the knife, ready to cut them off.

Gasping for breath, Kyle found her staring at him. He was pretty sure he saw a flicker of pity. She dropped her gaze and released him, then stood and collected up his socks and ragged shirt. "We'll use these to stuff our pillows," she murmured, handing the clothing to one of the men, who in turn stuffed it into a knapsack he carried over one shoulder. "Be safe, kid."

The whine of a cruiser increased, and to Kyle's horror it came in close as if to land. It didn't, though. It simply hovered there, waiting.

The woman jerked her thumb skyward. "You're all over the news at the moment. They're waiting for you to get beaten to a pulp so the mayor can crow about it and show people what a rotten hellhole it is out here." She scowled. "Best head east beyond the tech-zone where they can't reach you. They'll forget about you after a few weeks. Then you can come back."

*Yeah, looking forward to that,* Kyle thought.

The gang walked away, strolling without a care in the world. Kyle rolled onto his stomach and watched them go, filled with indignation, shaking with anger. How *dare* they? How could they be so heartless? Wasn't he in the exact same predicament as them? How about a helping hand, an offering of peace, an act of simple kindness by *leaving him alone*?

Shaking, he knelt in the street wearing only brand new pants that still had a price tag hanging from them. Now he could add two more problems to his list—staying warm, and avoiding severe lacerations to his feet as he ran.

* * *

If anything positive had come from his run-in with the gang, it was that he felt a little more emboldened. Sure, there would be other gangs, probably worse than the last one. But he'd come through his encounter and earned his first battle scar, slight as it was. The gang had been kind, in a way. They could have kicked him, stabbed him, left him bleeding. The woman could have cut off his pants and left him naked just to add to his suffering. But he'd gotten away with his health and his pants.

He met nobody at all during the next two hours. The old, abandoned town started to peter out, the buildings becoming few and far between. He was heading out into the open area.

The problem was that the cruisers knew where he was. They'd been following him all along. Kyle had stopped hiding from them, had even taken to sauntering along the streets in full view, looking up at one hovering vehicle after another, wondering why they didn't descend and collect him. At first he thought they were just waiting for a clear landing place, but that wasn't it. Many of the streets were wide enough to land in, especially this far out from the Wall, on the fringes of the city that had been here before.

No, it was something else. Maybe the gang leader was right, that the mayor was letting him run. Maybe these cruisers were just watching him, *filming* him, hoping he'd suffer a horrible death so it could be broadcast all over the news as a warning to others.

Was that it? Were they simply recording his progress on cameras, waiting for a nice, juicy action scene where he was set upon by a *really* vicious gang? His parents would be watching, and Byron, too. This was good in one respect; they would know he was still alive. But his mom would be worried sick, seeing him shirtless and shoeless like this, wandering about in this dangerous place. And if he was attacked, and it was shown on the news . . . well, that would be awful.

His simmering anger kept him moving. He ignored the pain in his feet from various cuts and grazes and focused his attention on the horizon to the east, which was opening up before him as he left the streets behind. There was the Tower, marginally closer than it had been a couple of hours ago. How long would it take to reach it? A day? Two? It was hard to tell. The landscape looked open and completely flat at a glance, but Kyle knew it wasn't really. There were dips and rises, rivers and rocks, a whole mess of awkward terrain that could tear his feet to shreds and wear him down long before he reached the Tower.

If only one of those cruisers would give him a ride, at least some of the way. If only they were as helpful as the crowd had been outside the Repurposing Factory.

He suddenly remembered the bearded old man who had allowed him to escape through the emergency door—a door that had previously been on lockdown. He'd used his implant to unlock it, then had locked it again. Why? Who was he?

Kyle sighed. He would never know.

It was scrubby out here, the ground baked dry. Ahead looked more promising. He saw clumps of trees and bushes, and a strange ridge that glittered and shone. He couldn't fathom what it was.

Something caught his attention to the left, and he made a detour to check it out, aware that a cruiser was lagging behind, fifty feet up. "Get lost," he growled, trying to ignore it.

The large object disappointed him. It turned out to be one of those automated road-cleaning trucks—taller than him and wide as a hovercar, a bulky, rectangular machine fitted with brushes, hoses and nozzles underneath. "What the heck are *you* doing in the Ruins?" Kyle said, walking around it.

There was nothing of use to him here. Being largely computer operated, there wasn't even an internal driver cab to shelter in. The truck had a solitary seat hanging off one side along with a few levers and a control panel, used only for occasional manual override. Kyle had seen many of these driverless machines shuffling along the streets collecting trash and hosing away all the muck that collected in the gutter.

It had seen better days. Resting on the ground, sand was piled up on one side, blown there over several months or years. Kyle climbed up into the operator seat and sat there staring ahead at the Tower. If he was going to make it all that way, he needed to think ahead. He needed water. He needed clothes. He needed a way to make fire, to learn how to catch wildlife for food. He needed a way to defend himself.

He sighed, resting his elbows on the stubby levers and placing his head in his hands. How did people survive out here?

As he was staring down at the small control board, he noticed that one of the lights was blinking on and off. Kyle rubbed his thumb over it, removing the layer of dust to read the label. It read CHARGED.

His mouth dropping open, Kyle glanced over his shoulder. His seat was high enough that he could see the top of the machine, which was fitted with the usual solar panels. If this thing had power, then maybe Kyle could fiddle with the wiring, create a spark or two, and make fire with a handful of dry grass. It was the middle of the afternoon, yet already he was worrying about the chilly night ahead. He could make camp right here, hunt for rodents, and roast them on a roaring fire.

Or . . .

He pressed the button marked POWER. Lights flickered on, and the droid began its boot-up cycle.

Maybe he could just drive on ahead.

*Chapter 16*
**Logan**

The kalibacks moved as one, veering right to dodge the rock Logan had thrown at them.

He vaulted over a large pile of rubble, pushed off sideways from a standing wall, and landed on all fours just shy of an expanse of standing water. Although it looked stagnant, undrinkable, it was a sign that water collected in the ruins. He needed to find a clean source. But first he had to elude the kalibacks.

He ran along the water's edge, fearful of the debris that surely lay submerged in its shallow depths.

Two of the kalibacks had no such qualms. They splashed into the water, narrowing the distance by half. Their dual mouths opened and closed with excitement. These big predators were trouble by themselves. Being hunted by a pack . . . Logan didn't like his chances. Nor did he want to be on the receiving end of their massive segmented tails or poison-tipped tongues. They moved swiftly, their muscular legs propelling them steadily through the water.

Logan had to come up with a plan. Running would get him pulled down. The pack leader issued several commanding grunts and warbles. The other two kalibacks at its side raced down a crumbling alley, seemingly abandoning the chase. Where were they going? Logan knew kalibacks were clever, the most intelligent predators in Apparata. Facing one was bad enough. Five would be a death sentence, especially since he couldn't summon a Breaker to beat them off. He sensed a trap in the works.

He narrowly avoided tripping over a large metallic cylinder wedged into the ground. Sidestepping to his right, he leaned too far forward and stumbled. He rolled several times, fearing that to stop moving would result in piercing jaws clamping down on him.

He sprang to his feet and saw that the waterlogged kalibacks were almost beside him. The pack leader bringing up the rear had slowed and now paced toward Logan with entirely too much leisure and confidence. It bobbed its head with deliberate cunning.

This signal spurred the closest kaliback to pounce.

Logan brought up his makeshift weapon in a wide arc, willing its glass head not to shatter. Miraculously, it sliced into the exposed underbelly of the predator with ease, releasing a rain of blood and organs as the disemboweled kaliback sailed overhead. Slippery ropes of innards dropped on him. He batted them away.

The kaliback landed and rolled over and over. The gaping wound to its midsection tore open even further. When it came to rest, it lifted its head weakly then stilled.

Time froze. The leader glared at Logan but didn't move or speak. The kaliback in the water stood stock still, indifferent to the pronounced plips and plops of the water dripping from its hide.

The leader was the largest kaliback he had ever seen. Only two of its four eyes were in working order. The two on its left were milky white and bisected by a jagged scar running from its ear nub down to its left lower jaw. The dual mouths were horrible. They opened and closed constantly, revealing rows of sharp yellowed teeth. Even through the gathering fog, Logan could see that bits of meat and gristle riddled the creature's teeth. Its eyes were rimmed with black fur like a mask, sharp contrast to the yellow and grey contained in the rest of its shaggy coat.

Most of its mass gathered in the front while its back half tapered to a very maneuverable posterior. Despite the creature's armored tail being over twelve feet long and of substantial mass, it could whip it about with astonishing speed. All four legs were thick and muscled with the hindquarters fringed with jagged ridges. Logan had seen a kaliback use its tail to sweep its prey into the proliferation of ridges, impaling them on the piercing array.

The leader's head moved slowly from side to side, bobbing down each time it returned to the center.

It was up to something. He drew in ragged breaths. Running was hopeless, and the pack outnumbered him.

Logan urgently surveyed the city around him. Many of the buildings now rose three or four stories before showing signs of damage. Could he escape by going inside and up? Out in the open, the kalibacks' speed was an advantage. They had room to maneuver. Inside, they would encounter far more obstacles. But Logan had no idea the condition of the buildings' interiors. He might just be rushing into a crumbling dead end.

Farther down the street, toward the west and the Tower stretching to the clouds, the fog thickened. He had thought it his ally, that ducking into its embrace would keep the kalibacks from finding him. But he knew that was a false hope.

He had to get inside. His best chance was a building across the street to his left, its small windows on the lower level whole and in place. The door was battered in, possibly offering enough room for him to slip through but not his pursuers. The only thing standing between him and the sanctuary it afforded was the large pool and the kaliback that now waded toward him.

He took a step in the direction of his salvation.

The pair of kalibacks that had disappeared earlier came hurtling toward him from up the street, racing out of the thick fog, warbling and grunting their battle cries. At the same time, the leader began pacing toward him again, all too assured in its movements. It would let the pack take Logan down. It was clear the leader didn't need the kill but would surely be the first to make a meal of him.

Logan splashed into the water, racing up onto a large rock that hung out of the water. He spied four more stones above the water line and hopped across them in turn. The kaliback ahead thrashed about. It was in the deepest section of the massive pool, the water rising up to cover all its legs. It tried to rear back and failed. It churned the water as it resumed its laborious wading.

If he jumped down into the water with the kaliback, the water would come up to his waist and hinder him from putting up much of a fight. He had to wait for the kaliback to get closer. He hoisted his glass axe high, eager to take a whack at the creature.

Looking back revealed the pair of kalibacks were now at the water's edge. The first to arrive bounded onto the large rock closest to the shore. Waiting was over. Logan sprang forward, letting loose a howl. He brought the axe down hard and fast. The kaliback in his sights froze, shocked it was being attacked.

He realized too late he had misjudged his actions. The axe didn't bury itself in the creature's meaty shoulders but sliced into the top of its head. It hit the beast's thick skull and shattered.

He tried to swing his legs up and around, attempting a forward flip in order to land on his feet atop the creature's broad back. If he could do that, he could launch himself farther afield and avoid the deeper water.

Instead, he landed on his back and glanced off into the water. He sputtered to his feet, amazed at how heavy his waterlogged clothes felt.

The other two kalibacks were now in the water and slogging toward him through the deepest section.

Logan willed his legs to move, trudging through the waist-high water until it was only to his thighs. When it was down to his knees, he was putting good distance between him and the three floundering kalibacks. He smiled. He might get out of this alive.

His hopes died when he heard the pronounced warble of the pack leader approaching. While Logan had been wading through the water, it had doubled back along the shore and was now racing toward him. At the speed it was going, it would easily cut him off from reaching the open door less than twenty paces away.

He lifted the axe, now no more than a heavy stick as he unsheathed his hunting knife. He exited the water, a weapon in both hands. If he was going down, he would fight to the last breath.

The leader arrived and stepped between him and the door. The intelligence in its eyes told Logan it knew his plan.

The three kalibacks behind him splashed out of the water.

Their leader roared at its pack.

Rather than finish him off, the three slunk around at the water's edge, chided by their leader to hold back.

*Now it wants to do me in itself.*

He took two more steps forward. The pack leader could easily swipe its front claws and slice through his leg. Logan knew this, but he didn't want to show it any fear.

Logan put on a bold front and took two more steps forward, knowing the pack leader could easily shred him to bits. He couldn't help flinching when the creature warbled, its two good eyes glowing with avarice.

Its back legs stiffened. Then it lunged forward, bringing its front claws up to rake across Logan's torso. He swatted the club downward, knowing nothing would stop the beast's murderous charge.

Out of the corner of his eye, he saw a large object drop from the roof of his sanctuary onto the pack leader.

Logan staggered to his right. What had pounced on the great kaliback was a spirit, a Breaker. And it was not tethered! It should've passed harmlessly through the kaliback. Untethered spirits couldn't affect the physical world.

But it did. It slammed into the kaliback, tusks first, hammering the predator into the ground.

Logan heard someone shout *run*. His brain froze for the briefest of seconds, overwhelmed by the velocity of the drama unfolding before him.

Something snapped deep down and he stirred. He stumbled forward and slipped neatly through the half-open door. No way could any of the kalibacks fit through such a tight doorway. He took in two measured breaths before looking outside.

The Breaker was nowhere to be found.

The large kaliback lay crumpled, unmoving. The three remaining members of its pack stared up at something on the roof, their six pairs of eyes wide in abject fear. They quivered in unison, then fled, leaderless and unhinged.

Logan slumped against the lower half of the broken door, his muscles all but dead to the world. He let the wooden axe minus its glass head clatter to the ground. He pulled the knife close to his chest and sobbed.

For several minutes, he sat there watching more of the fog roll in from the west until he could no longer see the edge of the expansive pool.

Someone had come to his rescue. He didn't know how to explain it, but knew his rescuer was long gone.

Inside he was consumed with an absolute certainty.

Whoever had been on the roof had *not* come from any of the seven enclaves.

*Chapter 17*
## Kyle

Kyle looked all around, fearful of a trap. Could this road-cleaning truck really be in working order? How could it just be standing here unused like this? Wouldn't some gang or other be making use of it if it still ran?

After the boot-up sequence was complete, Kyle tentatively pushed forward on the left lever. The truck shuddered and started to turn to the right. It scraped on the ground and halted with a squeal from underneath.

Peering down past the rounded cage floor below his feet, Kyle knew the truck should be sitting higher, at least a foot off the ground rather than touching it. Maybe that was the problem, why nobody had bothered with it. It wasn't much good if it didn't work.

He searched for the control that would switch it to automatic. When he pressed it, several lights lit up and the truck jerked, then bucked, nearly throwing him from his seat. But the machine rose a few inches and swayed like a large animal just woken from a deep sleep. Now it was hovering. The problem was that automatic mode meant the computer wouldn't accept any override commands, so he wouldn't be able to direct it to the east. It either did its job alone or an operator took over—not both. It seemed almost petulant in that respect. Kyle could almost imagine it saying, "Look, if you want me to do this job, then let me do it my way. Otherwise do it yourself."

*Dad says the same thing to Mom sometimes.*

This simple reminder of the family he'd left behind stopped him dead for a moment. Meanwhile the truck waited, apparently confused. Its mapping system recognized none of its surroundings.

Kyle sighed. If he wanted to get anywhere on this thing, he would have to switch back to manual. He jabbed the button, and the machine thudded back down into the dirt with a bone-jarring crash. Now he understood why it was standing here untouched. It didn't work. If he were a Mechanic, he could probably get into the computer's neural registry and fix it. Clearly there was no mechanical problem; it was just some sort of programming error.

The terrain ahead was littered with small jagged rocks in some areas and dry brush in others. It would be rough going with bare feet. He decided to have a go at powering down the machine and rebooting, something that worked for Byron when his software got muddled. Most people were dummies when it came to that stuff. They operated heavy machinery and delicate instruments without ever questioning how they were doing it. To them, tech just *worked*. If something went wrong, they called a Mechanic. Or there was a Mechanic already there on hand.

Kyle, on the other hand, had spent a lot of time maintaining what was essentially an old service robot adapted to include Byron's brain and reprogrammed with unique software. It was either that or wait years for multiple new body parts while his brain floated in a large jar. It was Uncle Jeremiah who had suggested the mechanical body after the accident, and the insurance company—unable to find a loophole—had dutifully funded the unorthodox solution. Byron had been famous for a while, the city's first fully mechanical boy.

The power-down switch wasn't anywhere near the operator controls. It was located at the rear of the truck behind a small panel. He flipped it and waited, listening, as the road-cleaning machine wound down. Kyle could hear servos and motors whirring deep within its guts, finally quieting at the same time that every light on the control panel went out.

Then Kyle flipped the power back on. Immediately the whirring and clicking restarted, and something rattled and clanked momentarily. The operator lights flashed and steadied, and a display indicated that the reboot was 13% complete, now 16%, climbing slowly.

He looked back toward the city. The dusty town sprawled for miles, dwarfed by the Wall and the gleaming high-rise buildings in the distance. How quiet everything was without the constant drone of traffic. And how much cleaner the air was away from the smog-filled city center.

A distant group of people wandered into view between crumbling buildings. Kyle instinctively ducked. The gang was larger than the one he'd run into earlier, at least seven of them. They were too far away to be a real threat, though. Kyle felt he could run and hide if they spotted him. Still, it was unnerving to think that he might have bumped into those thugs at any time. He might have ended up dead instead of waiting here for a rusty road-cleaning machine to boot up.

77% ... 82% ...

When the reboot was complete, the truck rose off the ground. Kyle refrained from shouting his delight. Instead, he checked that the gang weren't looking his way and climbed into the seat.

The truck was still in manual mode but hovering correctly. The reboot had worked, somehow fixing its corrupted software. Kyle pushed the levers forward and mentally clapped himself on the back as the clunky contraption started moving, brushing over low bushes without a pause, gliding gracefully over every bump and dip.

This was more like it.

Kyle imagined he was riding a canyon clacker, one of those ugly great rock worms that were seen out here in the Ruins from time to time. They surfaced when it rained hard enough, and it was an awe-inspiring sight to see a herd of them sliding along in bizarre, pulsing movements, each fifteen feet long and as high as his chest. Awe-inspiring, that is, when viewed through his miniscopes from a great distance. Nobody wanted to get near those beasts when they let out a screech loud enough to blast boulders into small chunks.

Aware that he was still being spied on by a cruiser from afar, he was sorely tempted to send it a rude gesture or two. But for all he knew, that might be all the excuse the mayor needed to blast him to smithereens. He opted to ignore the cruiser and enjoy his small victory in private.

The truck was slow, but Kyle made far better progress than he would have hobbling along without shoes. As the sun beat down on his bare shoulders and back, he started to worry about sunburn—and the rapid temperature drop at nighttime. He needed to think about how to make a campfire before it got too dark. There was time yet, though. It was still late afternoon, not even dinner time.

Right on cue, his stomach growled. Something else to think about! He'd missed lunch and would likely miss dinner, too. As he adjusted his direction to point toward the distant Tower, he wondered if he should perhaps head for one of the shores instead. The idea of fishing appealed to him more than catching whatever critters lived out here.

He pictured a map of the city encircled by the Wall, with the capitol and rich areas in the center and all the drab, poor suburbs out near the perimeter. There were coastal outcrops to the south, west, and north, even a couple of ancient settlements, but mostly there was nothing but ocean. To the east lay a relatively narrow strip of land where the Ruins sprawled. Though a good two- to three-hour walk across its breadth, it was rather like a bridge when viewed on a map—a bridge from Apparati to a long-forgotten world where the terrain spread wide and rose into the mountains. Perhaps there was something there, something worth a long journey far away from the city and beyond the Ruins.

Of course, everyone had the same fanciful ideas. Since tech didn't work that far out, airskimmers and cruisers and even lightweight spy-eyes were useless. There were no pictures of the far east, no film footage, no evidence of anything at all beyond what had been written into history books and passed down through the generations. Nothing but the Ruins. And nobody in their right mind would willingly leave the city to make a journey like that on foot.

Except exiles. Deadbeats with nothing to lose.

From time to time, Kyle came across the dusty, skeletal remains of a man or woman, with random bones protruding from filthy rags that fluttered in an occasional breeze. Kyle tried not to think about how they might have died. Beaten by gangs? Stabbed by robbers? Perhaps even shot down by city troops?

If the latter were true, Kyle considered himself lucky. At the back of his mind, he couldn't help thinking he'd gotten away easily. The cruisers had needlessly pursued him from the city center; General Mortimer could have made a simple call to troops patrolling the Wall and prevented his escape rather than arrive too late. And even as Kyle had wandered about the Ruins, they could have locked in and shot him at any time. He had the sneaky suspicion they'd allowed him to escape. Nothing filled curious stream screen viewers with more horror than the sight of a helpless boy or girl falling victim to the violence outside the Wall. Though exile was an option for adults, the mayor liked to remind everyone that repurposing was a far more humane way to die.

Movement caught his eye. Kyle gasped and instinctively yanked back on the lever, but it was too late—the service truck skimmed low over some ugly bushes and disturbed a heaving mass of small creatures huddled within. He pushed forward on the lever, eager to leave them behind, but the machine was cumbersome, taking forever to pick up speed again. A dozen of the creatures left the nest, hopping angrily, their tiny jaws snapping and letting off short bursts of blue flame.

Orb scavengers were best left alone. Adults usually flew around in groups, their ultra-light bone structure and membranous flaps of stretched skin allowing them to bob and weave on the air currents. Kyle had seen plenty of footage of packs descending on the dead and picking the flesh from the bones in a frenzied blur of motion.

They hid their nests among jagged kilbatoo bushes, of which there were plenty in these parts. Kyle should have been more wary. Now the tiny underdeveloped scavengers were hopping mad. Each was the size of his head, and though he could knock them away if they flapped too close, a dozen coming at him together was a problem. He waved his hands frantically as the screeching creatures leapt at him. He felt a sharp nip on his shoulder, a burn on his ear, multiple pricks on his back as they clung on with hooked claws, and all the while he spun and flailed in his seat.

He was lucky they were too young to have mastered flight. It was bad enough that they could leap and soar, attacking him with razor teeth and claws and blasts of fire as they hurtled past. He couldn't imagine the horror of a full-grown swarm descending on him.

And just as that notion entered his mind, he glanced upward to see a pair of adults converging on him.

*Chapter 18*
**Logan**

After the incident with the kalibacks and the Breaker, Logan stumbled outside, hoping to spy whoever had been on the roof. Try as he might, he couldn't see anyone and sensed whoever had come to his aid was long gone. He returned to the interior of the building searching for a way up to the roof. Discovering a door that led to a stairwell, he was disappointed to find the stairs blocked by a cave-in. Unable to inspect the roof, Logan returned to the first floor and did a little exploring.

He had selected some sort of store for his shelter. There was a large area in the front where shelves and display furniture sat empty, their wares long ago sold or pilfered. He also found a storeroom, its metal shelving bare. He marveled briefly at the craftsmanship of the metal shelves. No Weavers in the Enclave could manipulate metal to the extent he saw in those shelves. Adjoining the storeroom, he found a small room with a simple desk, a broken chair on wheels, and a long overstuffed couch. After slapping out most of the dust from the weathered cushions, he locked the door, slid the desk next to it as a barricade, and curled up on the couch to rest. With being consigned to the Pens and his escape the night before, the lack of sleep had caught up with him, and he quickly dropped off.

He sank into a frantic dream almost immediately. He stood on an ornate balcony, looking down over a stunning cityscape. The buildings were loftier than any in Apparata, including the trinity of the Hallowed Spires in the capitol and the reaching heights of the ruins, taller even than the Broken Lands' Tower. Below, he saw hundreds of people running in every direction along winding walkways and bridges that crisscrossed every open area. Spots of greenery defined small parks and gardens.

They were few and far between and appeared more planned than natural.

What frightened him about the dream was not just the scope of the city. Yes, it was huge, but what unsettled him even more were the long machines winding their way through the city atop metal paths that not even the finest Weavers could dream of constructing in their lifetimes. Most mastered wood and stone. Manipulating metal was reserved for smaller scale objects and structures like weapons and windmills. He playfully envisioned the vehicle threading along the path below as a giant metal serpent, stopping at several points while openings along its side belched out people from its hidden innards onto a wide platform. They exited, indifferent to having been swallowed by the beast.

What power these people held in their hands to create such impressive machines and buildings.

The dream ended with a commotion next to a large building. It appeared a crowd had gathered. They waved signs about. Larger citizens wearing what looked like armor waded into the crowd, attempting to clear a path.

Before the dream completely dissolved, he saw the disturbance erupt into a full-scale riot.

Logan snapped to attention as best he could, his head still groggy from his brief nap. He felt around for his knife, finding it where he had left it on the small table next to the couch. He slipped his fingers around its hilt and scanned the small room.

It wasn't difficult to remember his dream. It hung in his head, defying the usual conventions of dreams to wane upon waking. He couldn't dwell on it now. He had to get moving.

Logan guzzled down the remaining contents of one canteen before storing it in his satchel. He wolfed down three strips of dried brindle meat and a fresh leeg seed muffin his mother had packed for him. With no windows in the office, he had no idea how long he had slept.

He pushed the desk out of the way and pressed his ear to the door, listening for any indication he had uninvited guests. Hearing nothing, he swept open the door and dashed out and to his left, skirting behind a large stack of flat wooden frames whose purpose escaped him.

Logan peered intently through the numerous openings in the stack. The storeroom was flooded with daylight through its high windows. He had no idea how late it was but felt he had slept most of the day.

He shuffled quietly to his left, traveling down a narrow aisle between two towering rows of shelves. The dust around him swirled as if excited at being disturbed after such a long time. He coughed and tried to swat away the cloud of fine airborne particles.

He froze, taking in every nook and cranny of the storeroom, expecting the three remaining kalibacks to come charging at him.

A small bird with red markings on the tips of its wings flew to the back of the storeroom. He had never seen that species before and wondered how many new creatures he would find in the Broken Lands. He allowed the thrill of discovery to briefly overtake him. Maybe that would give him a purpose. He could catalog all the new plants and animals he found. But to what end? He couldn't go marching back to the enclave raving about his startling new findings and expect to be welcomed with open arms, could he?

Satisfied he was alone, he headed toward the swinging double doors leading to the front of the store. He peered out one of the inset windows before pushing the left door open enough for him to squeeze through. The door creaked harshly as it closed. He winced, his eyes flitting toward the open door that led to the street.

Nothing lurked in the front either. Outside, the fog had mostly dissipated. This surprised him because, from a distance, the fog had looked ever-present.

He padded over to the door. The fallen kaliback lay next to the puddle, its immense back to Logan. It had not moved. The Breaker had really done a number on it.

There was no sign of its pack. *They must be as spooked by the Breaker attack as I am.*

Just as he was about to exit, a blue flash of movement in the air caught his eye. Above, a swarm of orb scavengers swirled about, their upper arms threaded together to form their distinctive mode of transport. When they weren't hunting solo, orb scavengers flew in an intertwined mass, linking together to form a balloon shape thanks to their stretchy skin from their wrists down to their ankles. This arrangement kept the group aloft by their combined flame alone, allowing their wing flap muscles a respite. The creatures had slender, hollow bones and rode on air currents aided by the warm jet of flame they could expel from their tiny mouths. Because the creatures were almost always spotted in the air, no enclave citizen had ever discovered how they could generate such flame and not burn their throats or tongues. If they came to ground, it was in large swarms and only to feed. No one in the village was foolish enough to approach a swarm of feeding orb scavengers. Better to let them have their fill and then allow them to take back to the air undisturbed.

An orb scavenger by itself was not a threat. But a swarm, especially one as massive as what was drifting to the ground before Logan, went beyond dire. They were an impressive configuration. While each individual was no more than three feet tall, their combined bulk was twice the size of the fallen kaliback.

He didn't move, didn't dare breathe as he watched the swarm land on and around the kaliback carcass. He counted over forty with still more dropping from the sky. As they landed, the orb scavengers wasted no time tearing into the dead kaliback. With their tiny teeth, they ripped into its flesh, feasting with relative cooperation. As more set on the meat, a few disagreements erupted. It was almost comical watching the orb scavengers hock fire at each other in an attempt to stake small territories of ripe flesh for themselves.

Logan backed away, taking a slow breath and exhaling with just as much caution.

With the size of the kaliback, the swarm would take at least an hour picking it clean. Noting the sun already dropping in the eastern sky, he knew he couldn't wait that long. It would be dark before they finished their feast. He had to find another way out of the store and skirt well away from the street laden with the orb scavengers.

He shuffled back, pushing the door open to enter the backroom. The hinge let out a pronounced squeak, and he froze.

Outside, through the narrow opening of the door, he saw the orb scavengers pause, swivel toward him, and cock their small heads quizzically.

In unison, they shrieked and took to the air, darting into the store at an alarming speed.

Logan swung the door shut, hoping it would take out several of the lead scavengers.

He had found out something new about this mysterious species. Apparently, orb scavengers fed on more than just the dead.

*Chapter 19*
## Kyle

"Go away!" Kyle screamed as the adult orb scavengers streaked toward him from high above. With their spindly arms and legs and the skin that stretched between, their silhouettes against the hazy sky were almost square in shape, angled downward so that they cut through the air. Each was a little more than double the size of the babies, and he'd seen enough wildlife infostreams to know they could hook their claws into his skin and cling on while gnawing rapidly through his eye sockets and the flesh of his cheeks and mouth.

He pushed hard on the lever, urging the clunky service truck forward. It would be quicker to sprint—if he had shoes, and if the entire nest of baby scavengers weren't zipping all over the place and raking at him. He huddled in his seat and wished these road-cleaning clunkers were equipped with cabs. Instead, he perched on the exposed seat that stuck out from the side of the droid protected by nothing more than a waist-high cage and a panel of instruments.

*A panel of instruments.*

He started jabbing at buttons with his free hand. Immediately there came the roar of huge circular brushes as four of them descended from underneath and kicked up great clouds of dust. The dozen young orb scavengers that were attacking him screeched and scattered as the dust storm swept upward and enveloped Kyle and the truck. Alarms started beeping, and a message flashed GARBAGE FULL. OVERLOAD WARNING. Coughing and blinking furiously, Kyle deactivated the brushes, fearful of a crippling malfunction.

The roaring noise ceased, but the screeching continued. The dust was everywhere now, a choking cloud that blocked out the sunlight. Kyle scanned the dull sky and caught a glimpse of two shadows sweeping by overhead. He hunkered down, keeping the machine moving and hoping the adults would stay away.

Hardly able to believe his good fortune, he realized the baby scavengers were dropping back—and the adults were floating down to check on them, leaving Kyle alone.

He'd always heard that orb scavengers preyed on the dead, that they steered clear of the living unless provoked. If that were true, perhaps they'd accept Kyle's inadvertent attack as a mistake and let him be. *No harm done, right?* he thought nervously, craning his neck and keeping a watchful eye on the adults. They were on the ground now, herding their brood back to the nest—a curiously tender moment even for vicious, ugly critters like these.

By the time the nest was settled and the dust cleared, Kyle had steered his truck to what he considered a reasonably safe distance. One of the adult orb scavengers turned to watch him, and a sense of dread settled on Kyle as it raised its arms and spread its skin-flaps. With a hop, it launched into the air and flapped hard, soaring upward, coming for Kyle.

On impulse, he flipped a switch, one he'd noticed earlier. With a grinding sound, the rear of the truck opened up and forcibly ejected a huge mound of garbage—much of it collected from the streets of Apparati, the rest just a few minutes ago. As the junk and choking dust spewed outward, the orb scavenger veered away.

"Now leave me alone," Kyle shouted, "or I'll start cleaning again!"

That seemed to be the end of it. He nursed his sore but minor wounds and made good progress astride his road-cleaning truck. He tested other functions to see if he could muster a few more defensive weapons if needed; the washer might have been useful if it released a stream of water from the powerjet nozzle, but the tank was empty and emitted a dry hiss instead.

*111*

Still, the orb scavengers were far behind now. He kept a sharp eye on the scrubby ground, giving a wide berth to the prickly kilbatoo bushes that orb scavengers liked to nest under, and started to pay attention to the shiny, glittering ridge just ahead. He'd noticed it earlier that afternoon and barely given it a thought. Much closer now, Kyle came across hunks of machinery lying around in the dirt, some of them embedded in bushes—hoverbikes, robots and droids of all breeds, even a jetpack. The vast majority of the abandoned tech was some form of transport large or small. Kyle steered his ride around the wrecks, his heart sinking. He was nearing the end of his truck's use. Pretty soon it would be out of range of the city, and it would die and join the knobby backbone of metallic clutter stretching from north to south.

Everyone knew there was a massive field of energy that allowed tech to work. The field spread far outside the city in all directions, a gigantic invisible circle. Logic dictated that the field's outer perimeter, where machines stopped working, would determine the gentle arcing of this ugly metallic ridge . . . only the arc seemed to bend the wrong way as though the energy field was generated from a point far to the east.

It was an illusion. It had to be. The arc was so gradual that it suggested a circle of energy of unimaginable size, with a center point an impossible distance away, far beyond the Ruins, beyond even the Tower on the horizon. And its entire purpose would be reversed, allowing tech to work *outside* the field but inhibiting it within—which would be crazy. Why would anyone out in the Ruins prevent tech from leaving the city?

The ridge's arc was one of Apparati's unexplained mysteries, something that conspiracy theorists liked to harp on about, and what the mayor always shrugged off as a product of overactive imagination. Still, now that Kyle was out here in the Ruins, looking along the line of clutter from north to south, he could actually see the gentle arc—bending the wrong way as many claimed.

Puzzled, Kyle pressed ahead, weaving between rusted sand buggies and family hovercars. Much of it had been dumped out here by citizens, some by the authorities. The mayor seemed fine with the idea of tossing junk out, perhaps because it increased the entertainment value of deadbeats trying to break through the non-tech limits. A military utility tank sat nose-down in a shallow pit. It was solid black all over, its tracks loose and its four multi-jointed appendages sticking up in the air. There were quite a few scouts, too, their all-seeing eyes completely dead and half buried. Squat robots stood still and unmoving. Some of the humanoid types lay sprawled on the ground, frozen in a crawling position.

When Kyle came upon the ridge and started to rise above the piles of junk, his heart fluttered at the prospect of pushing through and getting farther than anyone else. Then the controls sputtered and lights blinked in alarm. The truck faltered and started to shut down. Not wanting to give up his ride just yet, Kyle yanked the thing into reverse. It shuddered and rattled, threatening to die, but obeyed its instruction and backed up. Once it had retreated from the ridge, the lights steadied and systems seemed to whirr back into life.

Kyle knew he'd have to continue on foot. It was such a shame to leave his ugly but faithful metal companion behind. They'd gotten along so well. "See you around," he said, patting the control panel and then deactivating the systems. The machine went into hibernation mode, just the way he'd found it. If he needed to return, he'd come back for it. For now, it looked like a useless piece of junk.

Picking his way across the ridge was difficult in bare feet. He winced and swore all the way across. Once he was clear, the terrain ahead promised relief for a while—flat and uninteresting until he reached some dips and rises and a few clumps of trees, by which time the sun was beginning to descend in the east.

The good news was that the annoying cruiser was unable to follow him. When he was a safe distance away, he turned and offered the rudest gestures he could think of—and then realized his mom might be watching and flushed with embarrassment. The cruiser hung in the air near the ridge, silent and ominous.

His feet were sore and blistered by the time he made it to the first patch of trees. He lost sight of the Tower after that. The ground was grassy here, becoming even greener as he pushed deeper into the woods—but darker, too. He descended a gradual slope into an enormous shallow bowl in the landscape, surrounded by trees and pockmarked by rundown houses that were utterly smothered in ivy. In the middle of it was a lake, clear and still under the reddening evening sky.

Kyle was amazed. At no point had he ever seen a grassy haven like this while looking out across the Ruins with his miniscopes. He'd seen only the trees sticking up *around* the haven. There could be hundreds of similar places across the Ruins for all he knew. He didn't recall the mayor ever mentioning these green patches, either. The wastelands were always described as dry and barren with occasional abandoned towns. It had never occurred to Kyle that some parts of the Ruins might not only support life but actually be some kind of paradise.

He contemplated that fact as he hurried down the open, grassy hill to the lake. Imagine *living* here in this strangely picturesque place in the middle of nowhere, just outside the ridge that marked the end of technology. Here he was, stripped to his pants and not a single possession to his name. It was like a sign from the gods to start over.

That gang he'd come across had owned a weapon, probably more than one. Maybe they lived in a camp filled with useful gadgets tossed out from the city. Yet here, past the ridge, mechanical devices were useless. Very few would stray this far if they couldn't bring their gadgets. Then again, some would relish the chance to shrug off technology and start a simpler life away from the city's spy-eyes.

Kyle splashed water over his face and shoulders, gasping as it touched his hot skin. He drank deeply, knowing that it probably wasn't good for him to guzzle unfiltered lake water but too thirsty to care.

As he drank, he saw his reflection in the water—and reality slammed home. His parents, his younger brother, the city, the girl at school who he'd never managed to pluck up the courage to speak to—all of it was behind him. He was on his own. Tears squeezed from his eyes. He lurched forward, choked, and dry-heaved as repressed shock and terror bubbled up.

With his grief came anger. How could his parents have approved his repurposing? Despite them, despite everything, he was *alive*. And not just alive but kneeling on the bank of a beautiful lake that represented hope. Deadbeat or not, there was no need for him to die. His dad in particular had been unrelenting on the subject, choosing to end Kyle's life cleanly rather than give him a fighting chance. What *right* had he? What right had *anyone*?

He pounded his fists into the shallow water, splashing wildly and yelling obscenities until he exhausted himself. Panting, he sat back and waited for his heart to stop thumping so hard.

When he was ready, he got up and walked along the grassy bank, marveling at how fresh the air was compared to the smog-filled sky over the city. And it was so *quiet* here. All he heard were birds chirping. This sure beat repurposing. He paused, throwing his head back and gazing up at the early evening sky with its lazy, drifting clouds. This was a far cry from dashing about the streets of the deserted town back near the Wall. This really was some kind of paradise in comparison. Could he live here? Maybe he should forget about the Tower and just—

Soft footfalls from behind made him jump and swing around. A small balding man with a shaggy beard was strolling down the hill, raising a hand in greeting.

"Good evening, young fellow."

Instantly suspicious, Kyle looked this way and that, seeking others that might be hiding somewhere. But the slopes were open, and although the grass was knee-high, it didn't seem possible for would-be attackers to crouch out of sight.

"New to the Ruins, eh?" the man said. He stopped in front of Kyle and looked him up and down. "I see you ran into Meredith and her clan."

"Who?"

"Blond, green eyes? With her two brothers and young sister?"

Kyle frowned. "How did you know?"

"Because they took your clothes. If you'd bumped into any of the other gangs, they'd have taken your life as well." The man nodded, apparently satisfied he was correct in his assumption—which he was. "Most exiles head for the shores to the north and south, but quite a few stick around the towns where stuff is thrown down to them from the Wall. You probably passed by six other gangs, not to mention lone wanderers. You're lucky. None of them would have let you walk away. Food is scarce, you know."

This caused Kyle to shudder. He swallowed. "Who are *you*?"

"Call me Archie. Are you hungry? Come with me. I'll get you some food and clothing. I have a camp in those trees." The man pointed vaguely, though Kyle saw nothing of interest.

He was torn. He *was* hungry, and he *did* need clothes. It was getting late, and he didn't want to be fumbling around in the dark, hungry and cold. But could he trust this man? Could he trust anyone at all out here in the Ruins? This was a lawless place. Then again, the laws of the city hadn't exactly kept him safe either.

"All right," he said tentatively.

Archie beamed. "Splendid. This way, young man."

He marched off up the slope, striding through the long grass without once looking back to see if Kyle was following. Kyle shuffled after him, glancing all around, half expecting a legion of thugs to come rushing out of the trees.

He consoled himself with the fact that he was a stranger in a strange land, and if a violent gang wanted to rush out and tear him limb from limb, there really wouldn't be a lot he could do about it. The danger was there no matter what, and extending a smidgen of trust to this small Archie fellow might at least earn him a meal and some clothes. Perhaps he'd learn a little more about the Ruins in the process.

Still, he couldn't shake the awful feeling that he was being led into a trap.

*Chapter 20*
**Logan**

Logan heard the first few orb scavengers slam into the double doors. He ran toward the far end of the storeroom, glancing at the office for only a second. It wouldn't do to hole up within as there was no way out.

The building had to have a back entrance. He hurtled past empty shelving, scanning the far wall for any egress.

The sound of thunderous battering made him cringe. The double doors heaved forward, buckling under the combined attack of the orb scavengers. Had the entire swarm set their sights on him? Wasn't a stationary meal far better than one that flailed about?

As he pondered why the orb scavengers were so driven to make a meal of him, the doors swelled open and the first of the swarm flew in. Both doors started to close again but one caught, leaving just enough of an opening for the swarm to enter one by one.

They no longer drifted in the air. It was a marvel of ingenuity to see how they manipulated their skin flaps and their fire to turn themselves into high-velocity projectiles. He spied a line of over twenty orb scavengers angling toward him. A few zipped through the generous openings in the lattice of the shelving units. One careened off a shelf, landing on the hard floor and bouncing end over end for a distance before righting itself and taking to the air, its eyes feverishly tracking Logan the whole time. Why were the animals in the Broken Lands so dogged in their pursuit? What made them so vicious and unforgiving? *The harsh environs, surely.*

So intent was he on his pursuers, he barreled forward, his head cocked back, paying no attention to what lay ahead. He slammed his right shoulder against a run of shelving. Bouncing to the left, he spun about and nearly toppled over. Ahead were two metal doors with no discernible knobs or handles. They sat in a stout metal frame surrounded by a wall of shiny steel. A small panel holding two buttons stood at waist height to the right of the doors. He had spied this earlier during his casing of the backroom and not investigated it, thinking it was not worth his effort to try to open.

He accelerated toward the doors. If he could get them open, maybe they would withstand the onslaught of the swarm. It was better than doubling back to the office and hiding behind a simple wooden door. No telling if orb scavengers could tear through wood or light the door on fire to get to him.

Did the buttons control the doors? He knew that some in their enclave had started inventing devices that went beyond crude tools, fashioning miraculous machines that worked levers, gears, and wheels to move objects. Maybe there were such things hidden behind the broad steel wall.

He slapped at both buttons several times to no avail. The doors stayed closed.

Behind him, the angry screams of the orb scavengers escalated. The nearest wave was less than fifty paces away and closing fast.

Abandoning the buttons, he wedged his blade in the slight groove between the doors. He pulled to the side, attempting to pry them apart. He expected his actions to fail but was surprised to feel the doors give. He sheathed his knife, slipped both hands into the opening, wrenched the doors apart, and slipped his head through the gap. It was dark, but he thought he saw a rope hanging in the center of the small room beyond. He squeezed through the opening and tumbled forward, landing on a metal floor that rang loudly at his impact. Logan spun about and pulled at the doors, attempting to close them.

They inched shut. He had the gap down to the width of one of the orb scavengers if they were to draw tight their wings.

From the gleam of intensity in the eyes of the lead creature, he imagined they would do just that.

As he pulled, two orb scavengers shot through the opening. Both slammed into the far wall of the darkened room as Logan finally got the doors shut. He heard the muted thuds of the rest of the swarm as they pelted the metal outside.

It was dark, but faint light came from somewhere overhead. Logan spun around, whipping his knife out and holding it at the ready. One of the scavengers hobbled toward him, its right wing bent at an odd angle. The little thing was permanently grounded. The other spryly bounced off the far wall and dipped down and to the left to avoid the two ropes that dangled in the center of the room. It flung itself at him, blasting flames his way. He swiped his blade down, just missing the winged attacker.

The orb scavenger crashed into his shoulder, sinking its teeth into his exposed neck. With his free hand he grabbed hold of it and tossed it hard at the ground. It bashed into the metal and didn't move. He stomped on it to be sure. He then turned and did the same to the other, which was diving at his ankles.

Logan slumped against a side wall made of stone and caught his breath, ignoring the pain from the bite. He didn't have time to clean and dress it. Outside the chamber, the orb scavengers continued flinging themselves against the closed doors of his haven.

He scrutinized his surroundings. The two side walls were made of rectangular stacked stone while the far wall was more of the shiny metal. The floor had a large metal loop where the ropes threaded through and a small trapdoor. Should he try there? It didn't make sense to go down into the earth. Were there catacombs underneath the ruins? Even if there were, he doubted they would prove passable. When he looked up, he was shocked to see the ceiling lay far away. The ropes reached all the way to the top, some sort of braided metal.

A slim shaft of light filtered in near the ceiling. Somewhere up there was an opening to the outside. If he climbed, would he gain access to the roof? He had no idea if more scavengers perched up there awaiting their turn at the kaliback. He hoped not.

The metal doors rattled against the onslaught of the swarm, pressing him into a decision. While he knew they couldn't get to him, he couldn't stand around here all day. He sheathed his knife and grabbed hold of the metal ropes. He pulled himself upward, wrapping his legs around them as soon as he was off the ground.

He climbed slowly, hoping he was not heading into an even bigger gathering of orb scavengers above.

*Chapter 21*
## Kyle

The small, balding man who called himself Archie led the way up the grassy hill and into the trees on the northwest side of the lake, which annoyed Kyle as it meant heading in the wrong direction. Glancing longingly to the east as he walked along the embankment, he could just about see the Tower over the treetops in the darkening sky.

"Down here," Archie called.

A small campfire burned, sending up a lazy trail of smoke. Nearby was a cave under a fallen tree. The trunk formed the front part of a sturdy roof structure, with lesser branches laid on top and fanning backwards down to ground level, then covered with ferns. Dirt had been painstakingly scooped out from below the trunk and piled up on top of the roof structure so that, from the back, the camp was invisible. Kyle stared down into the low entrance with distaste.

"Come in, come in," Archie said, gesturing for him to take a seat.

The space was ample for one, adequate for two. Kyle had to stoop to enter, though, and roots protruding from the dirt ceiling tickled the top of his head as he found a place to perch. A small glass lantern illuminated Archie's home, which was packed out with blankets and piles of clothing. Sheets had been tied and staked to cover the rounded dirt walls. Dozens of salvaged objects lay about, most on shelf-like recesses in the walls. He probably considered these things as ornaments, but Kyle saw only pointless clutter.

"How long have you been here?" he asked.

"Thirteen years," Archie said cheerfully. "Welcome to my home. What's your name, young man?"

"Kyle."

"Well, Kyle, can I get you something to drink?"

"Uh . . . sure."

"I filter the lake water," the man said, reaching for a jug. "It's perfectly clean and safe—unlike the filth you drank earlier."

"How do you filter it without power?"

Archie chuckled. "You think we need power for everything? We don't. People used to live a simpler life out here in what everyone calls the Ruins. There are dozens of ancient towns scattered about. One of the biggest is to the west—the one you dropped into when you were exiled. But there are plenty of other settlements, all old and abandoned." He nodded sagely. "Everyone moved west. Crammed themselves into one big area, then built the Wall to seal themselves off from the rest of the land. Everything out here was forgotten."

Kyle sipped his cup of water. He had to admit it was clean and fresh. "Why?"

"Why indeed!" Archie laughed. Instead of answering, he simply grinned inanely.

Raising the cup to his lips once more, Kyle looked away. Maybe Archie was just a little crazy after being alone for so long. Anyone would lose their mind living in a hole in the ground with nothing but random piles of clothing and junk. Hopefully this particular kind of crazy was harmless eccentricity.

"What *is* all this stuff?" Kyle asked. Making conversation was more useful and far less weird than sitting in awkward silence.

Archie spread his hands. "You'd be surprised what I keep in here. Look." He dug around and pulled out a rolled-up parchment. With the utmost care, he smoothed it out on his lap. He turned it so Kyle could see, and brought the lantern closer. "I found this in one of the houses. Most of the old homes have been picked through over time, but sometimes, if you look hard enough, you can find something of real interest. This is a map of our land."

Intrigued, Kyle peered at the map. The land was like two misshapen lumps joined by a narrow strip. He recognized it well enough, yet it was ... different. The familiar city of Apparati and its surrounding Wall were completely missing. Only the Ruins were shown, and in far more detail than he'd ever seen. One word stood out in large but faint lettering, spanning the entire land from one end to the other: APPARATUM.

"That's weird," Kyle said. "It's spelled wrong."

Archie shook his head and pointed to the left side of the map. "See this area? This is where Apparati stands as we know it today—only it's not marked because the map is much older. The city has only been around a couple hundred years or so. Before that we all lived in Apparatum, spread out across the land. The Ruins you passed through? And the Ruins farther east? That's what's left of Apparatum." His finger moved east of the Wall. "This is where we are right now. See this tiny splotch? That's a lake. There are lots of small lakes around. I've visited some of the closer ones, and I figured out that this is mine."

Kyle said nothing. His gaze roamed the map hungrily, zeroing in on faint markings that showed forgotten towns and roads, and words written in a language he recognized. "These are names?" he finally managed.

"Yes, yes. Whoever drew this map had traveled well, from the west all the way to the east."

His mouth falling open, Kyle saw just as many names and markings at the far right of Apparatum as the left. "Have any exiles traveled that far?"

"Sure. But there's nothing much to see, just a whole lot of nothing. The Ruins go about three-quarters of the way east, and there's a big old city there, falling apart ... but then the Ruins peter out and the last quarter of the land is kind of empty. Apparently nobody built beyond that point. It's untouched."

*124*

"What about the Tower?"

Now Archie pursed his lips. "The infamous Tower must be newer than this map. Newer than the Ruins. I marked it, see? It's a pretty boring structure, though."

"You've been there?"

Archie shrugged. "Years ago. Nothing but a staircase and an empty room at the top. Good view, but nothing much to see other than what I just told you. Drink up, boy. You look parched."

They both fell silent. Kyle's mind was buzzing with ideas as he sipped. "Nobody has ever seen a map like this! At least, *I've* never seen one. Do you think the mayor knows about this? I mean, everyone knows about the Ruins and that our ancestors lived out here hundreds of years ago, but nobody has seen an actual map or—"

Archie laughed. "Kyle, you shouldn't believe everything you hear, especially when it comes from Mayor Baynor. The man's corrupt, and so is General Mortimer. Look, the mayor wants you—and everyone else for that matter—to believe that the city of Apparati is all there is, that the Wall is the end of the line. There's a reason exiles are never allowed back into the city—because people like me would spread the news that there's more out here than just crumbling buildings. People could really live a nice life out here if they wanted to—without technology. Who needs all that smog anyway?" He gripped Kyle's arm. "Do you know why the Wall is there?"

Kyle shook his head, captivated. He felt strangely dizzy. "To keep exiled people out?"

"Or to keep people *in*," Archie countered. "Actually, both answers are the same. The Wall is simply to keep his citizens close. He doesn't want good, decent people heading east. If they did, he'd have to spread his resources thin to manage a larger territory, and that would lead to a looser grip. To Mayor Baynor and all the mayors before him, letting people out of the city to explore would be a slippery slope. Keeping everyone contained within the Wall gives him more control."

"But . . . but are you saying there are people living in these old houses in the Ruins?"

"Why, sure. Doesn't it make sense to take over an abandoned home when you have nowhere to live? All the exiles over the years have to go somewhere, right? So they set up wherever they can. Most go to the shores. I prefer here by the lake in this forested haven."

"In a cave?" Kyle protested, feeling faint. He screwed up his eyes and blinked rapidly. "Why choose a hole in the ground when you could live in a proper house?"

Archie's smile faded. "I don't *live* here. I told you, this is my *camp*, for when I need to hunt and eat out under the stars. As a matter of fact, I have several homes." He drew himself up. "In the Ruins, a man can be rich indeed."

Kyle stared doubtfully around the cave. "It just seems like there's a lot of stuff here." He squeezed his eyes tight and pinched his nose, then stared into his water. "What's wrong with me? I'm so tired."

The man tilted his head. "You're exhausted, Kyle," he said quietly. "City folk aren't used to the big outdoors. Go to sleep. Lie down on these nice blankets and rest."

Kyle swayed from side to side, letting the cup of water spill from his hands. He stared dumbly at the cup as it leaked its contents onto the blanket. His gaze shifted to several pairs of shoes and a seemingly random collection of shirts, sweaters, and pants. Why would a man collect such things? And more to the point, where had it all come from?

He leaned back against the wall. "Did you . . . did you put something in my drink?"

His words came out slurred, and his limbs felt heavy.

Archie steepled his fingers. "I'm sorry. I have my family to think of."

Kyle thought of his own family and, for a moment, understood why his parents had ordered his repurposing—to avoid something much worse. He knew he was in trouble. The cave was spinning as he fell onto hands and knees and tried to crawl outside, hoping the fresh air would help clear his head.

If anything, it made it worse. He collapsed in a heap, the trees swirling, a rushing sound in his ears.

*Chapter 22*
**Logan**

By the time Logan climbed to the uppermost reaches of the metal ropes, his hands were raw and his arms almost worthless. The opening that had produced the shaft of light stood directly across from him and was large enough for him to jump through. Beyond lay a gravel rooftop. Luckily, not a single orb scavenger perched on the edge of the building from what he could see. That didn't mean they weren't situated around front, though the opening only gave him a view of the back half of the roof.

Logan steadied himself by slowly sucking in a breath, then sprang forward, vaulting across with relative ease. His boots hit the gravel roof, and he was once again out in the bright sun. He flung up his arms to shield his eyes, overwhelmed by the sharp difference in light.

He spun around to see he had the roof to himself. He treaded toward the front half of the structure to see if the scavengers were still there, feeding on the fallen kaliback.

Logan leaned forward. The kaliback teemed with orb scavengers. They ranged over its entire body, feeding with singular focus. Several more exited the store and joined in. His pursuers were giving up the chase.

Now and then the expansive coat of scavengers parted, revealing their handiwork. Shredded muscle and white bone stared back at him. They worked fast. He shuddered and backed away, relieved he had not shared the kaliback's grisly fate.

His hand went to his neck. He probed the bite with his fingers, wincing at the sharp pain lancing through his neck and spine. His fingers were covered in blood. He used the back of his hand to wipe the wound, which no longer seeped. *Good, not losing blood as fast as I feared.*

A squabble arose from below. Not wanting to risk a return to the roof edge to see what had the swarm irritated, he refocused on his next course of action. His injury could wait until he had gained some distance from the scavengers. He needed to get down from the roof.

He walked the back edge of the building, looking for a ladder or ramp leading to the ground. He found a series of metal steps switching back and forth along the side, but the structure only reached halfway. The missing half lay twisted in the narrow path between the buildings.

He looked at the buildings nearby. Could he jump across to one and find his way down? It was a long drop to the caved-in roof to his right. He didn't want to vault into such an unstable structure, nor the one on his left. But the building right behind him looked manageable, a few arm lengths away. Even better, his landing would be farther from the swarm, making it less likely they would detect his escape and give chase.

For at least four buildings, it looked like he could hop from one to the next before his rooftop path dried up. The fifth building was just a pile of rubble. With five buildings to pick from, one of them had to have an open route to the ground. Better than his chances of waiting out the swarm and going back down the shaft with the metal ropes.

Logan inspected his scarred and blistered hands, rubbed raw from his ascension. They felt worse than they looked, mostly surface abrasions with very few deeper injuries. He wiggled his right thumb, perhaps the area most inflamed and scraped up. Even that would look better once properly cleaned.

Logan steeled himself as he paced out the exact run up to his jump. He'd have to kick up the gravel in order to get enough speed. Would that set off the swarm? He'd have to chance it.

Dropping to a crouch, he examined the sun. *No more than an hour or two left in the day.*

His priority was getting down then find a safer place to hole up for the night, putting as much distance between him and the orb scavengers as he could manage. He didn't want to travel at night. *No telling what kind of predators came out to hunt then.*

He drew in a sharp breath and tore off. At the roof's edge, he slid his arm against his satchel and canteens so they wouldn't go flying and launched himself forward with all his might.

He careened toward the lower building. He slammed into its gravel roof, rolling to reduce the impact and strain on his ankles. To hobble himself now would make him easy prey. He winced at the horribly loud racket produced by his landing. Springing to his feet, he assumed a wary stance, his knife at the ready.

Not a single orb scavenger emerged to investigate his disturbance. How could they not have heard that?

He waited, not wanting to drop his guard and have the swarm creep up on him while he tried to find a way off the roof. Again, the skies remained clear.

His shrug was slight; fortune was shining down on him for once.

Keeping his knife out, he paced around the roof. Finding no exterior ladders or metal stairs, Logan tried to pry open the door attached to the raised shack at the center of the roof. It was metal and locked. Had it been wood, maybe he could've battered his way in.

He would have to try the next building.

Luckily, the next two buildings were closer to the same height as the new roof he occupied, and he easily crossed over. Both had locked metal doors. When he jiggled the latch on the second one, something large thumped against the interior, trying to get out.

He wasted no time leaping to the next roof. This one was partially caved in. He approached the edge of the steep hole. It dropped two floors, filled with jagged debris. A section of the roof near his foot gave and dropped, shattering into pieces against a large white basin.

Logan searched all sides of the roof, finding another series of intricate metal stairs that switched back and forth. This one descended farther, but it also had its lower section missing and littered the ground below.

Thwarted, he kicked at the gravel, sending it flying into the air. The fog was slowly returning as the temperature dropped. He spun around, seeking to spot the Tower before it disappeared in the dense cloud. He saw its slender spire rising up above the ruins. He couldn't make out anything distinctive about it other than it dwarfed all others in stature, but he sensed that it lay at the end of his path, that the Tower was significant.

With slightly renewed determination, he leapt across the wide gap separating him from the last standing building in the row. His landing was awkward. He stood, brushing the gravel from his front. The metal door leading into the building was twisted open, its upper half torn free from its hinge. Large claw marks scarred the door and, when Logan stuck his head in, the odor of death and decay hung heavy in the stale air.

Logan would only enter the building if he found no outside means of climbing down. He didn't want to go in, fearing that he would be entering the lair of some great beast. He shivered, suddenly overwhelmed with fear. Something below had him unsettled.

He tiptoed to the far side, next to the demolished building. *No going down that side*, he thought. Nothing helpful awaited him in the front or back either.

He slumped as he walked to inspect his last prospect. It looked like he'd have to brave entering the building.

His eyes widened as he spied his salvation. A long metal ladder ran down the side of the building all the way to the alley below. He scanned the alley for any sign of a threat. Seeing nothing, he slipped onto the top rung and gently shook the rusted framework to test it. It rattled but felt secure enough to hold his weight. He descended quickly, stopping twice when he heard movement from within the building. He passed a broken window on the second floor and again smelled the fetid atmosphere of the interior. Was the building the den of the kalibacks or home to something far worse? He didn't want to linger and find out.

Once to the ground, he raced down the alley toward the street to the north of the orb scavenger's location. He skidded out into the open, and took stock. Other than a few birds gliding too far away from him to identify and a family of truggle rats that scattered at his arrival, he saw nothing that amounted to a threat.

He moved to the center of the street, giving the open doors and broken windows a wide berth. No sense risking being attacked from within. He imagined a tentacle or long clawed arm of some strange new creature snaking out from one of the buildings and grabbing hold of him. *No, better to stay in the center of the road.* While it made him easier to spot, at least he could see the attack coming and thus have time to react.

He covered a good distance before realizing he had very little daylight left. Behind him the sun dipped behind the horizon. In the lingering light of dusk, he found a small building he deemed defensible.

Logan quickly explored its much smaller interior and was pleased to find it had two back doors, both intact. Once he locked them and pushed a large wooden cabinet in place across the open front door, he sat looking out the main window at the fog working its way like something living through the cluttered streets of the Broken Lands.

As he drifted to sleep, he was struck by the distinctive roar of what could only be another turn of good luck. The sound was unmistakable and, now that he was no longer caught up in listening intently for any further attack, he was certain that what lay close ahead was a large body of flowing water.

Logan smiled, pleased with how he had survived his first day in the ruins.

*The night,* a niggling thought protested, *might not afford me the same good fortune.*

*Chapter 23*
## Kyle

It was the motion of being drawn upward, and the pain of the rope cutting into his ankles, that woke Kyle. The moons were bright in the evening sky, and he was hanging upside down from a tree, swaying from side to side, spinning slowly as the man called Archie tied off the rope with swift, assured turns around a stake in the ground.

As Kyle's view steadied, he peered first at the branches above, seeing how the rope wasn't just thrown over a bough but looped through a pulley hanging underneath. A *pulley*. This man had done the same thing before, maybe many times. A pulley avoided wear and tear on the rope that would otherwise scrape over the rough bark—and it made it easier to hang large, captive animals upside down.

Captive animals? Or *people*?

He shook his head. Archie was just a cowardly thief. He was playing it safe, stringing Kyle up so he could—

So he could what? Steal Kyle's pants? If that were true, why hadn't he taken them already? Tying him upside down by the ankles was the worst possible way to get at them.

What, then, did the man want? He'd mentioned something about having a family to feed, hunting in the woods for food . . .

A terrifying thought struck Kyle. Was he *kaliback bait*?

Archie went to fetch something, kneeling by what looked like a sports bag as he dug around inside. Kyle heard the clash of steel.

Trying hard to stay calm, Kyle made the mistake of looking down at the ground. He gasped, seeing in the moonlight a black stain that ran away down the slope and into the bushes.

*Dried blood?*

"No, no, no," he murmured, looking around frantically. There had to be something he could do to get out of this.

He reached for his ankles, straining to pull himself up. If he could just get hold of the rope with his hands . . . but he wasn't strong and flexible enough to bend that far. He dangled helplessly, terror threatening to overwhelm him. For a fleeting moment he longed for the Repurposing Chamber. Anything was better than this.

"You're awake," Archie said, sounding surprised. He stood there by his bag holding a long knife. He slowly wandered closer, and Kyle began to wriggle and squirm, unable to contain his moans of fear. The man stopped and held up his hands, knife and all. "Whoa, relax. It's okay, Kyle. I'm not here to torture you."

Kyle quit twisting. Hope flared inside. "You're not?"

Archie shook his head. "I'm not a monster." He let his arms fall to his sides, the knife out of sight behind his leg. "We get kalibacks around here sometimes. That's the problem with living so far from the Wall. Have you seen any? Nasty critters. Four eyes, two mouths, yellow teeth, vicious armored tails. It's the horrible warbling sound they make that gives me nightmares. The thing is, they're really hard to kill." He tapped the side of his head and narrowed his eyes. "Smart hunters, you know. Better than us feeble humans. And they eat all the time."

"Why are you telling me this?" Kyle gasped.

"I'm just saying food is hard to come by." Archie looked uncomfortable as he faced away into the trees. "I never managed to kill a kaliback. Others have. I guess I wasn't a born hunter." He laughed, then sobered quickly. "They take all the food, Kyle. It's not fair. It's hard enough living out here as it is. I have a family to feed."

"So what am I? Kaliback bait?"

This brought a frown to Archie's face. "What? No, no. That wouldn't work. Kalibacks like the thrill of the hunt, and besides, they're too smart to come sniffing around such an obvious trap."

Now Kyle was puzzled. He stared at the enormous bloodstain on the ground below his head. "Then what do you *want* with me? You're not just going to—"

He broke off as Archie brought his knife into view.

"My family is everything," the man said stiffly. "A wife and three children. We live in a house not far from here. I provide the best I can."

Despair gripped Kyle so hard that it felt like his life was being squeezed out there and then. "You're gonna kill me."

"Yes, but not while you're awake. You just didn't drink enough of my water. Usually people down it all. You drank from the lake first, so I guess you weren't as thirsty." He shrugged. "Well, look, I'll be right back. I'll get some more water, you can drink it, fall back asleep, and then I'll bleed you out while you're unconscious. You won't feel a thing, I promise. Like I said, I'm not a monster. Okay?"

He stared at Kyle with an expectant look on his face.

"You're gonna kill me," Kyle said again. "And feed me to your family."

Archie nodded, let out his breath, then turned and walked away. When he'd gone ten paces, he glanced back over his shoulder. "Won't be long."

"Take your time," Kyle muttered.

So he had a minute or two to escape. *Good luck with that*, a voice in his head told him.

*Think, think*, another part of his brain urged. *If you can't reach up to your ankles, can you reach down? Can you swing?*

Kyle tried both. With his hands dangling, the ground was still just out of grasp. He started swinging, having no idea why he was bothering. There was nothing to reach for, and he certainly couldn't arc high enough to reach the bough he was dangling from. It was a futile exercise.

*But better than hanging around doing nothing.*

He quickly picked up the pace. It reminded him of the tire at his Uncle Jeremiah's house in East Morley. The air rushed past his ears as he swung like a pendulum, first one way, slowing, stopping, then back the other way, slowing, stopping, over and over, all the time listening for Archie's returning footsteps.

Just as he'd decided it was hopeless, he choked back a cry of excitement. As he'd seen earlier, the rope looped over the pulley was tied off to a stake in the ground—and his seemingly ineffectual movement was causing that stake to shift. He watched it closely, throwing his weight around, trying to jiggle about and yank the stake free of the ground. The stake shifted bit by bit, lifting a half-inch at a time.

Or was he imagining it?

He yelled and doubled-up, launching himself into the swing, then twisting and arching on the way back. He was reaching farther now, though still nowhere near enough to grab hold of the tree trunk or anything else that would assist him. The rope simply wasn't long enough for that.

Archie returned, and he stopped dead when he saw what Kyle was doing. Kyle screamed at him, a torrent of fury and frustration spilling from his lips, and kept swinging just so the man would have a hard job getting hold of him.

"My," Archie said, coming forward with a cup of water in one hand, the knife tucked into his belt. "Aren't you industrious? I don't think that's going to help, though. Listen, take a drink and make it easy, okay? Or I'll end up sticking you while you're awake, and that's something I've only ever done once. I hated it. It made me sick to my stomach. I'd much rather—"

The stake came free, and Kyle, almost at the end of a swing, hurtled on through the air and landed with a jarring thud on a patch of stinging nettles that set his skin on fire. He was temporarily winded and shocked, but he broke out of his paralysis when Archie threw down the cup and came after him, his eyes wide and a look of fright on his face.

The small, balding man drew his knife as he approached. Kyle struggled with the rope around his ankles. It was just a noose, but even when he pulled it off, his feet were numb. Pins and needles hammered his feet and he curled up in agony even as his captor circled him.

Archie was silent, obviously afraid. The man was a coward. Kyle rolled around on the ground, moaning loudly, exaggerating his misery until he was ready. Then, ignoring the heavy numbness, he sprang at Archie, ramming the top of his head into the man's chin. He heard a crack, felt a terrible pain, and collapsed.

Groggily, he blinked, climbed onto hands and knees, and came face to face with his enemy. Blood leaked down Archie's chin from a split lip.

Kyle leapt past him and snatched up the knife, which glinted at him from the grass. Triumphantly, he turned back to Archie and held it out in front the same way he'd held the scissors in that doctor's face back at the Repurposing Factory. "Don't—" he started to say.

But Archie was already leaping to the attack. His eyes opened in surprise when he suddenly found the knife plunged deep into his chest right below his throat.

Both of them staggered. Kyle sank to his knees, his feet still tingling. Archie fell onto his backside, legs splayed out, staring in shock at the knife's hilt. "What did you do?" he gasped.

*Chapter 24*
## Logan

Logan was disappointed in himself. His time in the Broken Lands had been spent with far too much sleeping and resting up. As he rose from the makeshift bed comprised of rags he had found in a small storage closet of the building, he was immediately beset by a feeling of unease. He gathered his supplies and brandished his knife, his gaze stealing over the crooked silhouettes of the ramshackle environment outside the large window. He wished it was morning. Being in the Broken Lands at night was unsettling.

A scrabbling of claws against the cabinet he had wedged in front of the open door made his blood run cold. Whatever was outside chuffed as it set upon the wood. As Logan's eyes adjusted, he made out the immense outline of a creature far larger than the kaliback pack leader. Despite the fog, the closeness of the beast allowed him to make out several distinct physical attributes.

Its armored hide was a muted grey with dark blue splotches, all four legs thick and muscular, terminating on tree trunk-sized feet. It was the long claws on its front legs that the creature was using to dig into the wood of the cabinet. Its bulk reached higher than the window. A ridiculously stubby tail stuck out from its posterior.

He couldn't make out the head. It was behind the cabinet. But not for much longer, he feared. The tall furniture wobbled, and he gasped.

The creature paused.

It beset the cabinet with even more vigor. The wooden furniture splintered further and slid backward. Logan took several cautious steps toward the rear of the building. With its size, even if it knocked apart the cabinet, he doubted it could work its way in. If he retreated to the back room, maybe it would lose interest in him and move on.

The animal growled and yipped in rapid succession. It drove its claws and head into the cabinet, finally knocking the obstruction to the ground, and shoved its head into the doorway seeking the source of the noise.

Its face was a nest of nasty quills. Large red eyes glared at Logan, blinking several times as dust from its barrage filtered down. Its mouth was housed at the end of a long snout that bobbed forward by an arm's length. At the tip, a circular row of small teeth flexed open and closed as it wheezed with glee at being so close to its prey. It was a quill fiend. He had never seen one in person.

The flexible snout waved around but couldn't extend far enough to reach Logan. The creature roared in frustration and heaved its bulk into the building. The entire structure groaned and pitched slightly.

The front of the building endured another hit. Logan was beginning to doubt his safe house could hold up to much more punishment. He had to abandon it. He didn't like the prospect of being chased from his sanctuary and forced out into the night, but he had no choice.

The quill fiend slammed into the door frame again. It gave, and a solid section of the ceiling sagged.

Logan darted into the back, racing to the door farthest from the main entrance. He tried to recall if the alley next to the building was wide enough for the beast to fit through, but his memory failed him.

He put his hand on the metal handle of the door. Behind him, the quill fiend savaged the front of the structure. The entire building groaned under the onslaught. The creature trumpeted in victory.

He guessed it would keep after him regardless if the building fell down on its armored hide. It was certainly large enough to weather a roof or two dropping on its thick back. Logan had never seen a creature of such scale before. Even the largest kaliback paled to the massive proportions of the quill fiend.

He unbolted the door and whisked it open. He left it to swing in the chill night air as he tore off down the alley.

\* \* \*

After crisscrossing through a maze of back alleys and climbing over several mounds of rubble, he could no longer hear the trumpeting cries of the quill fiend.

Logan eased back onto the main street. He could not make out the Tower but had another destination in mind.

He listened. For the past few minutes, the sound of running water had grown louder. He was certain that ahead lay a river.

He would keep moving forward. Judging from the low-hanging moons, most of the night was behind him. In a few hours, Apparata's sun would return and illuminate the Broken Lands, and hopefully drive back to their dens any hungry nocturnal predators.

He caught his breath and took a deep swig of water. Emboldened by the prospect of a large source of fresh water just ahead, Logan took a second drink, even pouring a little on his head to cool down.

He sealed the canteen and eyed the open street. He resumed walking, passing a small strip of woods wedged between two long buildings. Several sculptures and fountains dotted the landscape of the woods, almost lost in the overgrown grasses and bushes that choked them. He was positive teeth and claws waited within; there was no way he was going to inspect any of those statues. To drive home that point, the grasses rustled near the edge.

He eased away, keeping the woods in the corner of his eye. Ahead lay a deep chasm in the road, which he capably crossed along a fallen metal post.

The sound of water was just ahead over the hill.

Logan crested the slope, surprised at how much he had quickened his pace. He was being reckless. For all he knew, he was walking into a busy watering hole, racing into a herd of beasts that, once their thirsts were slaked, would turn about and descend on him.

He crouched and sidled to a small pile of rubble. Spying a length of metal pipe lodged in the rubble, he excavated it. While slightly bent, it would make a decent club. It had more reach than his knife. It was slender along its length with a hollow socket on either end. It was a tool, that much was clear.

He peered over the pile, his courage stoked by the addition of his newest weapon.

His eyes widened as he took in the scene before him. He had stumbled upon a gathering, but not one of common creatures out to appease their thirsts.

Winding through the city was a wide river, its current swift and dark. Debris rested throughout. The water looked deep. There were no creatures using it as a watering hole. What stopped him from running down to fill his canteens and swell his stomach was the throng of spirits that amassed at its shore.

Every type of spirit was present. There had to be fifty or sixty of them.

They hovered in the air, forming a tidy line that matched up with the shore of the waterway. They all seemed to be striving to move forward, toward the center of the ruins—for what reason, Logan had no clue.

He had never seen so many spirits congregated in such a small area, but that wasn't the truly stunning aspect of their gathering. No, it was how they plunged forward and bounced back with alarming regularity. Was there an invisible barrier that prevented them from crossing the river? When that thought crept into his consciousness, it felt right, like he had known it all along.

Logan had always assumed the spirits had the run of the entire Broken Lands. Now he was faced with the notion that an invisible barrier held them back. But held them back from what?

Several Breakers charged toward the river en masse. They glanced off the unseen barrier and drifted back, dazed and offended at being thwarted. Two Fixers glided higher and floated down, seeking to pass through from a higher elevation. They encountered resistance and turned back, facing each other in silent consultation. Panic raced through him. If the spirits' progress was impeded, would his be as well? Would he be denied the precious water that coursed through the river?

He sensed that this was a ritual, something the spirits did every night.

He leaned back, checking around for any indication that a predator had gotten the jump on him while he had so intently examined the spirits.

Nothing stirred nearby.

He glanced across the river, lingering in his attentions with the far shore. Nothing. No animal life. Did that mean the barrier blocked spirits and animals alike?

This prospect was unnerving. If neither spirit nor animal could cross, then where did that leave him?

His deliberations were interrupted by an angry trumpeting coming from the street behind him. Racing at alarming speed was the massive bulk of the quill fiend, its head lowered as it prepared to ram into him with its array of nasty face quills.

Logan staggered toward the river. From the corner of his eye, he saw the spirits had spun about, turning their attention to him and the rampaging quill fiend.

He crept down the incline. Maybe he could dodge the beast and have it bash into the invisible barrier. If that didn't work, maybe it would drown. It certainly didn't appear all that buoyant. He vaulted over a ditch and slipped past a large pile of rubble.

The quill fiend halted at the top of the hill and issued a strangled battlecry. It scuffed the ground twice then charged.

Logan moved closer to the spirits. They allowed him through. He passed through their intangible forms, knowing they could not impede the attack.

He stuck his arm out and probed for the invisible barrier. His hand encountered no resistance. Maybe he wasn't close enough yet. He took three more steps and again flung his arm out. No barrier. He looked at the line of spirits behind him. He was well past where the barrier should be. Another step and he would be splashing in the shallows.

So the barrier only kept out the spirits. Well, that meant he'd have to sidestep the charging beast and hope it tumbled into the deep part of the river. Maybe it would get mired in the soft muddy bank.

He girded himself. For his plan to work, Logan needed to wait until the last possible second.

The quill fiend roared down the hill.

The spirits all tensed at the same time. Logan watched as they shimmered briefly. The moonlight was playing tricks on him. They looked more solid, but that couldn't be. A spirit only gained physical influence if tethered. No one could tether an entire army of spirits.

He watched as the spirits descended on the quill fiend. They rushed forward, their arms outstretched, their expressions resolute.

Astoundingly, they swarmed over the beast, lifting it into the air and using its own momentum to fling it halfway across the river.

The bulky creature spun about in mid-air, its serpentine snout wagging helplessly as it trumpeted in dismay.

It kicked up an impressive splash then sank, the swift-moving waters of the river swallowing it up.

Logan waited a long time for the beast to resurface. It didn't.

Realizing he had been holding his breath the entire time since the spirits had latched onto the beast, he exhaled loud and hard.

The spirits drifted to the ground, their bodies again looking diminished and unconnected to the physical world.

"Incredible!" Logan said.

A voice to his right replied, "It is indeed. But very taxing. I'm afraid I may have overreached with that little feat, young Logan."

A slender old man with white hair stepped from behind a tree and approached.

Logan's head swirled. He sensed that the stranger would bring a wealth of answers, along with even more questions.

*Chapter 25*
## Kyle

Despite the horror of what he'd been through, and the revulsion at what he'd done, Kyle already felt the adrenaline ebbing away, leaving him drained, angry, and cold. "It's your own fault," he said.

Archie, lying on his back and staring wide-eyed at the knife sticking out of his chest, blinked back tears and nodded gently. "I know. Can't believe I'm not dead yet. An inch lower . . ."

He wiped his brow and looked up through the trees. The knife's handle rose and fell with every breath, and the bloodstain widened.

"Can you go get my wife?" he whispered. "She'll know what to do. North side of the lake, big house with a barn and a bunch of durgles running around. Her name's Colleen." He closed his eyes. "Do me a favor. Don't tell her about . . . about all this. She thinks it's kaliback meat I bring home."

Kyle's anger boiled up again. He stood and looked around, seeing only darkness. "Which way to your camp? I need clothes and shoes."

"Follow Piracus," Archie said, sounding like he was half asleep. Kyle instinctively looked skyward at the moons as Archie struggled on. "Take what you want. Just . . . just don't leave me like this. Get my wife. She was a doctor, once. She can fix me up."

"I'll think about it," Kyle said, and hurried away.

Of the three moons, Piracus was the largest, just visible through the trees. Using it as a guide, he took off through the undergrowth. To his surprise, he came upon the camp almost immediately and breathed a sigh of relief.

The fire was still smoldering near the entrance, and the small glass lamp burned softly inside. He crawled around, sifting through the piles of clothing, his lips curling at the thought of all the people Archie had murdered just because he was too weak to hunt animals. There was more to it than that, though. The man could have found another way to feed his family if he'd tried. Instead he'd *chosen* to kill any man, woman and child who happened to pass by.

Maybe he enjoyed it in some sick, twisted way.

Fighting his distaste, Kyle threw on a couple of layers of clothes. He was pleased to find shoes that fit him well. However, the small piles of socks and underwear didn't appeal in the slightest.

A blanket would come in handy ... and a cup ... and a pocketknife. He dug around, looking for anything else that might be useful. Then he remembered the map, which he rolled and gingerly placed in the knapsack, imagining that it might crumble to dust if he wasn't careful.

By the fire outside was a wooden shaft with something thick and black wrapped around one end. He sniffed it curiously, then touched it, finding that his fingertip came away with a dark smudge. Holding the shaft at arm's length, he dipped the blackened end into the flames of the fire. The torch caught alight immediately.

Satisfied, Kyle snuffed out the lantern, thinking it would be better to use in confined spaces than a flaming, smoking torch. The glass was still hot, and it was a little delicate to carry around, but it was worth the risk. He carefully wrapped it in a bright red shirt before stashing it in his knapsack.

He set off into the night, holding the torch aloft to light his way out of the woods. Though desperately needing to curl up and sleep, it was better to get far away from this place of death first.

He tried to put Archie out of his mind. Let the man die a slow, painful death for all he cared. Kyle found it hard to feel bad about what had happened. They'd struggled, Kyle had gotten free, then swung around and held up the knife to protect himself, to warn the man away—but before he'd been able to shout his warning, Archie had flung himself forward to attack and ended up stabbing himself. The whole thing had been an accident.

It wasn't Kyle's problem any more. He had more important things to worry about. He was going to find a place to sleep and head onward to the Tower in the morning.

\* \* \*

With his torch held high, Kyle stood twenty yards from the large house waiting for someone to come out. Despite his vow to forget about Archie, here he stood outside the man's home on the north side of the lake. Not wanting to get too close, he'd thrown small rocks at the door to draw attention to himself.

A huge barn stood to his right. Durgles ran around his feet, squawking and flapping their tiny wings. Kyle shoved one away with his foot. "Go to bed," he muttered.

He'd never cared for the fat, waddling birds. Hardly anybody ate them because they tasted so bad, and their eggs were tiny. Still, durgles were plentiful and easy to breed, and Archie's family had thirty of them loose in the yard. Surely they were preferable to human meat? And if not durgles, what about the gentle morribies that supposedly roamed the forests out here in the Ruins? Kyle had seen a morribie at the wildlife reserve back in the city along with most other gentle game, and admittedly they were long-legged and flighty, probably hard to catch—but a determined hunter could trap one if he really tried. Or how about the stubborn, armor-plated shufflers? An adult's plump body offered a hearty meal for four.

Kyle sighed. Archie was a sadistic killer, and Kyle should just let him die. Instead, here he was waiting for the man's wife to emerge so he could advise her to go save him.

"What do you want?" the woman called, finally coming out onto the porch. There were no lights on, and she remained in shadow. "I have a loaded crossbow, and I won't miss even at this range. Say your piece and leave."

Three smaller figures appeared in the doorway behind her. Archie's children. So he'd told the truth about them at least.

"Are you Colleen?" he asked. The woman said nothing. Kyle had only mentioned her name to get her attention, to help her realize that he wasn't a complete stranger. "Archie's in trouble. He needs you up by his camp. He says you're a doctor, that you'll know what to do."

The woman caught her breath, and even though she was a silhouette, it was clear that she lowered her crossbow. "What's happened to him?"

"Stabbed himself," Kyle retorted. "He can tell you all about it, but you have to hurry." He turned to leave, confident that he was now done with Archie and his family. The burden of responsibility had been passed on. But he paused. "He did it while hunting. Do you know what he was hunting?"

The woman turned to the tallest of the shadows behind her. "Go get my bag—quickly." The older child ran off, her long hair swinging, and Colleen flung her crossbow over her shoulder and stared at Kyle with a frown. "Kalibacks, probably. But you say he *stabbed* himself? He wasn't bitten or clawed?"

The two remaining children bobbed and weaved in the doorway. One looked about twelve, the other much younger. How could he tell this woman and her family that they were unwitting cannibals? That their papa was a callous murderer, feeding them human meat just because it was easier than doing some actual hunting? He was a monster—but the children weren't, and maybe Colleen wasn't either.

"I've got to go," Kyle said. "You'll find him near his camp, where he ... where he strings animals up and kills them."

The eldest child returned with a bag. She had to be fifteen or so, with long dark hair much like her mother's. Kyle turned to head away. "You're not going to help me?" Colleen called. "If I have to carry him back here—"

"I'm done," he said firmly. "Sorry, but you should talk to him. *Ask* him."

"Ask him what?"

"Just ask him if there's anything he needs to tell you."

He left it at that. It wasn't his problem anymore. He was washing his hands of the whole thing. He hurried away, ignoring the high-pitched pleas of the three children who were begging their mother not to leave them alone. Colleen assured them she wouldn't be long and told the eldest to lock the door and keep watch from the upstairs window. It sounded like they had a routine down. They had to, given that Archie was away murdering people so often.

Soon back out in the open, the woodland fell behind and Kyle was able to look ahead to the horizon—not that there was anything to see in the darkness except the three moons. If he were back home in Apparati, he'd be curling up in bed right about now. Instead he was traipsing about in the middle of nowhere.

He yawned, suddenly ready to drop. He halted and looked around. Where should he sleep? He could quite easily lie down right here and fade away, but that would be foolish. What if there were kalibacks? Kyle had seen shows about the beasts and always shuddered at the idea of coming face to face with one. They were rare near the Wall because of the smog, which offended their keen senses. Now, well away from the polluted city, there was a real chance he might run into one. Or more of those hideous orb scavengers.

In the distance, the Tower was almost lost in the night. Still, it was notably closer now, perhaps a day's travel at most—provided he didn't get strung up by sadistic murderers or eaten by kalibacks along the way.

It took a monumental effort to trudge a little farther. There was a blocky silhouette ahead. Some kind of small building? It turned out to be a high-topped, four-wheeled wagon on the side of an old road. He was on the brow of a hill, and before him, down in a valley shrouded in darkness, was another town. Sighing, he made up his mind that he'd gone far enough for tonight. He would tackle this new hurdle after a good night's sleep.

The wagon was clearly designed for long-distance travel, of ancient build but probably used in recent months judging by its dirty but intact canopy. Abandoned now, though. Wagons like these were usually hitched to powerful hustles—docile creatures with six legs and long bodies that reminded Kyle of giant insects. They weren't very fast but had incredible stamina. What had happened to them? Why had this wagon been abandoned right here on the side of the road? More questions that would never be answered.

Kyle didn't much care right now. Ignoring his growling stomach, he carefully extracted the wrapped lantern from his knapsack and spent a weary moment using the torch to light it. Then he threw down the fiery shaft, kicked dirt over it to put out the flames, climbed inside the wagon with his lantern, and promptly fell asleep on some musty old blankets.

*Chapter 26*
**Logan**

The spirits parted for the stranger.

Logan didn't know what to think. Was he from another enclave? If so, where was his spirit? The man wore a black knee-length coat made from a reflective material. His boots were well worn, and his pants and shirt were brown with a line of light blue trim that ran along the seams. Around his neck was a device made of metal, looping up around the back of his head like a half-raised hood. The metal collar's surface was smooth except for a border pattern that reminded Logan of roots. The pattern glowed blue, casting a sinister light across the stranger's face. He was old, his skin wrinkled and weathered. The top of his head was bald, but white hair flowed around the sides and back, disappearing into the cowl. Equally bleached was his long beard. He held a metal staff as much for support as a weapon.

The man stopped a few paces away. The spirits closed in around him, but none passed through his solid frame.

Logan's nerves were frayed. The spirits converging on him were drifting in and out of his person. The fact that none of the spirits did this to the stranger lent him a weighty presence. Was it fear that kept the spirits at bay? What would this man do to him? Would Logan have been better off facing the quill fiend?

"You accounted for yourself well against the beast." The man slid his right hand higher on the staff, his sleeve dropping down to reveal another mystery. Fastened to the back of a thick brown glove was a wooden carving. It was of excellent craftsmanship, a series of ornate curls and spirals that defined its shape, their handiwork such that any Weaver would be in awe. The man's left hand was not gloved, and was instead adorned with three rings.

The stranger nodded. "Take it all in. Observation serves you well."

"You are not of Apparata?" Logan asked, but it came out less a question and more a timid musing.

"I am and I am not." The man coughed. "I know you don't want riddles. You'll forgive me. The opportunity to converse with others occurs so rarely for me anymore. As much as I prepared for this moment, I still find myself lacking. I ask you be patient with me."

Logan said, "Do you know me?"

He nodded. "I know who you are, where you're from, and where you're going." He frowned. His head sagged and he shook it. "Ah, there I go again, being cryptic." He pointed to the spire almost lost in the fog and distance. "It is to the Tower."

Logan tried to contain his excitement. Something about the man seemed familiar. Though their exchange so far had been vague, he felt that the stranger knew him and wanted to help, perhaps even owed him his allegiance. Logan would trust him. For now. "So you'll accompany me there and tell me what you know about everything?"

"I can't walk with you. I must be somewhere else for a time." He placed a hand on Logan's shoulder. "But I will be there. Climb the Tower and I will answer all of your questions." He held his gaze for longer than was necessary with what appeared to be pride.

The man turned and began walking back to the woods. A Breaker soared toward him, its face twisted in anger and frustration. Would it be the first to violate the stranger's presence by passing through him? From its fervent appearance, that was what it desired.

The stranger brushed his fingers over the wooden carving on his right forearm and the Breaker bounded away, its expression immediately distressed and subservient.

There was power contained within this strange old man, a power both creative and destructive. As much as he felt a kinship with him, Logan would have to be on guard. The stranger was adrift in the Broken Lands. As whole as the man appeared, there had to be something fractured within for him to make this wasteland his home.

Logan blurted out, "You know my name, but I don't know yours."

The stranger threaded through the forest, his long coat never once catching on any of the scraggly vegetation around him. "Abe Torren." He looked back at Logan. "Be at the Tower before the sun sets."

Logan drew in a breath, his thoughts more focused than ever before.

As dawn fast approached, he set himself to finding his way across the swift-flowing river.

\* \* \*

Logan strayed far from the spirits and the site where the quill fiend had disappeared into the water in his efforts to find safe passage across the river. He knew swimming would result in being pulled downstream by the swift current. Traversing the river would have to be by a natural or manmade bridge. He searched for both. On several occasions, he found enough debris to hop more than halfway across, but that wasn't enough.

As he wound his way farther downstream, eliminating rocky routes and debris paths as too narrow or dangerous or both, his zeal lessened. He would never get to the Tower if he couldn't ford the river.

Logan paused in his search to fill his canteens. He drank directly from the river until his stomach sloshed with every step. He fretted over how long it was taking to get to his destination. It was now mid-morning and time was slipping by fast. As he topped off his second canteen, his route across fairly presented itself. He had paid so much attention to the water's surface that he had ignored looking any higher.

Overhead, a large tree canted toward the river, its trunk steeply angled but still climbable. Its length didn't create a complete bridge, but below the upper branches a series of rocks jutted out from the river, providing a safe route across the remaining distance.

He scrambled to the base of the uprooted tree, pleased with himself. As he clambered onto its trunk, he realized his plan had a major problem. The tree leaned across the river, but even the closest branches that drooped toward the river at its top were still too high up. If he dropped from the tree to the rocks below, he would break something. Logan paced along the thick lower portion of the trunk as he thought.

Should he risk it? If he landed just right, the result might just be a twisted ankle. No, that would still be too dire a complication.

When he stubbed a boot against a thick strand of vine winding its way around the sloped tree, Logan dropped to his knees and pulled at the limp vegetation, excited that it might prove the solution to his dilemma. He could tie it to the tree and lower himself to the rocks below. If he could work it free.

He tugged, surprised at how much of a grip the vine had on the trunk. He braced himself and pulled with the ferocity of a kaliback. It broke loose, and he cut it free with his knife. He tested its strength. It would hold his weight. He unspooled the vine, which was far more difficult than it looked. Eventually he had enough to serve as a proper rope.

Logan wiped the sweat from his brow, took another swig of water, then began working his way into the tree's upper branches. Soon, he had climbed through the thick nest of upper branches and was looking down at the rocks below. The torrent of the river was fast here. If he didn't gain purchase on the rock, which looked small and insignificant against the expanse of water rushing around it, he doubted he could use the vine to clamber out of the strong current.

He secured the vine to two thick branches and dropped it down. It caught on a lower branch, but he shook it free with ease. He rubbed his hands together and slipped them around it. He shifted, slowly adding his weight to the vine. The branches above his head sagged slightly but held. He climbed down quickly, at one point losing his grip and sliding far faster than he desired.

His feet landed on the rock, and he steadied himself against his makeshift rope for a moment before releasing it and striking a guarded stance atop the rock. Logan hopped across the seven rocks before him and soon found himself safely ashore, scrambling up a rather muddy slope.

He used the exposed roots of another tree to pull himself out of the mud and onto solid ground. Behind him the river churned.

Logan stood, brushed off as much of the muck as he could, and set forth again.

*Chapter 27*
## Kyle

It was a city unlike his own—quaint stone cottages, unpaved streets, and people dressed in strange clothes. There were no high-rise towers, no troop cruisers flying overhead, no maglev train whining past. And no smog.

The streets were crowded, and Kyle kept getting jostled. Within the crowd he saw a man who looked familiar. His dad? Yes . . . only he wore the same strange garments as those around him, and his hair was unusually thick and unkempt. He was unshaven and had tanned, weathered skin. Clearly this wasn't his father after all, but the resemblance was striking.

A pale aura rose up from the man's back and shoulders, shrouding his head like a ghostly hood. It was an apparition of some kind, a humanoid creature unlike anything Kyle had seen before, with tusks and tiny eyes, and an expression that radiated anger and hostility.

Staring in amazement, Kyle slowly became aware that the surging crowd was getting rougher by the second, bumping and pushing him as they passed, causing him to jerk and sway from side to side . . .

\* \* \*

Kyle woke suddenly, blinking in confusion. He was still jerking and swaying from side to side, only the scenery had changed. Now he stared up at a curious rounded ceiling, a dirty white canopy stretched tight over a thin metal framework that rose straight on both sides and arched over his head. The musty smell was overpowering, but he was oddly comfortable, lying on something soft.

He bolted upright with a gasp and rolled onto hands and knees, gripping the threadbare blankets with fright. He stared toward the closed flap at the front end of the wagon. Clearly it was daylight out, but he saw nothing through the stained fabric.

The last thing he remembered was falling asleep in this abandoned wagon by the side of the road. Why was it now moving? Who was driving?

Creeping forward, Kyle carefully pulled the flap aside and looked out. Blinking in the sunshine, he saw the back of a man sitting not two feet away, slightly to one side of the bench seat, facing forward and flicking the reins, urging a hustle onward.

"Good morning, Kyle," the stranger said crisply, turning his head just enough to show his profile. He was an old man, bald on top but with flowing white hair on the sides, a long beard, a pointed nose, and weathered, wrinkled skin. He wore the strangest clothes Kyle had ever seen—an ornate metal collar that surrounded the back of his head and neck, and some kind of coat made out of metallic material that reflected distorted images.

Kyle had seen this man before. "Wh-who *are* you?" he gasped, remaining where he was with his head poking out the flap. "You—you were the one back at the Repurposing Factory. You let me out of the emergency door and locked it again."

The man made a sound that somehow caused the hustle to slow and stop. With the wagon halted, the heartwarming sounds of chirping birds fell upon them. It was the middle of the morning, the sun already high in the somewhat cloudy sky.

The stranger began to climb down, retrieving a long staff as he did so. He was slow in his descent, but seemed strong and wiry as he walked around to the side of the hustle and patted its heaving shoulder.

The huge brown-furred animal stood as high as the old man. The muscles in its six thick, powerful legs flexed and twitched, and the short, stubby tail flicked back and forth. Its head was low, and Kyle saw only its ears sticking up and the tips of two curved tusks. Flies buzzed around, probably attracted by the overpowering scent.

"My name is Abe Torren," he said, turning to face Kyle. "While you were asleep, I found a herd of hustles and brought the most docile I could find. She's a beauty, don't you think?"

Kyle glanced toward the extremely large backside and hundreds of flies. "Why?" he asked.

The old man blinked. "Why is she a beauty?"

"No, I mean, why did you . . . ?" Kyle gestured toward the hustle.

"Why did I hitch her up and get this wagon on the road? Because, my boy, time is pressing, and I need you at the Tower by sundown tonight."

"You need—" Kyle blinked and frowned. "But *why?*"

The man named Abe stood his staff upright on the ground and smiled. "It's the only place I can talk to you both together. And it has a nice view."

Kyle finally crawled all the way out through the flap and onto the bench seat. As he prepared to climb down, Abe reached for the top end of his metal staff. It was bulbous and contained symbols that glowed a faint blue. Around the base of the orb, where it connected with the staff, were several rings, one of which the man twisted a few notches. As he did so, Kyle felt a tingle along his arms and around the back of his neck. There was a strange power in the air, and it scared him.

"There's nothing to fear from me," the old man said, smiling again. "Now, I'll let you get on." He tapped his metal collar. "This is the only thing holding me here, and the power is about to go. Now, be firm with your steed. She'll happily obey as long as you show her you mean business." He reached for the top of his staff again. "Remember, Kyle—the Tower before sundown. Don't be late."

Kyle gasped and jerked back in his seat as the old man suddenly twisted violently and vanished into thin air. It was as though giant invisible hands had wrung him out like a wet cloth, twisting so hard and fast that he had been spun into a fine thread. Suddenly, Abe was no longer there. A gentle buzz of static electricity crackled and popped in his place, and the smell of sulfur made Kyle turn up his nose.

It took a while for him to come down off the wagon and make sense of where he was. What he had just witnessed would have to wait. He was convinced he'd dreamed it. Nothing about the man—what he looked like, what'd he'd said, how he'd vanished into thin air—made any sense whatsoever. So he put it aside for a moment and concentrated on where he was.

When he'd crawled into the wagon the previous night, a town awaited him in the valley ahead. Now that town was far behind, a mass of low-slung buildings. Following the dusty trail back through the wide streets up the rise in the distance, Kyle judged he'd been traveling an hour or so, an unwitting passenger. He had to admit he was glad for the helping hand.

He turned to face the east. The Tower was closer, and he could make out the structure's thin metallic form with his own eyes instead of having to peer through miniscopes as he'd done on numerous occasions.

Judging distances was difficult, but Kyle decided he'd be able to get there by sundown. Then he chided himself. Why did he care when he got there? He was going to the Tower, sure, but only because he'd been heading there anyway. Time limits meant nothing to him. This weird old man, this *Abe Torren*, was just another crazy old coot. In fact, maybe it would be better to avoid the Tower for fear of meeting him again . . .

Then again, thanks to him, Kyle now had transport.

He gave that some thought as he studied the monstrous form of the hustle. It was waiting patiently, its enormous low-slung head unmoving as he crept around to study it. The creature's left eyeball rotated, following his every move. "Easy, girl," he whispered. "So, uh . . . you're broken in, right? That old man bested you? So you should, uh, do as I say, yes?"

The hustle stared at him unblinking.

Returning to the cart, Kyle climbed up into the seat and flicked the reins. Nothing happened, so he tried again, harder this time. The hustle wagged its short tail.

"Move it!" Kyle shouted.

This time the animal turned its head slightly, peering back at him.

"Yeah, you heard me. MOVE!"

He yanked the reins hard, and the hustle began to amble. Kyle knew these creatures could run at great speeds if they wanted to, but he was fine with a steady pace while sitting on the wagon. Still, he urged it on a little more so that it broke into a lazy trot.

He passed through and out the far side of the valley, across meadows and around small wooded areas, and the only living things he saw all morning were a small herd of galumpers tearing across the plains in the distance, each twice his height, their long, spindly legs taking enormous strides as they stretched their necks and stuck their birdlike heads forward. Their short pointed tails were rigid.

All was still for the next few hours, and it was well into the afternoon when he next caught sight of movement. By this time he was almost faint from hunger, and his throat was dry, so when he came upon a dozen morribies dipping their heads to drink from a small, sparkling lake, he sighed with relief and urged the hustle toward them. Morribies were harmless. They would scamper away long before he drew close.

Sure enough, the slender four-legged creatures turned to watch him as he steered his hustle off the road and started bouncing the wagon across the field. One by one they hurried away, their long ears pricked. There was no way Kyle could bring down one of these things without a long-range weapon. For a moment, he felt a pang of understanding for Archie's lack of success in hunting—not that there was any excuse for resorting to cannibalism.

He clambered down and drank heavily from the lake, getting soaked in the process. Then he remembered the cup he'd pilfered from Archie's campsite. He retrieved it from his knapsack and sat by the water's edge, dipping it in occasionally, drinking more slowly now. He wished he'd found something slightly more useful like a sealed container, something to store water in for later. He was coming to learn that survival in the Ruins came down to possessing the simplest of items. Still, he had a pocketknife if he ever managed to trap a slow-moving shuffler or some other large rodent. He could perhaps skin it, then roast it over a fire and—

Was his lantern still burning? He'd forgotten all about it. He'd hoped to keep the flame going so he could relight his torch when he needed it. And where *was* his torch? He'd doused the flame the night before and left it on the ground outside the wagon. Suddenly angry, he got up to look for it. If Abe Torren had ridden off without it . . .

A quick check inside the wagon confirmed his suspicions: the lantern had burned out, and the torch was missing. Sighing heavily, Kyle looked skyward and swore loudly. "Thanks a bunch, old man," he added.

There had to be something of use at the Tower: food, shelter, answers, that sort of thing. All the more reason to head that way. The ache in his stomach increased as he emerged from the flap, seated himself, and picked up the reins. Then he froze.

Three kalibacks were racing across the field in the distance, and the morribies were scattering in all directions. Animal experts had conducted experiments and figured out that kalibacks communicated with telepathy. Now Kyle witnessed that talent as they silently picked on one of the morribies and ignored the rest. As one kaliback chased from behind, the other two spread out to the sides to prevent their prey from veering off; it could do nothing but keep running straight. It was fast, but so were the kalibacks, and they were patient and had far more stamina. When the terrified morribie began to tire, the

*161*

predators suddenly converged and pounced. Seconds later they were tearing into the creature with abandon.

Kyle urged the hustle away, heading back to the trail with a mixture of dread and envy. The last thing he wanted was to be hunted down like the morribies. But the idea of just a scrap of that flesh roasting over a fire made his stomach ache even more.

The Tower grew on the horizon until, finally, his hustle plowed through a thicket and started up a hill. The grass was long, completely smothering the slopes, but it petered out near the top where the immense structure spiraled into the air. The Tower was tall, thin, and metallic, looking rather like a giant screw sticking out of the ground. Experts back in Apparati speculated that the structure probably contained nothing more than a single flight of steps and, at the very top, a viewing room or lookout post. But these so-called expert opinions failed to dampen the sense of mystery surrounding the Tower.

It was getting dark again. Kyle debated about where to leave the wagon and, in the end, decided to hide it in the trees. He didn't know what to expect, but he valued his ride too much to simply offer it up for someone to come along and steal. Nervously, he tied the hustle to a branch. It didn't seem to mind and ducked its head to graze on the long grass.

Hardly believing he was actually here, Kyle emerged from the long grass and slowly circled the base of the Tower. He found a door on the far side toward the east. It was metal, extremely sturdy, probably locked.

He tried it. To his surprise, it opened easily. Stepping inside, he found himself at the foot of a spiral staircase. Only the first few twists were visible, but he imagined it spiraling high up into the sky. He placed his foot on the lowest step, and its metal surface clanged softly. "Here goes," he muttered.

Then he heard snarls from outside. Swinging around, he saw through the open doorway a gigantic kaliback creeping out of the long grass—and a whole pack of them lower on the hill.

Gasping in horror, Kyle leapt for the door and slammed it shut with a clang. Had he really come that close to being eaten alive? Another half-minute outside and he certainly would have been in serious trouble. The kaliback thudded against the door and let out a low moan as if realizing it had missed out on a meal.

Kyle looked for a lock, finding a heavy deadbolt at the top. But as he reached for it, something gave him pause. He couldn't fathom what it was exactly—just a feeling, a clenching of his gut at the thought of locking the door, locking somebody out with those monsters on the loose. What if someone had entered earlier and locked *him* out? Then he would be pressed up against the door on the other side right at this moment, hemmed in by kalibacks, about to die a horrible death.

He withdrew from the lock. The door was latched, and that was enough. Kalibacks were smart, but they lacked dexterity. Kyle was safe.

For now.

*Chapter 28*
**Logan**

The fog had not been as bad this morning. Logan made quick time through the slight forest and found himself again entering the shattered streets of the ruins. The buildings were in better shape here. Would that be the case the closer he got to the Tower? They looked inhabitable. Did that mean there would be others like Abe deeper into the ruins?

While the city appeared more structurally sound, it was still being overrun. Greenery abounded. The amount of vegetation had exploded throughout the open areas and all over the buildings. Vines crept up the sides of buildings, engulfing entire faces, while resolute weeds invaded the streets and alleys. A few small trees had found purchase in the broken road. This part of the city was more open, less built up. Maybe that was why the plants had been able to better stake their claim in this section. It almost had the look of a paradise, but Logan knew there was danger here.

A pair of hustles grazed by a large fountain. Their impressive six-legged frames, while bulky, enabled them to outrun even the fastest predators. He wondered if they'd ever been ridden before. His current path would bring him very close. If they didn't spook, maybe he could try to ride one.

Of course, why would he need to? The Tower was close. All he needed to do was get there for right now. Maybe later he'd come back and try his hand at befriending one or both of the beasts.

The hustles didn't flee with his passage. They stayed rigid as he walked by. That was a good sign. *Remember where they are*, he thought.

Emboldened by their acceptance of his proximity, he said, "Stay awhile. I have some business at that Tower, but I'll be back. Maybe then we can come to an arrangement." He snickered, knowing the beasts lacked the intelligence to respond. The large one chuffed and resumed eating, clearly determining Logan was not a threat.

As he jogged down the street, he spied a swarm of orb scavengers roosting atop a tall building to his right. With their perch over nine stories high, they were too far away to detect him. At least that was what he hoped. He broke into a run.

Logan was surprised to be spared any further encounters with predators. This gave him time to truly take in his surroundings. The city was vast and so intact. He desperately wanted to enter one of the buildings, positive they would be filled with strange objects and wonders. Something told him that this part of the Broken Lands was not so barren. Did that mean he could meet others who had chosen exile? Was there a thriving society of people who had fled so far in? Would they welcome him or treat him as a threat? He tensed at this thought, briefly imagining an arrow flying from one of the rooftops and piercing his chest.

Shaking his head, he pressed on.

The city sloped upward. The Tower rested on top of a hill.

The slopes were overgrown meadows. He brashly entered the high grasses, his caution extinguished for the moment by the excitement of being so close to the enigmatic structure.

As he threaded through the waist-high meadow, he wondered why so many others in his village had such contempt for the Broken Lands. Their aversion was so strong, a palpable and constant undercurrent of all from the enclaves except for him. He had never felt hatred for the ruins, never felt hostility toward the wastelands.

If anything, Logan realized a growing strength was emerging. With every step deeper into the strange new world, he felt empowered. The Broken Lands welcomed him. *Well, maybe not the wildlife.*

He continued to ruminate on this bond with the world around him all the way to the top of the hill.

As he stepped from the last of the high grasses into a clearing around the Tower, he was shocked to see what awaited him at the structure's base. Treading back and forth by the closed entrance was the largest kaliback Logan had ever laid eyes on.

The creature turned toward him and growled. From the tall grasses on the slopes behind him, a pack of kalibacks emerged. Their heads swiveled in his direction as their leader roared and charged downhill toward Logan. The way they were converging, they had to be closing a trap.

To retreat into the grasses would mean his death. The only thing standing between him and the Tower door was the monstrous kaliback. It was almost a repeat of his earlier encounter. *Only I'm heading uphill and there's more of them.*

Was Abe watching from the top of the Tower?

He risked a quick look up, half expecting the stranger to be floating at its top and looking down at him. The man was nowhere in sight.

Logan had to act on his own. He launched himself toward the charging kaliback. It would all come down to timing. He had to get past the predator and inside. Despite the door being closed, he sensed it was not locked. He couldn't fathom why he was so certain of this. He just knew it was more than blind hope that drove him toward the door.

The beast had the advantage of higher ground, so he couldn't vault over it at the last minute. He'd have to go under and risk being raked by those menacing claws.

He hustled forward, pleased by the flash of surprise that raced across the predator's face.

He slipped the cold blade of his knife between his fingers, balancing the weapon as best he could as he raced uphill. Then he stuttered to a halt, counting under his breath, waiting for the kaliback to come closer.

The beast sprang into the air.

He let fly his knife and dove forward, keeping his trajectory low.

The kaliback spun its forelegs in the air, attempting to alter its descent. At the same time, the knife plowed deep into its lower right eye. A thick arc of blood spurted into the air.

Logan landed and scuttled uphill, watching the beast roll into a ball and claw at its wounded eye, batting the weapon free. The blade fell farther downhill, out of reach.

Logan didn't race to retrieve it. He kept scrambling, pushing his legs like they'd never been pushed before.

He snagged the door handle and wrenched it downward. He shoved his body into the door, and it flew inward. It was unlocked! He darted inside, amazed at his good fortune. Slamming the large metal door behind him, he gulped in several breaths. Outside, he heard the kalibacks roaring. The door rattled as the creatures took turns launching themselves at it. As strong as the door appeared, Logan didn't linger. He scoped out his options.

A wide metal spiral staircase wound upward. There was plenty of light thanks to the narrow vertical windows cut into the walls. He could only go up.

Who else awaited him at the structure's apex? Logan drew in a steadying breath and took the steps two at a time.

*Chapter 29*
**Crossover**

As Kyle climbed the spiral staircase, he heard a terrible commotion outside and froze. He thought he heard the door slam shut, which alarmed him—but if Abe Torren or someone else had just come in, at least the kalibacks were still stuck outside. The noise quickly faded, and he hurried on up the steps, not wanting whoever was down below to catch up to him in such a tight space.

He hoped he wouldn't regret leaving the door unbolted.

Narrow, thick-glassed windows let in shafts of light all the way up the staircase. He peered through one or two, growing excited at the increasingly elevated view of the land. But the windows faced north and south, toward the shores, which was a little disappointing. It was fine to see the glittering ocean in both directions, but he hoped for a better view at the top—a view of the land from west to east.

He patted the map in his pocket. It would be interesting to compare it to what he saw outside.

After at least three hundred steps, his legs were shaky, his heart hammering. He pressed on, sure it would end soon. The staircase had narrowed to nearly half its original width.

At last he saw a spread of light above. Relieved, bursting with anticipation though wary, he finally arrived.

At a dead end.

The light came from a series of glowing orbs set into the wall all around the room just above his head. Unlike light bulbs, they had an ethereal quality to them as though ghosts were trapped inside glass balls. Bathed in the soft illumination, a steel ladder was fixed to the wall before him. It ended at a solid metal ceiling above.

Frowning, Kyle climbed a few rungs and studied the smooth surface over his head. Barely perceptible cracks indicated a square hatchway notched along one edge to accommodate the ladder's rails, the hinges on the opposite side. Kyle pushed against the hatch and found that it rose easily. Natural daylight filtered down, and he squinted through the gap to see that the ladder continued all the way up to another ceiling high above. He climbed a few more rungs into the room, pushing the hatch open as he went. Once past the vertical, it fell and clanged noisily against the floor.

How could an old man like Abe Torren have made it up this far? Then again, the man had vanished in a shower of sparks, so maybe a flight of stairs and a ladder didn't matter to him.

With head and shoulders poking out of the floor, he saw an empty, circular room with windows all around. Abe Torren, wearing his heavy metallic coat and clinging to his staff, was looking out across the land.

"Good evening, Kyle," the old man said without turning. "I'm glad you made it. Come on up. Close that hatch."

Saying nothing, Kyle climbed the rest of the way into the room and turned to close the hatch. When it had clanged shut, he became aware of a gentle hiss all around. Vents in the floor seemed to be sucking air out, while similar vents in the ceiling blew air in. When the hissing subsided, the silence was complete.

With his feet clanging on the metal floor, Kyle stepped across to a window nowhere near Abe and looked out in astonishment.

This was the view he'd been waiting for. The full length of the land spread out to the west. There in the distance was his home—the city of Apparati with its high-rise buildings and hazy smog, and the Wall that encircled it, separating it from the Ruins and protecting it from the ocean all around. The haze of smog that hung in the early evening sky startled him. It looked like a mist had crept in over the city, yet everywhere else was clear.

The tallest building protruded from its gloom, including Mayor Baynor's grand residence at the very top. His apartment probably enjoyed the freshest air in the city as well as the most amazing view.

Still, the view from the Tower was almost as spectacular. Unable to contain his excitement, Kyle rushed to the other side of the room and peered east, fearlessly standing shoulder to shoulder with the old man he knew so little about. To his disappointment, he saw nothing of interest at the other end of the world. There was no city, nothing. Just more of the Ruins. In fact, hardly even that. They seemed to peter out, becoming an expanse of jungle at the foot of enormous mountains.

"There's nothing there," he said with disappointment. "I expected . . . something. Another city. People. There's nothing but trees and mountains."

The old man smiled. "There's more than you think. I'll explain in just a moment. When Logan arrives."

Kyle blinked in confusion. His head ached. "Logan?"

"He's on his way up. I just saw him outside dealing with the kalibacks."

They both peered out the window. Far, far below, tiny figures moved in the grass.

Kyle shuddered and turned to look around the room. The ladder he'd climbed led to another room above. That, too, was sealed behind a metal hatch. "What's up there?"

"Control room," Abe said. "Nothing you need concern yourself with."

There was a long pause. "Look," Kyle said, "what *is* this place? Why do you—?"

"A few more moments, please, Kyle," the old man said, holding up a hand. "I know you seek answers, but I do not wish to repeat myself. Logan will be here shortly." He cocked his head. "In fact, I hear him now." The man raised his voice. "Come on up, Logan."

Silence.

Kyle waited and waited, trembling, wondering what he had gotten himself into. He heard absolutely nothing. Either the old man's hearing was exceptional, or he was crazy.

He was betting on the latter.

\* \* \*

Logan's progress slowed. He came to a halt again, kneading his sore thighs, trying to coax more out of his tired muscles. His sprint up the stairs should've been easy. Something about the tower made him sluggish, out of sync. Back at the village he could run all day. What was it about the Tower that seemed to weaken him now? All this time trekking across the Broken Lands, his strength had been on a constant upswing, surging really. And yet, inside the curved walls of this Tower, he was out of breath and even more out of sorts. His focus was off. Even looking out the narrow slotted windows that peppered the north and south walls demanded a heightened effort that drained him.

As he caught his breath and eyed the grounds around the Tower through a glass window to his left, he watched the pack of kalibacks drift away from the entrance. Surprisingly, they had found other prey—a hustle stood tethered to a simple wagon along the hill Logan judged to be opposite the side he had scaled. Had Abe traveled here by wagon? It seemed such a mundane form of transport for the grand stranger. Could the wagon have been used by the other that Abe talked to above?

Logan heard snatches of Abe's voice echoing down through the Tower, but whoever he conversed with remained tight-lipped, unwilling to talk. *Or unable to,* he thought. Did Abe have someone up there all tied up and gagged? Was he walking into a trap?

Instead of retreating, this notion spurred him to continue. He was furious at the stranger. If he did have a captive above, Logan wouldn't stand for it. With every step, his conviction and outrage built. Something about the Tower had him rattled, his emotional state amped up. He couldn't explain why he felt this way, but his unfettered and escalating anger was either the Tower's fault or the stranger's.

He was certain Abe had lured him here. To do what, he had no idea—but whoever was up there, probably another exile from some other enclave, he wasn't going to let Abe do anything to them. Not if he could help it.

Logan reached the top of the stairs to find a ladder leading through the ceiling. He clambered up and shoved a trapdoor open. Floundering through the narrow opening on weary muscles, he almost lost his footing on the rungs. He hoisted himself through and stood.

"Welcome, Logan," Abe said warmly. "Come enjoy the view, then we'll talk."

Inside the small round room, Abe stood all by himself. No furniture, no captive, nothing. An array of windows rimmed the room, allowing a panoramic view of the land. Logan spied the ruins to the east, and the edge of the wastelands. He could make out the lush woods around his enclave and the high roof of Sovereign Hall. His eyes traveled along the view, taking in the ocean creeping in on either side to the North and South. He watched the land again widen as he looked west. More ruins. And in the distance, the fallen city faded, hemmed in by an expanse of untamed forest. He was disappointed to see so very little to the west. He had hoped to spy a far-off kingdom, but there were only ruins and the wild.

Abe looked at a spot to Logan's left and spoke to the air. "See, we're all here. Now I can begin." His gaze trailed to Logan and he arched an eyebrow. "Shall I?"

\* \* \*

When the hatch opened, lifting toward him, Kyle gasped and stepped back. As before, it teetered and fell, clanging down on the metal floor.

But whoever had opened it must have ducked back down the ladder. Kyle found himself waiting with bated breath for the mysterious stranger to make an appearance.

He never did. That didn't stop the crazy old man, though. "Welcome, Logan," Abe said warmly. "Come enjoy the view, then we'll talk."

Staring in amazement, Kyle watched as the old man's gaze followed a make-believe person across the floor. Something about the way his eyes moved unnerved him. They were clearly focused on someone or something in the room with them, standing right there by the window.

But there was nobody there.

"See, we're all here," Abe said anyway. "Now I can begin." His gaze trailed to the phantom. "Shall I?"

Wishing he could flee this place, Kyle looked toward the open hatch. As he started toward it, the old man nodded approvingly. "Yes, yes, please do shut it, Kyle. We need to keep this place free of contaminants. Especially the room above, which houses valuable equipment." As Kyle moved toward the hatch, the old man rambled on. "The control room has survived a few centuries sealed in up there. Let's allow it to survive a few more, shall we?"

Rather than make a run for it, Kyle realized too late he was closing the hatch. As soon as he did so, the vents started hissing again.

The old man grinned amiably. "My name, as I have said, is Abe Torren." He glanced at Kyle, then off to one side, then back again. "I'm very proud of you both for making it this far. But you're not home yet."

"Uh, sir?" Kyle said. For some reason he couldn't quite fathom, his heart was thumping hard and his hands were cold and clammy. Was he getting sick? The dull ache in his head suggested he was. "Could you please stop that? There's nobody else but me."

Abe bowed his head, then laughed. "Ha! How alike you are to speak at once and suggest I'm an old fool."

"I didn't say—"

The old man held up both hands. "Please, do not talk. It's hard for you to understand what's happening here, but I'll explain. Until then, refrain from speaking—otherwise I'll hear a babble when you speak at the same time."

*Oh my*, Kyle thought. *Yeah, he's crazy.*

He edged sideways and leaned to look out of a window. The frame was only two feet high, but very wide, one of six metal frames that surrounded the room, giving the effect of continuous, curving glass with only brief sections of solid wall between each.

"There's so much to explain, boys," Abe said, "but I want to get to the heart of it quickly since the transition is already taking place." He paused, nodded to himself, then took a deep breath. "You were both born with immense powers. Unfortunately, those with such potential often find themselves orphaned at a young age and oh-so-conveniently adopted by those in positions of command—such as your mayor, Kyle—or your sovereign, Logan."

*There he goes again, talking to air.* Kyle bit his lip as the old man continued.

"I didn't want that to happen to either of you. When you were very young, I switched you."

He waited for a reaction, glancing back and forth, but Kyle was too dumbfounded to say anything. Switched? What did that even mean?

"I stole you away from your homes," Abe went on, "and brought you here to the Tower. Once you were correctly phased, I delivered you to your new homes. Of course your parents knew something was wrong, that you were different. I cropped your hair in preparation for the city, Kyle, but I couldn't lighten your tanned skin or add a little weight, not in such a short space of time—nor could I grow your hair, Logan, and get rid of some of that puppy fat. And of course, though just toddlers, your vocabularies varied. You acted differently. You were essentially two unique boys. But you looked the same, and—to those in your new world, Kyle—your DNA was the same. So although your parents were frightened out of their wits by the subtle changes, no suspicions were raised with the authorities, which was the important thing."

"Why do you keep talking as if there's someone else here?" Kyle snapped, suddenly angry. He swayed and closed his eyes for a moment. "Why are you telling me all this? I don't believe a word of it."

"Completely understandable."

There was a long silence. Then Abe nodded.

"Indeed, Logan. But let me finish my story. You see, once everything died down, life returned to normal—or as normal as life can be for a family with a changeling in its midst. The reason for this switch was simply so your enormous powers could be hidden. Growing up in the wrong world meant you would both be remarkable in how utterly unremarkable you are. And those who don't stand out are safe from prying eyes, of no interest to the authorities."

"Except it nearly got me killed," Kyle growled. He couldn't understand the sick feeling inside him. It was like the room itself was disturbing his emotions and riling them up.

Abe closed his eyes and nodded. "But you escaped, and now you're here. You're no longer insignificant. When you leave this place and continue your journey, everything will be different."

\* \* \*

Logan was infuriated. What was the man talking about? "I don't have any powers. I can't tether to any spirit whatsoever."

Abe nodded at him and the empty spot he insisted was Kyle. "Yes, in your world, your Tethering Day didn't go the way you envisioned. Much like how Kyle found out he couldn't work any tech on his Implant Day. I will get to all that in a moment. Let me explain what you are experiencing right now."

The old man walked to the window facing east. "I imagine what Logan sees is his home in the distance. Out past the ruins, he is able to discern his village. And all Kyle sees beyond the scattered rubble are endless trees and tracts of open land. That will soon change. The two of you are out of sync. Having lived in the wrong reality for so long, you are no longer in phase with your place of origin. If Logan looks west he will see nothing, while Kyle will see the tall buildings of his city and the wall that lays blight around the Ruins."

Logan looked west. He couldn't see any strange city in the distance although the landscape appeared fuzzy, out of focus. His normally solid eyesight was failing him. Was that a result of the Tower's influence?

"The two of you are here to stabilize yourselves, to attune to the reality you will be returning to, the proper world where you are now needed. We are waiting for you to acclimate to your realities. This Tower is a waystation, a place linked to both dimensions. As you come in phase with your world, there will be a point where you can see each other. Right now, your emotions and senses are heightened, running hot and cold, a result of the Tower's influence. I imagine it's not comfortable, judging from both of your expressions."

Logan tried to wipe the grimace from his face. He glanced at the invisible boy. If what Abe said was true, would he suddenly see him?

Abe looked over at the empty spot again, answering so Logan would understand what Kyle had apparently asked.

Logan's head hurt. There was too much information swirling around in his head.

Abe stepped toward the phantom Kyle. "Calm yourself. I knew you would have the hardest time accepting this. With Logan's people, magic is a part of their everyday life. You have been immersed in a world devoid of such. With only tech at your side, you're operating at a deficit compared to Logan." Abe whispered conspiratorially to the invisible boy. "Although, truth be told, Logan's not taking it all that well either. Must be because you two are so extremely matched duplicates of each other. No other counterparts are so well paired. Good thing this was kept from the powers that be in your respective worlds. Otherwise, neither of you would have lived to see your fourteenth birthdays."

Abe paused, then sighed. "Now, may I tell you why your worlds are so separate?"

Logan nodded, his attention hardly on Abe. For now he could see the hazy arrival of Kyle. The boy was materializing into view as Abe began his story. As Abe spoke, Logan could make out his counterpart's expression. It was decidedly slack jawed and exactly the same down to his aquiline nose and wide brow. It was like staring into a murky mirror. He looked on as Abe launched into his unwieldy explanation.

\* \* \*

Kyle glimpsed something to his right and spun around. He gasped and jerked backward, then turned away to grip the window sill. He was breathing hard.

"Ah," Abe said quietly. "It begins."

"Wh-what's going on?" Kyle asked, unable to stop himself from trembling. He glanced over his shoulder toward the trapdoor, wondering if he had time to open it, drop down, and escape before this old man pulled out a weapon of some kind.

"Do you see Logan?" Abe asked, his eyes wide with interest. "What about you, Logan? Do you see Kyle?"

The crazy thing was, when Kyle slowly turned to look again, he *did* see Logan. It was just a faint, ghostly presence, but definitely there. And the apparition was staring back at him.

"It's . . . it's *me*," Kyle said simply.

Immediately afterward, the ghost's lips moved, and Kyle distinctly heard it speak though the voice was distant. "Yes, I see him."

All at once, Kyle's anxiety and fear seemed to evaporate. He was astounded, perplexed, unable to get a grip on what was happening, and yet the appearance of someone so like himself had a calming effect. It was like staring into a mirror, only the reflection showed a version of himself that wore his hair a little longer and had a tan. He marveled at how fit he looked, how determined his stare was. It was definitely himself he was studying, but perhaps a stronger, bolder version that made Kyle feel inferior. Still, there was a connection between them similar to the bond he and Byron shared.

"Explain," Kyle said grimly, and was aware that the ghost was repeating him, his voice faint and whispery.

"Forgive me," Abe said. "Kyle, please look again to the east."

When Kyle did so, he nearly collapsed in a dead faint. The earlier nothingness in the east was now a presence—an apparition of civilization with semitransparent clusters of tiny homes. "What *is* that?"

"That, my friend, is Apparata. Where Logan just came from, and where you, Kyle, were born."

Kyle rubbed his eyes, certain he had a film of gunk in them. "I wasn't born there. I was born in Apparati to the west." He jerked a thumb over his shoulder.

"No, Kyle," Abe said. "You were born in Apparata. Now you're going home."

"Home."

"And you, Logan, are going to the city—*your* home. Look."

Kyle turned, and found that the ghost boy did too. Together they stared west, moving slowly across the metal grid flooring to the window for a better view. Only Kyle's shoes made any significant noise, though he thought he detected the muffled echo of Logan's footsteps. It was truly bizarre.

The city of Apparati was still there but greatly faded. The Wall was almost transparent too, though the ancient structures just outside were solid and real, proving to Kyle's befuddled mind that it wasn't just a drifting cloud of smog messing up his view. The city seemed to be in the same state as the villages to the east—insubstantial, with the coastline showing through.

The ghost boy said something. Unafraid now, Kyle watched with interest, seeing Logan's lips move but barely hearing the words despite the smallness of the room and the close proximity of all who stood in it.

"Yes, Logan, that's the place you dreamed of," Abe said. "I sent you both a vision. A taste of the other side, if you will." He turned to Kyle and winked. "Logan sees the city now, slowly fading in the way you see it fading out. The opposite of what you both see to the east. When both cities appear fully substantial, we'll be halfway through the phasing."

They all stared in silence. A calm had descended over Kyle now, and he felt a strange, impossible kinship with Logan. After all, the ghost boy was—what? His twin brother?

Logan stared back at him, fleshing out by the second, becoming more and more solid. It was just about the creepiest moment of Kyle's life, yet he felt something wonderful was happening. As the crazy old loon Abe Torren had said, this marked the beginning of a new life.

Logan held up his hand, fingers splayed and gently curled as though he were pressing them against glass.

On impulse, Kyle did the same, moving his hand closer to his surreal mirror image. The illusion wasn't quite complete because both were using their right hands. And of course Logan was dressed differently, and had slightly darker skin and longer hair.

But they moved as one, tilting their heads at the same time, mouths hanging open, brows furrowed.

Their fingers touched.

\* \* \*

The hairs on the back of Logan's outstretched arm stood straight up. He looked at Kyle, his face equally mirroring his own astonishment he was sure.

Abe said, "The time with which you can interact is limited. Even as we speak, you are drifting away, aligning more with your true homes."

Both retracted their arms, sheepish grins creeping across their faces.

"This is important. You will both be powerful in your rightful realities, far beyond anyone else." Abe leaned on his staff and motioned for both to draw closer. "Your leaders will not like this." He pointed to Kyle. "When you reach the point where the spirits gather, you will be able to use your abilities." He didn't skip a beat, turning to Logan in kind. "And you will be able to control the machines they call tech in Kyle's world. When you come across a perimeter of dormant machines, you will know it is time to awaken what is inside you."

"What *is* inside us?" Logan asked.

He was trying so hard to commit to memory everything the old man was saying. Every utterance felt critical. He wondered if his so-called twin felt the same. Kyle seemed severely aloof, almost in denial. What sort of world did he come from that left him incapable of embracing a shred of wonder, of opportunity?

"The power to bring your worlds into balance, to undo the damage your corrupt leaders have wreaked. This world was once whole, but now it is fractured. With your respective returns, there is a chance Apparatum can again be cohesive."

"This is crazy," Kyle said.

Abe made a distasteful face. "I assure you that's not the case. Look, both of you face death if you return, and I'm afraid the phasing process is not easily reversible. Your affinity is shifting to your new worlds as we speak." He pointed both east and west. "See?"

Logan saw that he could now see a more solid massive cityscape, filling the western horizon with the audacious reach of the tall buildings. It was the city from his vision. He was positive there would be a long machine winding its way through the city but couldn't see from this great distance.

Kyle's eyes widened as he soaked up the far less impressive outline of Sovereign Hall and a smattering of other rooftops poking through the trees. Logan wanted to tell him there were more homes under the canopy but held his tongue. Something told him that whatever he said to Kyle had to have more import.

Abe said, "There's still so much to tell you, but so little time." He glanced out the window at the setting sun. Heavy clouds gathered outside as well, contributing to the thickening darkness. "Things have escalated with your brothers. Byron and Kiff are in trouble."

Kyle's eyes softened. With the mention of his brother, all his hardness and doubt evaporated. It was as if he had finally given in to the whole madness of the moment. At least that was how it looked to Logan. "What is it?"

Abe squared off with Logan. "The sovereign wants to end Kiff's life sooner rather than later. Your escape has spurred him to make an example of your family." He lingered, but not for long. He walked over to face Kyle. "And Byron's fate is identical. The general found out about his assistance in your escape. With what little he has left, repurposing won't come to pass. Byron also faces death and soon."

What did Abe mean about Byron having so little left? What was repurposing? Logan didn't like how so much was left unanswered but felt only one course of action rising to the fore. "Then why are we still here?"

He darted to the trapdoor, reaching it first. Kyle was right behind him. They ran into each other, their bodies phasing through each other slightly.

Logan leaned forward, determined to radiate resoluteness to his counterpart. "We are needed."

Kyle nodded, and they both dropped down through the hatch and beset the stairs.

\* \* \*

"Slow down, boys," Abe called down the stairs.

Kyle descended quickly, his footsteps clanging on the metal. Logan was right behind, his own noise a little muffled. The old man was surprisingly spry to keep pace with them.

"Can't hang around," Kyle said. "Gotta get back to Byron."

"I said *wait*."

The old man's sharp command caused Kyle to halt. He turned, seeing that Logan had paused also. The old man caught up at last and stood there a few steps above.

"You mean Kiff, of course," he said firmly.

"Well—" Kyle started.

"I want to make it perfectly clear that there's no going back. Your futures are in each others' worlds. You, Kyle, cannot save Byron—but Logan can. You must trust him. And Logan, the same with Kiff."

The staircase faded into gloom as the sun descended on the horizon, and only a weak shaft of light through a slotted window illuminated the old man's face. Gone was his smile. In its place was a mask of deadly earnest.

"Take us," Kyle said. "You have the power to ... to teleport. So take me to my city so I can save Byron. You can teleport us all out."

Abe smiled sadly and shook his head. "I can't teleport, Kyle. I can only phase in and out of these worlds. Besides, you're not listening." He leaned on his staff, peering down at them. "When you were babies, it took a monumental effort to switch you, to tune you to your opposite realities. It was possible because you were young and innocent, easy to displace. Here in the Tower, you're returning to normality, readjusting to your birthrights. This is part of what the Tower does. It resets things, makes things right. Now your minds are filled with knowledge, your hearts with longing for your childhood realities. Despite what you might think, your minds and souls won't allow you to switch again without a fight. You cannot go back home."

Behind him on the next step up, Logan sighed heavily, and Kyle felt a warm breath on his shoulder. "Maybe you should have helped us save our brothers *before* you brought us here," he griped.

"But don't you see?" Abe urged. "Switching places *empowers* you. Even if you could go back home, what do you think you'd achieve? Eh? Nothing, that's what. But if you trust each other and swap places, *then* you can help."

After a few seconds of silence, Kyle gave in. "All right, old man. I'll go on to Apparata." He turned to look up at Logan. "I'll save your brother Kiff."

"And I'll save Byron," Logan said, his voice sounding distant. He was fading fast.

"Watch out for deadbeats," Kyle said. Seeing Logan's frown, he added, "People in the Ruins. Exiles. Don't trust anyone."

Logan nodded. "Thanks for the warning."

A silence fell. Then Abe briskly rubbed his hands. "Splendid. So good to see you boys conversing in this brief interim period." He turned to continue down the steps.

After half a minute, Logan asked a question that was barely audible. Kyle opened his mouth to repeat it, certain that Abe couldn't have heard, but the old man answered promptly.

"Oh yes, this world. It's a rather sad story, you know. Everyone got along just fine for centuries, living a relatively simple life in what you now call the Ruins and the Broken Lands. With the swift rise of technology, things changed."

"What's that?" Logan asked faintly.

Abe chuckled. "Think of it as magic in another form. Anyway, technological advancements led to a whole new way of life for some people—but not all. Technology pushed boundaries and was seen by many as unnatural and dangerous, and in the end roughly half the population decided they wanted to return to a simpler way of life. An ambitious plan was hatched, and the land slowly divided."

"And one half became invisible?" Kyle said, skeptical despite everything he'd seen.

"*Both* halves became invisible, depending on your point of view," Abe said. "But not by design. Even after the worlds were divided, tension continued to mount—because so many people refused to obey the laws and brought their technology outside the city, often encroaching on the enclaves in the east. Meanwhile, untethered spirits roamed free, and the people of the city decided they wanted nothing more to do with what they considered superstitious nonsense such as tethering."

Logan sucked in a shocked, distant breath.

They were nearing the bottom of the Tower now. Abe slowed and turned to them, looking up with a sad expression. "Before you leave here, there's more you both must hear."

Both boys looked at him expectantly. Logan was almost completely transparent now, and Kyle had to blink to focus on him. "Like what?" he asked.

"I need to explain to you about the wink-outs."

\* \* \*

Abe had Logan's attention. And while Kyle was barely there, his physical form now no more than a pale ghost, he expressed intense interest.

"No one knows why they happen, but I guess you do," Logan said, surprised at his antagonism. The Tower's influence again.

Abe ignored Logan's posturing. "You have to understand, it wasn't planned that way. It's an aberration, a miscalculation that we haven't been able to undo. Our lands were divided, but people from the city regularly flew their machines all the way to the enclaves, a cause of great anger. They sent spy cameras. They hunted kalibacks for recreational purposes using powerful ground vehicles, thus pushing the creatures to the east. Despite their promise, the people of the city simply refused to let up with their technological devices. Meanwhile, the natural spirits of the world continued to roam the Ruins, often encroaching into the city and attempting to do what they had always done— tether with suitable subjects. This did not sit well with the city dwellers. So, those in charge devised a method of obstructing each other. Back in the city is an underground bunker where magic is plied, twisted, and projected outward to create a large radius around Apparati and well into the wastelands." He pointed east. "It stretches all the way to the river that cuts north to south and marks a boundary where spirits cannot cross."

Logan could no longer see Kyle but knew he was still there on the steps. There was a tangible presence.

"And back at your capitol city, your Hunter Enclave, there's a hidden temple housing a massive machine that sends out a magnetic pulse across the land, rendering any tech useless this side of the Ridge. These inhibitors did their jobs well. Too well. They sealed each other off, and the overlap of their large fields of influence spans into the ruins. Within the overlap, the area close to this tower, between the tech-ridge and the spirit-boundary, it is a no-go zone. No tech or magic will work. That's why you both came across boundaries where neither the spirits nor tech could pass. The Tower was built later by my group. We were a small band of thinkers who felt isolation of the two cities wasn't right. We discovered that what each had done to separate one from the other had repercussions to Apparatum's very reality. Both cities were shifting out of sync. A horrible offshoot of this is the wink-outs."

Abe listened for a moment, then nodded. "Tension eased, and life went on. Over the next two hundred years, the fracture increased to the point that the city and enclaves forgot each other existed."

Logan found that hard to believe. "That's just—"

But Abe held up his hand. "Please, Logan, let me finish. I understand your skepticism. How could an entire civilization be split in half and then forget the other half existed? Well, it's possible if the leaders of the city and the enclaves agree to *make* their people forget. Then it's surprisingly easy: a systematic erasure of public records, a brutal censorship on the types of stories passed down from generation to generation, an organized movement by the authorities over the centuries to cleanse their past and prevent the secret getting out. But no matter how much each tried to deny the other, their tampering with reality through their disruptors produced a bizarre consequence, one we are still trying to figure out. We know the why, just not the how of wink-outs."

Logan tensed, knowing what Abe would say next was dire.

"We can't quite explain it, but a result of cleaving the world in two also brought about the counterparts. At a certain point, and we know this because my group found a way to sync with both realities by what we constructed within this Tower, we witnessed the fact that a birth in one world matched with a birth in the other. Now, not all counterparts are so closely synced as the two of you. Most only share their gender and age with each other. Those who are tied more intimately are able to manipulate more tech and magic. Your governments hoard these rare individuals for their own nefarious purposes."

Abe paused a moment, then responded to something Kyle had apparently asked him. "It's true that I can exploit both, and have done so to assist in your journey here, but my abilities pale in comparison to yours. That's why when we detected the scope of your powers, we had to hide you away in the opposite realities until you were ready."

He paused, his attention again on where Kyle stood. He nodded at the open space. "I am getting to your brother, Kyle. Please bear with me. I am doing my best."

Logan nodded for Abe to continue.

Abe said, "Kyle wants me to *get to* how the wink-outs affect your brothers." He rubbed his forehead, pressing his fingers deep into his wrinkled scalp. "When one dies, their counterpart ceases to exist. So if someone fell from a great height or died of medical complications in one world, their twin would wink out. It happens both ways. Wink-outs occur in Apparata and Apparati and with more and more regularity I'm afraid, but that's a dilemma for another day. Right now, you two must help your counterpart's brother. If one of them is put to death, the other will wink out. Both must be saved. But it's not enough to come to their rescue. You must be a catalyst for true change to occur."

Outside, distant thunder sounded.

"You will reunite with your proper realities and be given access to your true selves. Your powers will be extraordinary. Make sure you use them to exact lasting change. Your worlds' leaders have strayed, become bloated, despicable wielders of influence and control. They must be dealt with."

Logan tensed. Abe was asking them to kill? He wasn't sure he could do that.

It was apparent from Abe's face that he knew they were reeling from his pronouncements. "Now, there isn't any more time. You must go, master your magic and tech and bring forth a new order." Abe waved at them to depart, then looked at Logan. "Kyle is leaving. You must too. It's looking and sounding more and more like rain. And you have enough obstacles slowing you down already."

Logan bolted down the stairs, holding back his tears as he realized his path was taking him away from Kiff, possibly forever.

*Chapter 30*
**Kyle**

Standing outside the Tower, Kyle could see the back end of his wagon in the trees where he'd left it, but the hustle seemed quiet, maybe asleep. Still, at least the kalibacks had disappeared.

The sky was darkening rapidly, and thunderclouds were rolling in. Kyle felt the first drop of rain on his forehead as he started toward the wagon, his mind in turmoil. Purely by chance, he came across a knife lying in the grass. He picked it up, wondering if it belonged to the old man. Or Logan. That seemed more likely, especially as it had something nasty plastered all over the blade. It was probably kaliback blood.

He absently—and rather foolishly—wiped it clean on his pants while he trudged across the clearing toward the wagon. How was he ever going to process Abe's impossible information? How was he to move forward with his life? To head on to these distant enclaves and integrate with an entirely different society, to bring down the authorities, to be reunited with his biological parents, to save a little brother who wasn't quite his? He shook his head. *Too much, too much.* There would be plenty of time for rumination on his way to the enclaves. He should be there fairly quickly if—

He froze, looking down at a huge blood stain where the hustle had been. The poor creature, hitched to the wagon and tied to the tree, had been easy prey for the kalibacks. No wonder they were gone. They'd dragged the creature away and were probably devouring it right now.

Well, Kyle hoped their bellies were full. He hoped they had settled down to sleep. He considered this as he tucked the knife into a belt loop and climbed into the back of the wagon to collect his knapsack. It contained only a cup, a pocketknife, and a neatly folded blanket he'd never even used—his sole possessions in the world apart from the clothes he stood in and the larger blade he'd just found. What about the musty old blankets he'd slept on? Should he take those, too? No, they'd be too bulky. Best leave them in the wagon where they belonged.

He was tempted to lie down again and stay the night, but he knew he wouldn't be able to. Not yet. He needed to walk, to clear his head, and to make some headway in his journey to the enclaves in Apparata. Besides, what if the kalibacks came back?

For that matter, what if he ran into more along the way? He shuddered and pushed the thought to the back of his mind.

As he set off down the hill, the rain started coming down hard. He groaned, thinking again of the wagon. Perhaps he should wait there until the storm moved on. But for how long? What if he waited all night and it was still raining in the morning? He couldn't afford to waste that much time—and Logan couldn't either. They both needed to push on.

He tucked his chin into his shirt, hunched up his shoulders, and plowed through the wet grass. When he glanced back toward the tower, he noticed something strange: a void in the rain shaped suspiciously like a man. Or ... like Logan. His breath catching in his throat, Kyle stared long and hard, then waved on impulse. Immediately he realized he was being ridiculous, that he was imagining things. Of course it wasn't Logan. How could it possibly—

The figure waved back.

So Logan, though invisible, still partially existed in this realm. The rain knew he was there. The grass he stood on flattened under his feet. But how could that be? And if Logan jumped up onto the wagon—assuming he could even see it—and bounced about, would Kyle see it shift? If so, where exactly was the delineation between realities? At what point did things stop being part of either Kyle's or Logan's world and start being part of the ancient Ruins, what might be considered a neutral zone?

Or was Logan's phantom outline visible in the rain simply because both boys were still adjusting to their new realities, at an in-between stage, blurring the boundaries?

Kyle patted the knife at his waist. It was Logan's, and yet now it was in Kyle's reality. Or rather he was in the knife's reality, where Logan had been originally . . .

His mind boggled. With an involuntary shiver, he hurried away, shuffling through the long wet grass, heading east.

\* \* \*

The rain was depressing. It was one thing being soaked to the skin but quite another to be dragging his feet through mud and sinking into ankle-deep puddles. Walking long distances was hard enough without the added slog.

He'd been trudging for hours. All three moons were hidden behind thick thunderclouds. The sky was starless and black, and he was cold, wet, and miserable. He thought over and over about the wagon and how much simpler his journey would have been with it. At first he had contemplated going back for it, perhaps searching for a herd of hustles and attempting to capture one. But he kept hoping he'd come across something else, some other form of transport to help him on his way. No such luck.

He passed plenty of buildings, though, and was now on the lookout for one to hole up in. They were remarkably intact considering their age. Apparently, this part of the world was devoid of deadbeats from what he could see. For all he knew, dozens of people were looking out at him right now, wondering why anybody would be stupid enough to travel the night in a never-ending downpour . . . but somehow he knew he was alone out here.

*Except for the wildlife.*

When he sank up to his knees once more, he groaned and dragged himself free, ending up on all fours. He waited there a moment, thoroughly exhausted. *Enough's enough*, he thought. *I've walked a long way. Time to rest.*

Kneeling in a pool of muddy water, he shielded his eyes to peer through the heavy rain. When lightning flashed, blocky architectural shapes revealed enough detail for him to choose his lodgings for the night. He picked himself up and staggered toward a square, three-story building, wondering idly what it had been used for hundreds of years before.

When he was just twenty paces away, an ear-splitting shriek filled the air. He threw himself down in terror. Wallowing in a muddy patch, he jerked his head around, trying to find the source of the hideous noise. It trailed off, then started again, and as it reached a crescendo, a dull crack and boom echoed across the fields.

Kyle couldn't decide whether to dig himself deeper into the mud and stay there or get up and run to the building. Lightning flashed vividly, and it was then that he saw the canyon clackers sluicing through the waterlogged field toward him.

There were three of them, eerie wormlike monsters, each the length of a car and nearly as high. They held their blunt, open-mouthed heads as if sniffing the air. The clackers used muscles along their entire bodies to push them forward, which then rippled and repositioned for the next lunge a second later. Anything that stood in their way would likely be pulverized.

In the time it took for the next bolt of lightning to illuminate the pasture, Kyle realized the hideout he had chosen was probably not the safest place to be. As the clackers advanced, the building ended up in the path of the one to the far right. Rather than go around, it let out a deafening screech, and Kyle imagined it punching through the rear wall. As the two visible clackers advanced around the side, Kyle imagined the third keeping pace inside, moving through the interior rooms. Seconds later it screeched again from within, and a small section of centuries-old stonework at the front of the building dissolved into a muddy paste in the rain. The giant worm lunged out of the hole.

Kyle watched with horror as the three canyon clackers continued through the field directly toward him. With a shudder, he picked himself up and started running, his knapsack swinging around on his shoulders. He stumbled, squelched deep into the mud, and ended up crawling.

The clackers moved impossibly fast when they wanted to. While two lunged forward and past, the third paused, lowering its head and sweeping it from side to side. From what Kyle knew of clackers, they had no eyes or ears, just a huge mouth to suck in dirt and pass it through their long bodies. They didn't care for the sun, which dried out their bodies, so they usually stayed below ground in the moist earth. They surfaced during downpours simply because it was easier to travel. Their mysterious migrations were helped along by sonic shrieks to loosen rocks that stood in their path. And they had a strong sense of smell.

They looked like giant worms but were very, very different. They were carnivorous, eating whatever meat lay in their path, absorbing all the nutrients as the food passed through their bodies—a slow and horrible death for anyone swallowed alive.

Kyle knew he would never escape this beast once it locked onto him. It was far more agile than it looked. As its head swept around no more than ten or fifteen paces away, Kyle fingered the knife looped through the top of his pants. He almost laughed at the absurdity of trying to tackle one of these loathsome creatures with what amounted to a tiny pricking pin. But a sharp, stabbing pain in the roof of its mouth *might* help distract it while he scampered away . . .

As he lay there quaking in the mud, he realized the clacker was confused. It paused, its huge maw dripping thick gobs of saliva that glistened in the lightning. The head lowered, skimming across the grass, slowing when it neared Kyle but never quite locking onto him.

And then realization dawned. He was covered in mud. It was catching his scent but couldn't quite detect him.

Kyle took a chance and bolted. He could hide in a crack in the ground until it got bored, or he could outrun it. They moved fast, but they had to pause between lunges. And since there were no ruts or crevices in the grassy, waterlogged pasture, running was his only hope—either that or lying completely still until the clacker finally sniffed him out.

As soon as he started running, the clacker's head whipped around. It *knew* he was moving. Yet it still seemed unable to locate him, and it shrieked in frustration.

Shrieking was one thing. What issued from the clacker was deafening, but the concentrated wave of sonic vibrations was worse. Kyle felt those vibrations pass over his head, and he ducked and fell again, gasping as the blast arced like a stream of water from a hose.

The clacker came after him. In one single lunge, it was right behind him. Kyle veered right as a shriek nearly blew out his eardrums.

Lightning struck again, and a wall materialized out of the darkness ahead. It was an old stone wall surrounding a cemetery. Kyle scrambled over it just as another shriek pierced the air, this one accompanied by a sonic blast. A round section of the wall behind him blew apart, and Kyle once more fell flat on his face as debris and chunks of stone showered him. He was pummeled and spattered as he lay there in the grass protecting his head.

The clacker lunged through the hole and paused three feet away from him, steaming in the cold rain. The stench was awful.

Kyle lay in the mud next to a gravestone, covered with bits of rock and wet dust, his own scent effectively masked, the top of his knapsack resting on the back of his head. Refusing to budge, he waited with his eyes clamped shut. If the clacker picked up his scent and shrieked, his brain would be scrambled.

Worse, it might swallow him whole *without* first turning his brain to mush.

It was the longest twenty seconds of his life.

Then, its grunts and moans revealing its disappointment, the clacker slid forward and continued across the graveyard. Kyle's eyes were open again now, and he watched with awe and terror as the monster's slick body lunged, paused, then lunged again, leaving behind a rounded indentation that quickly filled with rainwater.

A minute later, the clacker reached the far side of the cemetery and shrieked its way through the wall.

Kyle wasn't sure he could get any wetter, dirtier, or colder than he was right now, but all he felt was elation. He was still alive! Climbing to his feet, he stood trembling with exhaustion and emotion before stumbling away from the cemetery and down the slope of a hill. He no longer cared if he was still heading east; he only wanted to find a safe place to cower and sleep.

Several more shrieks in the night reminded him that the canyon clackers were everywhere. Every so often he caught sight of one as lightning flickered, but now he was vigilant and determined not to let them close in on him again. When he saw one sliding by ahead, he lay down flat and wriggled in the mud, turning over and over before lying still to watch it, barely breathing. He wished he was still plastered with dust from the collapsed wall, but the rain continued to pour and was even now rinsing the mud off his back.

Now that he had a chance to lie still, looking down on the landscape from the brow of a hill, he waited for the lightning and spotted something behind the pastures. It was like a break in the terrain, a dark, wide crack. It took a few more brilliant flashes of light to show him that he was looking at a river stretching from north to south.

He groaned. As if he wasn't drenched enough, now he had to swim as well?

The river could wait until morning. He could, at the very least, find a place to sleep at the bottom of the hill. He saw several squat buildings along the riverbanks. Any one of them would do.

Weary, ready to drop, he stumbled down the hill and toward a tiny stone cottage with half the roof missing. He didn't care. Any shelter at all would be a welcome relief. The door was wide open, and he plunged into the darkness. He had no light, no way to look around the place and check it out, no way of knowing if there were dangerous critters waiting for him.

He threw down his knapsack, collapsed against a wall, sank to the floor, and rolled onto his side, aware that the knife was pressing against his thigh but too tired to do anything about it.

*Chapter 31*
**Logan**

It was dusk. Another city awaited him out past the ruins. Logan drew in the chilly air. The sky had continued darkening and the stacked clouds had become more imposing. Abe had been right. While he had only a drizzle to deal with now, he was about to get rained upon and badly.

He looked back at the entrance to the tower, wondering if Kyle was still there. He thought he might be. Was he also caught up in the enormity of it all? He knew his doppelganger couldn't hear him, but he had to say it. "Keep watch over Kiff. Try to help him. If Abe is right and you hold such power, then change his fate. Don't let the Breaker take him. I will do the same for your brother if I am able." His cheeks grew flush. It had been the most he had spoken since entering the Broken Lands. And he was talking to an audience of none.

He gravitated to the wagon, eyeing the broken harness that had been attached to the hustle. Blood splattered the ground. Hopefully, the kalibacks had dragged their kill back to their lair and wouldn't return. A hustle had to be enough to feed a large pack.

He searched the wagon and found nothing but a blanket. He tied it to his satchel, amazed that objects from Kyle's reality were real and substantial to him. The wagon, on the other hand, judging from its hodge-podge construction, had to be a product of those who lived in the wastelands. Did that mean it existed in both worlds? He looked back at the Tower.

Rain poured, the dark skies finally opening up to deliver on their promise.

His gaze traveled to a space close to the tall grasses to the east. The rain warped, driven away from a select volume. The shape that hollowed itself out of the sheets of rain was human. Kyle. Logan saw the vague outline of an arm lift and displace the torrential rain. Logan returned the gesture. He watched as the grasses parted and the boy, his counterpart, began his quest.

Logan marched into the meadow carpeting the western side of the hill, his thoughts on what he would say to his new family.

\* \* \*

The rain didn't let up. He had been traveling for a better part of the night and was exhausted. The intense revelations at the Tower felt so distant, a lifetime ago when it had in fact only been hours.

He moved across a wide street, attracted to a column of smoke beyond the next ridge that rose up in defiance of the storm. Would he find people willing to help him reach Apparati? Would all of them be wearing strange metallic trappings like Abe? If so, would any of them use their 'tech' on him? He knew he was in a no-go zone, where both magic and technology were out of phase with their worlds, but how far would he have to travel away from the Tower before he was fully phased into this brave new world.

Right now, it wasn't a far cry from the Broken Lands—more and more ruins and the spread of plant life into the abandoned landscape.

The column of smoke had to be a simple fire, probably a campfire. So he was more than likely still too close to the Tower.

He huffed, spraying water ahead of himself from the rain that had been running rivulets down his lips and chin. Downpours like this were not good. If it kept up much longer, it would soften the ground to such an extent that the canyon clackers could burrow more freely and venture out from their rocky canyon home. Were there even such creatures here in the west? Or were there even scarier threats? He wished he had asked Abe about the possibility of kalibacks or any other sizeable predators on this side of the Tower. Why hadn't he picked up his knife? He was completely weaponless.

As he splashed through the growing puddles, he searched for a stick or length of pipe to arm himself. He wandered toward a storefront, keeping an eye on the column of smoke. Through the large smudged display window, Logan spied a long wooden handle, maybe a broom or some other tool.

He pressed his back against the stone front of the store, happy that the overhang above shielded him from the rain for the moment. The door stood half open. He scoped out the street. Relieved to see nothing bearing down on him, he sidled toward the entrance.

With his left boot, he kicked the door open and stole inside. He hopped over a toppled set of shelves, amazed that there were a few goods arranged neatly on several standing dust-free shelves farther in. He lurched over another pile of debris and fingered the wooden staff. Logan pulled it close to see it was a broom with its bristles intact. He snapped the cleaning head off, tossing it into the pile of rubble, and stared at its now ragged tip. With a little whittling, he could easily narrow it to a deadly point.

Lightning streaked outside, delivering a brief flash of light to the store's dark interior.

Logan stiffened. An old woman stood behind a long table, her back to a door leading deeper into the store. Had she been there before?

His eyes quickly adjusted. The person stepped closer, keeping the table between them.

"Really saddened to see you breaking my merchandise, son. One doesn't come by intact brooms so easily out here."

It was an old woman, her hair long and straggly and laden with detritus. She was missing a tooth, her skin a motley collection of blemishes. She wore a long filthy apron. In her hand, the woman waved a long sickle, its blade glaringly clean.

She saw his eyes track the movement of the sickle. "And it's not like you have much to trade for it, unless you got some choice goodies in that satchel of yours. Let me see it." She thrust her free hand at him. Black grime festered under her unkempt nails.

Logan backed toward the door.

"Uh-uh, wouldn't do that if I were you. Gus is just outside dying for you to try and escape. Hand it over." Her eyes were feverish and impatient. She motioned for him to transfer the satchel to her grubby hand.

"Are you a deadbeat?"

She laughed. "We all are out here, sweetie." She inspected him. "Although, from how cleaned up you are, I guess that makes you a new member of our fine club. Seeing as you're so fresh to this world, I'll go easy on you. Hand over the bag, and maybe I can talk Gus into only slicing off one of your arms. Nice filled-out limb like yours should have enough meat on the bone to keep us nourished for a while." She snickered.

Logan saw a shadow pass over the window outside. A big shadow. Gus.

*No escape out the front.* He'd take his chances getting past the crazed woman, hoping for a back exit.

"This is a store?"

"It is. It's my trading post. Got folks from all over coming to sample my wares." She waved a hand at the poorly stocked shelves. While they were tidy, their contents were meager. She moved around the far end of the table.

"You cleaned out and arranged only the back part, why?" Would the table support his weight. It looked none too sturdy. He nervously thrummed his fingers along the length closest to him. Her eyes darted to the movement. He wanted her to think he was nervous. His leg knocked against the table, bucking it upward. She would interpret the move as a result of his apprehension when it really told him the table was not heavy.

"Appearances. People come to my store by invitation only. Keeping the section up by the window all amuck gives the impression the place has been gone over, already picked clean." Her face soured. "But that didn't deter you. Had your eyes on a fine broom, did you?"

Gus shoved his weight through the door. He stooped to fit his tall frame through and grunted at the old woman. She shooed him and talked sweetly to him. "Not in here, Gus. Let me get him to rabbit. I'd prefer if you're going to gut him, you spill his nasty blood out on the sidewalk. A girl has to keep up appearances. What would it say to have these fine floorboards stained red?"

Gus grunted.

Logan tensed. If he used the table, he could spring toward the back door. A storeroom had to be on the other side. "Not much for words."

"Yeah, there's that. Poor Gus had his tongue cut out by a rival gang of deadbeats." She paused, lost in a memory. "That was Archie's fault. Still hold him responsible for that."

"I'll let Archie know you still hold a grudge if I see him." Logan held up the broom and jerked it at the door, wanting them to believe he was going to try to get past Gus.

She cackled. "Oh that's rich. Afraid that's not gonna happen. Word came down from his wife, lovely woman, really can stitch up just about any injury, that's he's not taking visitors. Fool stabbed himself while out hunting. Colleen came racing in a few hours ago. Really had her hustle in a lather. I don't like seeing people push their animals so. Not at all humane." She twirled the sickle. "His prospects for this world aren't looking too good. She couldn't afford what I was asking for the medicine. And it's not like she'd dare take it from me."

Time for Logan to say goodbye to the crazy shopowner and her stooge. He vaulted over the table, hearing it crack as he pushed off it. He tucked his legs up into his torso to avoid the wide swing of the sickle. The woman flew at him with far more speed than seemed possible.

He scattered the contents of the organized shelves, grabbing a faded bag that turned out to be heavier than it looked.

Logan plunged through the back door and straight into the open maw of a canyon clacker, its bulk filling almost every square inch of the doorway.

He paused, unable to process what he was seeing. There was no entry tunnel leading from the ground into the building. The long monstrous worm just lay in the middle, not even waving its head about in alarm over Logan's presence. Canyon clackers hunted by movement. And surely he had the beast's attention. He slipped farther to his left, moving each limb in slow motion.

The smell was what he noticed first. Then his eyes trailed along the length of the creature, registering the numerous spears and other weapons buried in the creature's hide.

It was dead.

The old woman and Gus stormed into the back room. "Ah, looks like you snuck a peek at my latest addition. Gus and some others dragged that sorry sucker in. Thing was all by its lonesome, no parent around to defend it."

She was right. While impressive in size, it was a young canyon clacker.

Gus moved toward him as the rattle of the rain on the roof above increased. Logan looked up, distracted by the noise. His stomach lurched.

"How long ago? How long ago did you bring it in here?"

"Couple days. Why? What do you care?"

He felt the floor under them vibrate. "Has it rained since then?"

Gus was almost on him. Logan swatted the broom at the oversized deadbeat. The mute warrior smiled and pressed forward.

"What? Why?" she said.

Logan snapped, "Tell me! Has it rained since you killed this thing and dragged it inside?"

"Not a lick. Been having a dry spell, you could say," the old woman replied. "That's why this fella's going to fetch a pretty penny. His licular glands are full of delicious syrup, especially in one so young. With a little fermenting, we've got ourselves a huge supply of grade-A wine."

How could someone who knew the properties of the clackers' glands be so foolish as to house a fallen one in her back room? He shook his head. Greed must have clouded her judgment, otherwise she would not have taken the risk. "You idiot! Don't you know they're intensely loyal, that they come back for their young, dead or alive?"

The floor under them buckled and shot upward.

Logan yelled, "The only thing keeping its parents from gathering it up was no rain! They don't like the sun. It dries them out. This storm, that's all it takes. You've brought the whole family down on you." He leapt toward a metal ladder running up a nearby stone wall, not caring where it went as long as he could climb it.

The old woman realized too late what he was saying. An adult clacker shot up behind her and slammed its open jaws down. Logan scaled the ladder as he watched the floor of the building turn into water, its once solid foundation pulverized by the sonic screams emitted by the two canyon clackers that now rose up and encircled their dead brethren.

Logan waved for Gus to make his way toward him and the ladder, but the dumb brute threw himself atop the nearest clacker, driving a long blade into the beast's thick hide.

That was when the screaming began.

*Chapter 32*
## Kyle

Kyle woke shivering. His clothes were still sodden, so he knew he hadn't been asleep long, just enough to revive himself and deal with the immediate problem of getting dry and warm.

It was still night. It had stopped raining, though the clouds were so heavy that the moons were hidden and unable to give him a clue as to the approximate time. He stepped outside and stood looking down the grassy bank at the river just a few yards away. He could barely see it in the dark, but he heard it clearly as it gushed and gurgled over rocky outcrops. Across the other side he saw a strange spectacle—ghostly auras floating around near the water, some of them pale blue, others green, another bright yellow. Fascinated, he stared for a long time as they moved in the gloom, flitting about like oversized fireflies.

It was hard to judge their size, but most of them looked slightly smaller than people. He hadn't noticed them earlier, but it had been pouring, and he'd been dead on his feet. Maybe they hadn't been out then. In any case, they were everywhere now.

He sighed. Were they dangerous? To continue his journey would mean crossing the river and walking right through the apparitions. *No way.*

Looking left and right, he quickly realized there was no way he was going to get around these phantoms. They lined the riverbank as far as he could see, sometimes darting toward the water—and then halting suddenly, bouncing back. Although they floated in the air, they seemed afraid of the river.

Kyle knew he had to cross and move on. But how? The water was moving too fast to swim, and it looked too deep to wade. There were rocks here and there—or perhaps piles of debris from collapsed buildings along the banks—but there was no decent route across, no handy stepping stones.

On the other side, the grassy bank sloped upward. There were more squat buildings lurking in the darkness, but he was unable to see over the hill. A little farther downstream he saw woodland. Upstream was crowded with buildings.

"There have to be bridges," he muttered. *Or maybe not. They probably crumbled away hundreds of years ago.*

How had Logan made it across?

The idea of his twin traversing the river gave him hope. However, being a city-dweller, Kyle wasn't used to this kind of terrain. Hiking in the city meant visiting a park and taking one of the winding trails through the trees—but all those trails were paved and fenced. There were no natural dangers anywhere that he could think of. There were rivers but none as fast flowing. And there were footbridges everywhere.

Suddenly annoyed at this obstacle, he edged through the long grass toward the river's edge. Though he was careful, he still plunged knee-deep into the cold, swirling water. He gasped but held steady and took another step so that he was standing with both feet in the river.

He could feel the current tugging at him. How far across was the other side? Fifty feet? More?

"You're gonna die," he told himself, and began wading out.

When he was waist-deep, it was so cold he found it hard to catch his breath. The riverbed sucked at his feet, and he started worrying that he'd lose a shoe. Meanwhile, the current pushed and pulled, twisting around him, forcing him to stagger.

Then his foot caught and he toppled forward. The river picked him up and carried him along, and Kyle splashed frantically, trying to plant his feet in the mud and avoid being pulled into deeper waters. It wasn't working. He changed tactics, lunging for the far side. The unrelenting river pulled him back again, sweeping him faster downstream.

By sheer luck, he slammed into a pile of rocks that stuck out of the water. He stubbed his toe and scraped his knee, but suddenly he was stationary, defying the river's will. He climbed out of the water and perched there on his tiny island.

"Great," he huffed.

He was two-thirds of the way across the river. He'd made progress at least.

The ghosts were still there, much closer now. He stared at them, seeing that each color had a distinctive form. They stared back, clearly aware of his presence. The largest glowed a fiery red, long tusks sticking out of its head and smaller tusks curling up from its cheeks. It looked twice Kyle's height, a mean-looking thing that seemed to radiate hostility. Only . . .

Kyle frowned. This phantom looked eager. Hungry.

He shivered, and not just from the icy cold water. Tearing his gaze from the spirit creatures, he looked around, wondering how to get out of his predicament—and which way to go. He *had* to continue east, but the thought of walking among the ghosts gave him chills. Could they harm him? Or were they as insubstantial as the wind?

*Even the wind can do real damage*, an inner voice muttered.

Stranded as he was, he had no choice but to slip carefully back into the water. This time he would be in control, heading for the bank instead of—

The current tore him off the island, and he went under. Fighting the panic, he felt for the riverbed, then struck for the surface instead. It seemed ages before he rose high enough to break through and suck in air. When he did, his fingers brushed against the low-hanging branch of a bent and twisted tree. He grasped it, not caring that it cut into his palm. He found himself dangling sideways, swept downstream by the river but hanging in place, fighting for a grip with his other hand.

When he did, he was able to crawl along the branch to the bank. Finding solid ground under his feet at last, he staggered up the grassy, boggy bank—and straight into the wall of ghosts.

They gave him no time to recover. Something engulfed him immediately, a shimmering pale green light, and he bucked in panic at the feeling of being smothered. He rolled over and crawled away, but the phantom rolled and crawled with him as though it were somehow attached, sticking to his body. "Get off me!" he yelled.

He had the strangest feeling that something was in the bushes just a stone's throw away. A shuffler, and a big one at that. Suddenly hungry, Kyle forgot about the aura that was enveloping him. It hardly seemed important anymore. What *was* important was the shuffler—his meal.

He got up and felt for his—Logan's—knife. It was right there, tucked into his belt loop. He drew it while darting through the grass. He couldn't figure out how he knew it, but the shuffler was just yards away, slinking through the undergrowth. Kyle was aware of the phantom surrounding his body, somehow part of him now, urging him on while nudging him from side to side, forcing him to duck and weave as if it instinctively knew how to intercept the scampering shuffler.

Kyle pounced. He could hear voices of reason in the back of his mind screaming at him to stop and take back control of his body, but there was also a strange and wonderful sense of power as he leapt over the bush with his knife held high.

He came down right on top of the shuffler. It was almost as long as his own body, its silvery grey armored body sleek and rounded, its tail fat and powerful. Kyle knew where to strike. As he landed heavily on the creature's back, the blade of his knife sank into the small unprotected area in the side of its neck where the body armor ended and the hard narrow head protruded. There was a gap filled only with muscle and flesh. It had to be that way or the shuffler would not be able to turn its head. Kyle plunged the knife all the way in, and the creature died instantly.

Panting, he stared at his meal and was suddenly repulsed and angered. "Get off me!" he yelled to the phantom within. He backed away from the shuffler. With a moan of effort, he got to his feet and staggered into a clearing—and shucked off the spirit.

It tumbled away from him, a man-shaped apparition with a long snout and horns, vicious razor-sharp teeth, and hideous flaps of skin behind its ears that puffed out as it twisted around to face him. It still glowed green, but more softly now. The creature stared at him, hovering there while Kyle stared back. Its head tilted to one side.

Then a flurry of activity distracted him. A horde of phantoms came out of nowhere, zipping toward him, most of them pale green but a couple that were blue and one a fiery red. He stumbled backward, but a green ghost with ugly tentacles around its waist hissed and reached him before any of the others.

As before, the spirit engulfed him and took advantage of his shock. It was like having a bucket of cold water thrown over him. Unable to react with anything other than a gasp, he stood there numbly while the aura surrounded him. All the other spirits veered away, barking and hissing their annoyance.

"What do you want with me?" Kyle moaned.

He turned and ran. He needed to get away from these things, and he knew exactly how. There were dozens of hiding places in the immediate vicinity, places where even these spirits wouldn't find him if he managed to shake them off. He darted between trees with phantoms on his tail. He could hear them back there making frantic barking noises, wails of frustration, and savage hissing.

But the noise decreased as he tore through the woods and up a slope. He was heading east, and with all the adrenaline pumping through him, he was sure he could run all the way to the enclaves. With a hiss, his passenger made it clear that *fleeing* was not the plan. The plan was *hiding*. And before he knew it, before he was even aware of what he was doing, he found himself sliding under a fallen tree and scooting up into its rotten, hollowed-out trunk.

He lay there panting, sweating from the exertion but already beginning to shiver in his cold, damp hiding place.

"No!" he growled, and slid back out. Hiding was one thing, but cowering like a rodent in a disgusting, rotten, filthy hidey-hole was too much. "Get out! OUT!"

And, as before, he ejected the phantom. It tumbled away, shook itself, and turned back to him with an intense look of surprise on its creepy subhuman face.

Kyle picked himself up. "Leave me alone," he said firmly.

To his surprise, he found the knife still grasped in his hand. Tucking it away, he brushed himself down and started walking, realizing only then that he'd left his knapsack behind. He shook his head, annoyed with himself. He hadn't given it a moment's thought when he'd stepped into the river. Still, what had he lost? A blanket and a cup? And a small pocketknife, though Logan's was far better.

Well, he wasn't going back. He'd miss the cup, and would probably miss the blanket, but could make do without either. He wasn't tackling that river again, especially with those phantoms lurking around the place. Those *spirits*.

*No more weirdness*. Those phantom-spirit things were tenacious but no match for him. He could shove them out when he put his mind to it. Maybe he could stop them from entering in the first place if he kept his wits about him.

As he resumed his trek east, picking his way through the woods, he became aware of a commotion behind him. Swinging around, he saw too late the fiery red glow of the tusked monster bearing down on him, its tiny, deep-set eyes full of anger.

When it engulfed him, he tripped and fell, banging his head on something hard. The feeble nighttime light faded into blackness as he slipped away.

*Chapter 33*
**Logan**

The clackers made short work of poor Gus. Logan felt bad for the deadbeats. But their fates had been sealed the moment they had taken the infant creature.

He crouched along a metal walkway, having exited onto the suspended structure from the ladder only moments ago. He didn't move a muscle. If the clackers sensed him, they'd rocket toward him. Could they reach that high? Three stories above the carnage and shrouded in darkness should be enough to ensure his safety. The rain thundered against the roof just above his head. This close, it was impossible to hear anything else.

He squinted, detecting the movement of the great beasts. Did they know he was up here? *Take yours and go,* he thought, attempting to broadcast the directive. He had his own family member to save. If he did his job and Kyle did his, then Byron and Kiff would be safe.

Logan wanted to leave, to soldier on, knowing time was of the essence, but couldn't. They'd detect any movement and pounce. He had to wait for the clackers to deal with their dead first.

Lightning flashed, flooding the room with light. The adult clackers were tunneling into the ground, preparing a wide exit for their lifeless offspring.

Logan choked down his sadness, empathy flooding through him for the giant worms.

He waited. Three more flashes of lightning allowed him to witness the worms at work. The smaller clacker nudged the fallen one onto its mate's back. With care, the adult carried its dead into the tunnel.

When Logan was certain they were gone, he retraced his steps along the swaying metal walkway, descended the ladder, and exited the store.

As he hustled down the street, he peeked inside the sack he had grabbed. Several bottles and vials of medicine along with bandages and clean rags. He flashed to thoughts of what the woman had said about the Archie fellow. His wife had come looking for aid and been turned away by the cruel woman. *Hunting accident*, she had said.

The rain had lessened. And while it was now fully dark, he could still make out the column of smoke from the fire he had been heading toward earlier. *Archie's place.*

He thumbed through the supplies in the bag. Archie's place couldn't be too far away. He wasn't so much overtaken with the compulsion to help as the desire to find someone out in this wasteland that would help him. Would this Colleen person feed him or let him borrow a hustle if he brought her the medicine? Having a ride would help him reach Kyle's city much faster. Surely it was more than chance that had led him to grab the medicine. He strode toward the smoke with a fire in his belly. He was about to face off with another group of deadbeats. *Make it quick. You have Byron to save.*

He broke into a run, determined to find the good in the next person he met.

\* \* \*

It took longer than he expected to locate Archie's home. It had to be close to dawn. The storm had passed and the woods around the homestead were filling with the sounds of activity, nocturnal critters shaking their coats dry and settling back into their perches and hidey-holes after a long night of playing either predator or prey. Logan was thankful none of the emerging cries was the distinctive warble of a kaliback. Maybe they weren't as plentiful in the western part of the Broken Lands.

*211*

Below, the small two-story cabin sat nestled in a wide valley. Two young boys raced back and forth from the home to a large barn. It was awfully early to be up, but then again Logan also had early-morning chores. Why not those trapped out here in the wastelands? It looked like they had saddled a hustle and were arguing over something.

Thoughts of Kiff welled up inside. Arguing over the silliest of things had gotten them in trouble on numerous occasions. These brothers, despite living in such a dreadful place, weren't much different. Their dispute centered on who would ride. The younger boy dragged his smaller saddle back to the barn, disappointed he had not been allowed to drape it over the animal. They had to have more than one hustle. Why else have more than one saddle? He needed to be extra persuasive.

He had yet to see the mother or injured father. The old woman had said the wife, Colleen, was a doctor. Then she'd welcome his arrival, right?

He raced to a large rock, in full view of anyone looking for the briefest of seconds. *Maybe I should deliver the supplies to the two boys by the barn. Less contact with the ruthless adults of the ruins, the better.*

He shimmied along behind the rock, dropping to his belly and crawling to a standing ridge of stacked stones. The wall ran down to the corner of the barn, marking the boundary of a field that had seen better days. He wondered how successful this family had been with growing crops. Not very from the looks of the barren rows and weeded patches.

As he crept closer, snatches of the boy's conversation wafted through the fleeting night air.

"Mom won't let you go. You're too young."

The smaller boy, his long hair spilling from out of his large brown hat, waved a strange metal tool around, pointing it at his brother as if he were aiming a bow and arrow. "But I got me a weapon. This blaster will make short work of any creeps that try to take me down. Pow! Pow!" He danced around, pointing the tool at his brother.

Logan eyed the device. It was tech, not functioning as a result of the inhibitor working its magic back in Apparata.

The boy's brother kicked the useless weapon out of his hand, sending it flying. It clattered against the stone wall near Logan's head, and its hilt sunk into the soft mud at the wall's base.

"Please let me come. I can be a good lookout. I have a knack for spotting kalibacks."

His brother shrugged as he cinched the strap of the saddle to the hustle. The beast grunted in protest and waved a tusk vaguely at the boy. "You're more like a magnet for those things. Mom wants me to go. I can be to the Horner settlement in a day. They'll give us credit and hand over the medicine she needs for Dad."

"And if they don't?"

The younger boy's eyes played over the scabbard hanging from his brother's belt. A sword lying sheathed inside it.

His brother didn't answer. "Go get Mom. Tell her the rain's stopped and I'm setting out early. Need to get a jump on this."

The younger boy ran toward the cabin. "Okay, but you know she's not going to like that."

The boy disappeared inside. His older brother walked into the barn and returned with a large satchel. As he tied it to the pronounced horn of the saddle, Logan hopped up on the wall and stood as tall as he could muster.

The boy clicked his tongue but kept securing the satchel. "Wondering when you was going to pop out from behind there. I don't want any trouble." The boy freed a hand and dropped it close to his sword.

"I don't either. Heard your father was in a bad way."

The boy froze and glared at him. "Yeah, how'd you hear that? Only word we got out about Dad was to Crazy Cass and her dim-bulb son. Any friends of theirs aren't welcome here."

"I ran into them. Not very friendly." He opted not to fill the boy in on their fate. "I took something from them I thought you might need." He held up the bag.

"And what would that be?" The boy sauntered around the back of the hustle. "Can't say I'm seeing you in such a good light here. You sneak up, outright brag how you're a thief, and then want to share what you pillaged. How does that make any sense?"

Logan's mouth moved, but he didn't talk. The boy was right. Why should the boy trust him?

A door slammed, and a tall woman ran toward them, stringing an arrow into a long bow. Her face was flush with anger. "Step back from Clint now!"

Logan, still holding the bag, put his hands up. "I'm not here to hurt anyone."

"Don't trust him, Mom. Something's not right."

"I have medicine."

The woman's face softened for a second, then she squinted in suspicion at him. She drew nearer.

He threw the bag to the ground.

She slipped closer and leaned down to pick it up, lowering her bow to do so. "Guess if you're going to attack, now's a good time, stranger." She yanked open the bag, and her eyes went wide. Her slender fingers danced over the wealth of medicine within.

"I just came to give you that," Logan said. "I have to go now." He wanted to hop down and run off but feared an arrow in his back.

Colleen rose and stared at him, recognition flashing in her eyes. "It's you, the one who told me what happened to Archie. You came back. I thought you washed your hands of the whole thing."

Logan was confused. He had never seen her before, had he? No, that was impossible.

*214*

"Yesterday morning, when you happened by, you wouldn't lift a finger to help. Why now?"

It clicked. Kyle. He looked like Kyle, pretty much. This woman thought he *was* Kyle. He shrugged. "Change of heart."

She retreated, keeping her bow down and not drawing it up to take aim at him again. "Thank you. I think this will more than do the trick." She looked at her son. "You don't have to go. This boy provided what we need. Get inside and help your sister wash up your father. Megan shouldn't have to scrub him down herself, should she? I'll be in shortly."

"But, Mom . . ." The boy eyed Logan with mistrust.

"Go, I can handle myself here."

She watched him go inside. Once he was out of sight, Colleen looked at Logan with heartfelt sadness. "I am so sorry what Archie put you through. He told me every horrible detail. I suspected, but said nothing all these years. After all, he was doing his best."

Logan didn't know what she was talking about. What had happened to Kyle with this Archie character?

"Would you stay and eat with us? I have some leftover bread and some lettuce. It's not much, but it's yours."

"Yes, I'll take it—and a hustle as well! I have to be somewhere else."

Suddenly, the door to the cabin burst open and out spilled the younger brother. He ran toward his mom, all smiles. "Clint told me! We have medicine for Dad. You can fix him up."

He slammed into her leg and hugged it tight.

"Yes we can, Rourke. This young man came to our rescue. He's a hero."

Rourke raced over to Logan, arms outstretched. He smiled nervously, the boy's demeanor reminding him of Kiff's explosive enthusiasm.

Rourke skipped past him, picked up the weapon earlier knocked out of his clutches, and presented it to Logan. He

*215*

bowed slightly and tipped his hat. "Then you require a reward. Take this. Maybe you can get it to work."

Logan took the device and held it up. Clumps of mud slid off its shaft.

Rourke frowned. "Haven't you ever seen a blaster before?"

"Uh . . . sure I have."

Suddenly, a warbling roar tore through the still air. He turned to see a kaliback racing across the field of muck toward them.

He shouted at the family, "Run! Get inside!"

If he didn't act, there was no way they'd make it to the cabin. He tucked the useless weapon into his belt and gripped the long broom handle, bracing himself for a fight.

*Chapter 34*
**Kyle**

Kyle again woke to darkness. He groaned. Would this night never end? Wincing, he sat up and looked around.

Ghosts surrounded him.

"Go away," he muttered, although in truth he felt more intrigued than scared. "What do you *want* from me?"

Then he remembered something was in him. He climbed to his feet, trying to get a sense of the invader. Its feelings, its instincts, its knowledge . . . all seemed to filter through into his mind and body. This one was different from the others. The first had made him want to hunt, the second to flee and hide. This one . . . this one . . .

He realized he was trembling. It wasn't so much anger bubbling up inside as a simple need to let loose and *destroy*. But there was nothing here to destroy, and besides, he'd never been the strongest fourteen-year-old on the block. Yet he felt strong enough to pulverize a traffic droid, something many adult citizens of Apparati dreamed of and joked about.

Not wanting to hang around, he started to walk, aware that the phantoms eased through the air after him. They were silent except for a barely audible murmur.

He got it. Only one could take him over at a time. If he evicted this one, another would jump in. Well, that was only if he let it. But before he shoved this one out, he wanted to see what it could do. His fear and loathing had faded. Now curiosity had taken over.

When he emerged from the woods and found himself on the outskirts of an ancient town, the first building he came to was a three-story structure, mostly a shell smothered with moss and overrun with weeds. Shaking with dark, barely suppressed emotion, Kyle leapt at the wall and tore at it with his bare fingers.

It was ludicrous to think he could make a dent in the stone blocks, but the demon within him rose up and lent him strength, and to his astonishment he found that his flesh-and-blood fingers actually carved out chunks of stone. The masonry came away easily, and he attacked it with ferocity, watching almost from afar as his weak and feeble body did impossible damage to the building.

When he stopped, panting, he stood in a pile of debris that he'd scooped out of the wall. Staring in amazement at his fingers, he noted they were undamaged—dirty, yes, but somehow intact.

As gnarly as these ghosts were, he admitted to being impressed. Knowing that he could get rid of them at any time helped. And there seemed to be plenty wanting to ride with him.

He turned to study them. There were dozens, just hanging in the air, shoulder to shoulder. Many were like the first—the one that had made him hunt, its long snout and fangs suggesting that it was born to kill. There were quite a few of the ugly run-and-hide phantoms, too, with their hideous midriff tentacles.

But there were others: slim figures with nimble hands and huge round eyes; eerie serpentine creatures that undulated slowly in a weird, hypnotic and entrancing way; small, plump, furry critters with legs like stalks; and, perhaps the strangest of all, a single birdlike apparition that stood tall and slender with elegant wings spread loosely to its sides.

"Okay, guys," Kyle said nervously. "Who's next?"

The monster within seemed to boil with anger at the prospect of being evicted, and it clung to him, pressing against his frame as if there were a million tiny hands all over his body.

"Out," Kyle ordered.

Even before he'd uttered his command, the invader was flung wide. It screeched, then turned and barked angrily, shoving its tusks forward.

"Yeah, yeah," Kyle said. He focused on the rest of the phantoms as they eagerly surged forward. He wanted to choose the creature with the wings, but one of the slim figures with round eyes nipped in first, diving at his midsection a split second ahead of the rest. All the other apparitions recoiled as though it were a repulsive deed to occupy a host at the same time as another.

*A host*, Kyle thought as the creature wormed its way into his body. *Is that what I am? A host for these lost souls?*

It wasn't entirely unpleasant once he got used to it. He remembered how his younger brother, as a toddler, had climbed all over his lap and dug his elbows in his chest as he fidgeted around. Allowing this phantom to take up residence was rather like waiting patiently while a toddler got comfortable—sharp stabs of pain along with a lot of pushing and shoving. But there was also a strange, cool sensation, an icy grip like freezing water being poured into his body through a hole in his chest. The sensation passed, though, and half a minute later he had a new companion.

"So what can *you* do?" he asked quietly.

Once the spirit had settled into his body, the compulsion to tidy up the mess he'd made of the building quickly overcame him, and he found himself stooping to pick up chunks of stone. He shook his head, bemused. Really? This spirit actually thought it could put the wall back together?

His mouth fell open when the rock he placed against the wall stuck there. It had no business staying put, but there it was—a curious lump sticking out from the huge indentation in the stone wall. He picked up another rock, then another, and placed them in seemingly random places, where they stuck. He quickly came to the conclusion that he could do this all day, replacing bits of the wall, inexplicably fitting them in the exact right place and making them stick.

"All right, all right," he muttered. "So you can build. One of you breaks things, the other builds it back up. Great." He studied the fanged monster with the snout and single horn. "You're a hunter." He looked again at the ugly tentacle monster. "And you run and hide. What are you, a coward? Or . . . just really good at slipping about undetected?" He nodded thoughtfully. That talent could come in useful when he arrived at the enclave.

The possibilities were opening up. These phantoms would be amazing pets if he could get them to come with him. It seemed like the ones who had been inside him already hung closer than the others. Maybe they were trained to some degree—broken in the way hustles were when bested by a determined rider. If he were to try each and every spirit . . .

He evicted the gentle builder and turned his attention to the winged creature. Again, one of the others leapt in—this time a serpentine creature that gave him the creeps. When it settled, Kyle stood there trying to make sense of what he was feeling. After a while he shook his head, confused. "Am I missing something? What do you do exactly? What's your thing?"

The spirit murmured gently, but Kyle couldn't understand it. He shrugged it off, finding it easier and easier to slip in and out of these things. There were only two kinds left—the small, furry critter on stalk legs, and the elegant bird-like spirit that seemed to regard him with amusement.

"Your turn," he said to one of the furry creatures, raising his hand to ward off the others. To his surprise, that actually worked. As he swept his hand around, the spirits backed up. It wasn't so much his hand as his intent that forced them away. With his mind alone, he could—

Realization dawned, and he mentally slapped his head as the furry critter bounded into his body. Of course. This was Logan's talent. Or rather, this was Logan's *failed* talent, the equivalent of Kyle's useless implant. Abe had said their powers would become evident. This was Kyle's. Controlling these spirits was his gift.

"Okay, my friend, what's your game?" he asked, unable to control his excitement. "What can you do?"

His guest—the furry critter with legs like stalks—seemed as useless as the last. Growing a little worried, Kyle scoured his mind and body for a hint of what this spirit's purpose was. Surely it could do *something*.

But nothing happened. There was no urge to hunt or break or fix, and certainly no urge to run and hide. There was nothing at all. Sighing, he ordered the spirit out and watched with amusement as it shot away, twisting and turning until it righted itself and hovered there, a strange, ghostly presence.

"Okay, now you," Kyle said, turning to the bird creature. "I hope you can do more than the last two guys."

When the spirit entered, it took him over more gently than the others. He felt a strange sensation on his back as huge phantom wings spread out. To his surprise, they moved when he wanted them to, flapping gently and leaving curls of translucent vapor. He spread them wide and looked upward. The storm clouds had wrung themselves out and dispersed, and the sky was brightening, turning orange to the west. The urge to soar into that clear sky overcame him. "I get it," he said, nodding. "You're a bird and you want to fly. Well, sorry, but I'm just a mere human. You should—"

With a gasp, he realized his feet had left the ground.

Without any effort, he floated up into the air. His phantom wings were moving but hardly enough to warrant this kind of lift—or any kind of lift at all. And besides, the phantom was *immaterial*. It had no substance. How could it drag him into the air like this?

"Put me . . ." he started, but trailed off, knowing he didn't want to be put down at all. As he rose above the rooftop, above the trees, his heart nearly pounded out of his chest. "This isn't happening," he moaned.

But it was. The ancient town spread out below, and the landscape all around was revealed to him. There were buildings everywhere, all empty and broken. Woodlands and grassy hills. Streams and ponds. The river he'd crossed during the night, somehow flat and still from up high, a mirrored surface. The crisscrossing trails left behind by the canyon clackers as they slipped and slid across the pastures. In the distance to the west, he saw the Tower rising high and gleaming in the sunlight. To the north and south, the land ended at the sea where vast expanses of water took his breath away. The world was enormous, and yet so empty.

To the far west, the city of Apparati was strangely absent as though the high-rise buildings were lost in a haze of smog. Kyle knew he was simply out of sync with that reality now. He saw only the ancient Ruins all the way to the distant coast. The city didn't exist to him anymore. His parents, his younger brother—all were gone.

To the far east . . .

Kyle gasped. The enclaves were there in the distance. He'd seen them from the Tower, but this was different. Now they were closer, and he was much higher. The land spread out all around, filled with mountains, forests, sporadic clusters of buildings, and several enclaves around the coast. And he had a bird's-eye view of it all.

"I can fly," he said simply.

The notion of being able to soar through the sky for the rest of his journey, of not having to trudge over hills anymore, filled him with relief. Suddenly, the spirits were more than useful pets. They were his friends, to be honored. They could give him so much, but he needed to earn their respect and had no idea how.

"What do you want from me?" he wondered aloud as the spirit began to glide east. The world eased by below.

The spirit said nothing. Kyle thought he saw the others darting along the ruined streets, struggling to keep up. Would they follow him to the enclaves?

He hoped so. He was going to need their help.

*Chapter 35*
**Logan**

The kaliback splashed toward Logan, slowed by the muddy expanse of the open field. Its long armored tail swayed back and forth.

*Keep the creature busy, lead it on a merry chase. Maybe land a few jabs with the broom.* Not much of a plan, but it was all he had time for.

He risked a glance back at the cabin. The door was shut, but Colleen was still outside, hoisting a ladder against the high roof of the dwelling. She scrambled up onto the roof, which was beginning to steam in the dawn sun. What was she doing?

Logan spun around to face the kaliback, yelling over his shoulder at the top of his lungs. "Get inside! They're good climbers!"

He heard no reply.

His eyes fell on the open barn door. Maybe he could lead it in there and trap it. The doors were large and possibly heavy. It was worth a try.

Logan took off toward the barn, screaming at the kaliback to draw its attention. It was at least two hundred yards away if not more. He thought he could make it to safety in time.

The predator's gaze drilled into him, filling him with unease. Beside Logan, the saddled hustle bolted, shooting off for parts unknown. Not that the creature would've drawn the kaliback's attention with a human around.

Logan swept past the barn door. Extending his free hand, he almost yanked the door closed but thought better of it. He wanted to lure the kaliback into the barn's tight quarters. Closing the door might cause it to give up the hunt and go for the more obtainable prey.

His attention turned to the interior of the barn. Darkness swallowed almost everything around him. He could make out a crude loft and a pen filled with durgles, all clucking and fussing about, rattled by the predator outside.

He pitched forward, splaying his hands outward in case an obstacle came up suddenly.

A shriek erupted outside. It came from the kaliback. What had it so upset? The creature's utterances were sing-song, distressed.

The door hung open, his view slight but enough.

Atop the roof, the woman fished for an arrow from her quiver. She held the bow out, clearly adept with the weapon.

Struggling in the mud outside of the barn door was the kaliback, two arrows sticking out from its shoulders. It pawed at the deeply embedded shafts, unable to remove either. The woman fired another arrow, missing the beast's head by inches. She shouted at Logan, but the beast's keening made it impossible for him to hear her.

He clapped his hands, drawing the predator to the barn's threshold.

The animal slunk into the barn, glaring at its easier prey. *One that doesn't have the higher ground or a long-distance weapon*, Logan thought.

"Come and get me! Yah!" He waved the broom about as he backed to his right.

The hay-matted floor of the barn was far less sloppy. The kaliback marched toward him, its determination revealed in its confident warble and easy-placed, stalking gait.

If only he had the power to call down another Breaker on the animal. Where was Abe when he needed him? A whole squadron of spirits could be crashing down on his attacker if the old man truly cared. He had done it back at the river. Then again, Abe had mentioned an inhibitor of some kind, its magic extending out from the city of Apparati, reaching as far east as that very same river. Logan was now in a spirit-free zone. Abe couldn't conjure spirits even if he tried.

The kaliback flexed the spikes lining its hindquarters.

Logan shuffled left, knowing he needed a better angle to dart behind the predator and rush out the narrow opening behind the creature. *Just need to bring it a little farther in.*

His thoughts flickered back to the no-go zone. He couldn't use any spirits anyway. What had Abe said? As he treaded toward Apparati, his powers to manipulate tech would manifest. He yanked the blaster out of his belt loop, slipping his forefinger against the small lever situated near its hilt. The young boy had played with it, pretending to fire . . . what? The device didn't look long enough to house any arrows. Did it fire some other type of projectile? Was he far enough away from Apparata's tech inhibitor for this strange weapon to work? Abe had said he would come upon a line of fallen tech, unmoving and unable to be stirred. Had he passed it and not noticed? If he hadn't, could he override the inhibitor and force the tech to work? Could he be that powerful?

The kaliback growled, pawing the ground and casting a wary glance around the barn's interior. It didn't like hunting in such an enclosed space. But Logan was running out of time. The beast was angling to use its tail.

He focused on the weapon, willing it to hum to life. He wasn't wholly sure how to activate it but thought tech control had to be mental, much like the commandeering of spirits. He tugged on the small lever, producing a series of clicks. Anger washed over him. A thin groove along the length of the weapon's shaft lit up then died.

Encouraged, he concentrated even more as he moved farther back into the barn. His brow furrowed, and he bit down on his bottom lip, pushing commanding thoughts at the tech. It again lit up, and he felt the hilt vibrate. He clasped it tighter and drew it up to point at the kaliback.

An arrow flew in through the narrow door and broke against a wooden support beam near the kaliback, drawing its eyes away from him.

Logan raced toward the door, his concentration split between escape and keeping the weapon powered up. He felt an energy spilling out from the weapon and up his arm. Was this how it felt to be tethered? Was he binding himself with this tech? In an instant, the knowledge of how to operate the blaster flooded into his mind. He embraced it, finding strength in the logic and science behind the weapon and its link to him.

The kaliback's tail, all twelve impressive feet of it, swept toward him. Instead of evading it, he swung the blaster toward the fast-approaching appendage and pulled the trigger. A fiery orange beam of light shot out and cleaved the tail clean off the animal. The kaliback rolled on its back and howled.

Logan pictured the settings menu of the blaster in his head. Despite never having seen such a thing before, he intuitively understood what he was looking at. His mind filled with a glowing rectangle. Lines were hatched through it at regular intervals demarking what he interpreted as power levels. Suddenly, details about the beam width and whether he wanted to stun or decimate his target flooded his mind. The farther along the rectangular bar, the deadlier the result. With a natural ease he nudged the level to the upper end.

In a split second, he re-aimed and fired at the beast's head. The beam again shot out of the blaster's shaft. Logan heard a sizzle, and the head disappeared, leaving a stump. The creature's legs twitched, and its abdomen erupted in a flurry of mini-quakes, then it stilled. An acrid stench of burnt flesh filled the barn. He coughed and stumbled out of the barn.

Already, the woman was off the roof and running toward him. "What did you do?'

Logan stood, his head throbbing. The connection to the blaster disappeared and his head felt the worst for it. He waved the gun at his side. "I don't . . . I used this . . . blaster. Took its tail and head off. It's dead."

He dropped to his knees, flinging the broom and the blaster to the side and slumping forward. What little food remained in his stomach emptied onto the ground.

Her face was white, her eyes wide. "You shouldn't have been able to do that. Tech doesn't work here."

Rourke barreled up behind his mother and swatted at Logan. "I saw the whole thing. You made it work!"

Logan wiped his mouth and stood. He retrieved the blaster and his makeshift spear and eyed Archie's family. The older boy stood at the doorway, uncertain whether to approach.

Colleen slipped up to the barn entrance and sized up the situation within. She looked back at Logan, newfound respect and awe across her face. "It's dead all right."

"I-I have to go. I can't stay." He took several steps away from them.

Rourke looked at him expectantly. The boy's eyes darted to the blaster.

Logan handed it to him. "It's yours."

The boy pushed it back at him. "Not anymore. Doesn't work for me." He tapped the back of his neck. "I'm too young for an implant. Anyway, I was born out here and not in the city," he said with a hint of pride.

"Take it. I fear you will need it again." Rourke's mother stepped up behind her exuberant son and slipped her hands gently around his shoulders.

"Thanks," Logan offered and gave a quick salute. He turned and broke into an easy jog, invigorated at what he had done. He had manipulated tech, and if the woman could be believed, far sooner than was possible. What did that mean?

He stuck to the grassy stretches, steering clear of the large tracts of boot-sucking mud in the open fields and the claustrophobic woods.

He passed by a large lake to his left, avoiding its shore when he saw two morribies. Both looked slick with sweat and tired. If these fast-moving animals were winded, that meant they were on the run. Was there a predator about nearby? He held fast to his new weapon, his assurance that he could work it again to deadly effect growing incrementally within. The lean herbivores raced along the shore, ignoring the ripe berries in abundance on the stickle bushes they passed through at the water's edge. Another sign that they were rattled. Morribies never passed up an opportunity to graze on their preferred meal of choice. The larger male looked at him and snorted. Both took off with dizzying speed.

Logan, more alert than before, continued on. Nothing jumped out at him and eventually his thoughts settled. The dense forest gave way to a simple path, one that looked well-travelled. Did that mean deadbeats or something even worse? Again, he tensed up. He saw random footprints mixed in with animal tracks. So this route was used by both. Most of the animal tracks were of the hooved variety, a detail that calmed him. If this path was frequented by docile herd animals like the morribies he had seen earlier, then he was relatively safe. He wondered if Kyle had traveled this very route.

Kiff loved identifying animal tracks around their enclave. He was good at it. Many times Logan had taken him along known paths with slight inclines, so that his brother's leg wouldn't be as much of a factor on the expedition. It was amazing how quickly Kiff could identify the slightest evidence of an animal trail.

Logan struggled to hold back his tears. Would he ever see Kiff again? From what he could glean from Abe's explanation of syncing up to a new reality, his chances didn't sound good. Would Kiff be lost to him forever? But he had another to save: Kyle's brother, Byron. With his purpose again at the forefront of his thoughts, he slogged forward with renewed determination.

After what seemed like an hour, he came across the tech boundary Abe had mentioned. At its center and spreading out along a tidy line were hundreds of strange metal wagons and machines whose purpose he could only guess at but was hopeful to employ. He looked at his blaster. Why had it worked back at Archie's place? Wasn't this the line indicating where any and all tech failed? How had he made the weapon work?

He felt the tech around him, its presence a rising hum in his mind. He wanted to explore all of it, unearth how to wield each and every one, but knew he didn't have the time. His mind was drained from his trek. He needed to rest, recharge. A quick nap would do the trick and then he would be on his way. Maybe he could even coax one of the elaborate carts into operation and travel the rest of the way to Kyle's city in style.

He found one with four circular brushes mounted underneath and slipped into the small seat hanging off the side of the machine. He sank deep into the seat, hopeful his hiding spot would help him avoid hungry predators stumbling across him as he slept. All he needed was fifteen minutes.

He curled up into a ball and wedged the blaster between his knees, available to him at a moment's notice.

\* \* \*

Logan awoke to the blinding light of morning. He stretched, rubbed his eyes with the heels of his hands, then yawned and sat up—and stiffened at what awaited him.

Hovering above him slightly to the west was a large armored man standing atop a floating octagonal platform. On the machine's underbelly, six nozzles shunted vast funnels of air, allowing it to defy gravity. Buffeted by the gusts, he drew his hands up to shield his eyes from the flying debris kicked up by the machine. It was flat on the top where its passenger lorded over a raised section of machinery. The man held onto a long rod attached to the assembly, making slight movements that were mirrored in the platform's airborne course corrections. He wore a black helmet with a visor pulled down over his eyes.

He glared at Logan and spat, "Well, well, why am I not surprised to see you back? What's the matter? Couldn't cut it out in the wilds of the Ruins, Kyle Jaxx?"

The man jerked his right arm, signaling for someone to approach.

Logan reached for his blaster and held it up at the warrior. It was obvious he faced the equivalent of a Hunter, and from his posturing, a great one at that.

The man's eyes settled on the blaster, and he smiled. "That's rich, Kyle—you threatening me with tech."

Logan felt his mind reach into the tech once again, only this time with far more ease and confidence. He selected stun from the menu and fired.

The beam sliced through the air, hitting the flying man square in the chest. He dropped off his platform and fell out of sight.

Logan sprang to his feet and hurdled out of the vehicle, scraping his stomach along the metal side as he did so. He soon found that the man in the sky had not come alone. All around him, other warriors in similar garb raised tech of various shapes and sizes and settled on Logan as their primary target.

He froze and dropped the blaster. *No way I can fight my way free from this.*

*Chapter 36*
## Kyle

The view from high above left him breathless with wonder, especially now that the sun was up. Everything that had happened to him over the past few days, all the hardships he'd endured, the dangers he'd faced—it all seemed insignificant now. His new perspective on life showed him that he wasn't just fit for repurposing. He wasn't one of the city's rejects, Mayor Baynor's garbage, a deadbeat. In fact he was someone special.

Unfortunately, he might not ever see the city again, nor his parents or brother. Logan would.

He had mixed feelings about it all. As he flew low over the warped rooftops and toppled walls of a sprawling town in the Ruins, he told himself that he would see his brother again. This mission of his was temporary. When things had settled down, he would travel back to the city, even if it meant visiting the Tower first and somehow phasing back to his own reality. It would mean being useless again, but that would be okay. At least he would be home.

For now, though, he would take Logan's place and Logan would take his, and they would save their brothers and complete their missions.

Whatever those missions were.

He saw three kalibacks scampering between the buildings. Kyle thanked the moons that he was able to fly. Walking these streets would have been dangerous.

So what *was* his mission, exactly? He still wasn't clear on that. Abe had talked about corrupt leaders and the need for change, and Kyle understood that all too well, but what was he supposed to do about it? Whatever happened, he was sure life in the city would be much better without the likes of Mayor

Baynor and General Mortimer—and probably the same could be said of the enclaves since their existence apparently mirrored the city's.

Kyle made excellent time and would have been faster still had he gone on ahead without his faithful spirits. There was no doubt about their allegiance, though. They zipped around below, whipping around corners, in and out windows, and sometimes plunging straight through walls in their effort to keep up. It was a shame they couldn't fly higher and pick up the pace, but if they could, then there wouldn't be anything particularly special about spirits with wings.

That said, the winged phantom hardly used its wings either. They moved from time to time, but most of its flight was by will alone, gliding and soaring and swooping without any effort. But this was just a spirit after all. Perhaps it had once occupied a flesh-and-blood creature that had used its wings in the proper manner. Of course, if that were true, then it stood to reason *all* these spirits had once been living, breathing animals, as much part of the wildlife as kalibacks, galumpers, and orb scavengers were today. Yet they were strangely unknown to the people of Apparati. What had happened to these bizarre beasts? Why were their spirits left behind like this, haunting the land?

Kyle kept his arms tucked into his side and his knees slightly bent, though it probably didn't matter one way or another. Oddly, the rush of wind in his face was slight. It reminded him of the times his Uncle Jeremiah had taken him for a ride along the back streets of East Morley in his road-rumbler, the roof back and the wind whistling around the windshield. Looking back, he saw a long, pale green contrail that he likened to the exhaust from his uncle's rattling vehicle.

"This is so cool!" he suddenly shouted.

The Ruins eventually petered out, and he came across what he took to be an enclave—a sprawling mass of quaint buildings. It all looked so old and primitive that Kyle gaped. There were no paved roads, no maglev trains, no gleaming structures of glass and metal. People *lived* here? It seemed incredible.

There were other enclaves in the distance, too. From his vantage point high above the land, he counted five more settlements around the coast and one clustered in the peaks of the nearest mountains. The enclave farthest south was notably larger than all the others, with one particularly impressive building in the center. The timber and stone structures were tiny compared to the high-risers of Apparati, but judging by this enclave's far-reaching outskirts, Kyle guessed the leaders resided there.

But was this where Logan came from? Flaws in the so-called mission abounded, and Kyle shook his head in disgust. There was no point conjecturing about where one fourteen-year-old boy lived in this wide expanse of land. The only way to find out was to ask people.

Still . . .

Instinct told him to check out the enclave nearest the Ruins. It seemed to make sense for Logan to live there since he had wandered into the Ruins with his brother in tow. Kyle found himself drawn toward the town. He circled around and around, studying the simple but sturdy homes with their timber walls and stonework bases. He was fascinated by the slim towers poking up from each building. Gray smoke drifted lazily from them, and nobody in the streets seemed to care. Kyle was reminded of the factories in the north of his city, which burned fossil fuels and, many claimed, caused most of the smog.

There was a large building near the center of the town that Kyle guessed had to be important. It was three times the height of neighboring structures with its gigantic and steep pitched roof. Was it a good place to check out?

He flew toward it, running questions through his mind: *Excuse me? I'm looking for Logan . . . uh, Logan Somebody. I don't know his last name. He lived around here. Maybe in this town, but maybe not. He's fourteen, if that helps? Looks a lot like me.*

Having decided that landing in full view of everybody was a sure-fire way of getting some quick attention, he landed in the middle of a street. It wasn't paved, and Kyle was amazed at how muddy it was in places. These people lived in the middle of dirt trails? Yet he had to admit that, with the sun shining down, it was a pretty place with all its quaint cottages and heavy log structures—and the air was fresh.

Nobody paid him much attention, and this blew his mind. Hadn't he just come down from the sky? He turned in a circle, checking to make sure that he was, in fact, visible and not a ghostly apparition like the spirit that engulfed him. A few people nodded to him as they passed, and Kyle relaxed. So, apparently, people floating around in the sky was a common thing around here.

*Same as back home*, he thought, thinking of Logan's probable reaction to all the high-tech troop cruisers and hovercabs. *It's the same, only different.*

He noticed several guards standing on the wide stone steps outside the grand entrance to the enormous building before him. A sign over the double doors read SOVEREIGN HALL. There were six guards, each with a bow over one shoulder and a quiver full of arrows over the other. They carried short swords and wore armor over their shoulders and chest. Their helmets were shiny and ornate, their cloaks a deep red.

One guard was frowning at Kyle. He came down the steps and into the street. "Hey, Glider-boy," he called. "Do you have a message? New evidence or a petition for the sovereign? If so, you'd better make it quick. He's just about to hand down his sentence."

Kyle stood there dumbly. "What?" he finally managed. He stared in amazement as something appeared at the guard's shoulder—an apparition of some kind. A spirit. It was very similar to the first spirit Kyle had encountered during the night, the one that had guided him to hunt and kill a shuffler.

The guard stopped before him, his spirit rising up out of his shoulder and baring its fangs. "You're new," he said, nodding. "Just got your wings, eh? Well, lucky you. But you won't last long as a messenger if you stand around gawking instead of passing on your message." He frowned, tilting his head to one side. "Wait. Do I know you from somewhere?"

Another guard slowly approached, his eyes widening. "That's impossible," he muttered. Then, as if talking to a child, he spoke in a stern, clear voice—while raising his bow and reaching into his quiver for an arrow. "Don't move. If you attempt to fly away, we'll bring you down. Dead or alive." As he spoke, his own spirit started to emerge, horns first, then the snout and razor-sharp teeth.

"Who is he?" the first guard asked, stepping closer and clamping onto Kyle's arms. His spirit was rising higher, its long snout sniffing the air, skin-flaps flaring behind its pointed ears.

"That's none other than Logan Orm. Here to see his little brother's sentencing."

Kyle said nothing as the guard deftly confiscated Logan's knife. A dozen possible actions had been flitting through his mind, none of them good: launch into the sky and escape, feign innocence and tell them he'd been mistaken for Logan all week and was getting fed up with it, scream for help, fight and disarm them, break down and beg for mercy . . . But once the guard had hold of his arm, Kyle felt resignation settling in. All right. He'd go with them quietly. At the very least, maybe he'd get to meet Kiff.

And his parents.

The notion of coming face to face with his biological mom and dad, who probably looked a lot like the mom and dad he'd grown up with, struck him as both exciting and terrifying. How would they react? Would they know who he really was?

His hands were pinned behind his back and his wrists clamped in lightweight but sturdy iron manacles.

Once secured, he was led inside. Sovereign Hall was rich with ornate wood panels adorning its walls. The high vaulted ceiling, with the thickest rafters Kyle had ever seen, showcased an enormous arched window at the far end, under which impressive statues lined a circular stage. Between the statues, in the center, were what looked like thrones—two of them, both unusually oversized, with intricately carved wood frames and wooden backrests. Two men sat in the seats, stiff and regal, bathed in the auras of their spirits. One of them was droning on about food rationing to a packed audience.

Kyle disliked both men from the moment he laid eyes on them.

"Here," the guard behind whispered.

It was awkward sitting in a wooden pew with his hands behind his back, but Kyle sat, biding his time. Looking around, he was startled to note that the vast majority of the audience had come along with their own spirits. Many were bright and easily visible while others were either hidden away or absent. He spent a moment identifying the ones he could see and concluded they were the same kinds as those he'd already encountered. Seven distinct spirits.

He wondered where his own were. On their way to the enclave, hurrying to catch up? One was still inside him, of course. He was barely aware of it now, but the moment he thought about it, the winged spirit seemed to awaken.

"Watch it," the seated guard warned.

Kyle suppressed the urge to fly away. Manacled or not, he was sure he could float up into the air and zip away—that is, if someone had left the door open for him.

". . . And now let's move on," one of the seated men on the stage said. He was fat and ugly, the jowls of his neck wobbling as he spoke. "Chancellor Gretin?"

The other seated man, gaunt with a thin neck and beaklike nose, unrolled a parchment. He spoke in a rumbling, gravelly voice that carried across the hall. "Sovereign Lambost, before we get to the Orm boy, there is the not insignificant matter of overdue taxes from the Glider Enclave."

The sovereign sighed so loudly that Kyle heard him clearly. He was amazed. The acoustics in this place were excellent. "They *still* haven't paid their dues?" the man on the stage complained, shaking his head and causing the flabby folds under his chin to swing horribly. He leaned forward and pushed himself up onto his feet. Beside him, the Chancellor followed suit and stood up with him, straight and tall.

The sovereign addressed the audience. "Protesting about tax increases is one thing, but I take a dim view of those who seek to alter laws by breaking them. Such anarchy will not be tolerated. Our egotistical friends in the mountains rate themselves above everybody else and refuse to comply with the laws of our land. They need to be, ah . . . brought in line. What would you suggest, Chancellor Gretin?"

Judging by the glint in his eye, the sovereign already knew the answer before he asked the question. So did the chancellor, who replied without pause. "An immediate cessation of imports from the other six enclaves for a period of one month, a heavy fine plus interest on overdue taxes, and . . . an example."

The sovereign nodded sagely. "Ah, yes, an example." He appeared to give the matter some thought, but it was obvious he had already done so. "Chancellor, send a company of Hunters and Breakers to the mountains. Have Lord Brutin of the Gliders shackled and brought to me at once. For execution."

This statement caused a ripple of astonishment throughout the audience. Looking around, Kyle could see that people were outwardly shocked, murmuring to each other and shaking their heads. If the sovereign had been hoping for a celebration, he'd made a grave mistake.

*237*

Yet it seemed he'd expected the consternation. "Yes, my friends, this will be an unfortunate end to a promising leader. You'll note that I judged and sentenced him in a single breath, and you're likely asking yourselves how any man, even a sovereign, can skip the tribunal and associated proceedings. Well, it's quite simple."

He paused and waited for absolute silence.

Then: "Because I can. Because I, as your esteemed leader, have the power to do so. Because from time to time it is necessary to remind you all how fair and just I am in all other matters. Quite simply, my chancellor doesn't *need* to organize a tribunal for every little matter that we discuss here in this hall and back at the capitol. But I allow it anyway. I come here out of the goodness of my heart simply because I believe in being fair and just. You see?"

He smiled briefly, a sickly grin that caused Kyle to shudder. But then the sovereign scowled.

"Do not mistake my kind and just nature for weakness. I will not tolerate an uprising. Refusing to pay taxes constitutes a very serious crime indeed. And after Lord Brutin is executed, there will be no more complaints of tax increases and unfairly rationed food. *Is that understood?*"

A murmur spread throughout the crowd, and many heads nodded hurriedly. Even spirits seemed unusually cowed, and they ducked down within their hosts.

Sovereign Lambost smiled again, and waved at Chancellor Gretin. "Next?"

The chancellor lifted his parchment, peering at it down his nose. "Um, next we have the matter of Kiff Orm who, at the tender age of eight, recklessly entered the Broken Lands a few days ago with his older brother and was inadvertently tethered. This morning he must exorcise the unwelcome spirit from his body—or die."

*Chapter 37*
**Logan**

A squad of soldiers marched Logan into a large flying ship. As one secured him to a hard metal seat built into the wall, Logan's mind registered the tech on the man. His longer weapon was a vapor cannon, used more in crowd control. The specs and proper usage of the gun flooded into his mind, bombarding him in seconds with all the training he would need to use it. It was unnerving how swiftly the tech divulged its secrets. Secured to the man's right leg was a putty saber. He concentrated and soon knew the ins and outs of dispensing the sticky restraint webbing with the flick of a finger. Even the small communication pad mounted on the soldier's chest opened up to him, pelting him with a string of ones and zeroes, the coding to manipulate all its capabilities.

The man grunted at him and snapped the belt tight against Logan's chest before crossing to a line of seats. He and the rest of his squad secured themselves and stared back at him with a grim intensity.

Logan's gaze settled on a flat rectangle of tech held by one of the soldiers. The man's hand darted back and forth across its surface. Logan's mind reached out and he slowly wrapped it around the tablet, soaking up its capabilities and limitations.

A moan broke his concentration. Two soldiers hurried past, carrying the man he had shot with the blaster. They pulled down several seats from their wall housings and hoisted their human cargo atop them. They were far enough away that Logan only caught fragments of their conversation. Surprisingly, the injured man had the most impressive volume of the three.

"I'll get fixed up once we have him secure. We were told he couldn't use tech whatsoever. What's—" He coughed.

One of the soldiers strapped four buckles along the man's length, being careful with the one that crossed the point of injury. "Sir, calm yourself. The fugitive has been apprehended." The soldier whispered more to the prone man, but Logan could hear nothing further. The two soldiers soon joined the others across from him and signaled the pilot to take off.

The pilot nudged backward some sort of stick jutting up from the floor between his feet. Their ride rose, rocking gently.

Logan cast his mind farther out, soaking in the details and intricacies of the large machine that defied gravity like a Glider. It's functional designation was 'vehicle,' a people carrier. He wished he could look out a window, but all viewing areas were in the fore and aft sections of the Oberon Interceptor. His scan gave him an overall familiarity of the immense ship's hardware but only a rudimentary awareness of how to fly it. Was this what Abe had described? If so, it was impressive.

Logan had synced up in some fashion with every piece of tech he had encountered so far. Did that mean Kyle was experiencing the same with the spirits? Logan had never heard of anyone tethering to more than one. Would Kyle be able to herd a Breaker for a brutish task then switch over to a Glider to race to one of the other enclaves? That sort of power would be sure to unsettle the sovereign.

A soldier approached, nursing a small object in his hands, what looked like a long needle. Distracted by thoughts of his counterpart's plight, Logan failed to recognize the danger until the soldier jabbed him with it. His mind snatched at the tech piercing his skin, desperate to identify what the man was pumping into him. It was a vascular uploader, and it was pumping him full of sedative—Klyozene Beta something. His link with the tech dropped off.

The soldier's words spilled out. "Mayor's going to be real interested in how you . . ."

Then everything went black.

\* \* \*

A hand slapped Logan hard on the side of his head. He slumped forward then sat up straight, swinging his arms up to find they were bound together by some sort of restraint. His mind tooled around the tech, revealing he was subdued by Arc Manacles. As the device shared its inner workings, Logan penetrated deeper into the interface, seeking to unlock the cuffs. Another blow to his skull broke his focus, and he glared at his surroundings, his vision swimming from the sedative and the blows to his head.

The man who had captured him and been blasted by Logan stood by his side. He walked stiffly, clearly still in pain from being on the receiving end of a stun beam. Surprisingly, he had lost the intimidating helmet but was in no way diminished by its absence; his impressive stature and gruff demeanor more than made up for it. Tightly cropped thinning hair atop his head matched his grey beard. His skin was weathered, and the proliferation of wrinkles around his deep-set eyes suggested he was much older than Logan's father, maybe somewhere around the Chancellor's age. Two soldiers, both young, stood by an impressive metal door emblazoned with tech that surely would need to be cracked if Logan hoped to escape. He squelched his curiosity to read the tech and assimilate its workings. He needed to focus on the living and breathing in the room.

The bearded man paced, drawing his arms to his lower back as he addressed Logan. "What's your story? You escape, disappear out in the Ruins, and come back all fired up and able to work tech."

Logan felt the presence of all the machines in the room. The chair he sat in had simple diagnostic capabilities that submitted Logan's vitals to somewhere else. No windows adorned the stark white room, but he did spy a sizeable rectangular machine that had to be a larger version of the tablet the soldier had used in the interceptor. He reached out to envelope the wall-mounted tech and was assaulted by hundreds of streaming images in his mind. It was a stream screen, but activated only for Logan. He sensed that wasn't how the viewing device normally worked. His powers were ramping up the screen's capabilities, freeing it to project hundreds of video clips of information directly into his cranium. It was overwhelming. He retreated, tamping down his questing mind, putting the brakes on further exploration.

"General Mortimer addressing you here, Kyle Jaxx. I was given to understand from your father that you would be very cooperative. Now answer me. What happened to you? Why can you suddenly manipulate military tech when you had zero aptitude three days ago?" The man winced as he leaned toward him. One possible outcome of firing a stun beam was cracked ribs. The information dashed into Logan's mind from an earlier clip that had assaulted him out of the dormant stream screen.

His mind again nudged outward, thirsty. He cringed and forced it back inside, bottling it up as tight as he could manage.

Mortimer placed his hand on the bandages secured to Logan's neck. "Looks like you got yourself hurt out there. Not the best dressing I've seen. I can get a medic in, fix you up good as new." He pushed his thumb into the soft bandage, applying steady pressure.

Logan gasped, but didn't pull away from the general.

His interrogator hissed, "Just tell me what I want to hear and you can get patched up."

The door slid open and two figures walked in. One was tall and thin, wearing a long white jacket. The other was shorter, rounder, and exuded a presence that fouled the very air. Most of his hair had fled his head, retreating to a thin slick of oily black strands that ran from ear to ear. His grin was broad, but not friendly.

The shorter man said, "General, let Doctor Pollard work his magic and assess the patient's needs."

Logan ignored the doctor, instead tracking the other's movement with mild agitation. Here was a leader, that much was clear. Was this the leader Abe said needed to be dealt with?

The squat man extended a hand and then immediately retracted it. "Oh, not very thoughtful on my part. No handshake pleasantries for you. Not with those cuffs on." He straightened the front of his blue jacket and announced, "Mayor Lorne Baynor. You've really gotten the city all riled up, young man. The number of protests has escalated since your rash departure. I'm not too happy about that. Had to allocate far more soldiers than I want to crowd control and docility interviews."

The doctor ran a red wand up and down Logan's chest and around the back of his neck. Doctor Pollard shot the mayor a distressed look. "What's up with him? There's no tracker to tell me what's wrong. He's a blank."

Mortimer's eyes lit up, intrigued by yet another mystery Logan presented. "We were wondering that too. Surveillance said we picked up a brief signal from the Tower—Kyle's tracker—but it vanished quite abruptly."

Mayor Baynor looked physically ill. A rim of sweat presented itself along his forehead. He tried to settle himself, but Logan could tell he was upset. "Probably faulty equipment or operator error."

Mortimer snapped, "Like how Pollard messed up the implant, writing this one off as a lost cause. Well, I've got the cracked ribs and bruises that say otherwise." He stabbed a finger toward Logan. "He capably handled a Series Seven blaster. Not sure where he got hold of such old tech, but he did it without an implant."

Mayor Baynor made placating gestures with his hands. "Settle, General. Pollard was right. The boy had no aptitude, one of the poorest set of results in a while." The mayor scrutinized Logan, squinting at him with distrust.

Pollard now had a long rod with several nozzles and lenses mounted on its narrow end. He abandoned the tech and leaned back, examining Logan with determination.

"He didn't have such long hair when I saw him. How did it grow so fast?" His skinny fingers kneaded Logan's left cheek, probing his skin before darting down to his upper arm and feeling at his muscle. "And his complexion shows extensive sun damage. His musculature is far more defined than before. If I didn't know better, I'd say this wasn't the same boy, that Kyle walked off into the Ruins and a nearly identical twin came back in his stead."

"Ridiculous. Are you suggesting something transformed him out there?" The general sniffled with impatience.

Doctor Pollard's eyes unnervingly widened. He lifted the hair on the back of Logan's neck and focused his inspection there. "It's not Kyle. There's no scar from the insertion of his implant, not even a scab. This is someone else."

Mayor Baynor grinned. "Yes, that's quite an imagination you have, Pollard. Really might want to see about psych testing if this is how you handle such a clear-cut case."

Pollard shrunk back, cowering at the implied threat.

"We all know that the Tower causes some sort of instability with tech," the mayor said. "Probably why you can't detect his tracker right now. Give him some time and maybe you'll get a signal. But not now. I need to have a private chat with our little escapee. He should be filled in on what's been going on since he left."

Logan, feeling emboldened by how nervous the mayor was acting, said, "Where's Byron? You can't execute him."

The mayor gestured at Logan. "See, he knows his brother's name. It's Kyle."

Doctor Pollard looked ready to protest, but the general grabbed him by the arm and led him to the exit, leaving behind a small tray of medical tech on the table to Logan's left. His mind wanted to access it, see what he could do with it, but he thought better. If he was about to confront Baynor, he needed his wits about him.

The door closed behind Pollard and Mortimer. The mayor dismissed the two sentries as well, chiding them about worrying over him.

With the room empty except for Logan and the mayor, the wretched man's demeanor slipped into coldness. He pulled a small hand gun from his belt and passed it back and forth between his hands. "You're not Kyle. I know this, but the others don't. You're from the east. You're his doppelganger, aren't you?"

Logan didn't respond.

The mayor laughed. "Oh, I know all about your little magical enclaves and all the mischief your people cause with your spirits. I know everything just as my predecessor knew and every mayor before him. It really was a pity you had to make your way over here for nothing."

Logan thought to what Abe had said about the leaders of each world keeping their people in the dark. This man was the sovereign's counterpart. He had to be.

"What I don't know is why you can work tech. You don't even have an implant."

Logan stayed quiet. He felt his mind reach out and surprisingly latch onto the tech within the mayor's left eye socket. He slipped in to find Baynor's eye was artificial, a technologically enhanced insertion. Briefly, he looked through the device, seeing his battered self slumping in the large chair. Logan watched his own lips move. "You are a small man. I know someone just like you back home."

The mayor gasped and pushed away from Logan. He clutched at his eye. "I *felt* you in there. How did you do that? That's *medical* tech. Mortimer said you wielded military tech out in the Ruins. How did you *do* that?"

Logan didn't say a word.

The mayor's fist bashed him in the chin.

Logan coughed and spat out a string of blood.

The mayor shrugged. "You can work more than one type of tech. That's useful to me." He fidgeted with his blaster. "Just how powerful are you?"

He strode back to Logan and yanked the bandage off his neck, not caring that the rough treatment opened the wound, allowing a trickle of blood to seep down Logan's neck. The mayor pointed at the tray of tools Pollard had left. "Fix yourself up. If you can do that, then maybe you have some use."

"What about Kyle's brother?" Logan said.

Baynor smirked. "As for Byron, I am assuming you know of him because you ran into your twin out there. Well, he's out of reach. His execution is a few hours away. If Kyle sent you here to save him, then you failed. None of your concern. Heal yourself and we'll see what can be done with you."

"If I do what you say, impress you with my tech, will you spare Byron?"

Baynor walked to the door, his back to Logan. "Work the tech to fix yourself up and then we'll talk."

The mayor left him alone. Logan closed his eyes and sent his mind out to gather up the medical tech. It only took him a minute to figure out which devices he needed. He glared at the stream screen in front of him as his powers made the appropriate tools dance about in the air and tend to his injury.

He didn't trust the mayor. Even if the foul man offered to save Byron, Logan knew the man wouldn't honor his word. He'd have to find another way to save Kyle's brother.

As he worked the tech, he plotted his next crucial move. Abe had said true change could only transpire if the corrupt leaders of Apparati, the mayor definitely one of them, were taken out. He set his mind to planning just that.

*Chapter 38*
**Kyle**

When a side door opened and Kiff Orm was dragged into Sovereign Hall by two burly guards, a whisper spread through the audience. Nobody looked particularly happy, though several poorly tamed spirits hooted and barked with excitement.

Kyle strained to see over the heads of the people in front, and the guard to his side gripped him by the shoulder and warned him to sit still. But Kyle bobbed and weaved as Kiff, chained at the wrists and ankles and held upright by the arms so his feet dragged on the floor, was paraded to the front of the hall then up the stone steps to the circular stage. A third guard came from the opposite side with a chair, and Kiff was dumped into it.

The boy was having trouble restraining his unwanted spirit. His brow was slick, his face white, and even his shirt had great damp patches where he'd sweated profusely. He was shaking uncontrollably, and sometimes his eyes rolled back in his sockets. But mostly he scowled.

A sob broke free from the front row on the opposite side of the aisle, and Kyle strained to see who it had come from. The rows of pews were angled toward the stage, and he eventually caught a glimpse of a woman in tears—though her hair covered her face.

"Sit *still*," the guard to his left hissed.

"Is that Kiff's mom?" he whispered.

"Shut up."

The sovereign ambled closer to the prisoner. "Young Kiff Orm," he said sadly, patting the boy gently on the shoulder. "I do wish youngsters would respect the laws of the enclaves and refrain from venturing into the Broken Lands. Laws are made for good reason, you know."

Now that the audience was still, Kyle stared between heads at Kiff. He saw something familiar in the boy's face, a blast from the past—his own younger brother. The last time he'd seen Byron's face was four years ago, and although kids changed a lot between the ages of four and eight, there was definitely a strong resemblance. Kiff's skin was darker than Byron's ever was, and although scrawny he seemed to possess a wiry strength, ready to spring loose of his manacles, his small fists bunched and his face set in a defiant scowl.

Even though he'd never met Kiff before, Kyle instantly felt proud of him. And then it hit him. *This* boy was his brother, not Byron. *This* boy was his flesh and blood. They shared the same mother and father.

The guard to his left leaned close and whispered in a stern, threatening voice. "When the time is right, I'm going to take you up there and hand you over to the sovereign. And you'll go along with everything he says. Got it?"

Kyle frowned and said nothing.

"If you know what's good for you," the guard continued, "you'll make Sovereign Lambost look good. If you want *any* chance of living, you'll play along with whatever explanation he concocts. Understood?"

This time, Kyle nodded. He hadn't yet formulated a plan but had no intention of putting the guards on alert with an antagonistic display of resistance.

The sovereign circled the prisoner like a vulture. "Tethering at such a young age is a breach of the law, but sometimes a spirit leaves the Broken Lands and enters our enclaves, and a tethering occurs. It's extremely rare and most unfortunate. But you, my boy, blatantly broke the law and entered the Broken Lands. What happened to you is your own fault."

Another whisper swept through the audience, and Kyle heard a stifled sob from Logan's—no, *his*—mother.

"I'm a reasonable man," Lambost said softly. "You will be afforded the same courtesy as any other that has become tethered at such a tender age. You must exorcise the spirit. For this we have invited a Banisher into our midst. She will be on hand to send the spirit back to the Broken Lands—but she can only do so after you exorcise it."

As if by magic, a young woman sidled onto the stage. Her hair was so black and tightly pinned that it might as well have been applied to her head with an oily brush.

"She cannot draw it out for you," the sovereign went on. "Only you can do that, boy—if you have the strength." He smiled. "If you succeed, then your family will pay a simple fine for your transgression in entering the Broken Lands and you will all go on with your lives." Now his smile faded. "If, however, you cannot exorcise the spirit, then we will have a problem. A mere child tethered to a powerful Breaker? We can't have that. As according to the law, you will be deemed an unnecessary risk to the Seven Enclaves and sentenced to death."

Kyle wondered where his own spirits were. One still resided in him, and he now knew this was the type represented by those tax-evading folk in the mountain—the Glider spirit. The Glider stirred as he probed around, and this caused a rush of escape plans to flood his mind, all culminating in him soaring for the sky.

But flight wasn't an option in this hall. Whipping around like a trapped bird would just make him a target for archers. He needed help from his *other* spirits.

As if they had been awaiting this mental command, the spirits arrived. The first Kyle knew of them was when a woman screamed in the back row, and then several men yelled. In seconds, pandemonium ensued as the audience ducked low in their pews to avoid the blur of activity over their heads—six different phantom creatures of varying sizes darting around like mischievous children bent on terrorizing their victims.

"What are they doing here?" a man somewhere behind Kyle exclaimed. "This isn't possible! They *can't* be here!"

The chancellor's booming voice cut through the noise as he ordered everyone to sit down and cradle their young. Kyle realized this was exactly what the adults were doing already—holding their children close and shooing the spirits away. Their own spirits had emerged during the excitement, and the hall was filled with a haze of phantoms.

A woman was running down the aisle—the Banisher. She stopped near the back of the hall as close to the invading spirits as she could get, held up her arms, and shrieked, "Untethered spirits! Begone from this place!"

As she spoke, she opened one of her fists and blew on her palm. A fine golden dust filled the air, sparkling like glitter and spreading quickly—and impossibly—all the way across the hall. The six spirits recoiled from it, zipping over to the far side of the hall in a panic. They twisted and turned in the air, and Kyle knew they were about to plunge through the wall and leave.

"To me!" he shouted, leaping to his feet.

Even in the commotion, heads turned his way. The oily-haired woman swung around, frowning.

The guards by his side jumped up and gripped his arms, hoisting him inches off the floor. Kyle grimaced. It was bad enough that his hands were shackled behind his back without these goons suspending him helplessly. But he shouted again, louder this time. "Spirits! TO ME!

After the tiniest of pauses, all six spirits zipped toward him, shooting right through the golden-speckled air over the pews. Everyone gasped, including Kyle himself, as the spirits plunged into his chest one after the other, all together, filling him up and sending a wash of emotions through his body—the urge to run and hide, the desire to hunt and kill, the overpowering need to go on a rampage and *break* things.

As the seven spirits fought within him, his guards released him and stumbled backward in shock, and those in the seats nearby screamed and tried to push their way out of the pews and into the aisles.

Kyle broke free of his shackles and stared dumbly at the separate rings of iron around his wrists, wrenched into two pieces with nothing more than a shrug of his shoulders. He felt dizzy, but at the same time empowered with a strength he had never before experienced—not just a brutal, physical strength, but a thirst for knowledge, hunting instincts he had no business possessing, a crazy desire to help and heal, and much more. The conflicting emotions and thoughts threatened to tear him asunder, but he rose above it all and got a grip on the situation.

A strange hush fell over Sovereign Hall. Every member of the audience stared at him. Most were twisted around in their seats, some were standing, others paused in the aisles. Even the sovereign and his chancellor were frozen in shock. The Banisher woman looked aghast.

On impulse, Kyle reached sideways and grabbed a guard by his wrist. He clung so tightly that the gasping man couldn't pick his fingers off. In that instant, a stream of noisy thoughts poured into Kyle's head as though his touch had opened the floodgates of the guard's mind.

*. . . don't hurt me, don't hurt me . . . what kind of magic is this? . . . this isn't possible . . . nobody can tether with all seven at once . . .*

Kyle dug deeper, and the man stopped squirming and opened his eyes wide. Buried behind the jumble of exclamations and incessant chatter was valuable information. Kyle absorbed it all in the blink of an eye as though he'd just downloaded data from a slip drive.

The seven spirits identified themselves in his mind: Hunters, Creepers, Breakers, Weavers, Skimmers, Fixers, and Gliders. Thinking back, he'd used the Hunter to track and hunt a shuffler in the woods, and the Creeper to run and hide afterward. The Breaker had taken over and angered him into tearing out chunks of a wall, and the Weaver had calmed him and rebuilt it. The Skimmer . . . well, nothing had happened, and now he knew why. Skimmers read minds, and there had been nobody around to read. But he was using the Skimmer spirit right now to absorb this information. The furry little Fixer had been dormant, too, its healing abilities having no use at the time. But then Kyle had invited the Glider into his body and flown east.

Now he had them all at his disposal, except according to this guard, to *everyone*, it was impossible for a single person to be tethered to more than one spirit. Especially for someone like Logan who had flunked even that.

But Kyle was not Logan.

The guard snatched his hand away, and time seemed to start moving again. With no easy exit to the aisle, Kyle hopped up onto the wooden seat, wondering if he could jump into the next row and escape that way. It seemed impossible—the place was too crowded, and more guards were already moving in from all sides to grab him. Amid the rising background noise, the chancellor's booming voice called for order in the hall.

Kyle allowed his Glider to take over. He leapt into the air and over the audience, aware that a guard was nocking an arrow to bring him down. Somersaulting through the air, Kyle landed in an aisle crammed with bustling villagers. Their presence protected him from the archer, but it was hard to make any headway—until his Creeper took over and guided him with dizzying speed through all the gaps, making him twist and duck like he were a puppet. At some point he crawled between legs, hurdled a pew, and slipped sideways between a sea of startled faces.

Bursting out of the milling audience, he found himself at the front of the hall near the stage, just yards from Kiff. He tore up the steps and, without hesitation, used his Breaker's strength to wrench the manacles from Kiff's wrists. They snapped like brittle wood. Kiff stared at his freed hands in amazement while Kyle bent to rip the irons off the boy's ankles. It barely took an ounce of effort; the Breaker seemed to guide his hands, and the manacles simply broke apart.

"Get him!" the sovereign screamed, stumbling backward.

The chancellor was already there, moving toward Kyle with a knife in one of his outstretched hands, his gaunt face twisted into rage. The chancellor's spirit was a Creeper, but it seemed to be of no use at the moment. Kyle could almost see its torment as it urged the chancellor to flee, but the man was too busy trying to grab the runaway.

Just for a moment, Kyle allowed the towering figure to latch onto him. As the chancellor tightened his grip and started yelling to the guards, Kyle tried to ignore the knife pressed to his throat and conjured up his Skimmer to peek into his captor's head.

What he saw there shocked him.

*Chapter 39*
**Logan**

Logan synced up with the two cameras hidden in the walls. He could disable them, but he knew the mayor wanted to watch him patch up his neck with the medical tech.

His mind stretched farther afield. He sensed the tech of four guards just outside of the door, surprised that one even had a cybernetic arm like Mortimer. Six weapons in all if he counted the blaster housed in the arm. He fussed with several sonic grenades clasped to one of the soldiers. Those could come in handy if he needed a non-lethal approach to escape . . .

Logan froze, frightened at how calculating his thoughts had become since learning how to tether to the machines and tools of Apparati. It was a talent, but one he needed to temper with compassion. His goal was to end the mayor's rule.

He washed his mind over the medical equipment, quickly ferreting out the proper tools and steps to address his injury. He sent the first tool airborne, fully exploiting its self-levitating feature, making sure to manipulate it clumsily. No sense letting them know how much control he had. Control wasn't the word for it. Mastery fit better. Outside of the Oberon Interceptor, every piece of tech he had tackled had easily revealed its secrets. That vehicle had been too big, having contained too many systems for him to wade through in such a short time. He stared at the dormant stream screen. The screen was a bit like that too, but he thought he could parse out its information if he honed his approach to it.

He wobbled the medical tech as it approached his neck. He kept his gaze off the stream screen, but that didn't stop him from accessing it. He worked slower this time, unspooling the video clips and information streams one at a time. Despite working in this fashion, he was able to digest a plethora of information about this new world.

As he educated himself on Apparati, he maneuvered the sterilization doser across the gash, wincing at the cold mist against the cut.

He ran through clip after clip about repurposing, horrified at what his counterpart had almost endured thanks to a nonfunctioning implant. He was lucky to have escaped! A replay of the security footage revealed Byron's part in the breakout, and Logan was shocked to see that the boy was housed in a robotic body, actually a full-form motility construct. He ran the specs, cataloging the numerous antiquated aspects of Byron's tech and sifting through the various ways to update it. If he could save Byron, he could give him an upgrade.

Other than Byron, the only citizens to receive tech replacement body parts and organs were those of the soldier class. That explained the general's arm. Did that mean the mayor was adept at using military tech? He didn't look the part.

His attention turned back to the pocket cellular regenerator. The tool deftly regrew the affected subdermal tissue. He took several forced breaths after that step, hoping to show the mayor how much the act took out of him. *Not really.*

He plowed through more data streams, learning exactly where Byron was being detained, the setup of his execution site, and the number of troops scheduled for the event. It sickened him to see the news of the execution spreading through media channels, absorbed by so many watchers.

He combed deeper, unlocking classified documents detailing the corrupt acts of Baynor and his predecessors. He found a peculiar file behind several firewalls and hacked into it.

He arrayed the dermal sealer over the cut, using its lowest setting. It would take longer, but his skin would look like new, the scarring almost impossible to detect.

The well-guarded file was marked Torren. Logan dove in—and that was when things got interesting.

\*\ \*\ \*

He finished his neck restoration in under an hour. The mayor didn't return. Another hour passed, and he soon grew tired of plumbing for information through the stream screen. He had what he needed for now. He had a complete picture of just how nasty Baynor was, the fragmented history of Apparatum, and who had worked alongside Abe to construct the Tower. Although pertinent information was conspicuously absent, what he found in these files opened up an entire new path for him, one that he was positive both he and Kyle would need to travel together.

But that would come later. Right now he had to escape from this place and free Byron.

And then . . . And then what?

He had no idea what came next.

He mentally tinkered with his manacles, unlocking them and relocking them numerous times. His mind was abuzz with purpose. He could do so much in this world.

The door opened and Mayor Baynor strode in, grimacing. Three guards entered as well. None of them wore any tech that Logan could detect outside of their implants and trackers. Instead, two brandished hefty clubs.

The mayor kept his distance from Logan. "So, you've been busy I take it?"

Logan angled his neck to display his injury-free skin. "I healed myself up. Now what about Byron?"

"I'm afraid I can't honor that deal."

"What?" Logan tried to sound incensed but had known the mayor wouldn't be a man of his word.

"You did much more than I asked. Did you think us stupid? That we wouldn't detect your encroachments?" He clicked his tongue. "We have evidence of you accessing the door locks, your manacles, the cameras, all the weaponry my men were outfitted with earlier, and the stream screen."

Logan's mind quested outward. The guards outside were now also bereft of any tech except for their trackers and implants.

The mayor drew closer. "What did you see? Our techs can't make sense of all the places you accessed through that." He harshly pointed at the stream screen. "You worked too fast, they said. But you left a trail and, slowly, they'll uncover it for me."

Realizing the mayor was itching to make a pronouncement, Logan asked, "So what happens to me?"

Adjusting his neck as if alleviating a kink in his muscles, Baynor said, "You're too dangerous to keep around. You can manipulate tech far more extensively than anyone on record, but then you know that now, don't you? That and a bit more. I can't have ordinary citizens, much less fugitives, knowing more than I do. What sort of leader would I be?"

Logan didn't answer.

"You're too much of a threat to my well being and to that of my city." He looked at his watch. "You have just under an hour left. You and Byron will participate in a joint execution. Two problems go away like that." He snapped his fingers.

He didn't know what to say. The mayor had just given him exactly what Logan wanted: an audience.

"A shame you couldn't be brought in line. You would've proven quite useful." The loathsome man trundled out, his guards exiting behind him.

Logan unlocked his manacles and threw them to the ground as he stood to stretch. As he walked around, flexing his tightened leg muscles, his mind worked at an unparalleled speed to formulate his endgame.

*Chapter 40*
## Kyle

Kyle reeled away from the chancellor and again used his Breaker's strength, this time to backhand the man hard across the face. Chancellor Gretin spun and fell, knocked cold, his knife clattering to the floor.

What Kyle had seen in the man's head disgusted him and left a nasty taste in his mouth. A lifetime of brutality, some of it out in the open but most behind the scenes—endless beatings, vicious tortures, and outright murder, not just of civilians but his own guards and soldiers as well—and all supposedly for the good of the Seven Enclaves.

Shaking with revulsion, Kyle turned his attention to the sovereign. As a stream of guards and several archers struggled through the audience, he grabbed the chancellor's knife off the floor. He made a leap for the fat leader, who had seen his comrade fall and turned to waddle off the stage. As they tumbled together, the sovereign shrieked for help, but Kyle straddled his back and held the knife high. "Stop!" he yelled to the approaching guards. "Stop, or he dies!"

There was no way he would be able to stab the sovereign, to drive a blade into the man's body. But the fat man didn't know that. Nor did his protectors. He blubbered and moaned for them to stay back. The archers looked uncertain and halfway aimed their bows toward Kyle, but the burly guards held up their hands and retreated.

Kyle felt his Hunter spirit pushing to the surface, begging to take over and finish the sovereign as though he were an oversized shuffler. It was a struggle to keep the spirit at bay. Abe Torren was right in saying this awful leader's reign had to be ended—but not by way of murder.

With the shiny blade trembling over the sovereign's neck, a long silence fell over the hall, a moment of breathless anticipation. Then the audience started murmuring, and Logan's name was repeated several times.

His Skimmer spirit took over again. This time it seemed like Kyle was being dipped into a cesspool. The depth of the sovereign's greed and cowardice was staggering. Just the thoughts at the forefront of his mind right now were enough to make him sick:

*... get him off me! ... kill him, sacrifice yourselves if you need to, just protect me! ... you incompetent fools, I'll make sure your families will suffer for this ...*

But beneath the desperate pleas of an unfeeling coward was a history of vileness that seemed to bubble and boil like a volatile compound in a technician's lab. He was as bad as the chancellor but in a different way—all lies and deceit, manipulation and greed, a slimy politician who cared only for himself and couldn't care less about the welfare of the enclaves—unless ignoring problems happened to threaten his career. He did as little as he could for his people with an eye for as much personal gain as possible.

And he knew about the fractured world of Apparatum. He *knew*. He was aware that some children were born with enormous powers capable of taming all seven spirits at once, and that those children were a danger to the sovereign's rule. Nobody could stop someone with seven at his disposal. Lambost was afraid of the existence of such a person, and he took care of the problem early, nipping it in the bud by testing children at a young age and arranging 'unfortunate accidents' for those who attracted the attention of all the spirits.

A guard edged closer, and Kyle looked up at him. If only he could make the man see what was inside the sovereign's head. But this guard had a Breaker rising up from his shoulders rather than a mind-reading Skimmer. In fact, Kyle now knew from the stream of information he was receiving that there were relatively few Skimmer spirits in the enclaves, and the few that existed were kept at a safe distance from the sovereign. And no wonder! If they saw what was going on inside the leader's head . . .

The silence broke. Sovereign Hall erupted into a cacophony of noise as the chancellor picked himself up, shaking his head and touching his chin as he blinked and looked around. Kyle watched him warily, his gaze darting back and forth between him and the guards and the restless crowd, looking for a solution to this stalemate. He couldn't sit on the sovereign's back all day holding a knife aloft. He had to *do* something. Yet his mind was blank.

Logan would know what to do. Logan was stronger, tougher, trained with the knife, probably used to hand-to-hand combat and wrestling with loathsome creatures. Kyle wasn't. He was a thinker and a tinkerer with a thirst only for *knowledge*—

Then an idea came to him.

The nearest guard lunged at him. As the man's weight came crashing down, Kyle twisted aside and caused the guard to topple off-balance. Kyle ended up sandwiched between two bodies—but he still had the knife, and he grunted with effort as he maintained his grip on the handle and leaned into the guard, determined not to be knocked from his mount. He and the guard squirmed atop the sovereign's back.

Kyle used the physical contact between them as a conduit for his Skimmer.

He had no clue if it would work or not, but he commanded his eager spirit to share the thoughts he'd extracted from the sovereign's mind. Instantly, he felt the information streaming out of his body and into the guard's like a computer virus unleashed into the datahub. The man froze as though he'd received an electric shock.

All the while, the sovereign was bucking feebly beneath, trying to turn over or get up. He was big and heavy but clearly too obese to right himself. "Help me!" he screamed.

Guards rushed in from all sides, reaching for him. Kyle yanked on the sovereign's hair, pulling his head back, and pressed the knife to the man's throat so hard that a bead of blood welled up. "Stay back!" he yelled.

The ring of guards flinched and backed off. Behind them, the chancellor's face was red with anger.

Meanwhile, Kyle's Skimmer continued streaming information. Kyle hardly needed to keep his mind on the task; his faithful spirit was handling it behind the scenes. All he needed to do was stay in contact with the guard, which wasn't difficult as the man had an iron grip on his shoulders. He twisted around and was gratified by the expression he saw: big wide eyes and a deepening frown as the sovereign's life story was downloaded into him.

He gasped and shook his head. Keeping a grip on Kyle's shoulder with one hand, he used the other to reach for one his colleagues, grabbing him by the ankle. "You have to see this!" he shouted. "Take a look! Pass it on!"

Now there was a chain of three, and the new guard went through the same range of expressions before his face darkened into anger. He grabbed the arms of those next to him, and the downloaded information spread rapidly, the chain expanding.

The chancellor was yelling angrily from behind them. "Arrest him, you imbeciles!"

"Quiet!" a guard barked.

The archers were brought into the chain, and then the first row of audience members. The sovereign's dark, cowardly lies and deceit spread as men and women joined hands and reeled from the shock of what they saw.

Realizing what was happening and unable to push the knife-wielding Kyle and heavyset guard off his back, Sovereign Lambost slumped and gave in. The noise from the restless audience was beginning to rise again as more hands joined and the sovereign's despicable lies were spread throughout the hall.

"No!" Chancellor Gretin roared, shoving his way through the ring of guards. He dropped to his knees before Kyle. "Get out of his head!" He lunged and tried to push Kyle off, then fell on the guard and tried unsuccessfully to wrestle him away. "You don't know what you're doing! You can't let the people see what he knows! You'll ruin him. You'll ruin *me*. You'll ruin the entire land!"

Neither Kyle nor the guard said anything. They simply maintained their connection, allowing the information to stream from Kyle's head to the rest of Sovereign Hall.

The chancellor looked aghast. With a frenzied effort, he batted at Kyle's face. Kyle closed his eyes and took the abuse, knowing it would just be a few bruises, nothing more. He ducked his head and hunched his shoulders, imagining himself to be a shuffler curling into a ball and presenting his armor plating to a predator. If his Breaker were in control, he could simply knock the chancellor flying—but it was important that his Skimmer continue streaming, so he bore the attack without complaint, knowing somebody would surely extract himself from the chain and come to his rescue any moment now.

The chancellor grabbed Kyle's knife hand and began wrenching on his fingers. Gretin's grip was strong, and a second later he had yanked the knife free—

And stabbed Kyle in the side of the neck.

He gasped with pain and shock and fell sideways, cutting off the stream of information as he broke contact with the guard. His Breaker took over, grabbed the knife, and plucked it out. Blood spurted, and Kyle clutched at his throat. People screamed.

As Kyle slumped to the floor, his Fixer took over. He watched a pool of blood spreading out around him as dizziness and shock overcame him . . . but then he felt a warm, tingling feeling in his neck and the flow of blood halted. Guards exclaimed and pointed. Sovereign Lambost, finally free, rolled onto his side and struggled to get up, moaning to himself.

The knife-wielding chancellor stared in horror as Kyle healed before his eyes.

Hardly able to believe what was happening himself, Kyle climbed to his feet and held up his blood-drenched hands. A hush fell over the entire hall.

"He's healing!" someone screeched. It was a woman in the front row. "My son—he's *healing himself*."

Kyle singled her out and focused on her. She was the same as his mother back in the city only leaner, a little younger in some ways. Right now she looked astonished, her hands to the side of her face.

"How's he doing that?" someone called from behind her. "Has anybody *ever* healed themselves before?"

Several others shook their heads.

Next to Kyle's mom was his dad, as gruff as always but with perhaps a hint of pride in his expression. He said nothing, just held his head high.

And there was Kiff, still sitting in the chair on the stage. Though freed, his face was twisting with the effort of restraining his Breaker. He gripped the sides of the seat and writhed, oblivious to what was going on around him.

*I need to get that Breaker out of him*, Kyle thought.

He reached up to touch his neck. His wound was gone. He was still sticky with his own blood, and weak from the sudden loss and shock, but his injury was gone.

"Where were we?" he said. He moved toward the prone sovereign again, raising his voice so everyone could hear. "It's time everyone saw the truth about this man. He's just like the mayor back in my city. Some of you have seen already, but a lot of you haven't. Join hands, everyone, and I'll show you everything you need to know about your so-called leader—and his henchman."

He glared at the chancellor, who knelt a yard away looking defeated. Kyle reached for the sovereign, who now lay on his back, pressed down by guards.

"No!" Chancellor Gretin shouted. He scrabbled in the pool of blood for the knife, and shouts of alarm went up as guards broke the chain and rushed toward him. "You don't know what you're doing! What the sovereign knows about our world is too much for our enclaves to bear." He snarled, his thin face stretching into a wolfish grimace as he waved the bloody knife at the sea of faces around him. "You'll ruin us all. Things will go back to the way they were hundreds of years ago. Don't you understand?"

"Put the knife down," an archer snapped, raising his bow. "Put it down, or I'll put *you* down."

But the chancellor yelled, lunged, and stuck the knife deep into the sovereign's heart. An arrow zipped over his head. Gretin yanked the knife out and stuck it in again and again, three times, four times, killing his esteemed leader over and over, giving Kyle no hope at all of using his Fixer spirit.

Amid the screams of horror, another arrow zipped through the air—and this time it passed right through the spot where Chancellor Gretin had been kneeling. The projectile continued on and clicked harmlessly against one of the statues.

The chancellor was gone, vanished into thin air.

Another silence fell as everyone stared dumbly at a dead sovereign and an empty space where the chancellor had been. Only his clothes remained, along with the bloody knife lying nearby.

"He's gone," someone said. "Winked out."

"What are the chances?"

Kyle, shaking and breathing hard, swallowed and nodded. "The chances are good. I think the exact same thing just happened in the city."

"City?" someone repeated on the far side of the hall. "What does he mean by that?"

With a heavy sigh, Kyle looked around. At least a third of the people here, including the guards, knew the truth about Apparatum, about the two separate lands and how they were out of phase, and about how the sovereign and his chancellor had systematically destroyed all evidence of such a past and ensured that anyone with Kyle's capabilities was removed from society early on before he or she became a threat to the leaders. And these huge secrets were just part of it. There was also an endless list of horrible lies, a history of greed and corruption sure to destroy any lingering delusions of a fair and just sovereignty.

And all of it had been broadcast in vivid detail to dozens of people in the hall, leaving a nasty taste in their mouths.

Kyle knew that, in the last few hectic minutes, he'd made the difference Abe had hoped for. Things were going to change around here. And the chancellor had killed his sovereign far too late. Kyle had already absorbed enough of the man's memories to impart them as secondhand knowledge to the rest of the enclave. To *all* the enclaves.

Kiff suddenly let out a strangled wail of anguish. His Breaker spirit was thrashing, its phantom shape rising up and sinking back down as though it were trying to get more comfortable. With each downward lunge, Kiff shuddered, his face slackening. He'd tried so hard to contain the Breaker, but now, perhaps stirred by the excitement in the hall, it was growing stronger and taking over.

The boy's mom tried to rush forward but was pulled back by strong hands. People all around were scrambling to get away. And with every passing second, Kiff succumbed more and more to the possession.

Kyle staggered forward, tired and bloody. "Get out of him!" he yelled.

To his surprise, Kiff's body ceased its shuddering. The boy opened his eyes, but it was something else that looked out, something alien. This was the Breaker, beginning to manifest in physical form, taking over its host. Kiff's forehead warped as the spirit's tusks pushed through from the world beyond.

"I said OUT!" Kyle screamed, and threw every last shred of will and energy at the possessed boy.

With a sharp intake of breath, Kiff sat up straight as if plucked by unseen hands. The spirit tumbled backwards out of him, and it floated there behind the prisoner, clearly shocked and confused by the sudden eviction. Kiff's eyes rolled up, and then he slumped sideways, toppling to the stage floor.

When the Breaker realized it was floating free, a stunned audience staring at it, the first thing it tried to do was re-enter Kiff's body. But Kyle was waiting. He gave a sharp twist of his hands in opposite directions as if wringing out a cloth.

And, just as Abe Torren had done previously, the Breaker spun and vanished.

*Chapter 41*
**Logan**

Not more than twenty minutes after Baynor left, a young woman entered Logan's cell, forced him to clean himself up, and garbed him in the proper Apparati fashion worn by someone his age. Another person, this time a tall, aloof man, came to cut his hair, obviously to match Kyle's shorter hair, and scrubbed his face and arms with a sponge that faded his tanned appearance. They were making him into Kyle. The mayor didn't want the citizens to know his true origins. Neither attendant said a word or carried any tech. A lone guard wielding a simple club stood watch as they worked.

Logan was not fed or given water, which left him feeling wearier than usual. They wanted his mind dull.

The mayor didn't pay him another visit.

Half an hour later, a squad of eight soldiers walked him out of his cell, through several corridors and along quite a few skyways. Thanks to his abilities, he tracked exactly where he was and where they were taking him. None of them attempted to refasten his Arc Shackles.

They arrived at the execution site very close to the time of his scheduled demise.

It was an open courtyard. All around him the tall spires of Apparati shot skyward. He saw a few soldiers flying around on their vehicles, but they patrolled a good distance away. He reached out, pleased he could touch their tech. Evidently the mayor underestimated his reach.

He was marched up a long set of steps and escorted to a stage. He saw Byron being led to the same point, his robotic face emotionless. Despite having examined Byron's robotics inside and out via the stream screen, his appearance was still jarring. He moved with a stiffness, projecting a sad impassiveness.

Logan focused on the huge crowd. The first several rows of spectators had been stripped of tech and were held at bay by an army of soldiers, all carrying non-tech weapons of various types.

At the fringe of the assembly, a few citizens brandished signs of protest that were quickly confiscated the minute they were held aloft.

Byron finally arrived and was guided to stand beside him. Logan didn't know what to say. Should he play along and pretend he was Kyle?

Byron didn't look at him. "Care to explain to me why you look like my brother?"

Logan couldn't help himself; he probed the boy's cybernetics, knowing from his previous briefing through the stream screen that Byron housed no weapons whatsoever other than a small finger laser.

Byron flinched and angled his face toward him. "Hey, don't do that. How did you access my system? What are you?"

"I can't explain everything now, Byron. You just have to trust me. I'm here to help." As officials raced to greet the passengers arriving on a large vehicle to their left, Logan lowered his voice and said, "Kyle sent me."

Byron said, "Impossible! You're just someone the mayor augmented to look like him. If everyone sees you die, it's better than them thinking Kyle escaped and is still running around out in the ruins, I know it. Puts power back in his hands."

Logan marveled at the boy. Little more than a brain in a jar, deprived of a proper body, and still so very strong.

"I'm Logan. I came from the Broken Lands—er—the Ruins. I ran into your brother. We switched places. He's back in my world, facing a similar situation if I know the sovereign."

General Mortimer ascended the stage and stood behind Byron. Logan searched his cybernetic arm and found no weaponry. The General sent Logan a smug smile. "Pity I don't get the opportunity to break you down and make you mine. Would've been fun. Baynor tells me you can work all sorts of tech." He flipped open his vest to show Logan a tiny blaster tucked within. "Cautioned me not to bring any weapons near you. But you managing to work an outdated blaster isn't all that impressive." He patted the hidden weapon. "This baby is cutting edge, calibrated to only fire when held in my cybernetic arm. Doubtful you can commandeer it and mess up our fun here today."

Logan scanned the weapon and realized the general was right. While he could access the weapon, he couldn't work it unless the general gripped it in his cybernetic arm. *Then why show me the weapon if he isn't going to use it? He just wants to rub it in that he can wave about dangerous tech so close to me and still keep it out of my reach.*

He examined the blaster closer, desperate to find a way to utilize it. It had an override function that when triggered caused it to self-destruct. *Designed to keep it out of enemy hands.* The explosive yield was small, not enough to harm the general other than maybe some minor first-degree burns, but maybe enough to cause a distraction. He keyed in all of the code to trigger the override except for the final sequence. If need be, he'd light up the blaster and see what that spurred.

The mayor mounted the steps, carrying an impressive weapon. Logan scanned it—a large Bingham Assault Grinder, named for what it did to the brains of its victim. Point it at the cranium and witness the invisible waves of death turn the victim's mind to mush. A perfect weapon, especially for Byron.

Logan glanced at the robot boy. Adrenaline raced through him. He would not let Byron die.

The mayor turned to face the crowd. Logan saw the scene projected on a large stream screen on the side of a building at the opposite end of the courtyard. Baynor looked even more bloated up on the wide screen.

The mayor thrust the weapon into the air. "It is with a heavy heart that I attend this distressing event. Before us stand two who would spread destruction to our city. Byron Jaxx you know as the rare citizen granted cybernetics despite not being soldier class. For a time, he was idolized for his bravery of overcoming the hardship of losing his body."

Logan looked at Byron. The boy stared at the mayor, revealing nothing.

"I'm afraid his circumstances have soured his mind. We don't know how that happened. Possibly brain damage. Whatever the case, his recent actions reveal him to be unstable. Freeing his brother during his repurposing has been acknowledged as an act of terrorism. Afraid that he liberated his older brother as part of some plot to bring even more death and carnage to Apparati, we sent our men out to hunt Kyle Jaxx down in the Ruins. We found him and also discovered he had deliberately hidden his potential, shielding his massive abilities from the state. That is why such little amount of tech can be brought within his proximity."

The mayor paused for effect. Despite the deathly stillness, he raised his voice.

"We fear that, given the opportunity, he could wrest the nearest weapon or assault vehicle from one of our fine soldiers and use it to devious means and at great cost to our citizenry."

The crowd remained silent, caught up in the story.

"You want proof? Then simply watch." He swept his hand toward the stream screen. The image switched from the mayor on the steps to a shot of Logan shooting the General with a blaster. It jumped to him unlocking his Arc Manacles repeatedly, and ended with his manipulation of medical tech to heal his neck.

Many in the crowd gasped.

Baynor struck a somber expression. "As near as we can figure, he can manipulate all tech, across all classes. We believe he has others like him out in the Ruins waiting to invade our city." He took a deep breath. "Letting him live only increases the likelihood of another escape. We can't risk him reuniting with his fellow rebels out in the Ruins. You have my word that after these executions, General Mortimer will move in with ground forces and raze the wastelands, hunting down and killing all of Kyle's conspirators."

Logan wanted to scream the truth but knew now was not the time.

Baynor activated the grinder. The weapon hummed loudly as it powered up.

The mayor held aloft the weapon and pointed it at Byron—but eyed Logan with narrowed eyes. "By the way, try and stop me from firing this, I dare you."

The mayor was making it too simple on him. All he had to do was reach out, wrest the weapon from him, and blast the mayor's brains. He sent his mind out and was shocked to encounter a mental barrier.

Logan's expression of dismay registered with Baynor, who chuckled and said, "Nice little force field being projected in front of me, young man. Its source is miles away. No time for you to locate it and shut it down." He nodded to Mortimer. The general shoved Byron forward. He trailed behind the robot boy.

The shield hadn't been there before. Logan tried to reach out and touch the platforms and stream screen in the distance. He couldn't. The shield had probably been activated right after the mayor's speech. He cast his mind out to the sides. He could link up with tech in those directions. The shield was not a dome. Could he use that to his advantage?

"Any last words, Byron?" The mayor glowered.

Byron said, "You lie."

Baynor leveled the weapon at the boy's head. "It'll be painless, that's what they tell me."

Logan had to do something. His eyes fell on the general. Everything unfolded in a matter of seconds. He keyed the last sequence into the general's hidden blaster and dove toward him.

The override kicked in, producing a faint series of chirps. As the general reached to grab his blaster, the alarm on his face told Logan he knew what was happening. Logan slammed into the tall man and pushed him away from Byron and toward the mayor.

At the same time, the weapon in the general's vest exploded.

Soldiers raced forward, and Logan darted toward Byron. The general staggered about, clutching his chest and moving more out of reflex than from purpose.

Baynor looked flustered. He drew up his weapon and fired, sweeping the beam across the stage, not caring that its path tore the general's mind apart on its way toward Logan. Mortimer shuddered and toppled into the rushing squad. The man shook and scraped helplessly at his head. Logan raced toward Byron, barely ahead of the beam.

He realized his mistake almost right away. If he raced toward Byron, he'd allow the mayor to zap them at the same time. He couldn't let Byron lose the only thing he had left: his mind.

He changed course and barreled straight toward the mayor. Baynor looked put out by Logan's brazenness, but he didn't hesitate. He tried to realign his heavy weapon with even more urgency, forgetting about Byron for the moment. Logan leapt into the air, determined to bowl over his target even if his mind were reduced to mush.

And then the miraculous happened.

Mayor Baynor winked out.

His clothes, the mind grinder, and his bionic eye fell to the ground. Logan sailed through the now empty air, landing on all fours with practiced ease. Spinning around, he heard the crowd gasp.

The general's body still flailed weakly about, his mind gone. The large man took one last gasp, his eyes vacant and soulless.

Then he was still.

The crowd was confused, uncertain why the mayor would disappear at this exact moment.

But Logan knew why.

* * *

The first thing he did was send his mind out and shut down the shield. It took him a little over a minute to do this. In that time, the crowd exploded into hysteria. Soldiers found their hands full trying to quell them and halt a stampede.

Logan dashed over to Byron and took his hand. He sent his mind out to the giant stream screen and focused the cameras on the platform. He zoomed in on the two of them. His voice rang through the courtyard, carried now by the booming speakers attached to the screen. "Mayor Baynor lied to you. He has always lied to you. I have proof. I am not Kyle Jaxx. He is elsewhere. If you will listen, I can show you the truth that has been hidden from you all these years."

The crowd settled, their urge to riot tamped down. They looked at the screen as Logan played the video streams he had found the day before. He showed them the truth of their fractured world, of what lay beyond the Tower. The images showed a history the citizens had never known: a world divided, oppressive leaders, the harsh conditions out in the wastelands. He projected select info from Abe's file, detailing why the wink-outs occurred and hinting that there was a way to stop them and reunite the divided worlds of Apparati and Apparata. He left out the parts Abe had covered up, for now.

The screen went blank. For a long time no one said a word.

They turned to face Logan, shocked but slowly filling with belief.

"The mayor winked out because Kyle, my counterpart, must've slain his twin. I didn't want to take a life, but events slipped beyond my control. I am thankful this innocent boy was spared and two truly evil men fell."

He felt Byron's eyes on him but didn't dare look. Exhaustion was creeping in. Too much tech manipulation and too little food and water were a dangerous combination. Not to mention the hardships of his trek through the Broken Lands.

"We can make this right." Logan swayed, his fatigue finally catching up with him. "We can join our two . . ." The faces in the crowd blurred. Logan juddered to the left, stumbling over the weapon Baynor had used. He spoke but didn't make sense as he watched a throng of soldiers racing up to him, their clubs raised. His eyes closed as he gave in and spiraled into blackness.

*Chapter 42*
**Endgame**

Kyle chewed his mouthful, savoring the flavor of the roasted durgle before swallowing and attacking his plate again. He didn't remember meals tasting this good back in the city. Durgle was common and plentiful there, too, but somehow seemed fresher here, more tender and succulent.

When he commented on this, Leet Orm—his biological father—thought about it and said, "I've eaten wild durgles, I've eaten farmed durgles, and I've eaten durgles bred in cages. Truth is, it doesn't matter how they're reared. What matters is their *diet*, and how big and fat they are. Those that run around all their lives and get plenty of exercise are nothing but stringy muscle. The lazier, the better. Big and plump is what you want, nice and juicy, young rather than old. And their diet is crucial. I ate a durgle once up at the Breaker Enclave. It was horrible. Had a nasty fishy taste because of the junk they were feeding it. Not that I have anything against fish . . ." he added after a pause.

He frowned and stared down at his plate while his wife smiled and patted him affectionately on the arm. Kyle sensed that Logan's dad was trying his best to appear chatty and welcoming, but being sociable was not his best trait. In that respect he was worse than Kyle's own father back in the city.

*His own father.* Kyle was still trying to wrap his brain around the switch in families. These two adults sitting opposite him were his real bloodline. They'd raised him from infancy, coaxed out his first few words, been there when he'd started walking. Yet they were strangers to him now. They'd welcomed him into their home but only because Logan was missing—because Kyle had replaced him. The situation was awkward to say the least.

Kiff, too, clearly missed his brother. He said very little throughout dinner, just stared at Kyle with narrowed eyes.

With a sigh, Kyle put down his fork and stared at his plate, unconsciously mimicking Logan's dad.

"This is weird," he said at last, looking up at Logan's parents. "I . . . I don't even know what to call you. I mean, you're my real mom and dad, only . . ."

"Only you've been raised by others," the woman who looked so much like his mother said. "Call us Leet and Prima if you prefer. And you're welcome to stay here as long as you want." She paused to choose her words but in the end choked out, "You're still our son no matter what."

Kyle nodded and stared at the table. It had to be hard for Mr. and Mrs. Orm—her especially. Of course she loved Logan more, the son she had raised all these years, but Kyle was her actual flesh-and-blood. As difficult and awkward as this was for him, how she must be feeling was unfathomable.

"Is Logan coming back?" Kiff asked.

"I don't know," Kyle answered truthfully. "Look, I want to go home myself. But for now, well, let's just see how it goes."

He didn't want to tell Kiff that it might be impossible to switch back again.

A pounding on the door made them all jump. Leet scowled and got up. Without a word, he left the room. Seconds later, voices could be heard outside on the doorstep. They started off muffled, but Leet's volume increased steadily as the exchange went on.

"Look, I don't know," he said, clearly annoyed. "Maybe tomorrow."

"*When* tomorrow? Dawn?"

"No, *not* dawn. Give him a chance to rest up."

"When, then? Morning? Noon?"

There was an audible sigh. "Let's say after lunch. I can't promise anything, though. He's not my son, so . . ."

The voices dropped back to a murmur, and the door closed soon after. When Leet returned to the table, he was scowling and chewing his lip.

"Dear?" Prima prompted.

"They want to know."

She raised an eyebrow. "Know what?"

"Everything." Leet spread his hands and looked at Kyle. "The whole enclave wants to know what some of us learned in Sovereign Hall this morning. They want to see for themselves. They want proof."

This topic had come up in conversation earlier. "The sovereign is dead," Kyle said, "and so is the chancellor. I can let people see what *I* see, but will that be enough?"

"It should be," Leet said, nodding. He stared at Kyle long and hard as if trying to see through him into his head. "Skimmers never lie."

"But people do," Kiff piped up.

Everyone glanced at him.

"That's an astute observation," Prima said. "A Skimmer can be used to read a mind, but the report twisted to cover the truth. Do you remember when Chancellor Gretin enlisted Lancie Rayden to investigate a murder?" She turned to explain the case to Kyle. "Lancie used his Skimmer to read the mind of the accused and condemned him immediately, saying every graphic detail of the murder was lodged in the man's mind. The condemned was put to death."

"So?" Kyle said.

"So, Lancie Rayden later killed himself. Close friends were convinced he was consumed with guilt, that he'd lied at the reading—that the accused was innocent after all. His Skimmer had seen no such murder."

"So why'd he lie?"

Prima spread her hands. "Nobody knows for sure."

"The point is," Leet said, "that Skimmers don't lie, but people do. So you'll have to do more than tell everyone what you saw. You'll have to show them. The way you showed *us*."

Kyle thought of the audience in Sovereign Hall earlier that morning. A sizable number had received the sovereign's thoughts directly through linked hands. Could he do the same for the rest of the Enclave? For *all* the enclaves?

"I'll try," he said.

Leet grunted and pushed his chair out. "Do it," he said, standing. "After lunch tomorrow, prove yourself to these people. Leave them in no doubt about your powers. Show them a world beyond the Broken Lands." He stared at Kyle, then pointed at him. "You're not Logan. Don't ever pretend you are. But . . . you're still my boy. And you saved Kiff's life."

With that, he shook his head as if it hurt and hurried from the room. The front door banged shut moments later.

Prima made no apology for him, and Kyle decided that was okay. It was better to be open about the situation. "He's right," she said. "You're not Logan, but you're still our son. You *both* are. You're like . . . twins." She smiled and nodded.

"You're not as strong as *my* brother," Kiff said, his gaze roaming over Kyle's pasty-white arms. "I mean, you're strong in your *head*, but that's about all. Have you ever wrestled a shuffler into submission with your bare hands?"

*Yes, actually I have,* Kyle thought. But he shook his head. "I'm a city kid. I don't get out as much as Logan."

"Do you have a girlfriend?" Kiff challenged.

Prima laughed, rose, and started gathering up the plates. "If you're finished, I'll leave you boys to talk."

"Well, *do* you?"

Kyle thought of his friends at school. "There's a girl I like, but she doesn't know I exist."

Kiff's face suddenly lit up. "Hey—maybe you can start courting Nomi but pretend you're Logan. Then, when he comes

278

back, he can take over. He's too much of a durgle to approach her, but maybe *you* could and . . ."

And so the conversation went. Kiff gave a tour of the quaint stone cottage and the yard, and it was then his limp really became noticeable. Kyle desperately wanted to use his Skimmer to extract information about the injury, but he stifled the eager spirit and simply asked questions out loud. Kiff answered readily, with no shame or self-pity. He did, however, confess somewhat matter-of-factly that his classmates left him out of many activities because he slowed them down.

The comparison to Byron was painfully clear. He hoped Logan could help fit the boy with a new robot body.

Kyle touched his neck, feeling for the injury he'd endured in Sovereign Hall. Just how powerful was his Fixer spirit? It had healed his wound instantly. Could it also put right injuries that were years old?

He went to bed that night with his head full of ideas—and his body full of the mysterious and ethereal creatures from the Broken Lands. He'd kept them on a tight leash, knowing that the residents here in the enclave were uneasy with the idea of spirits in their midst.

It was time to get to know them better.

\* \* \*

Logan slept fitfully, slipping in and out of consciousness. When he woke, the room spun and he was tended to by a gentle woman who looked shockingly like his own mother. She brought him plenty of liquids and encouraged him to rest. She wouldn't answer any of his questions, and he noticed there was no stream screen in the room. Not that he could muster the strength to eavesdrop on any infostreams at the moment.

The fourth or fifth time he stirred, he stayed awake, his strength vastly improved. Daylight streamed in from the one window in the room, and he promptly exited the bed and walked over to peer outside. The woman did not rush in this time. He was positive with his mind now clearer that he had been watched over by Kyle's mother. Correction, his *real* mother. It felt weird to think that. He had no connection to her, no memories of her.

It looked to be morning in Apparati. Citizens went about their day, walking to and fro on the skyways. Below, he saw the snake train and scolded himself for thinking it a living thing earlier. It was a maglev. His thoughts reached out to the vehicle, passing over it faintly but not enough to register all of its aspects. It was a commuter vehicle, trucking around large numbers of citizens to their various destinations.

He retracted his mind to closer to home. Other than a camera in the corner of the room, there was no other tech. When he quested farther, he latched onto the weaponry of two guards outside his door. So he was still a prisoner. But as to why they had him in a residence and not back in the room where he had been shackled, he had no idea. He ranged around the entirety of the house, reading the tech that was lying around, a good deal of it mundane appliances that were reserved in their digital exchanges. A small tablet left in the front room proved a gold mine. It was Kyle's father's. And from it he learned he was indeed at the Jaxx's house. As he tried to access the media links in the tablet, the door to his room slid open with a whisper.

The woman he suspected was his mother entered. She was all smiles. She sat on the bed and waited for him to come to her. He strolled over and put one knee up on the mattress.

She tucked a length of her brown hair behind an ear. "Do you know what happened? They tell me you can retrieve information from any nearby media tech. Did you educate yourself in how much our city has changed in just one day?"

So she had deliberately left the tablet within reach of his mind. "You're Kyle's mom?"

She nodded and waited for him to continue.

He found he liked her patience; it reminded him so much of his own mother. He wondered if Kyle's dad was as brusque as his own. "I haven't yet. Just starting to feel clear-headed."

She frowned and raised her hand. "My fault. I gave you a sedative specifically designed to numb your neural centers. I figured in your delirious state, too much information so readily available to you might do more harm than good."

He nodded. Was she a Fixer like his mother, dispensing healing with unbound graciousness? He thought so.

"I can wait here and let you fill yourself in or I can tell you directly—that is if you trust me."

As much as he wanted to dive into the infostreams, it might be better to reach out to this strong-minded woman. He had a feeling she was already predisposed to being his ally. Why not show her he trusted her? For the moment. "I'd like to hear it from you."

She lightly cleared her throat and began. "Your bravery in coming here to Apparati was inspiring. The secrets you uncovered and broadcasted have caused the citizenry to demand change. With Mayor Baynor and General Mortimer gone, the government falls back into the hands of representatives of each district in the Hub." She caught her breath. "They convened late last night and came to some very critical decisions."

"They want to silence me?"

"No, nothing of the sort. While there are pockets of corruption in the seventy-nine members of the Hub, none approach anything like the sinister dealings of the mayor and the general. No, you awakened something in us, Logan." She leaned closer. "We have always gone about fitting into our roles, not questioning what our implants have assigned to us. Here you come along and show us the existence of something bigger than we ever dreamed of, a sister world filled with magic and our twins. It explains so much. We now know why there are wink-outs."

"So what's going to happen?"

"As revolutionary as your actions have been, change will be slow. The Hub will steer us toward the correct path."

"Won't a new mayor and general just rise up and take over? What's stopping them from denying everything?"

"Once the genie's out of the bottle, it's rather hard to put it back. They risk too much to try and discount your narrative. Even now, there's talk of expeditions to Apparata. Did I say that correctly?"

He nodded.

"And guess who they want to head the first one?"

He knew before she said it.

"You," she confirmed. "They want you to go back and be an emissary. Do you think your people will do the same for my son? Do you think he has inspired them as much as you have?"

He was wounded that she referred to Kyle as her son and not him.

Logan wanted to give her the right answer to make her happy, but he couldn't because he didn't know. He had no idea what his people would do without their sovereign and chancellor. He knew they were both gone. He was certain the mayor and general had been their counterparts.

She stood up and patted his arm. "No worries. We'll find out soon enough. Now, before you go getting ready to race off to the Ruins, there is one thing I need to know."

"What is it?"

"Throughout the night, you talked quite a bit in your sleep. The few times I checked on you, I have to admit to listening in quite intently. I'm sorry for that."

"That's okay."

"I couldn't help myself. You see, you went on and on about Byron, rattling off all manner of details about his cybernetics and such." She swallowed then said, "So, my question to you is, can you really do it? Can you give him a better body? Will you?"

*282*

Logan smiled, caught up in her excitement. He replied cheerfully, "I can. Just point me to the tech I need."

"Oh, I will. How does this afternoon sound?"

* * *

After lunch, just about every citizen of the Enclave streamed along the narrow streets. It was a good thing that Acting Sovereign Durant moved the proceedings to the northern outskirts of the village, at the foot of the impressive mountains, where there was far more room to cluster together. Durant was a wiry man, quite unlike the late Lambost in appearance. Still, he seemed nervous, and with good reason: word had spread that he was not a good choice for sovereignty.

Kyle caught snippets of dialog as he pressed through the crowds behind Prima, Leet, and Kiff:

"I heard he was in Lambost's pocket."

"We'll soon find out'"

The strange thing was that Kyle barely remembered much of what he'd seen in the fat sovereign's head. But in any case, it had all passed through to the guards, and then to the audience, and perhaps they'd made more sense of it all. They'd recognized faces in the sea of visions, picked up on sordid details that Kyle might have missed. As bad as it had been for him, the guards and villagers had seen worse. It had affected them deeply and personally.

The information was still there in Kyle's head, buried deep in his mind. He knew he could retrieve it and pass it on.

The proceedings were relatively informal. Kyle was ushered to the front and made to face the enormous crowd that had gathered at the foot of the mountain. He felt extremely small. Behind him, a spokesperson named Gamar, wise and old, stood on a cluster of boulders with his arms raised, his voice echoing off the nearby cliff face.

Acting Sovereign Durant stood off to one side with a few close aides. Apparently nervous, he kept shooting frightened looks at Kyle, clearly hoping this mind-reading business would fail terribly.

Kyle listened to some of Gamar's introductory speech but quickly tuned him out when he noticed a pretty girl in the front of the crowd. She smiled at him and mouthed "Hello," and he nervously smiled back, wondering who she was.

Then he spotted Kiff about twenty faces away. The boy was gesturing urgently toward the girl, nodding at Kyle as if to tell him something. Then he understood. This was Nomi, the girl Logan liked.

Well, his counterpart had good taste. And although Nomi wasn't the same as the girl Kyle liked back in the city, she was equally unobtainable. He sighed and stared hard at the ground in front of him, wishing he could just get this over with.

Eventually, a silence fell. Kyle realized everyone was staring at him. The old man's voice floated down from the rocks behind. "They're all yours, boy."

"Uh, okay," he said.

"Should we all hold hands?" someone shouted. "Should one of us hold *your* hand?"

Kyle immediately glanced toward Nomi, and then hurriedly looked away again. "Uh, yeah, we should," he muttered.

"Speak up!"

"Yes, we need to hold hands!" Kyle shouted back.

Several hundred people shuffled about, looking around to grasp those nearest to them. It took longer than Kyle would have imagined, but eventually the link was complete.

Except for the link to *him*.

The old man had climbed down from the rocks. He ushered Kyle closer to the crowd. Prima and Leet were there in the front with Kiff. However, seeing the pretty girl in the front row with an outstretched free hand, Kyle ambled toward her.

"Hi," he mumbled. "You're, uh . . . Nomi, right?"

"I am," she said, reaching for him. He felt a thrill at her touch. A huge balding man had hold of Nomi's other hand. "This is my father," she explained. "And . . . you're Kyle."

"Kyle, yes," he agreed. "Not quite Logan."

*Not quite Logan.* What kind of lame introduction was that?

She gazed at him intently, and he swallowed and cleared his throat. "Uh, so, okay then. Let's get this over with."

He closed his eyes, and as he did so, he felt his other hand being taken. The old man, Gamar, had a gnarled and tough-skinned palm quite unlike Nomi's, which was soft and warm.

*Focus*, he thought.

He called on his Skimmer. At first, the spirit seemed confused. *Whose thoughts should I extract?* it wanted to know. *The old man's, or the young girl's?*

"Mine," Kyle murmured. "Take mine. Take everything. Show them all."

After the briefest hesitation, the Skimmer entered the deepest recesses of Kyle's mind and did as it was asked, taking every last memory and sharing it all with this giant crowd. Kyle had nothing to hide. It was true that some of the things in his head were private, but he figured those incidentals would be lost under the avalanche of knowledge he was imparting. The villagers would be more interested in Apparati, the city to the west, and all its technology. They would look upon the Tower and Abe Torren with astonishment. But mostly, they would absorb the vile thoughts Kyle had lifted from the old sovereign and his chancellor before they had died.

Since his Skimmer was doing all the work, Kyle peered through his eyelids at the sea of faces around him. Most had their eyes shut, and those who didn't simply stared into space. All were slack-jawed. Every man and woman—and some of the older children—were linked by hands and arms, and some looked like they were clinging on for dear life as if the world were tilting beneath their feet. And it was, in a way. Everything they knew about their trusted sovereign was a lie, and his chancellor was worse.

Several women cried out, and a man swore. Their exclamations were in time with certain scenes that flitted through Kyle's mind as the Skimmer continued its work. Some of these people were seeing their loved ones or neighbors quietly and brutally removed from society for crossing the sovereign, for angering him in some way.

*So not accidental deaths after all*, Kyle thought with a stab of horror as he recognized what he was seeing. A father who gleefully exploited a loophole in one of the enclave laws and won himself a week's worth of rations was supposedly trampled by hustles the very next week—yet in fact he was set upon by seven of the chancellor's hired thugs one evening and left for dead in a field. Similarly, a pretty woman who politely declined the sovereign's advances was ravaged by kalibacks the next day—or, as the Skimmer clarified, was tied to a post in the Broken Lands and released only when the beasts had done their grisly work.

The truth was coming out. It was ugly, and Kyle briefly wondered if grief-stricken families should be spared these kinds of revelations ... but then, who was he to decide what to censor? These people had been lied to enough already. They needed to know.

What pained Kyle the most was what happened to the children like himself—those who showed extraordinary sensitivity toward the spirits and could attract more than one at a time. Those children were marked from an early age, often snatched away and disposed of in mysterious circumstances, or poisoned in plain sight. Kyle finally understood why Abe Torren had found it so easy to switch him and Logan at such a young age. And perhaps it explained why Logan's parents—likewise his own—had so readily accepted the swap. In their hearts, they must have suspected that overly talented children had oddly short lifespans.

When the Skimmer finished, Kyle felt tired and drained. The silence was disconcerting, but he could tell the information dump had worked. The crowd was numb with shock.

He found that Nomi's fingers were digging into his palm. When he looked at her, her eyes were squeezed shut. The old man, Gamar, released his own grip and stumbled away. The enormous crowd began to shuffle and murmur.

"So you can build the unbuildable and break the unbreakable?" an unseen man called.

Kyle blinked, confused. "What?"

The crowd parted just a little so that the man could be identified. Although his spirit was barely visible, Kyle recognized it immediately as a Weaver. "You can do what no other has been able to do with their tethers," the burly builder said. "If you can use a Skimmer to share the thoughts of others, and heal yourself from a mortal wound without even thinking about it . . . then you can help us dig down to the tunnels we discovered under the ground, to push through and explore places our best Weavers and Breakers have been unable to reach."

"Tunnels?" Kyle repeated weakly. He realized he was still holding Nomi's hand; she wasn't squeezing quite so hard now. "What tunnels?"

But someone else jumped in. It was a woman standing near Prima, and she touched Prima's arm as she spoke. "Never mind about the silly tunnels. What about the sick? We have only four Fixers in this Enclave—sorry, five now, with young Nomi here—and none of them have demonstrated the proficiency you displayed in the hall yesterday. Can you repair burns? Can you regenerate frostbitten fingers?" A hush fell, and she swallowed. "Can you cure my mother of her terminal illness?"

Kyle looked toward Kiff. He'd been planning to have a go at fixing the boy's limp as a demonstration, but now that he was on the spot and hundreds of eager people were staring at him, anxiety took over.

Seeing Nomi's hopeful expression and Prima's gentle nod of assurance, Kyle knew he had to try. And right now, in front of everyone.

*Can we do this?* he asked his Fixer spirit.

His head echoed with the incomprehensible voices of his other spirits bickering with each other. But one voice came through loud and clear. There were no words, just a stream of high-pitched clicking, which was apparently how these furry little Fixer creatures communicated. Still, Kyle understood.

*Yes, we can do this.*

Kyle approached the boy, and the crowd eased around him. "Show me," he said.

Anxiety spread across Kiff's face, but he sat on a rock and pulled up his pant leg to reveal the ugly, knotty scar and hard lump across his thigh. Several onlookers murmured and whispered.

On his knees, Kyle began prodding the boy's thigh. He allowed his Fixer to delve deeper, and a few seconds later the spirit went to work on the tangled tissues. This would take a while. He could sense, almost *see*, the terrible damage inflicted by the kaliback. No wonder Kiff limped! It was a wonder he could walk on this leg at all.

First the nerve endings would need to be disconnected, then the muscles straightened out and gently pulled into place, blood flow returned, cells regenerated, flesh kneaded . . . There was a lot to do. But he could do it. His Fixer worked fast. Though Kyle's hands barely moved on the boy's thigh, the spirit reached deeper and the pale skin rippled and bulged . . .

While he and his Fixer worked, Kyle wondered about his own brother, Byron, back home in the city to the west.

Was Logan keeping up his end of the bargain?

\* \* \*

Logan was so conflicted. His mother sat behind him, his real mother. And yet she had not rushed up to embrace him. She was warm and kind, that much was evident, but something held her back, a caution he couldn't fathom. Did she see him as tainted, less than what he should be? Why else be so distant?

They rode along in a pod. Logan had wanted to ride in a maglev train but had been dissuaded by her. His face was too recognizable. He would be mobbed. Better to whisk to their destination hidden behind the white shell of a pod. His tech wanderings had him thoroughly aware how to navigate the vehicle himself. Not that he wanted to. The operative who swept them along through these tunnels had sensed his probing and been suitably upset at his prying. And while he could've easily grabbed the reins and taken control, he had retreated.

As annoyed as the operative had been, she had also radiated a little awe at his presence. His mind was becoming more attuned to the tech and, through the implants, he was beginning to gain emotional impressions from those around him. This made him want to examine his mother's implant, to find out more of how she felt about him, but he didn't. It was too much of a violation. If she was to welcome him, it would have to be without him using his tech savvy to press the advantage.

She explained, "The appropriate housing for Byron has been assembled. It's a bit of a step up, maybe a little more than he's ready for, but the body they have prepared is what they use for those recruits savaged out in the battlefield. He'll look more like a young man than I want, but his new body will serve him for many years."

Logan wondered what sort of war they waged. He had not targeted infostreams concerning recent military actions other than those involved in forays into the Ruins. It might be worth a look later. He had yet to decide if he was still an enemy of the government here. While his mother had assured him the guards that accompanied them were for his protection, he couldn't help but still feel caged.

Then again, it just might be the city and its surroundings that made him respond in such fashion. As liberating as his newfound powers were, the city itself made him feel closed off, isolated from the world. Take the dark network of tunnels they currently threaded their way through. There was no life to the place. Only when he immersed himself in the tech did he feel alive here. He pined for a midnight chase through the woods with Nomi. His chest tightened as he thought of his friends back in the Fixer Enclave. What would happen to their village with the sovereign and chancellor gone? Would their enclave be made an example of? He shuddered as the pod slowed to a stop in a narrow shaft. It rose about fifty feet then went horizontal again, coasting along a section of track that led to a loading platform. The station was empty except for their pod.

*This station doesn't see much traffic*, Logan thought. *Where are they taking me?*

The vehicle's door opened, and he unbuckled. The guards stepped out first and strode to a solitary door at the end of a long walkway. His mother exited and waved for him to follow. He slipped out of the pod, watching it seal shut again and take off down the line. When its aft lights disappeared around a bend, he caught up with the group.

His mother said, "They are only doing this because they fear what will happen if they don't. I've never seen such pressure exerted by the people before. With Baynor gone, it's as if everyone feels free to breathe again." Her eyes softened, and she reached for him, pulled him close and squeezed tight. "I thought I was going to lose Byron like I lost you all those years ago. I should've looked for you, questioned why you'd been replaced, but your father—sorry, Josef—mollified me, urged me to put your disappearance behind us."

Logan didn't know what to say. He tried not to stiffen up as she started to sob.

She said, "Because you came back, Byron gets to live and better than before. No more salvaged parts, no more wondering if the government would decide to deny him any further upgrades."

Logan wanted to change the mood. He had thought he wanted her close but suddenly felt overwhelmed. He kept his response task-minded. "And they just presented you with the latest body for him? Why go from almost executing Byron to rewarding him?"

She disengaged and fell in step with the guards already at the next juncture in the corridor, again a little distant. Had his directness been too off-putting? "Because to put him to death now would make him a martyr. They aren't stupid. Neither should we construe their actions to mean they have our best interests at heart. They are still fostering their own agenda. It just happens to match what we want at this time."

Logan wasn't sure he understood what she was talking about. Just because he knew the oppressive history of Apparati, all the shadowed treacheries their leaders had engaged in, didn't mean he knew what the right move was. Should he go along with this and fix Byron? Did his victory here translate to helping a ruling party that would turn around and send him into exile or worse when the public lost interest in him? It was all a bit much.

They walked down a brightly lit corridor and slipped past two security checkpoints before arriving at a large circular room. Logan explored the tech arranged in the room. It was an operating theater. He glanced up and to his left to see a large viewing area.

While unable to see in, he probed with his mind to determine a citizen holding a tablet in hand, who was accessing the news sites, trawling for public opinion on Byron's reinstatement as a citizen and three armed guards awaited them within. He examined the implant of the tablet holder and was surprised to receive waves of satisfaction radiating from it. Whoever oversaw this spectacle was pleased with what they were seeing. Logan's mind stretched out and detected four cameras, all streaming live feeds to various media networks. He was being put on display.

His mother whispered, "Real change can happen for Apparati, Logan. I think what you do here will be a catalyst, even more than the deaths of the mayor and the general."

A door opposite the one they had come through opened. Two doctors entered, one pushing a bed on wheels with Byron strapped to it. Behind them came Doctor Pollard, pulling along another wheeled bed, this one holding Byron's new host.

Logan's mind dashed over to the new body, flitting through all the sleek tech contained underneath its flesh-colored outer skin. The facial features on the machine looked more expressive, and he combed through the various network of systems used to pull the pseudo flesh to create seventeen distinctive expressions.

He found several voids in the tech in the lower arms, areas where normally advanced weapons would be housed for a soldier. Not for civilians, though. Why weaponize someone who didn't follow their orders, who didn't report back to them in any capacity? He also searched and found three listening and tracking devices in the new body. He quickly shut those down. While he knew this wouldn't earn him any favors, he wanted to send a message to whoever was listening.

Doctor Pollard gave him a guarded look. "Will you need me to assist? These sort of transplants are extremely dangerous and require someone with years of experience to perform."

Logan grinned and said, "I can manage."

He stood between the two bodies and went to work. With all eyes on him, Logan set forth to give Byron another body, another chance at life.

Byron tilted his head toward him. "I saw everything. We're brothers. You went away for a long time."

He paused.

Logan sensed he was hesitant. He sent him a warm smile, hoping it would encourage his robot brother to open up.

Byron said, "Your home really is a world where spirits take people into the air? Where magic tethers one to phantoms that can read minds?"

"It is."

After today, he wondered, *Where will my true home lie? Where do I want to truly be?* He pushed such heavy thoughts to the side and poured all his focus into the miraculous tech before him, manipulating something he never thought he would ever work.

It was like magic.

## *Epilogue*

Kiff stood on tiptoes, bouncing from foot to foot, something he'd been unable to do for years. But even with his newly mended leg in full working order, he was too small to see over the shoulders of those crowded in front of him.

It was cold in the small cavern. Lanterns hung everywhere, and several men held flaming torches. Black smoke pooled under the uneven rock ceiling and drifted into the darkest crevices. All the Breakers of the enclave—twelve men and three women—were gathered together, spread across the confined space, eager to see what Kyle could do but uneasy with the idea of forcing their aggressive spirits together in such close proximity. The agitated phantoms bobbed and fidgeted, rising high above their hosts. Their ghostly auras helped illuminate the gloom.

Kiff wished he'd snuck in earlier. It wasn't like he was slow anymore. He could have dashed down the steep tunnel ahead of the group if only he'd thought about it. His mother was outside in the rock quarry with a few others; she'd wanted to come down, but Fixers were rare and best kept away from the danger of roof falls. His father, on the other hand, stood at the front of the group.

"Let's get this done," his deep voice rumbled.

Determined not to miss a thing, Kiff ducked and shoved through, squeezing between the restless men and women before they had a chance to grab him by the scruff and yank him back. A few complaints rang out, but their attention was diverted and Kiff made it to the front just before his older brother's twin got started.

Kyle stood in a deep recess in the wall, which was rigged with stout supports and beams ready for when the breakthrough was achieved. "Is it natural rock, or something else?" he said, touching the wall's surface.

The rock was a different color, lighter and with a wet-looking sheen. Nobody had mined this type of rock before. It was flat, perhaps an ancient wall, and had proved almost indestructible. There were slight abrasions here and there, but Kiff had seen for himself the pile of ruined picks and axes outside.

"We don't know. Tools hardly make a dent," Kiff's father confirmed as Kyle's fingers traced one of the discolorations.

"And you've tried going around?"

"Whatever this is, it spreads a long way. We could search for months trying to find a way around. But maybe you can do what we can't."

Kyle called upon his Breaker spirit. It reared up, generating its own eerie glow in the darkness of the cavern. Thick, curved tusks urged forward. The Breaker looked eager for action.

It enveloped Kyle's raised arm and fist. The spirit's entire essence channeled into that fist, causing a glare of light while the rest of the creature's aura faded. Yet when Kyle hammered at the mysterious wall, he succeeded only in scraping out a few tiny fragments of the rock.

A silence fell as Kyle frowned at his poor handiwork. He stepped sideways and tried again, this time on the darker, more familiar cavern wall. A huge chunk crashed down. All the Breakers sighed with awe at the amount Kyle had dislodged in one halfhearted swipe.

Yet he'd hardly dented the curious barrier.

"It's tough," he said, returning his attention to it. He thought for moment, then nodded, turned to the crowd, and spoke softly. "To me."

It took only a second for Kiff to figure out what was going on. With an explosion of dazzling light, fifteen Breaker spirits reared up and pulled loose from their hosts. Men and women stumbled and gasped as the tusked creatures shot away from them and toward Kyle. As each enveloped him, his aura glowed ever more strongly until it was blinding. At the same time, six other spirits of varying colors and sizes reeled sideways out of him, hovering with indignation at being ejected.

The crowd's collective shock echoed around the cavern. Kiff knew he was witnessing something unique and astonishing.

The Breakers jostled together, combined their energy, and focused it toward Kyle's right arm as he stepped back and lifted it high. He brought it down with a cry. This time, debris exploded across the floor in a mass of shiny pebbles.

The crowd gasped again, then cheered. A bowl-shaped dent had been carved out. In the center was blackness—a four-inch hole to the other side.

Kiff's father, looking as dazed as the rest of the men and women at the temporary loss of their tethered spirits, raised his flickering torch to the hole. After a moment, he turned to face the crowd. "There's a tunnel."

"I knew it!" a woman said. "Didn't I say so?"

"But a tunnel to where?" a man said.

As voices rose to an excited babble, Kiff's father patted Kyle firmly on the shoulder, causing a multitude of Breaker spirits to snap ineffectually at him. "Good work, son. Good work."

Kyle glanced at the man, and a half-smile crept across his lips. "No problem, Mr. Orm. I'll be through this wall in no time."

\* \* \*

Byron was uncertain why Logan had brought him to this part of the city so close to the Wall and the undesirable districts.

He'd been in his new body six days now. The procedure had gone smoothly, but to avoid further transplants as he aged, it had made sense to place him directly into an adult-size frame, one which he could keep well into his twenties and possibly thirties. Now he was four inches taller than Logan—and Kyle too, if he were here. But he wasn't. He was far away in Apparata dealing with much the same upheaval as Byron's family.

Logan paced around in an abandoned lot, his eyes scanning the ground. What was he doing?

Byron's new voice modulator made him a more natural baritone. "They voted in a new mayor. Everybody likes him." He knew Logan already had tapped into the infostream and had retrieved the news, but he hoped to spark a discussion.

Logan nodded. He crouched and swept his fingers through the sparse grasses.

"Trilmott likes you. He wants you to head the expedition to your home. I think he won't end up like Baynor." Byron flexed his upper arms, pleased at how the synthetic musculature tightened.

"We'll see," Logan said. He stood and waved at Byron. "You might want to move back a few yards. I'd prefer you be on the other side of the street, to be honest."

Logan's face scrunched up. Byron knew this meant he was accessing tech. Over the past few days, he had paid close attention to his new brother's mannerisms. The greater the grimace, the larger the tech he worked with.

"Thank you for putting me in this new body." He felt if he could keep Logan talking, he could prevent him from doing something foolish. For the last two days, Logan had grown more and more comfortable in his new home. With their parents warming up to him, Logan had almost settled into a cozy routine, his desire to fiddle with tech beyond the stream screen at a relative low. Byron had sensed that wouldn't last long. Logan was especially restless this morning. "I know you miss Apparata. And Kiff."

"Go," Logan ordered.

Byron spun about, maintaining his gaze on Logan despite now having his back turned to him. Thank goodness for the rotary aperture nestled in his shoulders that gave him a full 360-degree range. His older body had only been capable of 270 degrees. He crossed the street in three long, adult strides. "What are you doing?"

Logan pointed his outstretched hands at the ground before him.

Byron's sensory array immediately detected the tremors. They radiated from a point twenty feet in front of Logan. He watched as the ground of the open lot buckled and heaved. "You can't—"

Sweat covered Logan's brow. "Quiet. Almost done."

Byron knew his brother wasn't making the earth move, that he had to be manipulating tech below to create the sinkhole that was now appearing before them. Was he shifting around a long-buried vehicular relic? This close to the wall, it was possible that the city had even built over some locked secret storehouse.

With a deafening rumble, the ground gave away and a hole nearly a hundred feet wide presented itself. The rim of the chasm came right up to Logan's feet. He looked up and smiled, pleased with his handiwork.

Various internal alarms went off in Byron's systems. "What did you do?"

Sirens sounded in the distance. A convoy of soldiers or police were surely on their way.

Logan hopped down onto a crumbling ledge, until he was only visible from the waist up. Byron knew the hole was deep. He edged forward, watching as Logan carefully climbed down the sloped sides of the impressive cavity.

"This is dangerous. What are you doing?" Byron inched closer to the fissure. Below, dirt fell through a large opening. Two immense doors had dropped down into an underground chamber. He could make out the heavy-duty hydraulics Logan had activated off to the side, half buried in fresh dirt. Logan had indeed accessed a hidden chamber. The strange markings running along the doors' edges were not Apparatian. But how had Logan known how to communicate with such ancient tech?

"I was right," Logan said. "There's something down here."

"Like what?"

Logan looked at him and smiled. "Tunnels."

**THE STORY CONTINUES ...**

Kyle and Logan long to return to their families—or, better still, bring both worlds into phase so they can all be together. With Abe Torren's help, perhaps they can do just that.

Tunnels have been discovered deep below the enclaves and under the city. Within the darkness are signs of a lost civilization. But according to Abe, it isn't lost at all. In fact it's the third phase of Apparatum, very much alive today and filled with untethered spirits.

Only these spirits are flesh-and-blood creatures.

# UNEARTHED
## FRACTURED BOOK 2

Available Now!

## AUTHOR'S NOTE

KEITH ROBINSON and BRIAN CLOPPER (the authors of this novel) not only contributed exactly half each, they wrote alternating chapters at the same time. The basic plot had already been established during long phone calls beforehand, but the rest of the story, taking place in two very different settings, unfolded chapter by chapter. This was a collaboration in every sense of the word.

**Brian:** Keith and I wanted to work on something together. We talked about a joint novel. One of us, not sure which, suggested two stories that would meet in the middle. Each author would control their story and we would alternate chapters. I did the Logan chapters and Keith did the Kyle chapters. Early on we decided it would be nice to have one be a science fiction world and the other a fantasy realm.

**Keith:** We came up with the idea of doppelgangers, that each person had a twin in the other world. Of course, this logic wouldn't stand alone, because what would happen if one twin died in an accident while the other twin lived, got married, and had children? The whole doppelganger scenario would fall apart over generations. So we introduced the idea of wink-outs. That way, if someone died in an accident, his counterpart would vanish also. However, logic dictates that one twin still might marry and have children while the other twin might prefer to stay single, and therefore, while both twins would exist, there would be additional children in one world. Over time this, too, would mess up the logic of doppelgangers. So we deepened the idea to allow for those differences. Some twins are "pure" (sharing an identical family tree) while others are diluted or perhaps not twins at all. Kyle and Logan are "pure blooded," hence their finely tuned skills.

**Brian:** There were so many instances of our ideas bearing richer fruit than we anticipated. The wink-outs were like that. They gave us a wonderful endgame with the two sets of corrupt leaders. Another example is the crafting of the name for our respective worlds. When we came across Apparata and Apparati, we were initially playing off the word apparatus, which fits in well with Keith's world. Of course, we both realized that same root word could be a tip of the spiritual hat to apparition, which added so much to Logan's magical world of tethering to spirits. When we arrived at this, I felt yet again that synchronicity and a grand design were working through both our minds. It sometimes got downright scary how in tune our ideas and plotting would become. By the end, I realized we were becoming writing counterparts to each other much like the relationship Kyle and Logan had. Of course, our characters had vastly better hair than either of us.

**Keith:** I was fascinated by the idea of two worlds out of sync and what a traveler would see as he journeyed from one to the other—or rather what he wouldn't see. The wastelands between are visible to all, but the separate realities of Apparati and Apparata are not. A traveler from the city won't find the enclaves to the east; instead he'll find empty, untouched forests and mountains. So, too, will an exile from the enclaves who travels west.

But the distinction between these realities blurs in the middle. Logan drops his knife outside the Tower, then effectively switches places with Kyle, and it's Kyle who picks up that knife as they leave. Kyle's wagon, on the other hand, originated in the wastelands and is visible to both boys. Imagine if the hustle hadn't been killed and Kyle had been able to continue his journey riding the wagon. Logan would see that same hustle pulling what would appear to be a riderless wagon. The elements are affected also, for instance when Logan sees only a Kyle-shaped void in the rain; the rain knows the boy is there, as does the flattened grass and footprints in the mud, yet each boy appears to be alone. Strange things abound when two lands are not quite in sync. Is it merely their perception that's faulty?

**Brian:** I want to say Keith discussed the idea of Implant Day with his world and shared how it was an event that happened at a certain age. All I knew about my fantasy world was the image of spirits swirling around. In a desire to parallel Keith's implanting and his citizens' connection to tech, I thought of the idea of the enclave dwellers having to tether to a spirit. I then worked through that I wanted various types of spirits that carried out jobs that might exist in both worlds. I knew I needed a healer, a builder, and a soldier type to match what would be happening in Apparati. The image of a rough spirit that was destructive became the Breakers. The Skimmers and Creepers came along nicely and I recall Keith offering up the Gliders. I was pleased with the variety and set to work on thinking about their appearances, strengths, and limitations. Keith also pointed out we needed a way to contain the spirits to the wastelands so they wouldn't tether willy-nilly. He offered up the Banisher, which I gleefully accepted.

**Keith:** And speaking of spirits, it was a little daunting at first taking over the reins of Brian's world of Apparata. I found that I had seven different spirits to deal with as well as a menagerie of flesh-and-blood creatures in the wastelands. I delved through our notes and searched the manuscript (so far) for mentions of them all, and gradually put them together in my head. The details had to be accurate. If Brian had written that a creature had pink and purple polka dots, then I'd need to follow through with that too. This process actually turned out to be fun. It was like taking someone else's sketch and adding my own marks to it. I was free to flesh out these creatures and spirits (so to speak) with whatever details I wanted to throw in. In this way, the spirits and other creatures became as much mine as they were Brian's. And to my delight, I saw that Brian was doing a similar thing with the world I'd created back in Apparati. He was digitally remastering it and adding depth and many new bits.

**Brian:** Yes, and I saw where Keith made the kalibacks telepathic, a trait maybe Logan's people might not know about, but the city dwellers might have figured out from more tech-savvy study of the animals. Creating the flora and fauna was a real trip! It's always one of my favorite things to do in world building.

With Keith's world, I was worried I wouldn't do his science fiction theme justice. While I am a big science fiction fan, none of my other novels explore that genre. Thankfully, the foundation of Keith's world was so strong, it was a joy to come in and embellish. I loved letting Logan experience his full potential. With his former life always about his shortcomings, it was wonderful having him joyfully cut loose. I am eager to see what he does in Book Two.

**Keith:** This leads us to the "give and take" nature of this collaboration. Oh, and the fact that we had to leave our egos at the door. We had a skeleton structure to start with, something we talked about over the phone and in emails, spitballing until we had a basic plot and rough summary. The rest was organic. We had "markers" to shoot for; for instance, our characters had to be out in the Ruins by a certain chapter, at the Tower by another, and a specific amount of time had to pass during that journey so that our characters met . . . well, at the same time.

But other than occasional signposts, we were free to create whatever we wanted. We discussed anything we didn't agree on, and we were both more than willing to back down if the other posed a better argument. There were no egos in the way, and it actually felt good to relinquish control when appropriate. Sure, there might have been scenes or ideas we regretted losing—but look, if it ain't working, it's gotta go. To this day, neither one of us is interested in taking the lion's share of the credit (or indeed flack) for this novel. It's very much a shared work—for better or worse!

**Brian:** Of course, I'd tell Keith we should spend three chapters before they were exiled, then I'd turn around and ask him if we could take five or six chapters before hitting that mile marker. There was such a desire to delve deeper, to explore what we created. I also told him we'd keep the story tight and only have to contribute 20,000 words each. Ha! That soon went out the window. By the time the dust settled, we had our respective word counts around 44,000, shockingly close to each other. Keith can probably rattle of some more precise figures. He's good at that.

In fact, what I appreciated about the collaboration was how he made me work over my tendency to sweep along with my big, grand plotting and slow down to focus on smaller details. I feel my ability to apply nuance improved through his guidance and patience with me. It was a huge learning experience playing in each other's playgrounds. I dare say we learned a lot about each other and how to tinker with a book. I found out I need to be more comfortable with tinkering and massaging out a scene rather than leaving it be just because it was done and read well.

**Keith:** Actually the book came in at 92,500 words in total. But speaking of tinkering ... When it came time for beta readers to take a look, I admit I was nervous—as I always am with the first batch of readers of a brand new novel. Does it stink? Will it tank horribly? But when the first reader reactions came in, I breathed a sigh of relief, and overall the consensus of our entire list of betas has been favorable. Of course there are always things to fix. There are typos to catch, words and phrases to streamline, and entire scenes to trim down, alter, or remove.

We didn't agree with every comment, so it's not like we went into robot mode and automatically struck everything we were told to strike. Different betas have different ideas, so we had to be careful not to dump something that's perfectly all right. What if one beta hated something and we deleted it only to find that all the other betas loved it and were angry to see it go?

So we quickly dealt with obvious stuff, ummed and ahhed about other things, and vehemently rebelled against a few choice suggestions. In the end this book is ours, and what we say goes—but the decisions about what we ultimately keep, change, delete, and so on will determine how well the book does in the future. We thank the betas for their input, and we hope the changes we've made—and haven't!—satisfy them.

**Brian:** Yes, tinkering is a good watch word for the gestation of the book. Futzing with the story became a daily passion and obsession in this project. When we first thought of writing together, I quickly suggested alternating chapters and having us each write a story that met in the middle. This way, my desire to maintain control would stay intact. My perspective over the team-up was borderline shy and dismissive but not in a negative way. I'm so used to going it alone with my writing, it took me a little time to open up to the fact that I was living and breathing this project with another. In my mind, some of the initial remarks probably came off a little like this: *Yes, let's have them wander off into a wasteland. Oh sure, a tower would be good as a meeting place. Say, they could waltz on over to the other's reality and fiddle about. Let's go write.* My thinking was I could just close myself off and write like the dickens. Well, tinkering and collaboration reared its beauteous head in a totally organic way. We each asked hard questions, made astute observations, and sly criticism that resulted in making the book stronger and stronger.

Communication, the thing I tend to be shy about in many ways, became so critical. January, when the bulk of the novel was written, saw us sending back and forth over a hundred emails. And it never felt like a chore. Later, when we posted it on Google Docs and proceeded to edit, we laid down hundreds of comments. I again thought this step would get tedious and nitpicky, but each of us sprinkled our comments with playful asides and humor that poked fun at each other. It was the best creative experience I have ever had. It was challenging and made me a better writer when we exited the tunnel.

**Keith:** There he goes again, shooting past his allotted word count. Sigh. But ditto everything Brian just said. I want to finish with a word about Google Docs, which we used to joint-edit our manuscript. Quite simply, it's amazing. Two authors working on one document at the same time? How can that work? Won't one set of changes override the other? No, because all changes are auto-saved after the briefest of pauses, and since we're rarely working on the same part of the book at the same time, there's no clash whatsoever. But there were times when I saw Brian's cursor moving about on the screen while I was typing. And when that cursor fell still, I had the weirdest feeling I was being watched and would, while typing, suddenly insert "quit staring!!" into my text. So with one author in Georgia and another in North Carolina (an 8-hour drive), it's amazing just how much real-time communication we did.

And how much fun it was.

Printed in Great Britain
by Amazon